THE PREACHER

THE PREACHER

A Preacher Thriller

TED THACKREY JR.

ISBN: 1941298931
ISBN 13: 9781941298930

Published by Brash Books, LLC
12120 State Line #253,
Leawood, Kansas 66209

www.brash-books.com

A SERMON

Dear friends,

Our text this morning comes from the Book of Isaiah, fifth chapter, eighth verse:

"Woe unto them that join house to house, that lay field to field, till there be no place."

There is more to this verse—one final phrase, and I'll come to it before we're done—but for now let us consider only the first part.

The prophet speaks here to the children of Israel, telling them of the Lord's judgments on various sins. He warns not merely of the pitfalls of greed itself but also of the error of coveting the substance of others—depriving them of the richness of the earth and of the space upon it that God has appointed and ordained for each of his children.

He speaks to his own time, to the people of that time.

But he can also speak to us...

ONE

The game of poker is one of the great undiscovered tools of psychological investigation. You get to the core so quickly. Play seven-card stud with a man for seven hours, and you will know more about his basic character—about the springs that turn his clock—than his wife, his girlfriend, or his tax consultant will ever know. Played competently and with an ear for the language of the game, it can be a number one way of sorting potential friends from probable strangers. And it can provide a reliable lever for removal of the latter.

Which is what I was using it for now.

The chubby, surly boy in the thousand-dollar cowboy boots and eighteen-dollar blue jeans had been losing—and drinking— at a steady pace for about three hours, betting into me when he should have folded, dropping out when he had the cards to stay, and generally poisoning the atmosphere for one and all with his complaints. Now he had folded three kowboys on the third raise and watched me rake in the biggest pot of the evening on what I was careful to let him see was nothing more than a busted flush.

A grown-up or a gambler might have handled it by dropping out of the game or tightening up his play or at least going a little easier on the bourbon-rocks. But this was a smart-mouth richboy from east New Mexico, a tall-grown child of purest ray serene, and I wasn't too surprised when the nickel-plated .380 automatic I'd noticed earlier that night in a holster attached to his tooled-leather belt came out into the circle of friendly players and floated, wandering just a little, about an inch from the end of my nose.

"Hol' it right there," he said.

I just looked at him, past the wavering barrel, and wondered how he had lived so long.

"You nothing but a card mechanic," he went on when I didn't reply. "Cold-decking us all night long. Goddamn thief."

He blinked and he swallowed, and that checked it to me. I had spent the last hour bearing down on the little nose-picker, trying to ease him out of the game. But now he was trying to make up his mind whether to cry or shoot, and I didn't feel lucky enough to take a chance on which way he would go.

I had two options: He was either drunk enough or dumb enough to be holding the .380 within eighteen inches of my right hand, and I hadn't noticed him jacking a shell into the firing chamber. One quick move would either take the piece away from him entirely or break his trigger finger if he decided to be stubborn. It was tempting.

But it was no-go. Drunk, dumb, and obnoxious as he might be, this kid was the home team. Of the other five poker players at the table, all or more had probably known the boy since the day he was born, while I was a stranger—someone they'd never seen before tonight. They would live the rest of their lives with this youngster and his kin; me they could forget.

That left option number two.

"Why, hell and fireflies, son," I said, giving him the slow country-boy smile and keeping my hands rock-still on the table, "there's nobody around here done any cheating on you tonight. Never had to."

Whatever he'd been expecting, it wasn't that. I could feel some of the tension go. But the gun stayed put and so did he.

"Okay," he said, not ready to back off in front of witnesses, "go on…Let's hear you lie your way out of it."

"Plain truth," I said, still smiling and keeping track of the .380 out of the corner of my eye. "You've lost money tonight, and quite a few other nights, too, I imagine, not because you got cheated but because you purely cannot play the game of poker— or gamble at all, come to that—for sour owl shit."

"Yes, Lord!" the balding, owl-faced car dealer to my left mumbled, and there was a subdued rumble of agreement from one or two others. That shook the boy a little. He hadn't expected opposition from the five-dollar seats. But he still wasn't ready to quit.

"Liar," he said again. "I c'n play poker as good as any man in this room, and a damn-sight better than some."

I shrugged and took the chance of moving my hands, which were holding the cards. Never taking my eyes from his, I shuffled twice, cut, shuffled again, trimmed the deck, and set it in the middle of the table.

"Maybe I'm a liar, and maybe I'm a mechanic," I said. "But if you want to prove you're a gambler, I'll give you a chance to win back everything you lost to me tonight—and more. How about it, son?"

He blinked again, and I knew I had him.

"Liar," he said, licking his lips. "I bet you stacked that deck when you shuffled just then. I seen you…"

I kept smiling, though it was getting to be an effort. "Just a simple test," I said. "One simple wager to prove that you don't know how or when to bet, and never will. What do you say? You ready for this?"

He snorted, which probably meant yes.

"How much you got left on the table?" I asked.

He counted it with his eyes, forgetting to watch me and forgetting the pistol in his hand. It sagged away to point at the player to my left, who didn't like that at all.

"Two thousand," the boy said finally. "Maybe a hunner more."

"Okay," I said. "Then here's the deal…" I set the deck down, ace of spades looking up, in the middle of the poker table. "Sitting right here, just the way I am," I said, "I will bet you my whole stake—everything on the table in front of me against everything you've got left—that I can touch my right eye to that ace of spades without moving the deck or the table or my head. How about it, boy? Bet?"

I had him.

He took a full sixty seconds to think it over, looking at me and looking at the deck and looking at the money on the table. But I knew I had him. He'd seen me bluff that last pot, and he knew I was trying to do it again, and this time he was going to show me up. For sure, for sure.

"Okay," he said finally.

I looked around the table.

No one had anything to say.

Fair enough.

"The piece," I said, looking back at the boy and nodding at the .380 he still had in his hand. "It's part of your stake. Put it in the pot."

He didn't like that.

"It's mine," he said.

"It's in the pot, or no bet," I said.

For a moment, I thought he might back out. In that part of the world, richboys start carrying guns about the time they get their first wheels—which is usually too early on both counts—and he was going to feel virtually undressed without it. But in the end, as I'd hoped, the chance of showing up the out-of-town tinhorn was just too much. And besides, how could he lose?

The .380 thumped down atop the cash.

"Okay, then," he said. "I'll call you, bluffing sonofabitch. Let's see you do it—touch your eye to the cards without moving your back."

He grinned, knowing he'd caught me.

"Smart city boy," he said, thumping back down in his chair. "Smart sonofabitch in that preacher-black suit and string tie. Gambler man, gonna rook the country boys. Now looky here! Someone finally called him, and ain't that a pure-dee shame?"

He probably had more to say and was getting ready to say it, but I'd heard it all before, and I decided the rest of the players around the table had probably heard enough. Time to show openers.

Without a word—and being careful not to move my back or my head—I reached up and removed my right eye.

It's a good prosthesis, very lifelike, and I do my best to help people think it's a real eye. The richboy gunsel wasn't the first who'd failed to spot the counterfeit because he was paying too much attention to the preacher-black suit and string tie, which are a carefully selected part of the illusion, and not enough to things that count.

He sat stock-still now, frozen in mid-sneer, as I moved the eye across the table and put it down atop the ace of spades.

"All right, sir, then there, now," I said, slowly raking his money—and the .380—into the pile of cash and chips in front of me when I decided he'd had enough time to gape, but leaving the unsocketed eye out there in full glare. "All right, now, here's another bet for you: How about the papers to that shiny new Cadillac of yours, the one with the cow horns for a hood ornament and six-shooter door handles, that I saw out in the parking lot. You want to bet that car against my pile, that I can't do the same thing with the other eye?"

The boy thought it over.

You could see him want to go for it, and you could almost feel sorry for him, because there was no way in this world that he could make himself take the chance. The nerve simply wasn't there, and neither was the intelligence. After a long, silent minute he simply stood up and walked out of the room, not looking at anybody.

There were a few more moments of silence after he was gone, and I filled the time sorting money and stacking chips, waiting to see what the other poker players would decide to make of my play with the little gun-pointer.

He was a snotty, arrogant little customer, and I had moved deliberately to force him out of the game as a distraction from serious play, expecting no general outcry. But you never can tell about a thing like that, especially in a strange town, so I felt just the tiniest sense of relief when the prosperous-looking party across the table—Savile Row turnout slightly disordered by the wheelchair to which he seemed totally accustomed—eased back and began to laugh.

That set the tone, and in a moment or two the rest of the poker players were shaking hands, slapping thighs, and hooting. I had guessed right.

"You reckon Bobby Don will go tell his granddaddy?" someone asked.

"If he do, his granddaddy'll surely kick his no-good ass from here to Amarillo!"

"Dog! I like to be there when it happens."

That set off another round of good ol' boy cackling. I was careful to stay out of it, but the man in the wheelchair had evidently decided I was worth keeping.

"I think we all owe you a bit of thanks," he said. "Bobby Don's been nothing but trouble since the day he was born, and having him in the game is enough to sour a man on poker. Maybe losing that bet tonight will finally convince him that he's no gambler."

Ú"Maybe so," I replied. "But that first bet wasn't the one that really proved my point."

That called for an explanation, so I went on.

"Anyone could lose a proposition like that," I said. "Betting on another man's game proves nothing but a lack of experience. The situation where the boy—Bobby Don?—really demonstrated his lack of talent for poker was when he failed to take me up on the second bet, the one where I offered to do the same trick with my other eye."

I had everyone's attention now.

"A poker player's whole stock-in-trade," I said, "is his ability to think clearly under pressure. If Bobby Don had been able to do that, he'd have realized I could not possibly have been playing cards all night with two glass eyes. After all, the deck isn't marked in Braille. And I didn't come in here with a Seeing Eye dog…"

That took a moment for digestion and a few minutes for more hooting and snorting. A couple of the players sent out for fresh drinks. The car dealer lit a new cigar. One or two of the players headed for the men's room. But the man in the wheelchair never took his eyes from my face. And when he finally moved, it was to extend his right arm across the table, rising slightly from his chair to make the gesture.

"J. J. Barlow," he said. "My apologies, sir, but I'm afraid I didn't catch your name when the game began."

I stood up to take the hand he offered. Its grip was surprisingly strong.

"They call me Preacher," I said.

A SERMON
(CONTINUED)

We live in a world of spaces—emotional as well as physical—and those spaces are there for a reason. They are a lubricant. They keep us from intruding too deeply, from grating one upon another, in our daily lives.

Without that lubricant, that space, civilization would not merely be more difficult.

Without it, human society could not even exist...

TWO

We finally got back to playing poker a few minutes later, and the little scene with Bobby Don the baby badman had achieved just about the kind of effect I'd thought it might. The players had figuratively—and in one or two cases, literally—loosened their belts, settled down in their chairs, and shucked their shoes off. They still didn't know me, and they still had all the reservations natural to pack members trying to decide about a newcomer, but the first true eye contact had been achieved and nobody had blinked. I might be an alien, but I was neither a whiner nor a fool, and that can go a long way in establishing credentials for the closed circle of small-town acceptability. Until and unless I did something really outrageous, I would be looked upon as a potential acquaintance and ally. Innocent until proven guilty. An asset. Which would have gone heavy on my conscience if I had one.

For I was in the game—and in the town—under color of fraud.

To get there, I had been as up-front as possible: Before the first hand was dealt, during that shuffle-and-scratch time of getting organized, counting out chips, exchanging the latest home-folks gossip, and responding to friendly insults, I had told them as much of the truth as I thought the traffic would bear. I was from California. I was in town on business. My business was playing poker, and there would be no hard feelings if they didn't feel like having a professional in the game.

No one seemed to mind. I hadn't thought they would.

Poker is a game with a southern accent, and the watchful hospitality for which that region is famous extends generally to players from near and far, professionals included, as long as they are moderately honest, moderately courteous, and vouched for by an accepted member of the community.

My sponsor was about as accepted as you can get.

He had spent the past dozen years among them, tending the faithful as rector of the town's only Episcopal church and picking up added luster as organizer of charities, mainstay of Rotary Club meetings, four-handicap regular in Saturday-morning country-club foursomes, and enthusiastic leader of the town's biggest Boy Scout troop.

Later on, someone might take time to wonder how he came to be acquainted with a professional gambler and why he had made a point of introducing him to the local poker crowd before fading back into the woodwork. Later on, he might have a good bit of explaining to do, and I was glad it was him and not me who was going to have to do it.

For the moment, however, it was enough that I was accepted on faith for long enough to get into the game, size up the players, and have that carefully calculated run-in with poor, dumb Bobby Don.

A gamble, sure, but you can't win the money if you don't buy the cards, and while I might now be attracting a little more covert attention and speculation than I generally find useful, it was the kind of friendly attention and amused speculation that goes with acceptance. I was in.

And that was a dirty trick, because I had come to town and joined the game to prove one of them a thief. Or a killer. Or both.

This was to have been my slob season.

Winter is a close-to-home time in the little mountain town where I live when I'm not on the road, a snow-on-the-ground time that generally keeps the people who live there out of some of the more usual kinds of mischief.

A few of them go cabin-crazy, of course, but there is wood to split and there is ice to fish through and there are snowplows to run and even winter game to hunt if you're in the mood and need the food, and that can take some of the edge off the isolation.

Not that I ever get a chance to feel much isolation myself.

Sometimes I have to leave the town in winter. If we're short of money or if there is someone down-the-hill who might be ready to join us, I'll be gone for a while. But this was a fat year. An easy year, with the bank account full and the tempers even and the woodpile stacked head-high.

I was loose and contented, looking forward to the holidays in a way I hadn't for a long time, and sometimes skipping the morning t'ai chi workout, when the phone rang and I spent a few minutes talking to the Reverend Harold Jacob Spence.

Then I locked up my cabin and told Margery, my electronic-genius secretary, that I would be away for a few days, and caught a ride down-the-hill and bought an airline ticket to Amarillo and rented a car for the drive across the line into the next state.

The town of Farewell is on the far eastern side of New Mexico, about ten miles from the Texas border, and I think it might be a hard place to love.

A brochure put out by the chamber of commerce says it was established about a century ago as a five-way division point on the Santa Fe railroad and has been growing ever since. But the time that I spent there never gave me a single clue as to why.

East New Mexico and west Texas are a part of the country that God must have made as an afterthought, or while He was busy doing something else. It is not a desert; the land is fertile, and for a few days in late summer when the wheat is ready for harvest, I am told it can be as beautiful a spot as you will find anywhere on earth. But the people who say things like that live there, and so are apt to be biased.

Seeing it first in mid-November and recording that first impression for all time, I was left with a memory of featureless desolation. Bare land. Flat land. Damp land recovering slowly from one of the torrential rains that occur with unpredictable predictability at that time of year.

It is a landscape with missing details. No trees. No houses. No animals or crops in the fields. A red-brown canvas bisected at its base by the asphalt straightedge of the highway and topped by a sky of diamondlike intensity. Empty and hungry and waiting.

Driving in from the east that morning, I found myself wondering how Jake Spence had lasted so long in a place like Farewell.

I remembered him as a sensitive soul, a closet romantic who responded to beauty—physical, spiritual, or moral—in the way a desert bedouin responds to water, or a starving man to food. Clear skies could turn him near-manic, and gray ones send him scurrying to a proctor to confess sins of the imagination.

His vocation to the priesthood had been clear enough, but I'd wondered privately how he would survive the day-to-day grittiness of parish work. Somehow he seemed better fitted for a monastery.

Which is just one more unneeded proof of how wrong I can be when I really try.

The Reverend Harold Jacob Spence was that very rarest breed of cat, the born parish priest, capable of juggling the financial, social, and civic responsibilities without once compromising or losing sight of those inner considerations that bring a certain kind of man—the very best kind—to the ministry in the first place.

Jake was a winner, and it showed from the very first.

Ordained, claimed, and assigned to a circuit of three starveling congregations in darkest Kansas, Jake had closed one down and turned the other two into prosperous bastions of the faith in less than a year, which earned him a cordial smile from the bishop of Salina—and a call from a newly priestless congregation in New Mexico that could afford to pay the kind of salary that would permit him to marry the pretty girl he'd been engaged to since his first year of seminary.

I was anxious to see him and anxious to see her and curious to find out what on earth had kept him in a place like Farewell for all these years. But I never had to ask for an answer to the latter question; it was staring me in the face the moment I saw the church and the lawn around it.

Saint Luke's Church (Episcopal) was like its rector, a rare and collectible item. I have since discovered that it is the only true adobe church building of its denomination in North America, but I didn't know that at the time and I didn't care. Jake's aesthetic sense had found the right workshop. From the handmade bricks of the walls and buttresses to the carefully tended tiles of the roof to the obviously amateur-designed and lovingly crafted pattern of the stained-glass window, it was a jewel. One of a kind, amen. But the real explanation—complete and satisfactory, needing no embellishment—was outside the building, on a scuffed and battered expanse of green hopefulness that ended abruptly at the edge of a fallow wheat field.

Some kind of game seemed to be in progress there. About a dozen youngsters, the eldest perhaps five years old, were galloping, swatting, evading, and whirling at a breakneck pace, laughing like maniacs as they pursued a man in black canonicals.

I parked the rented car and watched them for a moment in silence. Then I looked at my own transparent reflection in the rolled-up window. "Dummy," I said to the man I saw there. He didn't seem to have an answer for that. I cranked him down, out of sight, and stepped into the chill brightness of a New Mexico winter afternoon.

Reunions with old friends can be awkward, even when it's a friend like Jake.

We shook hands and clapped backs and asked banal questions and walked into his office and closed the door and stood for a long moment in silence, stuck for conversation and trying not to be too obvious about sizing each other up. Twelve years is a good round dozen, and the occasional letters we'd exchanged were a bridge no thinking man would trust for a second.

Jake and I are only a month or two apart in age, and the framed seminary graduation picture on the wall behind him was a reminder and a reproach.

Had we ever really been that young?

Well, he had. And looking at him again, in the here and now, I could see that he still was. The Reverend Harold Jacob Spence was still easily recognizable as the smiling ordinand in the color photograph. The hairline had receded a bit, and I suspected that the clerical dickey was concealing five or ten more pounds than he'd carried then. But the face was still unmistakably Jake—fresh and eager and ready to believe that he could change the world. A prize and a wonder.

I wondered what he saw, looking at me.

A discerning man might just have been able to connect my face with the one in the seminary photograph, but it would have taken a lot of looking and a fair amount of luck. The left side was still much the same. But a mortar round at Khe Sanh had stirred a few items on the right, and the surgeons who had gone to work to repair the damage had moved a few more. That was only the surface, though. Other changes, the kind that don't show up on a photographic plate, were the important ones, and they were the part Jake would be noticing now.

"Long time," I said, to break the silence.

"Too long."

We stood another moment, thinking thoughts we would never confide to each other, and then he laughed. "Will you look at us!" he said. "Will you look at the two of us, acting like new kids on the block. You still take your coffee black?"

"And hot and strong."

"Good! So do I..."

He busied himself with a pot and cups from the table behind the desk, and I looked around the room where he worked. You can tell almost as much about a man by the kind of books he keeps near to hand as you can by getting him into a game of poker. Jake had always been a solid player—discounting a tendency to go after inside straights—but far too readable to make a living at the game. Now the books I saw told me that there were no more basic changes in him than appeared on the surface.

Moby Dick was there on the shelf, hard by Churchill's World War II series. *The Imitation of Christ* was shoulder to shoulder with More's *Utopia*, jostled by a clutch of Agatha Christie paperbacks and something by Luke Short.

Same old Jake.

I thought of the disorderly shelves at my place in the mountains and wondered what my old friend would think about the juxtaposition of Cruden's *Concordance* with the People's Anglican Missal, Asimov's guides to the Old and New Testaments, *Scarne on Cards*, *The Modern Witch's Spellbook*, and Arthur Orrmont's *Love Cults and Faith Healers*. Being Jake, he would probably give silent thanks that he hadn't found a grimoire or the Necronomican, and send out for someone to assist him at the exorcism.

"How's Helen?" I asked when we were looking at each other again from chairs on either side of the desk.

"Blooming!" he said. "Blossoming, and very eager to see you again."

I smiled a little.

"For true?" I said.

"For true, of course. Why wouldn't she be?"

I could think of a couple of reasons. And so could Jake, now that I mentioned it, but I could see the idea was new to him. Same old Jake.

"Oh," he said. "Well…"

Helen had been Sara's best friend in college. She had introduced us, included us on double dates with her and Jake, been matron of honor at our wedding, and stopped speaking to me when I joined the army instead of the peace movement. Sara had moved in with the Spences when I went overseas, and Helen had been there—but I hadn't—on the day Sara was killed.

"It was a long time ago," Jake said. "People change. They forget."

"It was yesterday," I said, "and nobody has forgotten anything. I haven't, anyway."

He looked at me out of those achingly young eyes of his.

"You didn't remarry," he said, pronouncing it more as an accusation than the mere fact that it is. Jake was giving me both barrels.

"No," I said.

"But Sara would have…"

"Sara's dead, and we never will know what she would have or wouldn't have," I said in a voice that was colder than I wanted it to be. "I'm not a monk, not a hermit, not a constitutional celibate, not a professional bachelor, and I haven't turned gay on you, but marriage is for the young and hopeful, not for one-eyed high-binders who play poker for a living."

He started to speak and then shut up, looking like an abandoned basset pup. It almost broke me up. The years fell away and we were back at Sewanee, and Jake had just discovered that beer-bust hangovers are just as prevalent among divinity students as among the laity. No wonder his congregation thought he was the greatest invention since the McCormick reaper. I wanted to pick him up, scratch his ears, and tell him all would be well in this best of all possible worlds.

"So," I said then, when the moment finally got too heavy to hold, "so…life isn't yak butter?"

The ancient joke and the need to communicate got a very small laugh and brought us back to square one.

"This garden spot." I glanced toward the dank, fallow field visible outside his office window. "It suits you? It's where you want to be?"

His face gave me the answer with no need for words, but he added a few just in case I'd missed the point.

"It's raw," he said. "It's lonesome, and the weather can make you wonder if the good Lord is having a fit of ennui. The people are decent enough—no different from most—but sometimes I think their potential for meanness, perversity, and plain wrongheadedness is rooted in the soil hereabouts. Like stinkweed."

"And you wouldn't be anywhere else."

He grinned and shrugged. "And I wouldn't be anywhere else."

"So," I said, finally working the conversation around to business, "the land is empty, the people are average, you're happy… and you call me down off my hill in the middle of winter because the stinkweed is growing faster than the wheat."

There was a double-beep from something inside the cabinet behind him, and Jake swiveled his back to me, dealing with it instead of answering. I heard pouring sounds, and he turned back a few moments later holding two mugs of coffee with one hand.

"Still no sugar?" he asked.

I nodded, accepted one of the mugs, and settled it on my side of the desk, warned against taking an immediate sip by the ess-curve of steam curling from the surface.

"I called you," Jake said, putting his own mug down within easy reach and picking up a pencil to keep his hands busy, "because you're an old friend, and because I may have abetted a mortal sin, and because I need a professional poker player to find out whether I need a refresher course in canon law and ethics. Old friend…you are just about my last hope."

A SERMON
(CONTINUED)

Yet, total isolation is death for most human beings.

Each of us spends a major portion of his time and substance in an effort to close these spaces, to achieve a unity of mind and body with others of our species.

Togetherness is more than the mere buzzword of a generation now passing its prime.

We seek friends, kindred souls, allies upon the face of the earth, as we seek food and shelter and clothing— not as luxuries, but as the necessities they are.

Why, then, this contradictory concern with space...?

THREE

Jake Spence is a gentle soul, and there is a kind of innocent haplessness about the surface he usually shows to the world that can lead strangers to draw false conclusions about him. In point of fact, the Reverend Mr. Spence is a clear, cool head, and far from ineffectual. Listening as he set forth the facts of his problem, I saw that the flinty core I remembered from another time was intact and functioning at full strength…with, perhaps, a seasoning of experience and understanding that I suspected might have made its owner something of a surprise to more than one member of his parish.

"You recognize the name Orrin Prescott?" he asked me.

I didn't.

"Try Pres Prescott," he said. "Think of the sports pages…"

Oh. "Wide receiver, first with the Steelers, then with the Jets…uh…after a two-year break for service in 'Nam."

Jake looked at me, waiting for me to go on. I culled my memory.

"About our age. Made All-American his last year at Michigan. Played quarterback there, but the pros retrained him…"

I shrugged. That was all I had.

"In 'Nam"—Jake took up the slack when he was sure I was through—"Pres was a helicopter pilot. Decorated twice. Came back without a scratch, married his childhood sweetheart the day he got home. Went back to pro ball as though he'd never been away. Played eight seasons. Made himself a millionaire and quit when the doctors said it was time. Used the money to start a good business back in his hometown...in Farewell."

Jake took a sip of his coffee, and it was still too hot. He grimaced, not just from the heat, and stood up. The east wall of his office was covered with photographs. Jake removed one of them, handed it to me, and went back to his chair.

It was a wedding party.

The groom—looming and bulking over the rest, including Jake—had one of those pleasant-ugly faces that make you smile to yourself without knowing exactly why. Pres Prescott, undoubtedly. The pretty girl in the bridal veil was...a pretty girl. I wondered who she had grown up to be.

I glanced briefly at the other faces and was about to put the picture down when something else caught my attention. The maid of honor. A blonde, like the bride, probably a sister or first cousin, judging from the soft-focused similarity of features. Something about her, though. I looked away for a moment. Looked back. No. And yes. The face was familiar somehow, but it had no name. I looked at Jake, but he was gazing out the window.

Okay.

He had handed me the picture for a reason, and he would tell me about it in his own good time. I put it down on his desk and waited for him to go on.

"The business Pres went into here made a lot of sense," he said. "He had inherited a full section of land out west of town, land that his father had farmed as long as he was able and rented out to other farmers when he got too old. Good land: A lot of it is still growing wheat for some renter. But Pres fenced off part of it to set up an office and a couple of steel hangars to house a brand-new Bell JetRanger helicopter and the kind of equipment you need to maintain one. He thought he could make a good thing of crop dusting, air taxi, and air ambulance work here, and for a while it looked as though he was right..."

Sipping coffee and staring into the middle distance, Jake told the rest of the story in a cool monotone that I could remember was his defense against emotional nudity. I made a mental note that the helicopter jockey might have been a pretty good man.

One of the drawbacks to setting up a new whirlybird operation, Jake explained, is the expense. Those things don't come cheap. But Pres Prescott had started with plenty of money in hand, and the banks were only too happy to set up the kind of revolving credit line any going business needs in order to survive, and to increase it as soon as there were enough steady customers to warrant expansion. Within a few years, Prescott Helicopters, Inc., had added a hefty LongRanger to the initial equipment, plus a little Robinson training bird for the locals who thought they'd like to learn to fly and had the price. A secretary, a bookkeeper, and a second pilot had been hired to help with the chores.

"Pres was a success in every way," Jake said. "He had no competition in the county, no need for elbowing or jostling. Besides, he was a hometown boy...the nice kid you're glad to see succeed. He and Marilyn, his wife, were members of my congregation from the time they got back to Farewell. If there was any major trouble in that marriage, I never could spot it."

And there he seemed to run out of gas.

"So," I said, picking up the ball, "they all lived happily ever after. And you just got me out here for a couple of drinks, a barbecue, and a little auld lang syne."

He looked back at me but didn't smile.

"The trouble began two years ago," he said. "About the time their second child, the girl, was born..."

The first intimation Marilyn Prescott had that her husband might be in trouble, Jake said, came when he drank too much at one of the country club's Saturday parties.

"I'd seen him do a little drinking in the past," Jake said, "and on those occasions the liquor only seemed to relax him a bit.

Bring out the overgrown clown. It was low comedy, like watching an elephant try to roller-skate. Harmless. But this was a different kind of drinking. Almost a different person. Pres spent most of the night holed up in one corner, leaving only to get another refill of vodka on the rocks. And when he finally did move, it was in the direction of J. J. Barlow…"

Jake took a deep breath. J. J. Barlow, he said, was chairman and president of the town's biggest bank. And chief trustee of the grain cooperative. And director of the local oil-and-gas marketing organization. And a power in the federal stockyard association, the merchants and manufacturers club, the chamber of commerce, the county and state Democratic central committees.

"And just about anything else you'd care to name," he said. "One of the two or three individuals without whom nothing much can be done in a town like Farewell."

"A .90 caliber," I said.

"A very big gun indeed," Jake agreed, "and all the more remarkable because of his physical limitations. Until Pres Prescott came home from Vietnam, J. J. Barlow was Farewell's one and only living, authentic war hero. The old man won the Silver Star—and lost both legs above the knee—during the Battle of the Bulge. Been stuck in a wheelchair ever since."

I thought it over and offered the first thought that crossed my mind. "Class of '45," I said.

Jake made a face. "You, too?" he said. "I know what Vietnam veterans think of the ones from World War II and Korea, but I'd hoped that you, of all people—"

"Jake," I said, stopping him before he could get us committed to the kind of debate that I'd quit trying to win a dozen years ago, "no one thinks anything, all right? The comment was just a mental note—that Pres Prescott and J. J. Barlow might have had a little trouble understanding each other on some points."

Jake sighed and nodded again. "You're right," he said. "I wish you were wrong, but you're right. Which makes what happened all the more difficult to understand…because up until that night, the two of them had what seemed for all the world almost a father-son relationship!"

Barlow had been in Prescott's corner from the very first, Jake said. In high school, when Pres first began to show signs of the size and talent that would make him a star, it was the wheelchair-bound banker who encouraged him, made sure that he studied enough to remain eligible for the team, and adroitly managed the behind-the-scenes wrangling that finally resulted in a full athletic scholarship to Michigan.

"And when he went into pro ball," Jake said, "it was J. J. who made sure Pres got the kind of manager who could and would protect his client through the bonus-baby infighting and then safeguard his interests when he had to take time out for that excursion to Southeast Asia."

"Valuable," I said. "A number one ally."

"More than that," Jake said. "Pres Prescott's father died when he was fourteen years old, and from that time on, J. J. Barlow was the man Pres went to for advice, for sympathy, and for the kind of emotional support that few real fathers can offer."

"Until that night," I said.

"Until then…"

Prescott had left his corner chair, Jake recalled, and was en route to the bar again when J. J. Barlow came through the door. There was the minor scurry that small-town protocol dictates: Bankers get the big hello and a lot of quick service, especially if they're in wheelchairs—and this was a man who was popular as well as powerful.

"But this time Prescott didn't join the rush," I said.

Jake shook his head. "He not only didn't join, he went the other way. Picked up a fresh drink at the bar, stood looking at J. J. for a moment, and then walked past him without a word—out the door and out of the clubhouse to the first tee, where he stood nursing the glass until it was empty, then got into his car and drove away, leaving Marilyn behind to make the apologies and find her own way home."

I thought it over and shook my head. "Saturday night standard," I said. "An earthshaker for the country-club set, maybe. But..."

"That was only the beginning," Jake said. "Or maybe just the first outward sign of something that had been going on for a while. I really don't know. Marilyn tells me the gambling had started a few weeks earlier."

I scored a tiny mental check mark. Gamble. The operative word. Now I knew why I was in New Mexico.

"Gambling, how?" I asked.

Jake looked the question back at me.

"Craps?" I prompted. "Horses? Las Vegas weekends? Lottery tickets?"

Jake shook his head. "Poker," he said.

"Your game," a woman's voice said from the space behind me...

It had been a long time, and a lot had happened to all of us. But I didn't have to turn my head to know who had spoken. In all my life I have known only two people who could enter a room behind me with such minimal noise, so little disturbance of the atmosphere, that the sound of their voices would come as a surprise and a startlement. Both of them were women, and one was long dead.

"Hello, Helen," I said.

I stood up and turned around. Helen Spence is a tall woman, only an inch or two shorter than her husband, and I remembered her as a beauty. The ministry, even in a place like Farewell, might agree well with a man like Jake, but I'd been wondering about her.

Ministers' wives get the worst of both worlds—all the restrictions that go with their husbands' calling, but none of the immunities. It can be devastating, and she wouldn't have been the first to find herself empty and drifting. The incidence of alcoholism among ministers' wives is comparable to that found among the officers' ladies on remote military posts.

But one glance told me everything I needed to know. Helen was still Helen, and there was a calmness now, almost a serenity, in the smile she offered in a package deal with the kiss and hug of welcome.

"You're skinny," she said when we unclenched.

"You're gorgeous," I said, grinning at her.

"You're a liar," she said. "And I love it."

We looked at each other for a moment, and I found myself wondering about Sara, how she would have responded to the real world if we'd ever had a chance to live in it. If I'd gone Jake's route...

"Sara would have fattened you up," she said, reading my thoughts. "And she would have kept you from wearing that perfectly awful black suit."

She put boldfaced emphasis on the word "awful," and I pretended to take offense. "Your husband's wearing one," I pointed out. "He wears one every day, and I bet you don't say that to him."

"He has to," she said. "He's a priest."

Which stopped the conversation for a moment.

We looked at each other, and the words that didn't pass between us were far clearer and more audible than anything we'd said aloud. Fair enough. Personal criticism and reproach are privileges I reserve to myself and to a very few others. But Helen was qualified. She'd been to see the elephant. And besides, there was nothing she could say or think that I hadn't said or thought for myself over the years. Absolutely nothing.

She glanced at the desk, saw the Prescotts' wedding picture, looked quickly at me and then at Jake, who answered with the least perceptible of shrugs.

"About poker," I said when the moment finally ended.

"About poker." She poured herself a cup of coffee and took up the tale where her husband had left off.

"Marilyn, Pres's wife—I can't get used to thinking of her as a widow—tells me he'd been playing in the poker game at the country club for only a few weeks before that scene with J. J. Tell me, are other little towns like this? Do they all have a poker game that's been going on for years?"

"Not all, maybe," I said, "but most. I used to have a regular poker route, playing in them; start the season just outside Cincinnati and continue, town by town, down through Kentucky to Alabama, Mississippi, Texas, and into Southern California. It's how a player learns his trade—like a stand-up comic sharpening his timing and his material in Des Moines and Paducah before he tries for the *Tonight* show."

"It sounds…"

"Different," I said, to keep her from finding the word she wanted. "A different frame of reference. A different sky."

She sipped at her coffee, not looking at me, and went on.

"At first, Marilyn thought it was harmless," she said. "But then she began to notice things: changes in Pres…"

The sometime wide receiver had always been a smiling man, Helen said, an outgoing person who made friends easily. The changes in him were subtle, and his wife noted them at first only in passing, sure that they were a temporary response to some kind of problem that he would finally share with her. But the time of sharing never came, and the changes continued.

"At first, he was simply preoccupied," Helen said. "He developed this middle-distance stare that insulated him from people. It got to be very hard to communicate with him. And then there was the thing with J. J.—whatever it was. Marilyn tried to talk to Pres about it, get him to open up and tell her what was wrong. He wouldn't discuss it, and finally she stopped trying. But it was wrong for Pres. All wrong. He needed J. J., depended on him, and not just the way any businessman has to depend on a banker. This was personal, always had been. And Marilyn could see it was eating Pres alive…"

The marriage changed, too, Helen went on. The distancing and preoccupation noticed by the Prescotts' friends began to extend to the children. The helicopter jockey had always been an affectionate and interested father; now he dropped out of the committee work he'd been doing with his son's Cub Scout pack and abandoned the playhouse he had been building for his little girl. But most startling of all, at least to Marilyn Prescott, was the alteration in their sex life.

"It diminished," Helen said. "And then it dwindled. And then it died. Marilyn says Pres had always been a goat, but now he moved into the spare bedroom. Tried to pass it off as courtesy— he was putting in some late hours at the heliport, and sometimes when he played poker he didn't get home till sunrise. Said he didn't want to disturb her sleep. But Marilyn was at her wits' end. Just a week ago, she was even thinking about a divorce…but of course, it never came to that."

I looked a question.

"Pres died three days ago," Jake spoke up. "A crash about ten miles south of town. He was dusting a wheat field."

"The official report," Helen said, cutting him off, her voice flat and metallic, "will call it an accident. That's what the sheriff says, and I don't think the Transportation Safety Board, or whatever they call that federal agency, is going to find anything to the contrary."

"But you don't believe it," I said.

"Not for a moment," she said.

I sat still a moment, looking at the two of them, sorting out the sticks and stones. The Reverend and Mrs. Harold J. Spence had come up with a very hot potato indeed—at least in their own terms. Especially if Jake had done what I damn well know he had done.

"You handled the funeral," I said, keeping my voice even and my face full of nothing. "You made the arrangements and you buried him in consecrated ground."

Jake nodded unhappily.

"But now there's reason to think that Prescott was a suicide."

Helen started to speak, but Jake cut her off with a look.

"There is reason," he said.

"And if he did, of course, you've been adding up the number of canon laws you've broken, and you've come up with a figure you can't live with, and you're wondering what to tell his widow if it turns out you have to do something about it."

Jake sighed and looked at the ceiling. He was out of words.

But Helen wasn't.

"My husband the martyr," she said. "I'm not going to argue the fine points with the two of you. I never had a course in apologetics, and besides, I don't think that particular question is ever going to arise."

"Helen..." Jake started to object, but she shushed him with a gesture.

"For the moment," she continued, uninterrupted, "the coroner lists Pres Pescott's death as accidental, and it may stay that way even when the investigation is finished. Or it may change. If it's suicide, a lot of people are going to be hurt, not just my straight-arrow husband and his scruples. But there is another possibility—one the federal investigators just might overlook."

It had occurred to me, too, but I held my peace and let her say it. Cathartic. Good for the innards.

"There are a lot of things about that crash that don't add up," she said. "Enough to make a reasonable person suspect suicide. But that isn't what happened."

She took a deep breath. "Pres Prescott didn't kill himself out there in that wheat field," she said. "We think he was murdered, and we got you out here to help us prove it."

A SERMON
(CONTINUED)

Here, then, is the paradox of the human condition, the basic conflict in the soul that has plagued us since first we fled, naked and ashamed, from the Garden of Eden:

We love solitude, but seek friends.

We rejoice in the unspoiled face of nature, but willingly pass our lives in cities.

We talk peace, but make war...

FOUR

By 4:00 A.M., the game at the country club was finally begin-ning to go my way.

I was a little money ahead.

And, hand by hand, I was beginning to know the other players.

Not that I'd exactly started cold; Jake and Helen had come up with personal background and character assessments that would have made a private detective squirm. Secrets die young in a town the size of Farewell. Still, all the Spences had to back up their murder suspicions was speculation—none of it even nar-rowing down to a specific name.

Which checked it to me.

Pres Prescott's sometime poker buddies were a cross section, not of the town itself, but of the power structure that made it go. The planners of housing development. The backers of charity drives. The builders of new hospital wings. The late-night telephoners to Santa Fe and Washington whose calls were always returned. Very little could happen in Farewell without their knowledge and consent.

But Pres Prescott had died broke, and no one seemed to know just why.

Without a word to wife and friends, the football-pro-turned-helicopter-jockey had spent the last two years of his life mortgag-ing everything he owned, beginning with the helicopter business and ending with the inherited land it stood on. Even his home in Farewell was heavily encumbered.

The one man who might have been expected to know all about it, of course, was J. J. Barlow. But the banker professed total ignorance. He told Marilyn Prescott that her husband had moved his bank accounts and financing across the state line to Amarillo the day after the still-unexplained scene at the country club.

"Left ol' J. J. right out there in the cold and dark," he said.

Glancing at the wheelchair-bound man who now sat across the table from me—the departure of Bobby Don and another player had left two empty chairs to my left—I tried to make that statement square with what I had learned during the evening of poker. And found myself in never-never land.

I had dropped out of the current pot after seeing my third card, and had a moment or two to watch and assess the other players.

J. J. Barlow might not have been a poker professional, but he was a strong contender, patient and watchful, bluffing rarely and milking the good hands with the finesse of a friendly cobra. At the moment he had a pair of fives showing, four of hearts mating one of the fives for a possible flush, and he'd paid to see the next card, gazing moon-faced at the wall while the other active players made their decisions.

Prescott might have moved the accounts away from his old friend's bank, but no way on this earth would J. J. Barlow have allowed a thing like that to deprive him of the kind of information that is the lifeblood of small-town power and economics. The old-boy network among bankers is one of the most effective in the world. It is international and it is accurate. If Barlow was pleading ignorance now, it could only be for some good reason, and I found myself wondering what it might be.

But he wasn't the only question mark in the room.

Idling to Barlow's left (he had dropped out of the pot a few moments before I did) was another: T. Bowering Woodbury,

M.D., F.A.C.S. Woodbury had performed the postmortem examination after a rescue crew removed Prescott's body from the wreckage of his helicopter. The doctor had come up with a finding of death due to massive cranial insult, adding (doubtless for the benefit of the widow) that Prescott had not been alive to suffer in the subsequent fire.

He had also—pointedly—included the information that the retired wide receiver's body contained no evidence of recent narcotics use: no cocaine, no amphetamines, no heroin, no marijuana, not even traces of alcohol. Jake and Helen had found it disturbing, perhaps even insulting, that the doctor had thought it necessary to mention such notions in his report.

I couldn't see it that way. In specifically ruling out drugs and alcohol, the doctor had effectively squelched the kind of leering speculation that has become inevitable in the violent death of anyone whose background includes professional sports. Or Vietnam. It was a thoughtful and intelligent move, totally at odds with the dim but affable face he showed to the world—a carefully dissembled persona that nonetheless had emerged in plenty of time to keep him from chasing an inside straight into the low-pair trap I'd set for him a few hands back. I wondered who else at the table could see the same man I did.

Barlow? Yes. J. J. Barlow, almost certainly. And also, perhaps, the player still fiddling with a pair of kowboys to the doctor's left.

His name was Edward Watrous. The Spences had identified him as Farewell's most successful merchant, and fully half the evening's conversational pauses had been preempted by what appeared to be a long-running verbal *guerrila* between him and the physician on the subjects of weight and girth.

Watrous's nickname—I would have offered long odds that it dated from grammar school—was Tiny, and it wasn't the kind of thing that would ever need explaining.

At first glance, from across a room, I had guessed him at 400 pounds. But closer inspection told me that was probably far too low. Tiny Watrous was the kind of fat man whose components are so totally in proportion that he takes on his true size only at close range—six feet two or three, I decided, and tremendously muscular under all the padding. If he'd been born in Japan, he might well have been considered for marriage into one of the better sumo families. In a town like Farewell, however, his size and bulk had probably been a social problem for him through adolescence and beyond, and he had evidently coped with it—as a few are preceptive enough to do—by casting himself in the easily acceptable role of Jolly Fat Man.

I wondered how many people over the years had found out too late that there are no Jolly Fat Men.

Galloping through their thumbnail sketches of my probable poker opponents, the Spences had mentioned that, in addition to owning Farewell's only department store, Tiny Watrous was a silent partner in the town's three indoor movie theaters, the 250-watt commercial radio station, six bars, a restaurant, and a rickety little dirt track where the local talent raced their stock cars every weekend during the summer. He was also a director of J. J. Barlow's bank and a former three-term mayor.

Jolly Fat Men do all those things, of course. But not by being Jolly Fat Men. Tiny Watrous might be only a fair-to-indifferent poker player—poor card sense and not enough concentration, a social player—but that didn't mean he was a loser. His running word-battle with the doctor never seemed to distract him so far as to make him incautious with his bets. His forays into the third or fourth round were always based on solid hands. After the first hour or so I had decided to be careful about betting into him, and noticed that those who did were usually sorry, because it was almost impossible to drive him out of a pot once he had decided to go for it and because he won the big ones as often as he lost them. For the night, he was a little behind, but no more than he could chalk up to necessary business socializing.

The player to my immediate right was another matter entirely.

His name, according to the Spences, was Leonard Kenneth Pemberton, but he had been introduced as Deke, and I never heard anyone call him anything else. When they spoke to him at all.

It wasn't ostracism, exactly. Deke Pemberton seemed to be well enough liked. "But somehow you just never know what to say to him," Jake had told me, and I could see what he meant. Some men seem to be old friends after a few minutes; big-town political chieftains and other truly dangerous confidence men have this faculty. With Pemberton, on the other hand, I suspected that a man could know him from childhood (at least two of the other players, I knew, could claim as much) and still be no more than acquaintances.

Deke Pemberton, Jake Spence had said, was probably the smartest, most successful, and least appreciated lawyer in the southwestern United States. Law school graduate at twenty-one, sometime clerk to a Supreme Court justice, Pemberton had seemed well launched in a prestigious Wall Street firm when he suddenly resigned and returned to Farewell on his thirtieth birthday to take a low-pay job as assistant district attorney.

"At first," Jake said, "people around here assumed he had either gotten into some kind of trouble back in New York or had political ambitions back here among the homefolks. He'd been born rich, and politics would have been a logical goal. After a year in the D.A.'s office, he took another short-money job as US. commissioner—that's like being a federal judge, only it's not for life—and a couple of his opinions are in the law school textbooks now. Deke could never have been elected to anything. Too chilly. But he'd collected enough IOUs over the years to take his pick of political appointments." Instead, Jake said, he had resigned and entered private practice.

No one ever asked him why.

Playing one night's poker against him hadn't answered any of the big questions, of course. But it offered hints. In this pot, for instance, he had backed an exposed jack-ten into the third betting round where he picked up a lovely queen to support the notion of an open straight. A solid betting hand if it was real, a solid bluffing hand if it wasn't. And there was nothing poker-faced about his expression as he waited for Tiny Watrous to come to a decision. As he sat it out, Pemberton's face revealed as much as it ever did—a collection of unmemorable features in cadaverous repose.

But there was a stillness.

A listening.

"Okay," Watrous said at last, pushing a stack of blue chips into the pot. "See your hundred and up fifty." He leaned back and took a deep, frog-grinning pull at what I knew was his seventh bourbon and soda. I think it was supposed to lull his opponents into a false sense of security.

Pemberton didn't seem to notice. Wordlessly, he tossed his possible straight into the discard and looked at nothing. No one seemed at all surprised.

J. J. Barlow hesitated the briefest of seconds, glancing pointedly at the fat man's kings before moving five blues into the pot.

The deal was mine, and now I handed him what I knew was the last remaining jack. It was another heart.

Tiny Watrous seemed unperturbed by the seven of spades that landed in front of him. "High pair bets," he said unnecessarily.

Barlow looked at his possible full house and finger-counted a double stack of blues. He had all the options; this was table stakes, and neither he nor Watrous was apt to run short. He waited for the fat man to make up his mind.

"Hundred," Watrous said finally, pushing ten blues into the center of the table without looking at Barlow.

The banker hesitated only a moment before meeting the bet. I dealt the final concealed cards and sat back to watch. The possibilities were endless, but—never mind the cards—I would have offered side action on the man in the wheelchair.

Tiny Watrous didn't see it that way, of course. "Go for broke," he said, counting twenty blues into the pot and grinning at Barlow.

Barlow seemed to think it over.

Despite Watrous's high pair, his possible flush was a strong betting proposition, and I was sure he hadn't failed to notice that one other king had gone into the discard earlier.

"By God, you don't make it easy, do you?" he said, fingering his chips again. "But I guess I'm in too deep to leave now."

His eyes never left Watrous's face as he stacked twenty blues, placed another twenty beside them, seemed to think it over—and then moved all the rest of his chips into the center of the table.

Watrous stared at the pile for a moment before leaning back to take another soothing sip of the bourbon.

He looked at Barlow and he looked back at the table and he looked at his bourbon and he looked at his hands and finally he looked at his first two concealed cards…which told me what he was holding. Barlow had been right. At best, the fat man was backing a full house, kings over; at worst, two pair. Otherwise, he'd have checked out the last card when he got nervous.

I wondered if Barlow knew it, too.

But the banker wasn't telling anybody anything they didn't already know. His attention was fixed again on the far wall, and his hands were quiet.

Watrous looked searchingly at him, and had a coughing fit.

"Well, I be damn!" he said when it was done. "I be damn if you ain't gone and trapped ol' Tiny." He turned his frog-grin at

Barlow, who looked back blankly. "Yes, indeedy," Watrous went on. "Trapped the ol' fat boy fair and square. No wonder you banker fellers wind up owning half the county."

He turned his eyes back toward the table.

"Well, sir," he said, "well, sir, now! Reckon there ain't much a poor boy can do but follow along, is there?"

He grinned widely again and—oh, what the hell—made a broom of his hands to sweep all his remaining chips into the pot. He clasped his hands behind his head and leaned back in the chair, which uttered a minor shriek of protest.

Barlow's face finally came alive.

Leaning forward, he used one hand to stack the fat man's final bet and his own in parallel. When he was done, five reds remained. He raked them back to the empty spot in front of him.

"Okay," he said. "Let's find out..."

Watrous shrugged, still smiling. Almost offhandedly, he flipped over his first two hole cards to show a pair of sevens for a full house. A nice betting hand. And not too badly played.

But Barlow's was better.

Nodding thoughtfully in the fat man's direction, he flipped his first two concealed cards over to display a pair of fours—and then a final four he'd caught on the last round to fill a winning hand that I knew must have surprised him as much as it did everyone else.

Even Deke Pemberton snorted.

But it remained for Tiny Watrous to pronounce benediction. "You," he said to Barlow, the emotion of the moment temporarily depriving him of the good ol' boy accent and vocabulary, "are a conniving misbegotten low-life indiscriminate fornicator of swine!"

Nobody seemed to want to go on playing after that, so we turned the chips back into money and left everything else for the club's morning cleanup crew—which, I decided on checking my watch, should be arriving at any moment. Dawn was a little more than an hour away, and as I stopped off in the men's room to put my right eye back where it belonged, it suddenly seemed time to remember that I hadn't been on close terms with a mattress for nearly twenty-four hours.

Suppressing a yawn, I refused with thanks an offer of transportation back to town, explaining that my rented wheels were waiting in the parking lot.

Walking out to reclaim the car might have been a good time to go through the mental sorting usual to the end of a long game. Hardening the lines around the personalities. Noting mistakes. Secretly congratulating myself for correct decisions.

But I didn't do that.

Just too tired.

Which may or may not explain why I failed to notice that the car wasn't where it should have been. Or, at any rate, had undergone some major alteration.

The transportation I had rented in Amarillo was a black Camaro, and unfamiliar though it might be, I was morally certain that it had still been a black Camaro when I parked it beside Jake Spence's aging station wagon at the far end of the club lot the previous afternoon. But the vehicle occupying that spot now was a new but battered Japanese-built pickup, its canary-yellow paint thickly spattered with the red mud of eastern New Mexico. It was the kind of vehicle that must surely contain a gun rack mounted beside the driver's bench seat, and I could see it had one. And something to go with it.

Leaning at ease against the open tailgate was six feet or so of B-picture country lout, gangling and dirty behind the standard equipment of green teeth exposed in a doggy grin. A nest of empty-and-squeezed beer cans on the ground nearby told me he had been waiting for quite a while.

"Hidey-there, preacher-man," he said, moving an inch or two to make sure I didn't miss the mail-order brass knuckles fitted loosely over his right hand. "Lookin' for something?"

It was beginning to feel like a long, long night.

A SERMON
(CONTINUED)

Some argue, of course, that this is all a part of God's greater plan...part of the destiny that He has prepared for us, His children...

FIVE

Surprise parties can be embarrassing.

Standing perfectly still and looking at my latest acquaintance in Farewell, I felt a momentary rush of shame and irritation—directed entirely at myself. Either I was getting old or I was getting careless or both, and that is the kind of thing that can be bad news for a man in my line of work. A poker player starves or prospers according to his degree of alertness and perception.

I made a mental note to consider a refresher with our resident *mahayana* master when I got home.

But I was fully awake now. *Nariyuki no matsu*...I turned my center still and waited with what I hoped was patience infinite while invoking *haragi,* the sixth sense that connects all living things. Greenteeth hadn't come alone. Listening with the pores open at last, I could fill in a partial picture of two others—height, weight, position, even the emotional pitch of waiting to move in on me—while they remained out of sight behind the truck. I wondered if their mothers knew they were out.

Greenteeth finally got tired of waiting. "That is sure a pretty suit you got on there, preacher-man," he said.

I just looked at him.

"And a nice hat," he went on when I didn't react. "Stetson, ain't it? You know, I always did want a pretty hat like that. Now, I wonder if it would kindly fit me. You reckon it would?"

He reached toward me and I moved back a step, turning a bit to keep my blind right side toward the place where his friends were still hiding.

"Aw, here, now," he said, flashing the green tusks again in a beer-friendly smirk. "Where you goin'? I ain't gonna hurt you for an hour yet."

He carried his right hand low but not out of sight, and I could see the fingers flex in the knuckle-duster. He was ready for business. And so were the other two.

Well, okay, then.

Having only one eye can be a frustration. It limits your perception of distance and cuts the effective field of vision by nearly a third. You have to turn your head to see things on the dark side. Still, there can be compensations. For instance, if you have learned to distinguish people and objects without visual contact, any action you take on the information can come as something of a surprise.

"Sorry, friend," I said, giving Greenteeth my brightest smile. "You've got the wrong man. I'm really far too tired to talk hats and haberdashery with you tonight. I'll just go back and phone for a cab…"

I started a turn to the left, back toward the distant clubhouse, and—who knows?—all things being equal, I might even have gone there and done that. Stranger things have happened. But no chance. As I'd expected, my retreat was a signal for Greenteeth's two buddies to break cover…which put the first of them in perfect position for the hook-kick I'd started with the left turn.

It connected with a satisfactory sound, and I felt its recipient's *wa* flicker, stunned, before erupting into pain and astonishment. A nice moment.

But not to be savored. Greenteeth had been almost as surprised as his friend. His brass knuckles were still fanning the space where I might have been when the final energy of the kick brought me back to face him. Now I moved forward, inside the danger range of his weapon, and grasped both sides of his shirt collar. He was about my height, so I didn't have to bend in order to bring my forehead into violent contact with the bridge of his nose.

Sudden white pain took away the breath he needed to scream. That left number three.

I'll say this for him: He didn't hesitate. The blade in his left hand was about four inches long, and he carried it in the tight but flexible grip of affection and long acquaintance. His eyes were bright with something more than beer, and his expression was one of pleasurable anticipation as he feinted to the right and attacked to the left.

I let him do it and waited for the low slash. When it came, I gave the movement a little help at the very end and managed a hard kite to the side of the neck as he went past.

Result: zero.

Whatever kind of controlled substance the little shitkicker was using, it didn't slow him down and seemed to make him relatively immune to pain. Sometimes I really wish I'd been a concert violinist like my grandmother wanted.

Over by the tailgate of the truck, Greenteeth was gradually recovering his grasp on the world, and I could sense a few signs of life returning to the youngster with the damaged jaw. Well, hell already! Finesse is a fine thing, and I like to measure the dose as well as the next, but enough is too much and I really had been awake a lot longer than I wanted to be.

"Hey, pussy," I said to make sure I had the knife-fighter's undivided attention. "Your mother still making it with the garbage man?"

Bull's-eye!

The knife point came straight for the middle of my face, and the whole weight of his body was behind it. I hardly had to move a muscle to intercept, and the force of his rush made the twist that broke his wrist almost reflexive. The knife skittered away across the pavement as my right shin connected with his crotch, and the bright eyes clouded. All the same, it took a double blow to the base of the skull to be sure of putting him away. Just in time to say hello to Greenteeth, who had lost his knuckle-duster and quite a bit of blood, but not his nerve. He was probably the best of the lot, and it seemed almost a pity to kick his left knee out from under him and break his face as he went down. But I was beginning to lose patience with the lot of them.

Two away, top of the ninth.

The third clown was technically conscious but not really back in the picture yet, so I had a few moments to spare and used them to retrieve his buddy's knife. When he was finally able to focus, he found the point less than an inch from his left eye.

"Do you like games?" I inquired conversationally.

The threatened eye rolled around the deserted parking lot, looking for erstwhile allies.

"Your friends were sort of tired," I told him, smiling with a lot of teeth. "They're going to take a little siesta now, and we don't want to disturb them, do we? No. Besides, they're no fun. Not like you. How's your jaw—working good? Hurt a little? Well, these things pass. You'll see, week or two you'll be good as new. Hey, you like games? Bet you're a real whiz, right? I know what let's do: Let's play Twenty Questions."

Hard to say whether he heard me or not. The eye kept moving around, but it always came back to the sharp point suspended above it.

"Okay, now," I said, still smiling at him. "Listen up! Here's the first question: What's your middle name?"

No response.

I shook my head gently in mild, schoolmasterly reproof and flicked the knife blade inside his left nostril, drove it sharply upward, then returned it to its former position. A single red droplet of blood oozed from the point, missing the eye by a hair and rolling slowly down his cheek.

"Wrong answer," I said.

That finally got through to him. I waited until the noise he made had echoed into silence and then repeated the question: "What's your middle name?"

He wanted to answer. His lips worked and he moved his tongue. But it took a deep breath and a swallow before he finally managed to make a recognizable effort.

"Har...uh, Harold," he said.

I kept smiling at him. "How's that?" I said. "Can't hear you."

"Harold," he said, throat and lungs working together at last, eyes still fascinated by the knife point. "My middle name's Harold!"

That earned him a friendly nod, but the end of the blade stayed right where it was.

"Harold," I said. "My, that's a nice name. There was a king of England named that once. Did you know that, Harold?"

If he did, he didn't say so.

"Now, that was question number one," I went on, "and I surely do think we are going to have a high old time with this game. You got a real talent! So here's question number two, Harold: Where's my car?"

The eyes wanted to lie.

He managed to tear his gaze away long enough to glance in the direction of the yellow pickup, and if you listened closely you could almost hear "I don't know" forming in the back of his brain. But when he looked back, that knife was still half an inch from where the buried fears live, and he just couldn't let it get any closer.

"Bobby Don," he said in a voice that had gone high and thin as a child's. "Ol' Bobby Don Thieroux, he drove it away. I don't know where he went to. Honest to God, mister!"

I nodded, readjusting my image of the richboy gunsel. He was dumber than I had thought.

"Bobby Don tell you to park here and wait for me?" I asked.

He bobbed his head up and down, eager to cooperate now. "Bobby come to Boo's house," he said, jerking his head in the direction of the still-sleeping Greenteeth. "Boo's daddy, he works out on the Thieroux spread, and we do favors for Bobby and the old man sometimes, you know? To be friendly."

"Well, now, that's nice," I said. "I like to be friendly myself. So I tell you what—just to show my heart's in the right place, I'm going to let you do some favors for me, too. Think you'd like that?"

Harold nodded vigorously to show he thought that sounded like a wonderful idea, and had sense enough to keep his mouth shut and his movements slow after I moved back to let him stand up.

It took a while for him to find his balance, and when he did it was in the posture of a man much older than he had been earlier in the day. With only the sketchiest supervision from me, he loaded his two damaged compatriots into the bed of the truck, slammed the tailgate, and turned warily to see what I wanted next.

"Open up the hood," I said.

He reached through the driver's door and struggled with a lever that finally caused the hood to pop upward with a rusty sound.

It was a six-cylinder engine and I had no idea what the firing order might be, but numbers two and four seemed as good a choice as any. I reached in, started to rip the distributor wires away from those two spark plugs, but thought better of it when I noticed the coating of grease and dirt.

"Come over here, Harold," I said.

He came, and watched blankly as I used the knife to indicate the proper wires. "Pull them loose," I said, and he did it without hesitation, looking back to me for further orders when he was done.

"Thank you, Harold," I said. "Now I want you to cut both of those wires in two."

I handed him the knife and watched the slow movement of his mind as he considered using it to resume hostilities. But the decision had really been made beforehand, and neither of us was at all surprised when he used it for the purpose I had suggested.

"All right, then," I said when the truck had been fully crippled, "just one more thing..."

A car was approaching slowly from the clubhouse side of the lot, but I kept my eyes on Harold.

"You put the knife blade under the sole of your boot, and break it off," I told him, and waited while he did it.

The car stopped behind me and I could hear the polite whine of the servos as they rolled down the window on the driver's side.

"Everything all right?" J. J. Barlow's voice inquired.

"Just fine," I said, relaxing a bit, but still not looking away from Harold. "This young gentleman and I have just been having a little discussion...kind of a philosophical dialogue, you might say."

"Heard part of it," Barlow said dryly. "Loud noises sort of carry at this time of day. Did you reach consensus?"

I spared a moment to glance in his direction. The banker's eyes were as guileless as a confirmation class.

"We did," I said. "Oh, neighbor, we surely did! But now it's time for meditation and mantra, so Harold here is going to get into this truck and use the keys I see in the ignition to start it up and drive it away. Aren't you, Harold?"

It took a moment for the words to register, but when they did, Harold wasted no time. The stump of the knife was still in his hand as he clambered into the driver's seat and started grinding the starter, but I saw him drop it to the muddy floor mat before he remembered to close the door.

The truck finally started on the third try. The engine didn't run too well on four cylinders, but it still had enough power to do the basic job, and Harold was able to nurse it out of the parking lot and onto the county road.

Barlow and I watched him go in silence.

"Welcome to New Mexico," the banker said when the coughing of the crippled engine had finally died away.

"Land of Enchantment," I agreed. "Fair fields and friendly folks. Tell me—who's got the main splint, bandage, and truss franchise hereabouts, and how much would it cost to buy him out?"

The banker nodded solemnly.

"Lot of that going around," he said.

Farewell had its own taxi service, but I accepted Barlow's offer of a ride back to town. He didn't ask where I was staying and I didn't volunteer. But that didn't seem to keep him from getting there.

As he'd observed, there seemed to be a lot of that going around.

A SERMON (CONTINUED)

Without the soul-sickness of war, would we love peace? Without the disillusionment of worldly success, would we value simplicity?

Without the final weariness of life, could we learn to accept death…?

SIX

Leaving the country-club parking lot, we rode for a minute or two in silence, and I spent the time using peripheral vision to admire the layout of Barlow's car.

It was a Rolls Corniche, about a year old and immaculate. Impressive. But the main attraction from my point of view was the effort, mental and technological, that had been brought to bear on the specific problems of its driver.

Ingeniously equipped motor vehicles are almost commonplace in modern society. Lift gates and special parking spaces enhance the lives of men and women who would have been permanently house-bound and dependent little more than a decade ago. Computer filters have given clear speech to the near-speechless. And I have personal cause to be interested in electronic research that seems to offer the hope of sight to eyes that no longer see...or even exist.

But Barlow's Corniche was something special.

Hand controls have, of course, been available ever since a wealthy and partially paralyzed President half a century ago decided he'd like people to see him driving his own car. But I think Barlow's must have been one of a kind: A console thoughtfully engineered to be within inches of his right hand supported the gear-setting mechanism, emergency brake, and radiotelephone controls, while foot brake and accelerator had been built unobtrusively into the back side of the steering wheel, offering fingertip control to a man who kept his hands in the two-ten position while driving.

No one seeing him on the road would ever have cause to pity the most successful banker in eastern New Mexico.

"Like it?" Barlow asked when he decided I'd gawked long enough.

" 'Admire' is a better word," I said. "I'm partial to machines that do what they are supposed to do, and this one seems to fit into the category."

He smiled thinly, acknowledging the compliment.

"It does the job," he said. "And then some. For what it's worth, I had more to offer than just jawbone back there in the parking lot, too..."

He touched the bottom of the special control panel, and a drawer snapped open to offer the butt of what looked like a .38 caliber automatic mounted on a .45 chassis.

"Belgian?" I asked, looking at it.

"One of the special Brownings." He nodded. "Re-machined a couple of times, now, and beginning to show its age. But it'll be a sorry day when I finally have to replace it. Old friends are old friends..."

I thought that over and decided he'd used the phrase intentionally.

I also decided not to take the bait.

"Got many local boys like the three I met in the parking lot?" I asked, not exactly changing the subject but altering the heading by a degree or two.

Barlow's gaze shifted back to the road, and something moved around behind his face. If we'd still been playing poker, I would have paid money to find out what it meant. But he let a moment or two go by before answering, and when he spoke again it was in a different tone. Crisper, less southwestern, with a fire-glow of anger somewhere in the back.

TED THACKREY JR.

"Yes, we have more," he said, locking his eyes on the road and keeping them there. "Every town has them. Always did. They've been there—and not by chance—ever since men first started hunting in packs and sharing the warmth of a common fire. The half-ape who could figure out where the game was likely to be found and how to make sure he ate it instead of vice versa couldn't carry out his plans alone; he needed other half-apes to get on one side of the bear and keep it interested while someone else rushed in on the other side to stab it to death with a stone spear...and you can bet the someone else wasn't going to be Mister Smart Guy!"

He paused for breath. I seemed to have struck a nerve.

"It went on like that," he continued, hardly missing a beat, "right through the ancient world. The sandstone engineers who designed the pyramids never raised a drop of sweat carving rocks or humping them into place; King Minos may have had a say in designing his palace and labyrinth, but he never turned a spadeful of earth.

"Medieval wars were fought as much to use up surplus manpower as to vent the greed and hubris of louse-ridden aristocrats. Immigrants who followed the Pilgrims to our fair shores were welcomed by industrialists who needed an eager and available workforce. Unemployment as we know it—a permanent percentage of the labor force for whom no jobs exist, not just the temporary displacement of previous societies—was born at about that time, and its creation was deliberate. Beat slavery all hollow! A slave owner had to feed his property whether there were any jobs for them or not, but a surplus employee could be told to go live on tree bark until he was needed again. So that's just what the marginal ones were told, and pretty much what they did, too!"

He paused for breath again as we negotiated the turn from the county road onto the state highway leading back to

Farewell, but I didn't interrupt. The man talking now was the one I had come to meet, and he was telling me quite a bit about himself.

"So nobody noticed—or cared, if they did notice—until the second half of the twentieth century," he said. "That's when the egg hit the fan, in the decade or so after my generation came home from its war.

"Early on in the fighting, Franklin D. Roosevelt and his buddies had decided, more as a public relations gesture than anything else, to offer a kind of bounty for the poor dumb bastards who had actually let themselves be dragged into the armed services during what is now remembered as the most popular war of modern times.

"They called their bright-as-a-penny soldier-hustle the G.I. Bill of Rights, and it put college education within reach of more than a million people who in the normal course of things would have quit with a high school diploma. Or less. Not all of them took advantage of the offer, of course, and not all wound up with degrees. But a lot of them did—enough, anyway, to touch off a technological revolution that created a whole new world. And that new world had no real place in it for a part of the population that had always been there but hadn't seemed like much of a problem until then.

"Always before, even during the depression of the thirties, people knew there were a few jobs that 'just anyone' could do. Swing a wrench on the assembly line. Carry boxes on a loading dock. Wash dishes. Dig ditches. Plenty of work for a man with a strong back and not too much imagination.

"But in the world that our wonderful new college generation made for itself, those jobs began to disappear. Automation cut most of the unskilled positions out of the assembly process, containerization raised hell on the loading docks, automatic dishwashers put the old kitchen pearl-divers out of work, and backhoes began to dig the ditches with a speed and accuracy that no human being could ever match.

"John Henry might have beaten the steam drill in the old song, but remember, he killed himself doing it—and modern personnel managers are there to make damn sure he never gets his hands on a hammer.

"For a while, education was supposed to be the answer. Retrain the adult unemployables. Keep kids in school long enough to learn the skills they need to cope with the computer world. Sounded good, and the government churned out all the laws and money to make it happen. Trouble is, it didn't work. A man who has spent half his life shoveling coal into a blast furnace simply is not going to become a salad chef, no matter how many special classes you send him to. And a high school kid who majored in hanging out in the smoking area isn't going to be much help around a stockroom where he has to read labels and add numbers, or even working in a garage where engine problems are diagnosed with a computer, no matter how many years you make him stay in school.

"What happens instead is that the guy who used to feed the blast furnace finally gives up trying to find a job and sits around the house wondering what the hell happened, and the kid who finally got out of high school without being able to read either finds himself a challenging career as a supermarket bag-boy— those jobs will be disappearing before long; you already use a computer to read the prices and make small change at the checkout counter—or he drifts away to a city where he can take his choice of dealing dope and dying young, snatching purses and winding up in the slammer, or spending the rest of his life sleeping under cardboard boxes because the skid-row missions just can't handle all the potential customers anymore…"

A line rig was bumbling along ahead of us on the two-lane highway; Barlow peeked around it and gunned the Rolls to pass.

The Corniche leaped forward in a kind of ghastly silence, slipping easily along the expanse of the double trailer and cab and dodging nimbly back into the right lane at least a second or two before it was rocked by the atmospheric bow wave of an onrushing semi.

I noticed that my right hand was clamped painfully around the door handle, and ordered it to relax. It did so. Reluctantly.

I had missed a sentence or two of the banker's monologue. But not enough to lose the thread.

"...found a use for them," he was saying. "The one that always seemed to work so well back in the Middle Ages. A man who isn't much at civilian life may turn out to be a real asset in war. You can get him to try any kind of a crazy thing, because he hasn't got sense enough to know it's impossible.

"They tried the idea out—just a little bit—in Korea. Instead of committing fully trained regular troops, the army called up reservists and National Guard units. Filled the empty files with conscripts who were either too dumb or too unlucky to qualify for one of the army's hot-shot specialist schools. And then threw them away playing out a semi-senile general's ego games up and down a godforsaken peninsula nobody really gave a damn about anyway.

"Even back then, a kid could wriggle out of the bind by signing up for ROTC in college or getting into one of the National Guard or reserve units that hadn't been called. A few people noticed what was going on, and they called it a scandal, but it never got much attention, and most forgot all about it as soon as the fighting was over. So naturally the idea went on the back burner and was trotted right out again good as new as soon as the next recession set in.

"This time they didn't even bother with window dressing. No nonsense about citizen-soldiers or Universal Military Service. Just a clear, cold choice: Stay in school or go to 'Nam. Be smart or be a target.

"Only it wasn't really a choice. Damn few kids who had the money and the grades to stay in school ever volunteered for the army; the ones who were drafted knew they were there because their folks couldn't afford college or because their brains weren't good enough to hack the classwork. Exceptions? Sure—the fighting went on a long time and some of the guys who had avoided the draft in college wound up graduating into the arms of the Selective Service System. But they'd all had a while to think and plan, and most of them either went into the service with commissions or angled into the same National Guard units that had protected their older brothers, or even into one of the advanced degree programs sanctioned by the Department of Defense. Nuclear physics. Medicine. Engineering.

"The result was about what you'd expect: A man who knows his life has been interrupted and endangered because his government thinks he is pond scum is absolutely going to have a major attitude problem. Especially when quite a few of the neighbors and fellow citizens that the draft board told him he was serving spit on him and tell him he's a baby-killer on account of having done what they told him to do. Nonetheless, there was an outpouring of general mystification and alarm when some of the prospective heroes decided to go live in Canada instead of swearing to defend the Constitution, while others either deserted or refused to serve and wound up in prison. Nobody could seem to figure it out…"

Barlow paused for breath, and I looked away from the road long enough to glance in his direction. He was staring straight ahead, his face full of an emotion I don't think he could have named. I'm not sure he still knew I was in the car.

"So finally that was over, and time passed, and there were pious congratulations all around about how much we had learned from our mistakes, and we were back to square one: What do you do with all the kids who just don't seem to be able to find a niche in the technological machine that was supposed to solve problems but, instead, ended up creating them? And the hell of it is, no one has come up with any new answers. All we can offer is don'ts. Don't use narcotics. Don't rob stores. Don't mug peaceable citizens. Don't dress like something from outer space. Don't make a nuisance of yourself."

He stopped talking again long enough to let a dusty sedan make a left turn in front of him at Farewell's main intersection, and I had time to decide that I could understand how the World War II soldier had been able to find common ground with a much younger man who had flown helicopters in Vietnam.

I might not be able to stand foursquare behind every single one of his conclusions. But I well and truly had to award points for the thinking that had gone into them.

"Sure, I know the manure-jockeys who jumped you," he said when we were moving again. "And a hundred or more like them. Known them all their lives, and their families before they were born. They are bone-lazy, vicious, stupider than a box of rocks, and God knows nobody is going to get all bent out of shape about them getting a few assorted lumps and limps. But they didn't invent the world they live in.

"And," he said, looking away from the road long enough to grin at me, "they sure as hell weren't waiting for you in that parking lot by chance."

We turned into the front driveway of a chain motel—where he appeared to know I was staying even though he had seemed to have trouble remembering my name earlier in the evening—and ghosted unhesitatingly past the main lobby to the door of the room where I'd left my suitcase before moving on to the country club.

"Jake Spence is a good man," he said, setting the hand brake and turning his head and shoulders to face me. "So if he thinks it's necessary to bring in a pro to see whether someone was robbed in the local poker game, I suppose I can understand it."

He paused, but there didn't seem to be anything for me to say.

"Orrin Prescott was more than a friend," he went on when I didn't answer. "I never married. Never had any kids...to speak of, anyway. So I guess a lot of people had it in their heads that I was playing father-and-son with him for all the years after he turned up in the backfield of the high school football team. But the truth is, he felt more like a brother—I never had one of those, either—and the older he got, the more it seemed that way.

"I don't know what went wrong. He didn't tell me and I couldn't ask. Maybe I should have. But I didn't and I have to live with the thought that maybe if I had asked he would be alive today, because I don't think the crash that killed him was any accident, and I don't think it was murder, either. But if he'd been cheated in the poker game, or been a heavy loser, I'd have known it, because I was at the same table every single time he played. Of course, you have only my word for that..."

He paused for a moment, and suddenly the tension was gone from his face and the powerful shoulders relaxed against the seat cushion. I waited, hoping for more.

But he seemed to be done.

"Lordy me," he said. "I do seem to be turning into a garrulous old bastard, don't I?"

I gave him my brightest preacher-man smile as I climbed out of the Corniche and closed the door.

"Lot of that going around," I said.

The eyes narrowed momentarily as he caught the echo, and then softened into a smile.

"Yeah," he said. "So I hear tell..."

We exchanged a few more words—unimportant but very necessary—through the car window before he finally put the machine in gear and wheeled its silent majesty around the parking circle and out toward the highway.

It was a joy to watch, but mingled in this particular instance with an unmistakable sense of relief. The ride back from the club had done terrible things to the muscles of my back and legs.

Unlocking the door to my room, I tried to think about Prescott and poker and helicopters and Barlow and what he'd had to say about Jake's suspicions. But it had just been too long between naps, and I wasn't even sure I wanted to risk a shower before melting into the mattress. Cold water would probably give me a heart attack, and if I made it warm, there was a good chance I would fall asleep in the stall...which can be dangerous.

Momentarily I toyed with the idea of picking up the phone to report the rented car stolen.

But Barlow had assured me that it wasn't necessary; the car would be back—washed, polished, and parked outside my room—by the time I wanted it again. I asked him if that meant he was going to tell Bobby Don's granddaddy on him, and he grinned but didn't answer.

I wondered about that—for at least a split second—as I closed the motel-room door behind me. But the questions were going to have to wait. The bed was a soft and seductive rectangle in the diffuse morning light that found its way through a rift in the draperies. The shower stall was totally inaccessible. No way to get there from here.

All right, then.

Enough.

Deal the Preacher out; he's dog meat.

But my hand never reached the light switch, and in an instant the thrill-spill of adrenaline had driven all the aches and pains to the very farthest edge of background scenery.

The day wasn't over yet.

I had company.

A SERMON
(CONTINUED)

Friends—kindred, allies upon the face of the earth—
have priority among us on a par with food and shelter
and clothing.

They are not luxuries.

They are a basic necessity of life...

SEVEN

My first, instinctive reaction was to present a moving target—roll away from the doorway and keep going. Pride and dignity be damned; the basic animal is terrified of the unknown and dedicated to survival. Run, do not walk. Its teeth may be bigger than yours.

But I didn't move.

There was enough light in the room, and I had spent enough time coming through the door, to give my visitor all the opportunity anyone would need if violence was really on the menu. Nothing had happened. So I subdued the craven beast with threats and curses and let my senses move around the room to pinpoint the intruder's position.

Wa is the Japanese word for the magnetism, or personal aura, that surrounds all living things. It is strongest and most perceptible in the human animal, and I've talked to psychiatrists who claim to use it for better understanding of their patients' emotional distresses. I don't know whether it really works that way or not. But I know it has helped me read more than one opponent at the poker table. And I put it to work now, assembling a picture of the person who had come uninvited into my personal living space.

The bed was empty, but emotional echo-ranging focused my attention at once on the couch backed up to the far wall.

At first glance, in poor light, it had seemed unoccupied. But, studying it more closely now, I picked up the outline of a somewhat undersize human form. Female? Yes. Absolutely. It was lying on its side, blending into the contour of its resting place with the help of a color-coordinated blanket. Regular breathing motions and the bland hum of the *wa* told me that my terror-inspiring visitant had gotten tired of waiting for me to come home and had gone to sleep.

I leaned back against the door and wondered what would happen if I just eased back into the bright morning and got the room clerk to find me another sleeping room. The idea was tempting. But curiosity—and basic meanness of soul—is a powerful force in this world, and in the end I couldn't resist bending over the couch to whisper words of doom into the defenseless ear.

"The men have come," I said, "to flood the beds for ice-skating."

Reaction was slow.

But rewarding.

The sleeper took a deep breath, stirred, and then stiffened with returning awareness.

"Jesus!"

I moved back, grinning just a little, as the recumbent form heaved itself upright and brushed a wisp of hair from shock-rounded eyes that struck me an almost physical blow as they sharpened their focus.

Rational thought congealed as I returned the stare.

Sara.

My dead wife was sitting propped up by one arm in an eastern New Mexico motel room, clutching a peach-colored blanket to her chin and staring at me without a trace of love or recognition…

On second glance, of course, I realized it wasn't Sara.

The hair was ash blond, not red, and there was the barest hint of a tilt to the nose that Sara's never had. Fingernails, slightly overlong and flawlessly laquered, were another difference; Sara'd never seemed to have time for anything like that, even if she hadn't been forever biting them.

And the deep brown eyes were different, too. There was a watchfulness, a wary privacy, there that defied deep contact and kept its own counsel. Emotional echo-ranging gave back its own image, and nothing else.

Still, the similarity was...

"If there is one thing in this world I really hate," my newly awakened guest said when the silent confrontation had gone on long enough, "it's someone with a sense of humor in the early morning."

She dropped the blanket to the floor and reached across to the luggage table, where I'd failed to notice a near-new pack of cigarettes and a throwaway lighter. I watched while she coaxed a Marlboro out of the crowd and set it on fire. When it seemed to be burning to her satisfaction, she put the pack back on the table and blew a cloud of smoke in my direction.

"You're shorter than I remembered," she said, looking up with what seemed to be honest curiosity. "Didn't you used to be taller?"

"It's my dissolute lifestyle," I said. "Whittles away at the moral stature, shortens the tibiae and fibulae. In high school, I was six feet six..."

"That might explain it," she agreed, and then we were silent again while she shortened the cigarette by half an inch.

I waited it out in silence.

"The Spences told me you were here," she said at last, stubbing the remains of the cigarette into an ashtray. "I knocked, and when no one answered, I decided to come in and wait."

I still didn't say anything.

"My own room's just two door's down, and I remembered that the locks they used in this place weren't all that fancy—my dad was in the hardware business and he sold the junk to them just before he died, believe it—so my key opened your door and I came in to wait. Guess I fell asleep."

She looked up at me in sudden exasperation. "Well, say something, goddammit!"

I shrugged. "It's been kind of a long night," I said. "Leads to bad manners sometimes, so I hear. Did you say the Spences told you I was staying here?"

"Of course they did! Wait a minute…Haven't you…? Oh, Christ!" She leaned back against the couch and screwed a fist into her forehead. "This is great," she said. "Perfect! You've been out all night, so naturally that means Jake and Helen didn't get a chance to talk to you, and you haven't got a clue about what I'm doing here. Beautiful! Terrific! Look—how about we start all over again. Okay?"

It seemed like the best idea I'd heard since breakfast.

"Deal," I said. "Uh…should I go outside and come in again?"

That got half a smile. Almost half, anyway. Call it forty-five percent.

"Suit yourself," she said. "But if you start talking about—what was it?—flooding the bed for ice-skating, all bets are off and you can spend the rest of your life wondering who the hell I was."

I nodded solemnly. "No ice-skating," I promised.

"Okay, then." She stood up and extended a hand. "My name's Dana Lansing. I'm Marilyn Prescott's sister, and she's kind of a basket case right now. So the Spences sent me over to see if I could help."

Sure they had.

Damn Helen. And damn Jake, too.

I stood there, staring into my wife's face and listening to the words it was saying and remembering the look that had passed between the two Spences when I noticed something familiar about the maid of honor in the Prescotts' wedding picture. I decided to have a serious word or two with both of them in the very near future.

Or maybe just with Helen. Jake's mind really doesn't work that way.

Room service wasn't working yet, and we adjourned to the hotel coffee shop for further discussion.

Dana Lansing was Marilyn Prescott's younger sister, and she had moved away from Farewell with her husband six or seven years earlier. The marriage hadn't lasted, but Farewell didn't seem to be one of her favorite places, and I gathered that this was her first visit home in a long, long time.

"And it could have been a lot longer as far as I'm concerned," she added, stirring sugar into her coffee. "One of the main reasons I married Harry Lansing was to see this town the only way I ever wanted to see it—in a rearview mirror!"

I looked around in mock astonishment. "Looks okay to me," I said.

She grinned. Almost a hundred percent this time.

"No wonder you win at poker," she said. "A man who can lie with a face as straight as that ought to be selling oil stock. Or Mexican prisoners."

"Fresh out of prisoners right now," I said. "But I have a bridge back east that needs a new owner, arid if you'll look under the edge of the booth I think you'll find an envelope full of money that someone seems to have left there. Now, all you have to do is put up a little money of your own…"

"Sold," she said. "Who do we get to hold the stakes?"

"My partner. He'll be along here any minute."

"And I bet he'll have a nice honest face."

"What else?"

"What else…"

She looked away, out the window and then toward the cash register and then out the window again. Whatever she was thinking wasn't much fun.

And I was having troubles of my own. No matter what kind of orders I gave myself, Sara's face kept wriggling in between me and the set of assumptions that are known as reality. I wondered how long it was going to last, and how much of it was visible on the other side of my face.

"Okay, then." Dana sipped her coffee and looked back at me, all business. "I suppose the Spences filled you in on the general situation at the Prescott household. Marilyn's widowed, broke, and pretty much out of it for the time being. I'm no financial genius, but I had a look at the checkbooks and talked to that banker, Barlow, who used to be such a big buddy of Pres's. He thinks we ought to take the insurance money—when and if it's ever paid—and sell the land and whatever's left of the helicopter business to whoever will buy."

I listened to her with interest. The Spences evidently hadn't known, and Barlow hadn't volunteered, anything about being back in contact with the Prescott family.

Not that the advice wasn't sound enough: good, solid banker-words to the widow of an old friend.

So why were my alarm sirens making such a racket?

"Your sister signed anything yet?" I asked.

"No, not yet. In fact she doesn't even know about any of this. I answer the phones and the doorbells. Anyone wants to see her has to get past me. And that's not as easy as it looks."

She didn't put any special emphasis on that last sentence, but it came out metallic all the same. I believed her.

"Okay," I said. "Let's keep it that way for a while, then. You don't stay at the house all the time, though…You have a room here at the motel?"

"Just for sleeping."

"No spare room at the Prescotts'?"

She shook her head. "Marilyn moved into the guest room the day Pres died. Master bedroom's locked up now."

Her face said she didn't think any more of that idea than I did. But, one problem at a time.

"You've been away for a while," I said. "Now that you're back, how well do you still know your way around Farewell? The people, connections, motives…"

She thought it over for a moment. "Things change," she said. "People don't. Not really. Anything I don't know, I can find out without too much trouble."

"Good. Then while I'm asleep—which I hope will be any moment now, all this horrible-tasting coffee notwithstanding— I'd take it kindly if you could come up with the name of a half-smart lawyer who isn't in bed with every power merchant in town, and someone who can talk about local real estate with a maximum of authority and a minimum of hard sell."

There was a moment of hesitation before she nodded, and I could see a whole phalanx of reservations formed up in marching order behind her eyes. On the whole, I couldn't blame her. After all, who was I to come barging into her family's life, throwing my weight around and giving orders? Just someone the Spences used to know…

"Look," I said, "I realize this is all pretty high-handed, and you don't know me from a can of paint. But—"

She shook her head with a trace of irritation. "I told you before," she said, cutting me off in mid-apology, "good old Harry-baby Lansing, my late lamented husband, was a born loser, and one of the things he lost oftenest at was poker."

Oh.

"We were in Las Vegas when we broke up. I didn't have the price of a bus ticket home—wouldn't have come back to Farewell anyway—so I stayed in town and went to work on the late shift

71

at the Sands with a cocktail tray, net stockings, and a three-inch skirt. That was one of Harry's favorite losing-places, and I had a ringside seat while he lost every cent he made at a job he got dealing blackjack down in Glitter Gulch, and then every dime he could borrow from friends and passing acquaintances, and then every dollar he could hustle out of the two-for-three boys who finally put him to work hustling tourists for a string of call girls when he couldn't pay up. And I was the one the cops called to identify the body and tell the coroner what to do with it when he finally got tired of seeing a pimp in the mirror and took a flying leap to hell off the fifth floor of a fleabag hotel downtown.

"Meanwhile, I was getting pretty well acquainted with all the nice friendly pushers, punks, pansies, powder-horners, and assorted sons of bitches who make up the general population of that little garden spot..."

She paused for breath, but I didn't interrupt.

She still had things to say.

"So I know you," she said. "You're the one they call Preacher. The poker hustler in the black suit, who plays it so cool and smiling and patient and never wants anything but mineral water when he's sitting around a table trimming the chumps. You live in California, and they say you travel all over the world to find games that are big enough to suit you, but you get to Vegas two or three times a year—and no one ever saw you go home empty."

My face doesn't usually tell people much. Call it a professional necessity. But Dana Lansing seemed to read my next thought before it was fully formed.

She shook her head. "No," she said. "Oh, no! It's not what you're thinking. This isn't a second-rate television movie, and you're not one of the people who broke poor dumb Harry. He did that himself. Strictly solo.

"But you're part of the scenery. Part of the life. So I'll go along with the gag and be as much help as I can, because it's something to do to pass the time and the Spences seem to trust you, and besides, it keeps you away from Marilyn, who doesn't need anything else to worry about right now. Only, just don't waste the charm and the hustle on me. Save it for the marks. I'm immune."

A SERMON
(CONTINUED)

Why, then, this seeming contradiction of the concern with living space?

The answer seems plain.

Space is freedom, room for that action which is basic to our search for those other necessities…

EIGHT

There didn't seem to be much to say after that.

We finished the coffee in silence and I counted its price, plus an outrageous tip, onto the check that the single on-duty waitress had dropped at our table before she disappeared from the face of the earth.

It was easy enough to tell myself that the surprisingly strong reaction I was feeling had to do with Sara, and not with the flesh-and-blood woman now gathering up purse, cigarettes, and sweater across from me. But I didn't believe it for a moment, and I had a definite impression that intellectual persuasion wasn't going to make a bit of difference. Apologia has its limits.

Our good-byes, at the door of my room, were punctiliously correct and professionally cordial. You could have cut glass with them. So all right. Enough.

Sufficient unto the day.

Frankly, my dear, I don't give a damn.

All the same, the air-conditioned chill of the room and its drape-dim anonymity left me empty and restless.

I wondered if there were any other poker games in town.

Which was ridiculous. Fumbling the dead bolt and spiking the key on the play-for-pay television set, I told myself I was merely too tired to sleep—that seemed to have been happening oftener than necessary of late—and stripped off for a long, hot shower. It turned out to be brief and lukewarm. But effective.

I switched off the lamp, flipped back the lightweight blanket, and let myself dissolve into the commercial ease of some mattress-maker's wholesale special. He had nothing to apologize for. Sleep came within seconds and I fell into shape-negative darkness without even token resistance.

Like a corpse.

But sleep was restless. Scientists who study such things assure us that everyone dreams. No exceptions. The ones who think they don't, they say, are simply unable to remember the dreams because their content is too revealing—too rich for the dreamer to handle on a conscious level.

They talk like that all the time. I bet it's a barrel of fun. If they are right, though, I suppose I must have quite a bit to repress, because my dreams have always been few and far between, and even the ones I do remember are nothing for the Krafft-Ebing crowd.

The one I was having now, for instance, was certainly a second-rate effort. A real programmer, banal plot and lousy camera work, with me in slow motion while everyone else was able to move at regular speed and a Rolls Corniche quietly drowning in quicksand while its owner squatted, serene in lotus, on the roof.

Somewhere in the distance, mortar rounds began pounding the far-too-familiar floor of the rain forest where all this was happening…and kept right on pounding when the scene dissolved.

I let it go without regret.

The blank wall of the motel room greeted me, and I only needed two or three tries to remember that I was in Farewell, New Mexico, and to realize that the ratio of waking to sleeping hours was still a long way out of balance. I sat on the edge of the bed and invited *saika*.

But the mortars were still pounding—from the vicinity of the door—and I finally gave up.

Too early in the morning.

Or too late.

I'd fallen asleep in the same costume I had worn for the shower, and for a moment I was tempted to deal with the noise without pausing for nonessentials. But in the end, wiser counsel prevailed and I took the time to pull on short trousers and a shirt before dragging myself to the door and putting my eye to the peephole.

The portal pounder with the mortar-fire cadence was a man. In uniform.

Twisting the dead bolt back into the open position and working the knob, I put three inches of New Mexico climate between door and jamb and waited for him to talk.

"Uh…I'm really sorry if I woke you up, there," he began.

The voice was incongruous. High-pitched and thin, all wrong for its owner. He was a big man—taller, broader, and far more formidable than he had seemed in the lens-distorted view afforded by the peephole. A bright-buffed deputy's badge, I noted, was pinned to the precise peak of a military crease painstakingly ironed into the uniform blouse, and the leatherwork of the regulation pistol harness showed the effect of patient stropping with a dog bone.

"Perfectly all right," I said, lying with a straight face and stepping back to leave him a clear path into the room. "I had to get up to answer the door anyway."

If he got the joke he didn't say so, and maybe it wasn't such a knee-slapper at that. I'm never at my best when I first wake up. But he managed to get into the room, and I closed the door behind him and stood leaning against it, waiting for him to tell me why he was there.

It took him a while to do that. First he had to dig a soiled little spiral notebook out of his pants pocket and leaf through it to find the page he wanted.

"You…uh…drive a black Ford Camaro automobile, Texas license plate…uh…1X4328D?" he asked finally, reading from the scrawled page with evident effort.

Maybe he needed glasses.

"I'm driving a car I rented yesterday at the airport in Amarillo," I said. "It's a black Camaro, but I don't think I even glanced at the license number."

He nodded earnestly. "You got the rental contract here with you?"

If this was J. J. Barlow's notion of getting the missing car back to me, I decided he was either a lot less intelligent than I had supposed, or was trusting the wrong people to do the work for him.

"No," I said. "I put the contract in the glove compartment of the car for safekeeping. Too easy to lose papers you carry around with you."

The deputy's eyes were immediately troubled. "Oh, you should never do that," he said. "See, if you do that and then the car gets stolen or something, you can't tell the police what license number to look for or even prove you got a right to turn in an auto theft report, or anything."

His distress seemed genuine, and I had a strong impulse to pat his head and scratch his ears. The town of Farewell was getting odder and odder.

"Well," I said, "I guess I just wasn't thinking. Sorry. I'll try to remember in the future."

He nodded and shuffled his feet. "Uh…yeah," he said, still unhappy. "Yeah, well…" He reached behind his back and brought out a gleaming set of handcuffs. "I don't guess I need to search you, do I?" he inquired hopefully.

I looked at the manacles and decided I must have missed a paragraph or two somewhere. They weren't in any script I had read. None of this was. The whole dream was getting entirely out of hand.

"I don't, do I?" he prompted when I didn't reply at once.

"Guess not," I said.

He seemed relieved. "Good," he said, reaching out to snap one cuff on my left wrist and then moving clumsily to turn me around. "Ain't no sense having trouble on these things, is they?"

"No, indeed," I agreed as he confined the other wrist, testing to see that they were comfortable in the small of my back. "But there is one thing…"

"Oh? What's that?" he said, turning me back to face him.

"I always like to cooperate with the authorities," I said. "And I wouldn't for the world want you to think I was planning to make trouble. But don't you think it would be nice to tell me why I'm wearing the nifty new jewelry?" I clicked the cuffs together to make sure he knew what I was talking about.

"Oh, darn!" The oversize deputy's features registered new apology. "Now, ain't that just like me?" he said. "Forgot to say you were under arrest or read you your rights or anything!"

He fished in his pocket once again and finally came up with a greasy little card, which he held at myopic distance, squinting a bit to read the small print.

"You have the right to remain silent," he said, launching into the standard Miranda admonition. "If you give up the right to remain silent, anything you say can and will be used against you in a court of law. You have the right to speak with an attorney…"

The dreamlike quality of the scene refused to go away. I let the words wash over me and decided it was very poor theater. Not really credible. A bomb. Should have fixed it in New Haven or let it close out of town.

The deputy paused, looking at me and waiting for something. "Do you?" he said.

I was fresh out of information and ideas.

"Do you understand each of these rights I have explained to you?" he repeated.

"Well," I said, stirring my hands to make a rhetorical gesture and thinking better of it. "Well, there was just one little thing there, Mr. Deputy."

"Manion," he said with an open-faced smile. "Name's Vollie Manion. Call me Vollie, everyone does."

"Okay, then...Vollie," I said. "Before I go giving up any rights, isn't there one other thing you ought to tell me?"

That seemed to shake him.

He looked back at the Miranda card and read it through again in silence. Nope. He was sure he'd said it all. "Well..." he began uncertainly.

"The charge," I said. "Before we do anything more, shouldn't you tell me I'm under arrest. And for what?"

"Aw, shoot!"

You absolutely cannot fake the kind of blush that started at his neckline and rose to his forehead in less than a second.

"The thing is," he said, "I guess you can tell I don't arrest people very often. Mostly, they just keep me in at the jail. But I was out on patrol tonight when all this happened..."

He had lost me again, and it must have shown in my face.

"Sorry," he said, shaking his head. "What do you say, let's start this all over: You are under arrest for the crime of murder. Uh...you want me to read you your rights again?"

"No, thanks," I said. "But there's still one little thing you haven't told me."

"What's that?"

"The name of the victim. Who am I supposed to have killed?"

I'd have sworn his look of astonishment was genuine.

"Why, my Lordy," he said, "ain't you heard? It's all over town by now. Even on the radio. Ol' Bobby Don Thieroux was found dead out on the county road—in the sheriff's territory, you know—three, four hours ago. In your rental car..."

A SERMON
(CONTINUED)

Examples of the contrary condition—and its terrible price—are all around us.

Muslim terrorists clash and kill and make war to drive one another from the face of the earth in the Middle East.

Christian terrorists clash and kill and make war to drive each other off the face of the earth in Northern Ireland.

Thousands disappear without a trace in Argentina...

NINE

Deputy Manion was proud of himself.

His first night on regular patrol—three other deputies were sick, they'd had no choice but to let him off jail duty—he had discovered what seemed to be a murder and was handling it all by himself without even having to bother the sheriff.

"They sure going to be surprised," he said as we pulled up in the sheriff's parking space behind Farewell's four-story courthouse. "Though I got to say it didn't take any great shakes of detecting to see who done what."

He helped me out of the car's enclosed backseat and kept a hand lightly on my arm as we entered through the basement door and waited for the elevator.

"The victim—ol' Bobby Don, you know—he was in that car," he said. " 'Course, I didn't know who it belonged to then. But I teletyped the license number to the Texas Highway Patrol, and they told me the name of the company owned it, and I phoned them up, and they give me your name."

We got out of the elevator on the fourth floor, which seemed to be the county's central lockup.

Farewell's courthouse had been built at the tag end of the 1930s, a federal make-work project that had survived the test of time.

Someone had gone to a good deal of trouble to keep it as clean and habitable as possible, considering its basic mission in the world. The booking room—where I posed for two photographs, let Deputy Manion roll and stamp my fingerprints onto a stiff FBI card, and deposited most of my personal effects in an envelope—disclosed little trace of the dinginess and detritus usually associated with such places.

Perhaps it was just lack of use. Moving down the hallway and along a double row of cells, I saw only two customers: a trusty in denim busy with mop and bucket, and a disheveled drunk still apparently sleeping it off in the holding tank.

Deputy Manion paid them no mind, marching me to the end of the cell block, then through a barred but unlocked gate and into a cell with a solid steel door, which he locked behind him.

I had been a bit surprised when he slipped the cuffs on my wrists again before we moved into the cell block, but decided he was probably just being extra cautious. Not every day a rising young lawman captures a desperate murderer single-handed.

Still, I saw no cause for concern.

A telephone call to Jake Spence would solve all problems. No matter whose car the late Bobby Don Thieroux had been driving, at least four of Farewell's most prominent citizens could vouch for my whereabouts at the time he came to his sad end.

I had just opened my mouth to remind Vollie Manion about my right to make a telephone call when his fist slammed into the inverted V of my ribs, removing all the oxygen from the world and turning it misty gray at the edges.

"Now, then," he said, never losing that friendly smile as he settled me gently into a metal chair and secured my manacled hands behind its back, "I did hear you say you wanted to make a statement without bothering any lawyers so early in the morning. I did hear you say that, didn't I?"

Leaning back in an effort to get just a little oxygen back into my lungs, I found myself wondering about a detail that seemed almost irrelevant for the moment, but seemed to take up a lot of space nonetheless: The smiling deputy's punch had come without warning. A total surprise.

And that was next to impossible.

I had walked into an ambush at the country club by acting like a civilian: slovenly, thought-resistant, and half conscious. But it had been an effective lesson. My senses had been tuned in to the world around me ever since then—give or take an hour or two for sleep—and there was absolutely no way I could have failed to sense the emotional heat, the sudden change in the *wa,* that had to have preceded such a blow.

Yet I hadn't felt a thing. And that left two possible—very unattractive—explanations: Either I was beginning to lose the ability to read and respond to other human beings, which would put me in the market for a brand-new line of work, or Vollie Manion had delivered the punch without heat.

If he could do that, I was in trouble.

"You ever study anatomy?" he inquired, talking over his shoulder while he busied himself with something in the corner of the cell. "I did. Most folks wouldn't believe it, looking at me or listening to how I talk, but I done real good over at the state university. Was third in my class before I quit. Could've been first, but I don't like to make a spectacle of myself."

He turned, bright as a button and friendly as a pup, and I had a chance to see what he'd been doing.

Modern college-educated policemen have a kind of mania for renaming. I think it has something to do with shedding the old-time image of the apple-grafting Keystone Kop. Prowl cars, for instance, have become patrol vehicles. Badges are magically transmuted into shields. Cops have become police officers.

But the old-fashioned nightstick just won't budge.

Official reports now refer to it as a crowd-control baton and administrators with Ph.D.'s in police science have approved the addition of a neat little extra handle sprouting at right angles to the regular grip—a development that makes it impossible to roll the thing with ankle-bruising force at the feet of a fleeing felon, as street-smart patrolmen have been doing for a century, and effectively tethers it to a steel ring attached to the leather gun harness, which has now magically emerged as the "belt, patrol utility, leather."

But the name "nightstick" has stuck; even the newest and fanciest of the modern crowd-control batons remains a nightstick in everyday non-official usage, and the item in Vollie Manion's hand was a classic—a battered old bum-basher with the chips and scars of long service, and a round irregularity at its tip to show where it had been hollowed out and filled with lead to give it extra authority.

Vollie had used the time while I was collecting myself to wrap the business end in a couple of off-white hand towels, holding them in place with rubber bands. He displayed the result now with pride and affection.

"The thing about wrapping the end of the stick with a towel," he explained genially, "is that you can just kind of tap a feller with it about as much as you want and not leave hardly any bruise at all, but he feels it almost as much as if the towel wasn't there."

He demonstrated.

The club bounced almost lovingly off the left side of my skull, and the shadowless geometry of the room was momentarily replaced by a chaos of light streaks superimposed on a background of inky velvet.

Point well taken.

Deputy Manion was definitely on to something here.

I decided there was just the tiniest chance that a sudden kick with my right foot might reach his testicles with enough force to let me get loose from the chair to meet him in a standing position. But even so, my hands would still be cuffed behind my back and his would be free. Besides, I had a feeling my reflexes might leave a lot to be desired at that moment.

All right, then. No kick.

Nariyuki no matsu...I began preparing the way to inner concealment, the place of hiding where the writ of pain does not run.

"That hurts a little, of course," Vollie said, still cheerful. "But that really ain't the main thing. See, when you hit a feller like that, a blunt blow on the top of the skull, like, it don't leave no sign outside. But inside there—on the brain, I mean—it leaves what they call pinprick hemorrhages—little bitty breaks in the surface? What I learned in the anatomy class, back there at the university, was that everyone gets knocks like that from time to time. And just one or two don't mean much.

"Feller who does any really serious drinking, he'll kill about that same number of brain cells every time he gets drunk. And if he keeps at it long enough, he starts to get sort of dumb. You seen people like that. They walk around peeing in their pants. Real sad.

"But of course that takes a long time. Years and years, usually.

"It happens a lot faster, sometimes, to boxers. They get hit in the head a lot, you know, they get punchy, which just means they had enough of those little hemorrhages that their brains don't work real good anymore. Never could understand why they let it go that far. I mean, they could stop anytime before that happens and be pretty much okay. And so could you."

This time the tap was harder and the darkness lasted longer.

"What would make me happy," Vollie said, bending a bit to look into my face, "would be for you to tell me just exactly how you killed ol' Bobby Don. Reckon you could help me out there?"

The padded club hit the right side of my skull and set off a pinwheel of blue sparks.

"Like, now, how did you get him into your car?"

A tap on the left.

"And did you beat him to death before you sent the car off the road, or was he only just unconscious in there when it happened?"

A tap on the right.

"You know, this could go on and on. We got all the time in the world…"

I heard the words and recorded them for future consideration, but they came from another world. A place far removed from reality. A dream place where mindless brutes played a game whose only rules were insanity. The nightstick blows still reached my head, but could not find the quiet mountain meadow where I sat sharing gossip with a low cloud that had wandered through the pass from the sea. There in the stillness I touched the grass-green fingers of the Enlightened One and asked him if he had enjoyed his many conversations with the rebbe from Nazareth.

His reply was glowing silence.

I touched the sky and filled it, immobile but moving at the speed of light, reaching for the infinite.

And stopped short.

Something had changed in the other world.

I tried to ignore it. But it wouldn't go away, and the instant of annoyance that I felt at the distraction was a molecule removed from the skin of a balloon. Vanishingly small, but disastrous. Reality collapsed around me and I was back in the shadowless little room, conscious of pain and fury.

"Vollie!"

A new voice. A stranger.

"Put it down, Vollie."

There is a technique taught in the military, a special force and inflection of speech known as the tone of command. The man who learns to use it effectively will seldom need to raise his voice to be sure of instant obedience. That is automatic. Irresistible. I heard that tone now, coming from the doorway. And so did Deputy Vollie Manion.

"I was only just—" he began.

"Put it down."

"Yes, sir."

Reluctantly, but with no real show of resistance, he unwrapped the towels from the end of the nightstick and leaned it on its lead-filled nose in the corner.

"Now unlock him."

"But—"

"Just do it."

Vollie wanted to go on arguing, but he didn't. I started to sit up as he moved behind me, but the sudden agony as he fumbled a key into the locks and unsnapped the manacles from my wrists came as a surprise. Circulation seemed to have been cut off for some time. I hadn't remembered the cuffs being that tight.

"Grab him!"

The deputy's hands caught my shoulders as I toppled forward at the waist and the world narrowed to a gray-upholstered tunnel. That was a surprise, too. I seemed to have been off in the other place, the real world, for too long. Things getting out of hand back here in kindergarten. Have to attend to them. But not right now.

"You need to lie down?"

My field of vision didn't improve much, but a new face moved into it. An older man. Dark skin tone. Mustache. Eyes like obsidian marbles, but not as warm.

"Be okay…in a minute," I told him.

"Sure you will."

The face moved out of sight, and a second pair of hands moved my torso forward until it was resting on my thighs. Someone pushed my head down between my knees and supported it there.

The edges of the world began to widen. I could see the floor and my own feet and the nightstick over in the corner.

"You want to throw up?"

I started to say no, but found myself less sure than I had thought. Might be worth considering. Something sour down there. Not sour enough, though, and not big enough to be worth the effort. The moment passed and I managed to shake my head a little. "Stomach's fine," I said. "But I keep getting these funny headaches, Doctor…you got an aspirin?"

That brought a grunt of what might have been amusement.

Or something else.

I decided it was time to sit up again, and after a moment of resistance the hands on my shoulders let me do it. The walls of the cell stayed put. I was back. For a while, anyway.

The man with the obsidian eyes moved back to where I could see him and picked up one of the towels Vollie had used to wrap the stick. He wet it at a sink in the corner and handed it to me.

"Go into the booking room," he told Vollie. "Sit down and wait for me there."

"I ought to go back to—"

"Do what I tell you. Now."

Vollie wanted to say something else but decided not to. He left, and the man who had sent him away looked back at me.

"Name's Frank Ybarra," he said. "I'm the sheriff hereabouts."

He didn't offer to shake hands, and I didn't feel slighted. We looked at each other for a few long seconds, measuring, but didn't seem to come up with anything definite. Not enough information. Later, maybe.

"Towel's for your nose," he said. "It's bleeding."

A SERMON
(CONTINUED)

We see these things.

We shake our heads.

We wonder.

But they are also a part of our own lives. They occur on our very doorstep. The difference is only one of degree...

TEN

Sheriff Frank Ybarra's office was on the other side of the building, and we went there when my nose finally dried up.

Big-city cops have an interrogation technique known as "good cop–bad cop" in which one member of a team is abusive and the other becomes your lifelong friend by saving you from him. It is so old and so hackneyed that television writers have almost given up using it to fill dead spots in their scripts. All the same, it seemed possible that I was getting the small-town New Mexico version now, so I kept my mouth shut as I followed the sheriff through the cell block, past the booking room, and through a sparsely furnished area that might have been the detectives' bull pen if the Farewell sheriff's department had any.

He closed the office door behind us and nodded toward a straight chair. I fitted myself carefully into it and waited for him to talk.

"Get you a doctor, if you like," he said when he was settled behind the desk.

I shook my head, still waiting.

Sunlight coming through the window behind him threw the sheriff's features into shadow—not by chance, I decided—and made them unreadable as he moved his right hand to pick up a smooth-polished stone that had been lying beside the telephone.

"Hell of a way to start a day," he said.

I couldn't argue with that.

The stone bounced in his palm, and I wondered if it was a kind of worry bead for him. Something to keep his hands busy while his mind was otherwise occupied. He bounced the stone again and put it down.

"Vollie Manion's new on the job," he said. "Sent him to the academy over in Albuquerque, but I don't think the training took."

"Try a mental hospital," I suggested. "They've got the kind of instructors he needs. Or maybe you could hire a keeper."

The sheriff's expression didn't change, but his eyelids came down for a moment, and something feral was still dissolving in the depths when they snapped open again. He took a deep breath and released it slowly.

"Thing is," he said, "there would be some real advantages to proving that an outsider like you, someone not from Farewell, killed the Thieroux boy."

He seemed to be waiting for some kind of reply, but I wasn't feeling helpful, and after a moment he went on.

"Sheriffs have to stand for election. They shouldn't; it's a bad system that got started a long time ago and never was changed, and it is purely hell on the professional objectivity. You sure don't win any votes by proving someone's husband, father, brother, or best friend is guilty of murder. So it's a good day when you can tell them it was someone they don't know and don't even have to make bail for. Everyone's happy."

He paused again, and I wondered if I was going to hear the good-cop routine after all. But no.

"The hell of it is," he said, "I kind of got out of the habit of thinking that way during the time I spent on the force in San Francisco—even before they sent me to the FBI academy. Department had sent me there because I was a senior detective, up for lieutenant, and in that town you either do some kind of postgraduate work or forget about making captain. Not that I ever made captain anyway. Guessed wrong about one street snitch, and he shortened my stride by half a foot before I could get the knife away from him, so I took my medical retirement and a plaque that said I was one hell of a police officer and came back here to Farewell and got elected sheriff because no one in town knew me well enough anymore to hate my guts."

He bounced the rock in his hand one more time and then flipped it suddenly across the room, scoring a direct hit on a wastebasket in the corner.

It had been a long speech, and I might have suspected it had left a bitter aftertaste in his mouth, but for the flat factuality of tone and the black-marble stare that remained fixed on my face. If it was a feint, it was a good one.

"You know," he said without any perceptible gear-changing noises, "that's a really fine glass eye. Took me all this time to spot it, and even then I wasn't sure until you let the left eye glance over to see where the rock went, and the right one didn't move with it."

"Sloppy," I nodded. "Have to work on that when I get some time."

"Vollie Manion never spotted it at all," the sheriff went on. "Put down your eye color without any other notation on the booking card. I know, because I looked the card over before I tore it up. You're free to go, unless you want to see a doctor or prefer charges."

I thought that over for a minute. "What about Bobby Don?" I said.

The sheriff sighed and leaned back to study the ceiling.

"Robert Donald Thieroux," he said, "died sometime after midnight and before dawn this morning when he drove your rented car off a downhill curve on the county road, out toward his granddaddy's place. Would've been no investigation, maybe, if Vollie Manion—he's not stupid, just got some kind of problem that seems to feed a natural streak of snake-meanness—if Vollie hadn't gone and spotted something wrong with the car's brake lines. They'd been knife-cut, almost all the way through.

"Just a guess—I'll have to send the damaged items to the state crime lab to make sure—but the way the job had been done, the lines most likely wouldn't have let go the first few times someone came to a stop. It would have taken a good solid foot. The kind you'd use if you wanted to slow down suddenly before starting a curve. So whoever did the cutting had to be somebody who knew his business. A mechanic, maybe, or someone who'd had a lot of experience doing it before. Don't know of anyone living around here who would fit in the last category, so there we are again, looking for someone new in town…" He glanced at me to make sure I was taking it all in.

I was.

"But you don't fit," he continued. "Three people whose word I have reason to trust have already told me you were busy playing cards right through the time when you would have had to be hacking away on the brake lines. Every one one of them put you out there in the back room of the country club all night long."

The sheriff let the tiniest trace of a smile slip past the corners of his mouth, and it surprised me. His face didn't seem like the kind of place where smiles happened very often.

"In fact," he said, "Deke Pemberton tells me you must have the greatest set of kidneys this side of the Mississippi. Says he never even saw you get up from the table to go pee. How the hell do you do that, anyway?"

"Early toilet training, long habit, and minimal liquid intake," I said.

He nodded thoughtfully.

"Worth knowing. Anyhow, you didn't have an opportunity, didn't have any reason to think Bobby Don was going to go stealing your car...and I just can't see where a little disagreement over a few hands of seven-card stud would be much of a motive. Especially for a man who makes his living playing cards."

Nice shot.

The sheriff had done his homework. Or asked more questions than he had told me about.

"Well," I said, "I'm sure glad to know I'm no longer a murder suspect. For the moment, anyway. But it still leaves quite a bit of room for speculation, doesn't it? Especially in one area that is kind of important to me."

"How's that?"

"Oh, just odds and ends you might say. Details. For example, I can't help wondering if the Thieroux boy was the intended victim. After all, I didn't lend him the car. Or even know he was going to take it."

This time it was the sheriff's turn to nod and wait.

"And then there's the matter of how he was able to drive it from the lot without leaving his own wheels—the fancied-up Caddy I noticed when I arrived at the country club yesterday. Unless he hitched them up and drove away Roman fashion, one foot on each hood, he had to have help, and I think it would be interesting to know who that was and why he was so obliging and what became of the other car."

Ybarra's face had resumed its fine-tuned blankness.

"And if those cut brake lines really were intended for me, then who knew what kind of car I was driving, where it would be parked, and how long I would be away from it? Also, I can't help wondering why anyone would want me dead, in a town where— as you mentioned earlier—no one knows me..."

I stopped for breath and perhaps in hope of some small reaction from the man across the desk. But all I got was breath. The eyes never changed, and the voice was empty of inflection as he agreed that it sure would be nice to know all of that. Yes, indeed.

"So, then, you'll want to be going back to your motel," he said, making it a statement instead of a question. Our conversation appeared to be at an end.

"Suits me," I said. "But not if I have to ride with your deputy. I don't think he likes me. Use your phone to call a cab?"

The eyes blinked but didn't lose their light-devouring opacity.

"Sure, if that's what you want," he said. "But Miz Dana—Marilyn Prescott's little sister—she's right outside there in the waiting room."

He took a moment to let that sink in.

"Fact is," he said, enjoying whatever it was he could see in my face, "you'd probably still be playing bounce-the-brains with Vollie Manion if it wasn't for her. She's the one called me out of a nice warm bed to come down here and spring you loose."

A SERMON (CONTINUED)

These things shock us.

But...should they?

The lion that lies down with the lamb is a charming proposition. But it is hyperbole. Not intended for literal consumption...

ELEVEN

The first few blocks back toward the motel passed in silence. I had questions to ask and gratitude to express, but the pain in my head seemed to be getting worse, expanding to fill whatever thinking space might have been left. And there were other mementos of recent history as well. Vollie Manion's anatomy teachers had been only half right. The towel-padded nightstick had no doubt done exactly the kind of damage he'd said it would inside my skull. The throbbing there was accompanied by a slight fuzziness of vision, the soft bottom-fog vagueness that sometimes comes with the better class of ethanol hangover. But the professors had evidently neglected to mention some of the side effects. Repeated blows to the head, especially from above, can also be a problem for the neck and shoulders, compressing vertebrae and wrenching tendons. It hurt now and would get a lot worse during the next hour or so.

Extending the thumb and forefinger of my left hand at right angles to each other, I pinched the web of skin and muscle between—and relaxed against the seat cushions at the sudden cessation of pain.

Dana glanced away from the road momentarily.

"If it's hurting that much," she said, seeing what I was doing and apparently understanding it, "I have a little training in acupressure, and there are a couple of points that might be more effective, depending on where the damage is."

I thought of nodding, but didn't.

"I know the places you mean," I said. "And thanks. But it's really not bad. I'm just doing this because it beats taking an aspirin."

A lie, but in a good cause. I needed to be back in the motel room, alone and without distractions, before I could begin any of the mental and physical exercises that would give more than temporary relief.

I tried to blank my consciousness, and conversation died again for a block or two, but then a question elbowed its way to the surface and would not be denied.

"How did you know where I was?" I asked.

"Luck," she said. "Came out of my own room just in time to see you driving away in the backseat of Vollie Manion's car. That was all I needed to know. Frank Ybarra's phone number isn't in the book, but my best girlfriend from high school is the chief operator at the phone company now, and I only had to threaten to tell her husband about a double date we had back in 1976 to get her to call in and have someone get it for me. I only met Frank once, but he got a hustle on as soon as I explained the situation to him..."

She slowed for traffic, swore under her breath, and glanced at me again.

"Vollie Manion was always a creepy little kid," she said. "A couple of classes behind me in school, but not someone you'd forget in a hurry. I remember he liked to hurt small animals and insects. Pull parts off and watch them try to move around? But most people didn't know about it, because he was sneaky and only did that when he thought no one was watching. Guess he's graduated to bigger and better things, now he's got that dandy badge and gun."

"Seems as if," I said.

"I been away for a while," she went on, keeping her eyes on the road now as we turned toward the highway. "But a town like this, things happen for reasons you'd never figure out if you weren't born here."

"Such as?"

"Such as don't blame Frank Ybarra too much for Vollie Manion."

"He's the sheriff."

"He's the *new* sheriff," she said, emphasizing the adjective. "First term. Which means he owes a lot of political favors around town, and one of them was maybe to some friend of Vollie's."

I thought it over.

"No," I said, finally. "Sorry, no sale. For one thing, I can't imagine any marker big enough—even in Farewell—to warrant hiring something like Vollie as a deputy. And for another, I can't believe that anyone would admit being a friend of his."

Dana snorted something that might have been a laugh but wasn't.

"That's just the trouble," she said, cornering neatly and bringing the car up to speed on the interstate. "Nobody ever wanted to be his friend, and his daddy never claimed him, either. Vollie's mama died when he was about twelve years old, and she never had been married. Didn't work, either. Never had a job anyone knew about, but she lived pretty well, and everybody knew she had to be getting the money from Vollie's father."

Traffic slowed for some obstruction ahead, and our car was caught between a pair of semis. Dana used the time to expand on her theme.

"Parents that never got married are nothing in particular these days," she said. "But twenty-five, thirty years ago—in a town like Farewell—things were different. Growing up a bastard had to be pretty hard on Vollie, at least until he got big enough that people started thinking twice before calling him names, and I always wondered if things might not have been different for Vollie if his daddy'd been around to stand up for him."

She took a deep breath and shook her head.

"I think," she said, "that is about enough of that. Let's change the subject. I talked to Marilyn on the phone just before I saw you leaving with Vollie, and she says she's had an offer to sell the helicopter business. A good one."

"How good?"

"Good enough to pay off most of Pres's debts and even have the house clear."

My head was still full of cotton and old auto parts, but I pushed enough of the mess aside to ask a few of the more obvious questions. "Who's the offer from?" I said.

Dana shrugged. "Came from some lawyer up in Tucumcari," she said. "He told Marilyn his buyer didn't want to be identified for the moment. I don't think Marilyn really cared. That's not too unusual, is it?"

"No," I said. "Probably not, but let's go on for a moment. Did your sister tell you whether this offer was just for the business itself—the name, contracts, goodwill, and so forth—or for the physical assets such as the hangars and equipment and the surviving helicopter?"

"The whole shooting match, Marilyn said. Lock, stock, and whirlybird."

"With the land it stands on?"

"That, too."

"What about the rest of Prescott's acreage? The helicopter operation only took up a corner of the full section he inherited. Does the rest of the land go with the deal?"

"Well, from what Marilyn said, I think—oh, *Christ!*"

The last two words squeaked upward into a range at least an octave above her usual speaking voice and were accompanied by a sharp twist of the steering wheel.

We swerved out of traffic onto the shoulder of the expressway, and I could see her front teeth clamp down hard on the end of her tongue as she stopped the car, set its hand brake, and rummaged in her purse, emerging after a moment or two with half a pack of tissues.

Silently, she folded a few of them into a pad and moved over to my side of the seat.

The engine was still running and sounds inside the car had to compete with the ferocious whoosh of passing traffic. But though her voice had dropped back into its usual low range, I had no trouble hearing all the rhythms of rage and long-burning fury that filled it when she spoke.

"That creepy little shit!" she said, dabbing at my upper lip and then pressing the tissue pad against the left side of my head. "That maniac. Sadist bastard! You're bleeding from the nose and ears. Sweet Christ…what the fucking hell did he do to you back there?"

The bleeding had stopped again by the time we got to the motel, and all I really wanted was to go inside and throw myself on the bed that someone had obligingly made up while I was gone. But Dana had other ideas, and I sat in the chair while she phoned for a doctor.

Waiting for him to arrive, she took one of the plastic sacks set out for some purpose or other in the bathroom, filled it with ice from a dispenser at the end of the breezeway, and wrapped it all in a hand towel.

"The shirt," she said. "Off."

I wanted to argue, but it didn't seem worthwhile, and I was facedown on the bed with the improvised ice pack on the back of my neck and Dana's fingers at work controlling pain in my upper shoulders when a knock at the door announced the doctor's arrival.

He was a surprise.

T. Bowering Woodbury, M.D., F.A.C.S., was the last person in the world I would have expected to see making early-morning house calls.

"I don't believe it," I said, squinting over my shoulder after Dana had let him in. "Don't they drum you out of the A.M.A. or something for things like this?"

"In most instances, yes," he said. "But from what Dana said, I gathered that I was being summoned to the scene of a disaster." He peered at her and then back at me. "Though from evidence at hand I'd have to say it looks more like an orgy that hasn't gotten off the ground yet."

Dana grinned at him maliciously. "Fine talk," she said, "from a man who propositioned me the second week after I went to work in his reception room."

The doctor drew himself up in mock resentment. "Proposition, indeed!" he snorted. "That, young lady, was a perfectly honorable proposal of marriage...and I might add that laughing yourself into a stomach cramp was one hell of an ego-bruising way to turn it down."

He moved to the bed and opened the bag, balancing it precariously on the nightstand. "I heard something about bleeding from the ear," he said. "Do you want to tell me about it, or would you rather show everyone what an iron-assed hero you are and let me guess?"

I told him.

When I was done, he nodded professionally and ordered me to roll over. We went through the usual procedure of checking the pupil for reaction to light. "Not much sense trying to see if it's the same size as the other," he grumped. "But how does the prosthesis feel: Painful? Or loose in the socket?"

I shook my head.

"All right, then. I'm going to turn my back and say some numbers. I want you to repeat them aloud, for as long as they're audible."

We plodded through the rest of the tests, one by one, and when they were done he took a small syringe from his bag and started to pump air into a bottle of colorless liquid.

"No shot," I said.

He looked a question.

"No offense, but I've kind of got out of the habit since I left the hospital a few years ago. There are other ways of controlling pain."

"It's to relax the muscles."

"Even so…"

He looked at Dana, but she only shrugged.

"Well," he said after a moment, "I guess you know what you're doing." He replaced the syringe in the bag and closed it. "No evidence of fracture that I can see, but you've got some pinched or compressed disks in the neck and upper spine, and they are going to hurt like hell for a while. The main problem, though, is concussion. Best thing you can do for that is rest. Lie in bed quietly for a day or two."

He paused to let someone assure him that this would be done, but nobody said anything.

"Failing that," he said sourly, "I guess the next best thing would be to avoid undue stress, exhaustion, and strenuous exercise…which, I suppose, is also just a contribution to the room temperature. To hell with you, then. Get up and bleed on the furniture."

He hefted the bag and started toward the door, but stopped short with one hand on the knob.

"For what it's worth," he said, "I think you came off damn lucky. Vollie Manion is a case of hormonal imbalance complicated by one or two genetic defects and situational stress. I've known him all his life, been his doctor on occasion, and I don't mind admitting that he gives me the willies. Stay away from him."

"You have my word."

"Uh-huh." He nodded thoughtfully, started to say something else but decided against it, and went out into the morning.

"Okay, then," Dana said briskly when the door had closed behind him. "Peel."

I looked at her.

"The pants," she elaborated. "Also, the shoes and socks. You got any pajamas with you? Nightshirt?"

I shook my head.

"Then out of the clothes—keep the shorts on if you're the bashful type—and onto the bed. Facedown."

"Look—" I began.

"No, you look," she said, cutting me off in mid-objection. "The only reason Bow Woodbury let you get away with that guff about not wanting an injection is that I was here and he knows I can do a better job than the needle."

She saw the look on my face, and it seemed to irritate her.

"I'm a trained masseuse," she said, with an edge on her voice. "And in answer to the thought that just passed through your dirty little mind: No. I learned it in Vegas, when I got tired of serving drinks to out-of-town drunks. But the training, and the job I got, were both legitimate. I've got a license that says I'm a headache-fixer and pain-reducer...not a hooker."

I still just wanted to be left alone, but the effort it would have taken to convince her was suddenly more than I wanted to face.

Silently, I kicked off the shoes and socks, dropped the wrinkled trousers, and let myself melt into the bed. A moment or two later, two sets of fingers began to work on the deltoids, slowly moving in toward the spine.

All right.

She seemed to know what she was doing.

There were things that needed to be said—plans to make and warnings to give. I wanted to make at least two long-distance telephone calls and I wanted to make sure Marilyn Prescott didn't sell anything and I wanted to talk to some people with specialized knowledge of the local scene and I wanted to rent another car.

I wanted to Seek Truth and Defend the Right.

But the muscles in my neck were finally beginning to relax and my head didn't seem to hurt quite as much and it was all more trouble than it was worth and who was I kidding, anyway?

The world narrowed to a single slit of blur-soft brightness whose edges wavered and vibrated, fracturing the structure of light and reciting the spectrum of visibility on an ever-ascending scale that shimmered and sang before fading, irresistibly, to total darkness.

A SERMON (CONTINUED)

Reality, for all living things, is strife.

Man, like all other viable life forms, is a food-seeking mechanism. He exists by consuming other living things...

TWELVE

Waking after a long sleep is usually hard work for me. The muscles have taken a set, and the head is full of foam rubber. This end up. Use no hooks. Do not expose to extremes of heat, cold, or moisture. Floor sample, for demonstration purposes only. I tried letting the darkness flow over me again, lulling reality back to dry storage, but it was no sale. Time had passed, and it seemed important to know how much.

I moved to look at my wristwatch.

Something seemed to be obscuring my vision on the right; I blinked, struggling to clear the obstruction, and then came fully awake.

No use trying that eye, stupid. The only thing you can do with it is trick richboy yokels who don't stay alive long enough to benefit from the lesson. Try the other. Ah! Better. Now: Focus...

The luminous hands pointed to the general vicinity of two o'clock, and a glance in the direction of the window said it was a.m., not p.m. I had slept for nearly sixteen hours.

My body said it still wanted more. But bodies always say things like that in the first few moments of wakefulness, and people who listen to them eventually grow mushrooms on their backsides. I forced a foot over the side of the bed, hooked the heel on the edge of the mattress, and pulled myself into a sitting position.

Dim night light outlining the drawn shades confirmed the outline of the room and the sense that I was alone in it. I allowed myself a single growl of protest before giving the mental order that brought me to a standing posture for the endless trip across the carpeting to the bathroom.

The human bladder will stand for just so much nonsense, and no more.

A few final tendrils of mist were still evaporating from the edge of the world by the time I reentered the main room, but I snapped on a light and looked around, taking inventory and sorting impressions to help speed them on their way.

Dana Lansing seemed to be a tidy sort.

Someone had committed a neatness with the clothes I had shucked off before collapsing on the bed. The coat and vest were carefully arranged on a wide-shouldered hanger with the trousers dangling from the cuff press, and the other contents of my single suitcase were displayed beside them. I wondered what Dana had made of the fact that my only change of clothes was another preacher-black suit, but decided she had probably taken it as just one more phony facet of my basically defective character. If she'd thought about it at all.

There was no immediate sign of the shirt or socks I had been wearing, but their identical replacements were stacked in the top drawer of the motel dresser, and my shoes were aligned on the floor of the closet next to the suitcase.

Fair enough...

The first order of business was to decide whether this was a mere intermission or the true beginning of a new day. No debate. Twinges and threats from various locations around the somatic landscape—and a sudden, specific pain message from my head—convinced me that nobody would be ready to play data-sharing games with me for a few hours anyway. So call it intermission.

Nonetheless, there were a couple of telephone calls that I couldn't put off.

I made them, dictating the numbers to a motel switchboard operator and enduring the long-distance protests of those whose sleep had been interrupted.

Then I snapped off the light and rolled back between the covers, barely remembering to leave a wake-up call before the curtain came down again.

Waking up was easier the second time.

I was already half aware, drifting in and out of the world, when the telephone rang and I forced myself to stand up before answering it and thanking the operator. Half an hour of t'ai chi, followed by a quick shower—warm at first, then stinging cold to get the juices flowing—put the finishing touches on the long night. Most of my pains were gone, and my outlook was almost disgustingly cheerful by the time I was dressed and ready for public exhibition.

I dialed Dana's room, but wasn't surprised when no one answered.

Find her later.

Find breakfast now.

I locked the motel room door behind me and took a leisurely course to the coffee shop, stopping off to spend a quarter at one of the newspaper vending machines just outside. But I didn't get past the headlines that told me someone with the unlikely name of Robert Donald Thieroux had been killed in a freak automobile accident.

Inside the coffee shop, I spotted Dana at a booth next to the front windows; a chubby little man in a silk business suit was seated across from her. She waved enthusiastically as I entered.

"Over here, dear," she fluted, in a stage-fluttery voice I'd never heard before. "Over here!"

The man with her didn't seem happy to see me.

"This dear little fat man," she said, still twittering along the top of the scale, "has been entertaining me while I waited for you."

The man shuffled his feet, started to move out of the booth, and then realized I was standing in the way.

"Look," he said, "I just—"

"He's very inventive," Dana went on, apparently paying no attention. "I mean, you absolutely wouldn't believe some of the things he said he would like to do with me if we went back to his motel room. I told him my husband was a minister and would want to hear about it, too, but I don't think he really believed me. Did you, dear little fat man?"

She paused, still smiling sweetly, and the man didn't seem to want to look in her direction. He pressed a shoulder experimentally against my left leg, but I pretended not to notice and favored him with a smile of my own.

"A pleasure, brother," I said. "Prime pleasure on this glorious morning to encounter a fellow laborer in the vineyard. Will you join us now in a moment of communion?"

All lechery had vanished from the face he turned to me, replaced now by a pained admixture of misgiving and disbelief.

"O Father of all goodness," I said, shading my brow with one hand while the other held him firmly in place, "bless this day to the building of thy kingdom and the furtherance of thy work. Look kindly upon this servant newly made known to us, and grant that his heart be uplifted and his body cured of all its many disorders and afflictions…"

The final words fell into silence. Every eye in the room seemed to be turned in our direction. You can weep, curse, or faint in a crowd with some fair hope of privacy, but public prayer never fails to shock and amaze.

I relaxed the pressure that had pinned him to the cushions, and his reaction was both swift and gratifying. In an instant he had slipped past me to freedom, scuttling across the room without a backward glance. The silk suit that had fitted so well earlier now seemed half a size too large.

"Prayer meeting at eight-thirty sharp," I called as he reached the door. "We'll be expecting you…"

He wanted to reply.

But he didn't.

When he was finally out of sight, I sank into the booth with a tiny rotten glow of satisfaction still warming the spot where remorse ought to have been hard at work by now.

"Shame on us both," I said, not believing a word of it. But Dana had stopped smiling and seemed to be having trouble looking directly at me. Something had changed. I picked up the menu to take her off the hook and let her pick her own time and words.

No accounting for mood swings.

"I had a long talk with Helen Spence yesterday," she said at last, about the time I had decided to give breakfast a miss and settle for coffee.

"Been meaning to do that myself," I said. "Always worthwhile…"

But Dana wasn't having any.

"Helen told me all about you," she said. "Everything—how you and Jake were roommates at seminary and were ordained on the same day. And the war in Vietnam and how you served two tours and lost your eye, and resigned from the priesthood."

Helen always did talk a lot. I wondered how I had come off, seen through her eyes, and what she could possibly have said to make this woman uneasy in talking to me now.

"And she told me about Sara…"

Oh.

Dana picked up a spoon and made a few unnecessary stirring motions in the half-empty coffee cup.

"So," she went on when we'd both had time for a paragraph or two of silent dialogue, "I guess I owe you an apology."

I started to protest, but she was already shaking her head.

"The trouble is," she said, "I don't feel one damn bit apologetic. Not really. Not at all, in fact. What I do feel is mad enough to throw this coffee in your face, cup and all, and then go back and see what Helen Spence has to say about a good solid clout in the chops."

The grin I gave her was absolutely genuine.

"If you really decide to do that," I said, "please take me with you, or at least give a little notice. I'd pay good money to watch. And maybe handle the betting line. I've seen Helen in action, and my money'd be on her…but not by more than six to five."

That did it.

"Bastard!"

Right.

Time is surely the best cure for embarrassment, but anger will do well enough in a pinch, and to carry out the plans I had for the day I needed a full partner, not a running apology. I watched her struggle through a series of emotions and come at last to a plateau where conversation—and even communication—might be possible.

"Well, anyway," she said, "I think it was a dirty trick not to warn you that I looked like…her."

No argument there.

"It would have saved a little wear and tear on the cardio-vascular system," I agreed. "But I guess Helen thought we'd be grown up enough to survive."

"All the same"—Dana's eyes were curious now—"is it…I mean, am I really that much like her? Like Sara?"

I thought about it, looking at her.

"On first impact," I said, "yes. Remarkably. Same size and build, same face. Even the same vocal range—when you're not chastising lecherous wimps. Hair and eyes a bit different, but all in all, close enough to use her driver's license."

"And on second look?"

"On second look, too. But maybe not on third. A lot of time has passed, remember. Impressions fade. Sometimes now I can't be sure if the face I remember is really Sara or an old photograph of her."

She nodded thoughtfully. "I know," she said. "It's that way for me sometimes, too. With Harry. Somebody told me once that no one is really dead while you remember him, so I guess that means poor old Harry is really gone. Take me a while even to describe him."

I wondered if that was really true.

None of my business.

"Anyway," I said, "when I look at you now, it's Dana Lansing I see. Not Sara. I'm not much for building monuments, in grave-yards or anywhere else, so whatever Helen may have had in mind doesn't seem to have made much difference. At least not to me. How about you?"

That got a smile, the first real one she'd offered. And it was worth the effort.

"Fair enough," she said. "Now—whose parade do we rain on first?"

In point of fact, the first order of business seemed to be a break-fast that would have buried a brace of lumberjacks.

Nothing like sudden human contact to sharpen the appetite.

Conversation languished while sausage, eggs, biscuits, and gravy—a country touch not to be sneered at; everyone has weaknesses and that's one of mine—met their destiny and were tamped down with more of the worst coffee I had ever tasted.

"Dear sweet Lord," I said, taking a final bite of biscuit to banish the acrid taste, "what do they make this stuff with, floor sweepings?"

Dana's nose wrinkled.

"Nothing wrong with the coffee itself," she said. "It's the water. Lots of alkali. People around here don't even notice. Been drinking it all their lives, so they think that's just the way it is. But if you go somewhere else for a while, you forget, and drinking it again can be a real shock."

"That would account for it." I nodded solemnly. "All the same, judging from the way you were able to rescue me from the clutches of the law yesterday, I'd say you were still pretty well plugged in to the local scene."

"I'm from here," she said. "Born and raised in Farewell, and that means I'm homefolks. Scenery. I could go away for twenty years—fifty—and come back and still be homefolks in a way that someone who'd moved in and lived here all those years never would. Damned if I know whether it's a good thing or a bad one. But that's sure how it is."

I nodded. "That," I said, "is more or less what I'd expected. And hoped."

She looked a question.

"Jake Spence gave me a bird's-eye view," I said. "He's been here awhile, and he's got the kind of job that gets him pretty well acquainted. Still, there are things about the town and the people in it that need the kind of gut knowledge you'd have and he wouldn't."

"Such as?"

"Such as, I played cards for a night with an attorney called Deke Pemberton. Jake tells me he is both smart and honest. A rare combination, if true. Especially for a lawyer. But I can only vouch for the smart part. Honest takes local on-the-ground information."

Dana fumbled a cigarette from her purse and lighted it, considering honesty.

"If he's not honest," she said after a moment or two, "then he must have changed a lot since I left. And I still wouldn't believe it."

Her expression said there was something more, and I waited to hear that, too. "Except?" I prompted.

"Except…well, Deke Pemberton just always scared the living hell right out of me. And I'm not the only one, either. Those eyes of his. You must've noticed them, playing poker with him. They look right through you and see everything and tell you nothing at all."

She inhaled deeply and blew the smoke away. "Honest, though. Yes, he's that for sure. Maybe it's just being born rich like he was and never needing to steal, but I always thought it was something more than that. Some people—and not stupid people, either—are just naturally that way. And I think he's one of them. Why? Are you thinking of changing your will?"

I grinned. "Might be a good idea," I said. "Second question, more personal: Your sister, Marilyn, has she given a definite answer, signed anything, on that offer she had to sell the helicopter business?"

"No way." Dana shook her head. "Before you went to sleep yesterday you mumbled something about how she wasn't to do that, and I've been stalling them anyway. Was that right?"

"Perfect. Now, one more question and we'll be ready to get out of here and start the day's work: I've already made a call that ought to get me part of the information I need, but to nail everything down and draw a diagram for the skeptical, I'm going to have to talk to someone with an insider's knowledge of Farewell real estate and financing. Particularly the financing. Any names in particular come to mind?"

Her response was immediate, but stopped just short of the voice box. Instead of answering at once, she tilted her head a fraction of an inch—and for a moment I was paralyzed.

Sara.

It was her mannerism, a memory I thought I'd buried and forgotten a long time ago—the slightly stagey way she had of picking her way around a question she could have answered but thought she shouldn't. I wondered if Dana had noticed anything in my face. Probably not. She was busy with thoughts of her own.

"You're not talking about J. J. Barlow," she said.

"Someone else, maybe."

"Uh-huh." She thought about it and her posture changed, and Sara was gone. My breathing resumed, and an almost painful relaxation spread across my shoulders and upper arms while I sorted out the residual shock. Fine way for a grown man to act.

Ridiculous.

"Okay, then," she said finally. "I guess I know who'd be the right one to ask. But I sure don't know how you'd feel about seeing him. Or how he'd feel about you."

I waited for her to explain.

"The one I'm thinking of," she said, "is richer than God himself. Owns half of this county and has a mortgage on the rest, and if there is anything he doesn't know about property and money hereabouts, he'll sure be after someone's hide for holding out on him."

"Sounds just right."

"Maybe. But he lives on a spread outside town, and you want to give him a telephone call before you go—he keeps a pack of dogs and they're blood mean—and even if he tells you to come ahead, you'll want to think it over for a while."

"Why would that be, now?"

"Because his name is Mose Thieroux, and he is the grandfather of the damn fool who got killed yesterday morning, driving the car he stole from you."

A SERMON
(CONTINUED)

But there is more to man than consumption; more to his life than a mere striving for sustenance.

Here is where he differs from all other life forms of which we have knowledge.

Here is the peculiar burden assigned him by the Almighty...

THIRTEEN

Looking at the world from the passenger seat of Dana's car on the way to the Thieroux ranch, I was force-fed another, more leisurely, jolt of east New Mexico landscape, and found no good reason to revise my original perceptions.

It was still big and raw and lonesome.

Yet the day offered a few compensations. Winter sun had dried the highway, and even the unmarked dirt and gravel track that cut away toward the horizon seemed tolerable. Metal signs attached to the fence wire warned us that we were on Private Property, and there were two gates. But they were unlocked, and the dogs Dana had mentioned didn't seem to have been set free with orders to kill.

Dana was silent throughout the trip. She hadn't wanted to listen while I used a pay phone to make the advance call to the ranch, and had expressed real astonishment when I told her that someone there had checked with the boss-man, and we were now invited guests. But she flatly refused my offer to rent another car and make the drive by myself.

"You'd find too much trouble to get into," she said. "I'll come along to scrape up the remains and give them a decent burial. Besides, that old man likes his privacy, and his place isn't all that easy to find."

Which was true, and not true.

Making the drive alone, I might very well have missed the gravel turnoff. But once on that road, there was no way to go wrong, because there seemed to be no side branchings, and its destination was not the kind of place that could be missed. Or forgotten.

One of the few folds in the steppe-like countryside concealed the main house and ranch buildings from casual highway observation, but this only intensified the effect when they came in sight on topping the first rise.

Mose Thieroux's tastes had evidently been formed in the early years of the century, and he had expressed them here without reference to local convention or aesthetics. The main house was of Victorian design complete with turrets, third-story dormers, and a forest of lightning rods surrounding the widow's walk at the very top. Its materials were a combination of red-brick and weather-napped wood, though on closer inspection I noted that the apparent weathering had been carefully arrested and preserved at a stage of silvering that must have been satisfactory to the owner.

Outbuildings—bunkhouses, machinery sheds, silos, stable, and a handsome horse-training ring—were of the same meticulous design and construction, the whole ranch unit surrounded by and interspersed with a stand of elm, oak, maple, and walnut trees arranged to create an impression of randomness and natural occurrence not really possible anywhere on earth, least of all here.

The workday had evidently begun, and an apostrophe of smoke from what appeared to be a blacksmith shop near the stable was the only visible evidence of life as we neared the house, but one of the double doors at the front of the house opened as we approached, and a rail-thin man in faded denim ambled out to watch us park at the edge of the driveway.

"That's him," Dana said in a stage whisper as we got out of the car. "Old Mose."

Viewed fleetingly and from a distance, Mose Thieroux gave the impression of easy vigor and assurance. His movements and erect stance were those of an active man of middle years, dried sharp and taut by sun and wind, and closer inspection changed only a part of this.

Roll-brimmed stockman's hat and unshined boots completed a picture of the quintessential southwestern cowboy.

But the belt buckle was a diamond-studded presentation model that had to have cost a good deal more than the car we were driving, and the eyes below the hat brim were those of a twenty-one-year-old gunfighter waiting in ambush behind a face that had seen at least ninety seasons.

All this, however, paled to insignificance when he spoke.

"Ayuh," he said with a flat nasality that summoned a clear and immediate image of clams and lobsters. "Ayuh! Shouldn't wondah you be the one they call Preacher...?"

The accent was pure Down East, and the violent contrast with its surroundings was not eased as Mose Thieroux ushered us through the front hallway, past parlor and formal study, to a kitchen where he used a pot holder to remove a steaming coffeepot from the stove.

"Like it black?" he inquired, pouring.

I nodded, accepted an oversize mug, and was about to take a sip when I hesitated, remembering the battery-acid brew at the motel coffee shop. But he noticed the hesitation, and the edge of his mouth twitched in what might have been a smile. The rictus changed his face and made it fleetingly younger.

"Son of a howah, boy," he said, the wording and cadence still jarringly incongruous. "You and the lady be company. I don't use alkali water for my own coffee, and I surer'n hell don't serve it to guests. That there is pure mountain spring, trucked in every day, and the coffee is brewed with fresh-ground Mexican bean and settled with eggshell. Drink up, b'Jesus!"

The old man did not lie. We live in an age of the almost-right substitute: Frozen foodstuffs and powdered condiments and instant beverages are not only a concomitant of modern urban life, but its very substance. Without them, millions would starve. Yet no benefit is without its price, and the levy in this case is that whole generations grow up without experiencing the true taste of fresh vegetables, unprocessed dairy products...or real true-brewed coffee.

Late breakfast at the Thieroux ranch was therefore an experience not to be missed or forgotten.

Coffee—a full, rich concoction carrying as much warmth from the Mexican plain as from the stove—was balanced by the unchilled sweetness of fresh-squeezed orange juice, scratch-recipe soda biscuits, and a jam that had no label but seemed to be some combination of jalapeño and hedge apple that I had never encountered before. The earlier meal notwithstanding, I managed to taste it all and do violence to quite a bit without making a total pig of myself.

"Homemade, the jam is," Mose Thieroux said, sipping his own coffee from a mug that had begun life as a German artillery stein. "Cook won't tell me the jeezly recipe, so I make sure she goes to get a checkup with the doctor in town twice't a year so she'll be sure to outlive me."

He twitched that decade-devouring smile across the corners of his mouth again, and then turned the gunfighter eyes full force in my direction.

"Ayuh," he said. "Reckon it's time to get down to it..."

I started to respond, but he seemed to have something to get off his chest and held home-court advantage. I shut up and listened.

"You," he said, "have got one hell of a nerve onto you, coming out here after my grandboy winding up dead, driving your car and you taking a wad of money off'n him in a gawdam poker game. Another time or another place—different circumstances, different people—a thing like that could sure-God get a body killed. I am one mean-tempered old son of a howah, and a town like this, that kind of killing could happen and nothing never come of it. Betcha ahss!"

He paused to take a deep pull at the coffee, and I kept my mouth closed and my face still while he did it.

"But if there is one thing on this earth I do like and admire," he went on with no notable change in tone, "it is a man who will face up to something instead of running away from it. Prime comfort to know they's still a few like that around. Get to wondering sometimes. And besides, I knew my grandboy better'n purt' near anyone else on this earth, and he was pure-dee pissant!"

The eyes blinked and the mouth tightened for a moment with a heaviness that was private and not to be shared. I didn't look away, but I didn't move or glance at Dana, either. He had more to say, and I wanted him to say it before I asked any favors.

"One or two of the younger, and dumber, hands here on the place turned up looking some feeble and lumpy the same morning Bobby Don died," he said. "I suspicioned the one thing might kindly have something to do with the other and talked to them about it, and after they got done lying and talking foolish, they told me some cock-and-bull story about a crazy man in a preacher-black suit who flat-out kicked their asses for them. Then I made one or two telephone calls around town and a few more out of town. Come up with some of the damnedest, by-Christ pack of nonsense I heard in all my borned days. So when you called this morning and wanted to come out, what it done was save me a trip into town. Now you're here, I can see for myself that the part about the preacher suit is true. But what about the rest? Way I heard, you really did start out to be some kind of jeezly Bible-thumper. Seminary and all. But that don't fit with playing poker for a living. And they don't none of it square up with you being some kindly kung fu ball-buster or, come to think of it, being here in Farewell at all..."

It was a long speech for a man I suspected wasn't usually much for talking, and I let it lie there for a while, cooling, before offering the only answer I had.

"Shouldn't wonder," I said.

The young-old eyes blinked. "Shouldn't wonder what?" he said.

"Shouldn't wonder I'd have another cup of that coffee, long as you're buying…"

For a moment I thought I had guessed wrong. The wire-thin shoulders stiffened and the eyes narrowed by that millionth of a millimeter that sometimes goes with a big raise on a low pair and guts, and other times means a sleeve gun. But it passed, and the climate of the room eased from formal to comfortable in the few seconds it took him to refill our cups. Contact had been established.

"Ayuh," he said, sitting down again.

Dana looked at Thieroux and then at me and then back at him again.

"What the hell just happened here?" she demanded. "Something sure did."

Thieroux favored her with a chilly little smile that was, none-theless, not unfriendly.

"Two dogs sniffing, deciding they could get along," he said, explaining as much as he could to someone he wasn't sure could speak the language. "You'll be the Hallowell girl. The one married that gambling man, name of Lansing he was, and moved away to Las Vegas and stayed there after he took and kilt hisself."

It was a statement, not a question, and left Dana no ready answer. But none was required.

"Wellsir, Miss Dana," he said. "I did hear tell that you was back in town to be with your sister in her time of trouble. Tragic thing, that was. Strapping young feller like her husband, and doing real well, what I heard. Tragic way to end up. Suicide."

He was quality. No change in cadence or tone, not a single sly peek at either of us when he threw the loaded word. Just a possum-quiet wait to see how we would handle it. I wondered how he would be at a poker table, and made a mental note to be circumspect to the point of paranoia if ever I had a chance to find out.

But Dana wasn't half bad, either.

"Funny thing," she said, cocking her head to one side in the way that once again stirred my memories of Sara. "You're the first one I heard use the word. Right out, I mean. Most people just think it."

"That a fact, now?"

"It is. And I'm grateful, because it gives me a chance to say that you're full of crap, and so is anyone else who thinks my brother-in-law would do a thing like that."

Thieroux nodded. "Careless, then," he said, still on the prod. "Or drunk or doped or had what they call that delayed stress syndrome—fancy name for being loony—like all the other fellas lost the war over there in the 'Nam…"

I wondered if that round had been target-ranging on me, but decided probably not. We'd passed the point of random fire, and his aim would have been better if he'd been firing for effect.

And he'd missed Dana, too.

"My brother-in-law was murdered," she said evenly. "Someone robbed him and then killed him and counted on everyone thinking just the kind of rotten, vicious things you said. But it's not true. No one who knew Pres Prescott would ever believe it…and you don't either, or you wouldn't be sitting with us now, poking around at the sore spots to see if we're worth helping."

Thieroux looked at her silently for a moment and then turned to me with another of his wintery smiles.

"She'll do," he said. "Ayuh. She'll do fine, b'Jesus. All right, then! Suppose one or the other of you tell me what the hell it is you come for…"

I ran through the story for him—Jake's original suspicions, my own assessment, and some of the reasoning that went into them—using as few words as possible. He asked one or two questions, grunted at my answers, and then sat looking into the middle distance while he ran the result through his personal mental filters.

It didn't take him long.

"Ayuh. Sounds about right," he said, the leathery features dour as they buried extraneous matter. "Fact is, it even fills in a few spaces I been studying about for a while…"

He turned his gaze on Dana. "You say the offer your sis got was for all the Prescott land, not just that little dab where her husband set up that helicopter landing field of his'n?"

"The whole thing," she said, "'Land, subsoil rights, and all improvements' was the way the offer was made."

Thieroux nodded and turned back to me. "I'll need to do me some telephoning here and about," he said. "Might take an hour or two—more, if'n I can't get hold of everybody right off—to nail the jeezly thing down, so mebbe you could kindly leave me the number of the motel you're at, and I'll call you up and let you know when I'm for sure."

I gave him the number, and we finished our coffee in silence. It didn't seem like a good time for small talk.

When we were done, Thieroux accompanied us back to Dana's car, and I saw that the ranch, for all its earlier appearance of near-vacant efficiency, was not entirely devoid of human life. Two children, a boy and a girl, were throwing sticks for a dog in the pasture next to the horse ring.

Thieroux followed my gaze, and I was startled by the mixture of pain and pride that began behind those unusual eyes and ignited the rest of his face.

"Mine," he said.

I stopped with my hand on the door handle and took a second look. The girl was about four, I decided, the boy perhaps a year older. Both were dark-haired, but the boy's face was broad and freckled in the black Irish mold, while the girl might have passed for pure Aztec.

"Bobby Don's bastids," Mose Thieroux said. "Two different mothers, ayuh, but my own great-grandbabies right enough for now, anyways. Sometime next week, though, soon as I can get the Christless court to sign the papers, they'll be my own children. Adopted fair and square."

The old man's attention never left the youngsters as he spoke, but he left no room for interruption.

"I get seasick," he said. "Three generations of lobstermen in my family, but I get seasick, and I purely hate the smell of fish, so when the army turned me loose in 1919, I come out here to New Mexico and went to ranching. Got married. Damn good woman she was, but she died having our only son, and like a damn fool I kind of dried up and left him to raise hisself while I got rich in cattle and the land business.

"Funny thing, he turned out right good quality. Good man, decent and smart and reliable. Don't that beat all? And so for a long time I went around feeling real smart and proud of myself, though if you'd asked me why, I surely couldn't've told you."

The old man's attention had moved to the far horizon now, and I wondered how many times he had played this recording for himself in the dark morning hours when sleep hides and dawn won't come. I wished I had some comfort, or even concealment, to offer. But I knew I didn't.

"So when he got hisself kilt, froze to death trying to save a Christless runt stray fifteen years backalong, I thought I would handle my grandboy the same way I done him...Come out the way you saw.

"Bobby Don.

"By the time he was ten, I knew I'd been wrong, but by then I reckon most of the damage had been done. Anyways, nothing I tried seemed to help, not even sending him off to that military school—reform school it is, really—down to Roswell. Come back here the same sneaky, arrogant little pissant he was when he left.

"Well, now he's gone, too, and everyone's telling me I'm too old to be raising any more young'uns. Too old and tired. Ayuh! And maybe they right, too.

"But I been doing every Christless thing my own way since before I can remember, and if some of it was wrong, some of it was right, and I be damn if I am going to stop now. Let me live another fifteen years…hell, give me just ten…and let me use the time to do as much work on my own blood kin as I done on making m'self such a rich old son of a howah, and who knows? The goddam Thieroux family might wind up amounting to something after all!"

A SERMON
(CONTINUED)

Man's purpose transcends simple survival.

And a good thing, too!

For if survival, per se, were the whole purpose of life, then there would be no purpose at all. For the sustaining of life is, ultimately, beyond us.

Our time on earth is short…

FOURTEEN

hree telephone messages and the keys to a new rental car were waiting at the front desk when we got back to the motel, so Dana left me there and headed for her sister's house while I attended to business.

Only two of the messages required return calls. The third was a simple estimated time of arrival, and I took time to convert it into another room reservation before leaving the main building to return to my own cubicle.

The rental was parked by my front door, and it wasn't anything I would have picked—fire-engine red is a nice color only if you want to be sure you'll be remembered, and I always thought roller skates came in pairs—but it didn't seem worth an argument, and I went inside without giving it much more than a glance.

The telephone was by the bed, and I allowed myself the luxury of returning the calls from a fully recumbent position. The day was still young and I'd had plenty of sleep, and of course a hardcase gambler like the Preacher never runs out of gas. He is immune to pain and fatigue alike; all-night poker sessions and back-room beatings are all in the average day's work. Part of the mystique. Hardly worth a mention.

Uh-huh....

Like hell...

By the time the call I'd awarded first priority was answered, the instrument in my hand weighed a ton and I was on board a

130

lotus barge, dreaming about some place with the unlikely name of New Mexico while a bevy of sloe-eyed lovelies whispered the riddles of immortality into the air that shimmered and sang around my head.

The words were soft seduction and the waters of Lethe were rising to flood—but none of it stood a chance, of course, when attacked by the bright and cultured persona of Mistah Dee Tee Price.

"You crazy bastard!" he thundered in a voice that might have devoured the miles between Farewell and Houston without benefit of A. G. Bell's little gadget. "What in Christ's kingdom you doin' in the wilds of east New Mexico? Wasn't 'Nam bad enough? And where the hell y'all get off waking me up at three in the morning to run your goddam errands, anyway?"

The lotus barge sailed away without me and I was back on the motel bed. Alone.

"Answering your tactfully phrased questions in order," I said in the tone of sweet reason that I reserve for conversation with Mistah Dee Tee. "It's small-minded and downright inaccurate to call me crazy, because the nice folks at the asylum gave me a paper to prove I was sane before they turned me loose. What I am doing in the wilds of New Mexico is the same thing you're doing off in the wilds of Houston—trying to cope with a hot game and a cold deck. And as for getting you up at three in the morning, you are just damn lucky it wasn't earlier."

He laughed. "Okay," he said. "Just makin' sure it was you..."

"Convinced?"

"Must be. Ain't nobody else talks so mean to me nowadays."

"So, then, Mr. smartass corporate financier and high-class heist man, what did you come up with?"

Dee Tee Price has made a lifetime career of being a good ol' boy from Texas, and I'd probably never have found out about the Rhodes scholarship or the business degree from Harvard if he hadn't been tied to the bed next to mine at the hospital where I was sent after my second tour in Vietnam. Talk was just about the only recreation we were allowed (I couldn't see, and he was still only partially convinced that he wasn't dead), so we had a month or two to become pretty well acquainted. Later, when we both were feeling better, we became allies in various small enterprises—such as our plot to kill one of the orderlies.

The pill pusher had made himself obnoxious in various ways, but might have been overlooked as a minor nuisance if he hadn't made a series of passes at the pretty wife of an artillery sergeant on our ward. The sergeant was having trouble enough getting used to the idea that he was not likely to be able to move anything below the waist for the rest of his life, and wondering what a thing like that would do to a marriage that was brand new when he was shipped out. Watching helplessly while another man tried to date his wife was not exactly the kind of therapy he needed.

So Dee Tee and I got an outpatient friend to bring us some steel wire, which we coated with soot from a candle and strung between our beds late one night: one wire at ankle height between the footposts to trip our man when he brought the late sedative cups, another tight between the mattress supports, the distance from the trip wire carefully measured to cut his throat as he fell.

It would have worked, too, I think. But some goody-goody warned the ward nurse, and we barely got the booby trap disassembled and out of sight before she arrived with the provost and two MPs.

Dee Tee and I were loud in our protestations of injured innocence, and no physical evidence could be found, so the whole thing blew over. But the orderly turned out to be smarter than he looked: He never came back to the ward, and I heard later that he had requested a transfer to West Germany but was shipped to the Southeast Asia command instead.

Things have a way of working out...

"First off," Dee Tee said, shifting to his business mode and dropping the thicker part of the stage-Texan accent, "I talked to a friend of mine over at City National—soon as it was time for civilized folks to be up and about, you night-crawling sumbitch—and set up the line of credit you wanted. I don't suppose it's any of my business—after all, it's just my entire reputation and financial future that's on the line—but what are you planning to do, buy Peru?"

"Something like that."

"All right, then, play 'em tight if that's how you're gonna be. See if I care. About the other thing you asked, though, let me warn you going in that J. J. Barlow and I are not strangers. Fact is, I've known him longer than I've known you, and so I could be biased in his favor. Fair enough?"

"Understood," I said.

"Okay. Well—I made me some calls here and there, and what I found out was more or less what I expected: The Citizens National Bank of Farewell made pretty much the same kind of mistakes everyone else did a few years back when Third World loans looked like a shortcut to fame and fortune. Especially fortune."

"And got burned?"

"What else? A man loans money at twenty percent or more—and keep in mind they could throw your ass in prison for charging that kind of interest a few years back—he has got to understand that there is a hell of a risk involved."

"So why did they do it?"

"Greed, my friend. Simple human greed…and I am by God entitled to say the word right out like that because I paid for the privilege. Took my lumps the same way, and for the same reason, as all the rest of the damn fools."

"So Barlow's bank is in trouble?"

"Not necessarily. Not at all, in fact, far as anyone I talked to seemed to know."

Most of the nation's smaller banks, he said, had jumped at the opportunity to stake out a piece of the international loan business when the field opened up suddenly in the late sixties and early seventies. Until then, giants like Citicorp and BankAmerica had dominated. But changed conditions—and new laws that made it easier for regional banks to syndicate their efforts—meant that just about everyone was invited to the party.

"But not all of the country cousins knew how to dress," Dee Tee continued. "Iron underwear is a must in that kind of company. Come about the time the price of oil started going up like there was no tomorrow, it was Katy-bar-the-gate. Energy loans were the coming thing, and a lot of the money got loaned to a bunch of little hill-Hitlers who hadn't been wearing shoes five years earlier."

"And then they stopped the music."

"They sure'n hell did, and you never heard such a wailing and gnashing of teeth in all your born days. All the members of OPEC that had been so buddy-buddy in the beginning had got just as greedy as the bankers, and every one of them was pumping twice as much oil as their quotas called for, and the price went into the dumper. A few of the bigger thieves in Africa and South America had already defaulted, of course. They sort of led the way. But now just about every single one of those twenty and twenty-five percent loans stopped paying off. And you could hardly hear yourself think for the sound of banks collapsing."

"Uh-huh," I said. "But the way I heard it, a few people were able to salvage a crumb or two from the debris."

Dee Tee snorted.

"You been reading my mail again," he said. "Okay, sure. Hell, I was one of the lucky ones. Got burned bad enough early enough that I could find a good strong safety net and survive more or less in one piece. Then turned it around and got even by picking up a few goodies later, when everyone was screaming how it was the end of the world."

"And Barlow...?"

"Did pretty good, too, far as anyone seems to know. Citizens' loan portfolio got some rough handling early on—couple of big ones stopped performing—but they wrote the paper off, and the stockholders hung tough, and Barlow was still in the saddle ready to play Lone Ranger when one of the other banks in his town was declared insolvent."

"I didn't hear about that."

"No good reason you should, probably. It would be old news by now. But there would have been quite a bit of fur and feathers flying at the time. The federal boys always talk a good game about maintaining competition and all that, but when they got a busted bank on their hands, it's 'Who's got the bailout money?' and the hell with anything else."

"Someone else tried to buy the insolvent bank?"

"Oh, sure. One outfit over there in Albuquerque and even a pretty big one in California...before it got into trouble of its own. But J. J. Barlow beat them all out and wound up skimming that cream away and leaving the feds stuck with the garbage."

"So he'd have been on solid ground by the time he did that?"

For the first time, there was an instant of hesitation on the Houston end of the line. "Well, now," Dee Tee said in a careful tone, "I don't exactly know as I'd say that. At least, not for certain sure."

"Damn it, Dee Tee, don't go all cagey on me."

"I'm not, Preacher. Really. But just talking about it here, I all of a sudden began to get kind of an interesting idea, you know..."

"Tell me about it."

"Well, hell, I just began to wonder how cozy things could get in a little place like Farewell. You know, one hand washes the other and all that cliché crap?"

I had a sudden vivid flash-memory of the faces around the poker table. Controlled, game-playing faces. But comfortable with one another in a way that comes only with a lifetime of practice at close quarters.

"It would be that important?" I asked.

"Hard to say. Thing is, I guess, nobody ever thought about J. J. Barlow that way, you know? Always real solid. Two, three cuts above what anybody'd expect for the head of a bank in a little bitty town like that. But it might could happen…"

"Keep going."

"Couple of bank officers—say, the president and the treasurer or chief financial officer—could cover their tracks pretty good for a long, long time if they needed to, and if they had some good reason to trust each other."

"You think that happened here?"

"Frankly, no. I don't, just because it's J. J. Barlow. When he took over that bank, backalong, it was in terrible shape, and it was him built it up piece by piece when the easy thing for him and for the shareholders would've been to sell it to the best bidder they could find as soon as it was on its feet and healthy. Barlow might not have any legs, but that wouldn't have had to hold him in a little place like Farewell. Man with his brains and energy, he could make it in the big time as good as anyone and better than most. So when we get to talking about how easy it would be for a friendly pair of thieves to play some fancy numbers games with a little bank like that one, I just have trouble fitting him into the picture, you see what I mean?"

"No incentive, then? No reason for him to do a thing like that, no matter how easy it would be?"

Again the hesitation.

"That's the hell of it," he said finally. "There could be. And it would fit pretty good, too."

I waited for him to explain.

"I can't see J. J. Barlow cooking the books to grab the money and make a run for Brazil or someplace, no," he said. "But there's another way it could be. Suppose he got hurt worse than anyone thought in the energy loan bust-up. Bad enough, say, that the bank itself would be on the line. That would be hard on him, of course, but not the end of the world, because he's not the type to hide all his gold bricks in one hollow tree. He'd be sure to survive. Make book on it. But a lot of his friends might not, and the town where he's lived all his life and where he's still a big local hero, it might find itself in bad shape, too."

He paused for breath.

"Keep talking," I said.

"Yeah, well, a certain kind of a man, now, he might find it sort of tough to face up to such a thing as that."

"He might," I agreed.

"And if that happened, the natural thing would be to hide it for a while, maybe with the help of that friendly bank officer we talked about. Or, hell, for all I know, with the help of the whole damn board of directors."

"But it would have to come out sooner or later, wouldn't it?"

"Not necessarily. As soon as he was sure the whole screwup was hid well enough to throw the feds off for a while, the next thing would be to scout around and find something juicy. A really big financial score that could also be handled on the quiet, far enough out of sight that the money could find its way back onto the books in some way that would look real legitimate— make the bum paper seem to pay off, and take the bank off the hook."

"No offense, but it sounds to me like the banking business isn't too different from the one I'm in. Only chancier, maybe."

Dee Tee's laughter shook the electronic firmament between Houston and Farewell. "Hell, son," he roared, "sometimes I think the whole thing's just nothing in the world but a damn back-alley crapshoot! All the same, if J. J. Barlow did do something like that—and mind you, now, I'm for sure not saying he did or even hinting at it—you'd still have to put him way over on the side of the angels."

"How so?"

"Well, like I said, the easy thing would be to either grab the money and run, or let the bank collapse and pick up what pieces you could for your own scrapbook. Sticking around to try to plug the leaks and make the damn thing seaworthy again would be strictly a labor of love. Hard-nose charity, not the flabby, whiney kind. Some sumbitch doing his dead-level damnedest for people who trust him."

"So, either way, he's still wearing the white hat?"

"Well...kind of a pretty pearl gray, anyway. That's if he did any of it at all, which is something I am going to make it my business to check out thirty ways to Sunday as soon as I get done talking to you."

"Thanks, Dee Tee. I owe you one."

He laughed again. "Damn well told you do! And don't you think ol' Dee Tee ain't gonna hand you the bill one of these days. When you coming to Houston?"

"Next time you round up some rich folks for me to play cards with."

"I'll see to it directly. Y'all take care, now, hear?"

The line went dead, and I hung up.

Fatigue descended like a waiting assassin.

Sack time!

The urge was powerful and insistent. No more nonsense...

But now and then you find a day that is just naturally longer than you mean it to be, and this was beginning to look like one of those times. Instead of lying still and making another call as I'd intended, I swung my feet over the side of the bed and levered myself, bones protesting every inch of the way, into a sitting position. The difference between thinking and sleeping for me can sometimes be a simple matter of posture, and the bed was just too soft.

The hell with it.

I decided to find out whether the new red rental car would move under its own power.

A SERMON
(CONTINUED)

What, then, is the purpose?

    Can it be comfort?

    Pleasure?

    Warmth? Security? Love?

    All these have their place, of course; they are, or can be, the grace notes to life…

FIFTEEN

Jake Spence was in his office at the church, but when I asked
about Helen, he told me she was hiding.

"Can't say I blame her," I said.

He was always an easy blusher. "Maybe I ought to be hiding,
too," he said. "I noticed Dana Lansing's resemblance to Sara, and
didn't warn you either."

"No, you didn't," I said.

He busied himself with the coffee cups and contrived to be
looking out the window at something or other when he handed
mine to me before taking his usual seat behind the desk.

"I heard you met our newest deputy sheriff," he said, still not
meeting my eye.

"Don't change the subject. Just what did Helen—and you—
hope to gain by giving me a heart attack?"

He squirmed.

"We didn't think it would be like that," he said. "Helen was
going to introduce her to you over at the Prescott house."

"So I could collapse among friends? What is this, Jake? You
were never like that before."

He looked at me with the punished-pup expression that must
have been pure larceny on the bank accounts of his parishioners,
and shook his head.

"Sure I was," he said. "You just never noticed. And so was
Helen. We both loved you and we still do. And seeing this girl—"

"She is a grown-up woman. And I'm a year or two past puberty, too."

"Seeing her and talking to her and liking her, it just seemed to us—both of us, not just Helen—that we might be doing the two of you a favor. If we were wrong, I'm sorry and I'm sure Helen is, too, but we didn't plan for it to be a shock. Who would have expected Dana to break into your motel room?"

"She didn't break in. The locks are cheap and the same key fits them all."

"In any case, we didn't plan to hit you in the face with it. That was an accident. And I apologize. I'm sorry about the deception, too."

"But not as much?"

"But not as much…"

Conversation languished for a moment while we both consulted the muse of caffeine. Say this for Jake's coffee, it had authority. The drowsiness and fatigue that had been riding the borderland, awaiting an unguarded moment, retreated to the horizon and stayed there.

"Okay, then," I said, dropping the subject but retaining my hold on the coffee cup, "the message you left at the motel said you had something to show me. Is it here, or do we have to go somewhere to see it?"

Jake swiveled to the table behind him and unlocked a drawer in its apron.

"This," he said, "was among Pres Prescott's business files. The accountant Marilyn hired found it, going through them to try and make sense of the estate."

He handed me a sheaf of papers. The top item was a business letter from a bank in Tucumcari, and a quick scanning identified it as a favorable response to a proposal for refinancing of the Prescott helicopter business.

"You'll notice," Jake said as I flipped to the next item, a similar response from a bank in Amarillo, "that the top letter is dated just three days before Pres was killed. The other is only a little earlier. Two answers within the same month, and both of them favorable."

I put the papers down on his desk.

"So," I said, "if Prescott committed suicide—don't look like that, dammit; we still have to consider the possibility, though I'll admit it's getting pretty thin—we'd pretty much have to rule out despondency over his business prospects."

Jake still wasn't happy. "What other reason could he have had?" he said. "If it wasn't the business..."

"The marriage?"

"Nonsense!"

I shut up and looked at him.

"Well, at least I'll never believe it," he said after a few moments of fidgeting. "Pres just wasn't made that way."

"Two days ago," I said, "you were telling me there had been trouble with the marriage ever since Prescott had his little scene with J. J. Barlow at the country club."

"Trouble, yes..."

"But not as bad as all that?"

"Lord, no!"

"How bad, then?"

"Well..."

"And how do you know? Did you live in the house with them?"

Jake started to answer, but stopped himself instead and sat looking at his hands, a time-killing mannerism I remembered from Sewanee. He is the only man I ever knew who could out-stubborn a cat. I waited him out in silence.

"A lot of things could have happened that I wouldn't necessarily have known about," he said, picking his words carefully when he finally decided to talk. "But if I didn't live with them, I certainly did know both of the Prescotts over a period of years, and the marriage was a good one."

I started to break in, but he held up a restraining hand.

"You didn't spend much time in parish work," he said. "The army got you too soon. But you had a few months of internship and worked at that Michigan mission with Sara for a week or so just before you were shipped out, so don't tell me you didn't learn to sniff the air when you went into someone's home—sniff and taste. Good marriages have a scent all their own; bad ones, too."

"Things can change…"

"The basics don't. Not, anyway, without a lot of effort on both sides, and the trouble here was pretty much one-sided. Marilyn kept trying. I watched her do it. She kept hoping right up to the end that the tide would turn or that at least Pres would tell her what was wrong."

He stopped again, visibly relaxing and shifting gears.

"Never mind," he said, taking another swallow of the industrial-strength coffee and putting the cup down. "I can show you a lot more easily than I can tell you. Helen's over at the Prescott house, and we're invited for lunch…if you promise not to kill her out of hand."

"I'll think it over."

"You do that. But don't take too much time. We're over-due already, and I want everyone on speaking terms before nightfall…"

The Prescott house was a surprise. I had expected something imposing in the way of Small-Town Affluent, but wheeling my little red roller skate up the driveway in the wake of Jake's wagon, I found myself making some drastic image revisions.

Either the house had been there a lot longer than any of its neighbors, or the builder and architect had gone to a lot of effort and expense to make it look that way.

Closer inspection told me I was half right. The broad hand-made tile expanse of the roof and foot-thick adobe walls were nicely imitated in a complex of rooms that had been added at the rear, but there were subtle differences that marked them as con-temporary in contrast to the assertive authenticity of the section closer to the street. No particular knowledge of southwestern architectural history was required to date the older part of the house into the latter half of the last century, though every brick and tile bore the imprint of loving care.

"It was the original house on this land," Jake said, notic-ing my interest as we walked toward the front door. "Working ranch house for half a century or more, but the people who lived here knew the worth of an honest building and took care of it—especially the adobe, which can be a bit of a problem when it rains."

I nodded appreciatively, noticing the slight imbalance in the walls of the older building.

"Someone's still at it," I said.

"Pres Prescott." Jake nodded. "He and Marilyn bought this house when it was about to be torn down. Supervised renova-tion and expansion themselves. Afterward, it was Pres himself who patted and shoveled the softened adobe back into place after every big storm."

The front door opened and a low, feminine voice that I took to be Dana's finished Jake's mini-lecture for him.

"And he did it himself," the voice said. "Never could get him to hire anyone for that particular job. He said he enjoyed it. God knows why…"

But the speaker wasn't Dana.

The woman in the doorway was an inch or two taller, with darker hair and a residual puffiness near the eyes that spoke of recent tears, a still-fresh mourning that the rest of the face had now consigned to those hours of night when sleep wouldn't come and time wouldn't pass.

"I'm Marilyn Prescott," she said. "And you must be the Preacher Helen and Dana have been telling me about."

"Lies," I said quickly, turning it into comedy. "All lies! I absolutely did not set fire to my grandmother. The dear old lady simply burst into flames one day, you know, and people jumped to conclusions because of that insurance money."

"Don't believe him," Jake chimed in. "He used that money for his first poker stake and never looked back."

Marilyn Prescott laughed—I had a feeling it might have been a while since she'd done that—and stepped back, moving the door with her.

"Grandmother or no," she said, "if you two don't get inside I'm locking you out. They can talk all they want about sun-drenched New Mexico…it's cold this time of year!"

The main doorway to the Prescott house was set into a small closet-equipped entranceway that opened on two very different rooms. To the right, I glimpsed a spacious chamber that I tentatively identified as a formal living room, something like the old-fashioned "company parlor" that my grandmother opened only for Sunday callers. Remembering what I'd seen and what Jake had said outside, I guessed that it was part of the new wing. But Marilyn ushered us to the left, into an older and more comfortable world cluttered with children's books and an array of bright Mexican blankets, all dominated by a fireplace that I decided must once have been the principal heating and cooking plant for the original ranch dwelling.

"This was the kitchen and main room of the original house," Marilyn said, catching the direction of my gaze. "A girlfriend of mine lived here—it was a real working ranch twenty years ago, long before they built houses on the land—and I always loved the way it felt, warm and welcoming in winter or summer. So it was vacant when Pres and I needed a house, and I couldn't bear to change this part when we needed more space."

"Didn't the cooking make the room awfully hot in summer?" I asked.

Marilyn shook her head. "Not really. It was hot close to the stove, of course. Had to be. There was a fire inside. But most of the heat took itself away through the chimney after it did the cooking, and the rest of the room stayed cool because of the thick walls and the way the roof keeps all the windows shaded. We have air conditioning now, but it's really just for the new parts. In here, you can still stay cool just by opening the windows and letting a little breeze through."

"It was seeing this place and others like it," Jake said, "that made me decide I wanted to build a church of adobe when we finally had enough money to begin construction."

"And what Father Jake wants, he gets, never doubt it." Marilyn smiled. "Until I met him, I always thought men of the cloth were gentle souls who breathed thin air and smelled flowers."

"I've sniffed an occasional cactus blossom," Jake said.

"And made it curl up in shame if it dared point a sticker at you." She turned to look at me. "Was he always like that?"

"He was!" I said. "I gave up trying to cheat on examinations about a month after we were assigned to the same dormitory room in college. Son of a gun would never tell the proctor, or even say anything to me. But I never did figure out a good way to handle all the sad-eyed disappointment."

"So he gave up and became the class valedictorian." Jake grinned, needling me in an exposed area.

"I'm impressed," Marilyn said.

"And so was I until I got to know him better," said Helen, joining the party, very brisk and businesslike, from a corridor that seemed to lead toward the rear of the house. "Dana tells me there's no chance in the world that you'll be hungry, because you've both eaten two breakfasts that would fell a farmhand. If so, then shame on you both, because we've fixed a meal that ought to be on the cover of *Gourmet* magazine."

Her eyes dared me to change the subject and berate her in front of Marilyn Prescott.

The smile I gave her was my very blandest model.

"Did you know," I said, turning back to Marilyn, "that Helen, here, studied high cuisine under no less a teacher than the celebrated matriarch of the d'Este family?"

"My goodness, did you really?" said Marilyn.

"No. Not really," Helen said. "And not at all. The son of a bitch is just showing off and being nasty, as usual, because he remembers that my college major was in history."

Marilyn's polite but puzzled nod said she didn't understand at all, so Helen was stuck with the punch line.

"The matriarch of the d'Este family," she said, throwing me a glance that would have sliced bread, "was Lucrezia Borgia."

A SERMON (CONTINUED)

Yet, grace notes are not the music.

They do not, in themselves, satisfy. And a life devoted exclusively to the pursuit of material success and acclaim and enjoyment leaves the pursuer hollow at the end...

SIXTEEN

Lunch at the Prescott house was friendly, quiet, and even better than promised.

As soon as she was sure Helen and I weren't going to get blood on the furniture, Marilyn led the way into the new wing, bypassing an impressive formal dining room on the way to a warm and cavernous kitchen where Dana and two children, a boy and a girl, were busy moving platters to a refectory table that looked as though it might have served several generations of cowboys before falling into the restoring hands of loving and talented friends.

"It can seat twenty people easily," Dana said, noticing my interest, "or more, if they're friendly."

"Then bring on the crowd," Jake said, glancing hopefully back and forth between his wife and me.

But his concern was needless. Helen and I had finally found our way back to the competitive but friendly relationship we'd had in a much younger and less threatening world. There was still an edge to it. There had been back then, too. But there was no way we could ever be less than allies.

My good friend, the critic…

"This," Dana said, catching one of the boy's ears and using it as a handle, "is Orrin Prescott, Jr. Call him Bubba, because he doesn't answer to anything else."

He escaped and scampered to the far end of the table, thumbs in ears and fingers wriggling.

"And this," she continued, feinting a swipe to the girl's left and folding her into a tight hug when she dodged, "is my very favorite niece. And namesake. She thinks her name is Missy, but it's really Dana Marie."

The girl relaxed and returned the embrace with interest.

"My children are so shy around their aunt," Marilyn Prescott said. "I really don't know what we'd have done if she hadn't been here this week. Or now, for that matter. I'm pretty much back in touch, but for a while I don't think anyone would have had a meal or gotten out of bed in the morning if it hadn't been for her."

"Everyone sit down," Dana said, neatly covering the compliment with a move toward the stove. "Soup's the only hot dish we have, but I'd like to get it into the bowls before it freezes."

Appetite is a sometime thing for me. I can go for a day or two with nothing more than a tuna sandwich and a few glasses of mineral water—and I often do, during long games when eating would invite a fatal drowsiness—so the two meals I had eaten that morning were already more than I usually consume during twenty-four hours. Accordingly, I had planned to pick at my plate during lunch, moving food into tight piles that appeared to have been partially eaten when they had not. But I did nothing of the kind.

The soup was *albóndigas agringadas*—with just the right amount of oregano and piñon nuts—and the first spoonful put me into a kind of feeding trance from which I emerged with an empty bowl and deep interest in the contents of the various platters.

"Tell me one thing," Dana said when I was half finished with the second plateful. "How do you do that and stay so skinny?"

"You're the second person this week who's called me skinny," I said, glancing at Helen, who ignored me. "Is it a compliment, or should I be thinking up something mean to say back?"

"Don't change the subject," Dana insisted. "A man who eats the way you do should either be working double shifts at a steel mill or weigh about four hundred pounds. How do you do it?"

"Clean life and daily devotions," I said.

She shook her head, watching with apparent fascination while I coped handily with *ensalada de pastor, coliflor fría,* and *garbanzos encurtidos,* dispatching the remains with a single pass of a flour tortilla.

"Well, whatever it is," she said when she was sure that I was really done, "if we could find some way of bottling it, all of our financial problems would be solved."

"Amen," said Helen.

"And speaking of finances," I said, jumping oafishly into a spot I couldn't have improved upon if I'd been writing the script, "reminds me of something I've been meaning to say ever since I arrived. I hope you won't mind mixing business with a wonderful meal, but I'd like to get into the bidding on the Prescott helicopter business…if I'm not too late."

For dessert Helen and Dana had prepared something special— *chongitos,* with plenty of cinnamon and vanilla. But it had to wait while I explained.

The fact that I was an old friend of the Spences' counted heavily in my favor, of course. Enough to rate an invitation to lunch. But selling a multimillion-dollar business is something else entirely, and I had deliberately chosen to toss the offer onto the table without warning: Hit 'em cold and find out what they're really thinking.

That's a poker player's play for getting acquainted in a strange town, and it works well enough in other situations, too. Jake and Helen were surprised; I hadn't yet told them what I thought was happening under the pleasant surface of their town. But they had reason—or thought they did—to trust my intentions, if not always the actions that went with them. Marilyn and Dana, however, had no reason to feel any such assurance, and it was time to find out just how far the sisters were willing to go on blind trust. The play that had been forming in my mind was going to need a lot of that.

"Have you...talked this over with Father Jake?" Marilyn said when the first moments of startled silence had passed.

"No," I said. "And I haven't talked to a lawyer, either, though I'd like us both to do that later today, if you don't mind."

There was more silence then, and I could see Helen was about to fill it with sound and fury, a long agenda of questions churning and boiling just below the threshold of speech. But I wanted the widow Prescott to do the asking.

"The price I had in mind," I said, "was one dollar...plus other good and valuable considerations."

That stopped the talk for a moment, and then got it started again on the fast track. Prolonged emotional battering might have left Marilyn Prescott's morale in bad shape, but there was nothing wrong with her brain, and one look at my face apparently convinced her that I wasn't trying to be funny.

"I think," she said, "that I'd like to hear more about those good and valuable considerations."

So I explained.

Playing one long night of poker with Pres Prescott's circle hadn't given me any conclusive answers about whether or not he'd been cheated—though if he had, it must have been by general arrangement; none of the people I'd seen around the table seemed to be able to manipulate the cards well enough to fit the image of a lone mechanic. But talking to people who'd known him and were acquainted with the town had given me the beginnings of a slightly different idea about what might have been happening at the time of his death.

"If anything was, at all," I said. "We still have no real evidence that this was anything but a series of normal business reverses."

The others drowned me in objections, and I waited for them to quiet down before going on.

"It was just too sudden," Jake said. "I've thought about it, and it simply doesn't make sense that everything should go so wrong so quickly, all at the same time."

"Other businesses here in town seemed to be doing all right," Helen agreed. "Why should Prescott Helicopters be the only one in trouble?"

"And our...personal problems seemed to start getting worse about then. A lot worse," Marilyn said.

I waited for Dana to have her say, too. But she was silent, looking at me and waiting to hear my response. I made a mental bet that she could have spoken the words for me.

"All right, then," I said. "Let's go with the idea that there was something more to the business problems than meets the eye. I've already got the bloodhounds sniffing around the edges of that, looking for a trail that makes more sense. But it's possible that we know at least a few of the answers already, without knowing that we know them."

This time everyone was ready to listen. I turned toward Marilyn.

"Dana tells me you've had one offer for the helicopter business already," I said. "Since I've already told you that I intend to make an offer of my own, it would be a bit unethical for me to ask what kind of a price was mentioned. But she said it was really not much more than enough to cover the outstanding debts and let you keep the house. That about right?"

Marilyn nodded.

"And they wanted the old Prescott wheat ranch acreage around it, wanted it thrown in as part of the deal?"

"Yes. I wondered about that..."

"And you were right to wonder," I said. "Let's ask a few more questions and then do a little speculating: I understand that the offer came from out of town—some lawyer fronting for the real buyer. Or buyers. Have there been any other offers? Or had there been, before the accident?"

Marilyn shook her head, but my poker-playing radar picked up a background trace of uncertainty. Not much. But enough.

"No," she said slowly. "Just the one, as far as I know."

"But…" I prompted.

"But it seems to me Pres said something—oh, it must have been months ago, way back before all the trouble began—about someone wanting to buy him out."

"I don't suppose he mentioned a name?"

"No. But the way he talked, I think it must have been someone here in town. Someone he knew."

"Why's that?"

"Because he laughed about it. He said he couldn't believe the person was serious, said they had to know he wouldn't be interested in making a deal that would put him out of business."

"Anything else?"

"No. He never mentioned it again. Do you think this new offer could be from the same person…right here in town?"

I certainly did, but it was far too early to say so. Always protect your hole card. "We can't be sure," I said. "But the letters Jake showed me, the ones from out-of-town banks that were so willing to set up a line of credit, have made me just a little bit curious."

Marilyn shrugged.

"Can't tell you much about that," she said. "I never heard about any of it until the tax man found the papers."

"Still, the very fact that those banks were ready to lend money to a business that was already heavily in debt and facing severe reverses tells us that they—and your husband—saw something, some major potential asset that we don't."

"And if they saw it," Dana said, speaking to her sister but looking directly at me, "then there's one hell of a good chance the

person making the bid for Prescott Helicopters has seen it, too…
and is hoping to make his deal before we figure it out."

Marilyn's shoulders squared. "I'll call them back," she said,
"and tell them to go to hell."

"No!"

My mouth was open to say the word, but Dana said it for me.
We looked at each other and laughed.

"I gather," Marilyn Prescott said, indignation momentarily
in abeyance, "that there's some good reason why I shouldn't do
that."

Dana glanced at me, but I wanted to make sure we were
both thinking the same way. Knowing your allies can be just as
important as understanding the opposition.

"I'm not a poker player," Dana said when she was sure I
wasn't going to make the explanations myself, "but I've watched
enough games to know a little about betting…"

She waited for someone to interrupt, but all the other faces
around the table were blank.

"The perfect situation," she went on, "is in a game of stud
where the first player to the left of the dealer is forced to get into
the pot, make an opening bet, whether he has anything in his
hand or not.

"They call this the trapping position, because it keeps him in
the pot without having to let anybody know whether he thinks
his hole cards are any good or not. If they're nothing, he can fold
or bluff…but if they're strong and he can pick up the right cards
to go with them, he can milk the hand—get other players to bet
higher against him than they otherwise might—because they
know less about his hand than they do about the others around
the table.

"The offer that was made for the helicopter business and its
land was something else, though.

"It's like the player who tries to drive everyone out by betting high in the early rounds. And from what I've seen, it's usually a sign of weakness...something you'd do if you liked your hole cards enough to get into the pot, but didn't get anything to go with them."

She looked at me again to see if I wanted to take over, but I kept my mouth firmly shut. The lady was doing just fine.

"So by keeping this mysterious other bidder on the string even though the helicopter business is off the market," she said, "Preacher is just playing a hand of poker without using cards. He's sitting there in the forced-opening position, backing a good strong pair and waiting to trap a big one!"

A SERMON
(CONTINUED)

Satisfaction, then, lies elsewhere.

Some seek it in spiritual exaltation, some in the life of the mind, others in the inner satisfactions of personal integrity...

SEVENTEEN

About an hour later I joined Marilyn and Dana in Deke Pemberton's law office to have him draw up the bill of sale.

But he balked.

"I'll do no such fool thing," he said when the proposal and its price were outlined for him.

"But it's what I want to do," Marilyn said. "And if I'm willing—"

"Then it's my duty as your legal adviser to change your mind," Pemberton interrupted, throwing me a glance that should have melted my boot heels. "You tell me you have a perfectly legitimate, financially adequate offer for the property and are rejecting it in favor of one that does not even make a full statement of purchase price. Mrs. Prescott, even if I were to draw up such an instrument, I must tell you it could not possibly be made to stand up in court—and I would quite rightly be defending myself against a disciplinary action for having been associated with such a thing. No, thank you very much indeed!"

Bravo.

Dana's judgment of people seemed to be right on the money. Pemberton's attitude here was intelligent, ethical, client-protective, and fully justified by the only facts at his disposal. It was up to me now to change his mind, if possible, while feeding him only as much information as he absolutely had to have in order to fall in with our plan. My plan.

She'd been right about something else, too.

Playing poker for a night with Leonard Kenneth "Deke" Pemberton—under less-than-brilliant lighting so that the faces were obscured in the accepted convention of the game—had not in any way prepared me for the eyes he wore in the clear light of early afternoon. They were gray almost to the point of being without color, and their gaze did, as Dana had said, seem well and truly capable of penetrating the clothing, skin, and skeleton. No wonder he did so well in a courtroom: Even a federal judge would think twice before incurring their wrath.

"There are three good reasons," I said, "for listing the price of the helicopter property at one dollar."

The eyes said I was a stranger, a liar, and a swindler of widows, but he held his peace, listening with that peculiar quietness that I had noticed two nights earlier, as I went on.

"First," I said, "it's that way because that's the real price. I have it in my pocket, and I'm going to pass it across to Mrs. Prescott in your presence so there should be no doubt that it is paid in full."

I had expected another objection. It never came, but the eyes continued to bore into me.

"The second reason is more important: I don't anticipate having to register the sale either now or in the immediate future. I have other plans for the document. But if push comes to shove and it does become a public record, I don't want any other people to know any more about the deal than they absolutely have to know. And that particularly includes the price."

Still no change in the eyes or the face around them.

"And most important of all, there are going to be two bills of sale…"

That finally got a visible reaction. Pemberton drew in a breath to tell me he wasn't about to draw up any phony bills of sale either. And he meant to follow it, I suspect, with a curt order to get out of his office. But I forestalled him by finishing my own sentence.

"...the second one undated but signed and properly witnessed, conveying everything back to Mrs. Prescott for the same one-dollar bill."

I shut up to let him think.

The eyes still wanted to throw me out. But the mouth still had questions to ask. I could feel the chilly tendrils of his *wa* turning the proposition this way and that.

I used the time to take a better look around the room.

Jake and Dana had both left me with the impression that Deke Pemberton's law practice was a busy and successful one, and so I had been a bit surprised when Marilyn was able to make an immediate appointment. Most of the lawyers I knew liked to keep clients waiting, whether there was any real need for it or not. I later discovered that Pemberton seldom made a personal appearance in court or at his office in Farewell. He had a phalanx of bright young law school products eager to handle those cases that didn't really interest him. And he was also a rare sight at the office he maintained in Santa Fe.

Only major clients or those whose problems rated special attention were invited to this room.

It was hard to see why.

Most lawyers' inner sancta are designed either with an eye to the comfort of their chief occupant or to impress his visitors. Careful stage dressing runs to Victorian legal prints and heavy red-leather furniture to lend an air of old-world solidity, while the professional ego is bolstered behind an oversize walnut desk. Somewhere—in Los Angeles, I suspect—there is a factory churning out such fripperies by the job lot.

But Pemberton's working headquarters contained no such trappings. If he thought about them at all, I decided, he had aimed at antithesis. And hit the ten-ring.

Pemberton lived outside Farewell on land that Marilyn and Dana told me he had bought when he returned from the East. They said they could remember a house and ranch buildings on the land long ago. But there was no trace of them now. Pemberton had obliterated all spoor of the original inhabitants, except for a few trees clustered near the shallow pond, and had replaced them with…nothing.

"Or as near to it as you'd want to get," Dana said. "Everyone expected him to build a house, at least, but he didn't do it. One day, after the land was cleared off, a couple of trucks came through town towing big, long trailers. Not mobile homes, either. I'm talking hook-them-up-and-drive-them-away-type trailers. And Deke Pemberton met them out at his place and showed the drivers where they were supposed to go. One for the office. A few people have been inside it, and that's where we're going to see him today."

"But if anyone has ever seen the inside of the living-quarters trailer," Marilyn said, "they certainly haven't told a soul about it. And the only car you ever see parked over there is his."

I thought about that now, using my limited peripheral vision to scan the office. It occupied most of the trailer—one end was blocked off, probably for the bathroom and storage area—and was almost featureless. No photographs, artworks, or citation plaques on the neutral biege walls—not even the framed licenses required by law. I later learned that the licenses were on display in the office reserved for his use in Farewell, a room he had not entered for at least five years.

In lieu of the usual legal library and personal files, Pemberton's trailer office contained a single cabinet that I decided must be a holding pen for data disks that could be run in the IBM computer that squatted, dark and mute, in the corner. A few chairs—bare, wooden, and not too comfortable, including the one behind the desk—completed the amenities. Traveling men, carnival bosses, and site supervisors for major construction projects have similar office arrangements. But all of them pick up more signs of human habitation in a single weekend than Pemberton's office had acquired in a decade. Twenty minutes' effort would have been more than sufficient to obliterate all trace of occupant and occupation.

"All right." The lawyer's voice broke into my impertinent speculations. He turned his head to face Marilyn. "Do you have a dollar bill?" he asked.

Marilyn hesitated for a puzzled moment and then nodded.

"Give it to me."

Pemberton took a yellow envelope from the center drawer of his desk while she was getting the bill out of her purse and, when she had handed it to him, sealed it inside and wrote her name and the date on the front.

"Now," he said, putting the envelope back in the drawer, "these people witness that money has changed hands and I am now your retained counsel—which means I can offer advice and keep secrets." He glanced at me again with a trace of impatience.

"It means," he prompted, "that she can tell me what you're up to without having to worry about whether I can keep my mouth shut. And unless you're planning a patently criminal act, I not only can but must."

I let him see my best poker-table face. "Marilyn Prescott's secrets," I said. "Not mine."

The eyes blinked and registered a moment of irritation, but it didn't last, and I could have sworn to the tiniest lift of appreciation at the corners of the mouth.

"Fair enough," he said.

"Fair enough, what?" Marilyn wanted to know.

"He means," Dana said, "that he hasn't told us everything he's planning to do—and he's not going to tell Deke Pemberton, either."

Dana had driven out to the lawyer's office with her sister. But after the sales contracts had been drawn up and printed out on the computer, signed in three copies, and distributed to all concerned, she decided to ride back into Farewell with me.

"Maybe," she said to Marilyn, "I can get the son of a bitch to talk about what he has in mind for the million-dollar company he just stole from you."

Once we were under way, however, she seemed to have other things on her mind.

"Okay," she said, leaning back in the bucket seat of the little red skate and gazing out the windshield, "now tell me that man isn't some kind of refugee from the loony bin."

I couldn't give her much of an argument.

"Odder than a square grape," I conceded.

"That trailer has got to be fifty or sixty feet," she went on. "All that space—and there he is, using up about ten percent. Or less. A person could go blind staring at those bare walls."

I grinned at her, looking away from the road for a moment. "Maybe he heard that old maxim about how less is more and took it for the word of prophecy?"

She snorted. "I don't think he'd take it for gospel unless it came out of his own mouth," she said. "Lord, if that's all he has in the one he uses for an office, what do you think the inside of the trailer he uses for a house looks like?"

I considered the proposition for a moment.

"Army cot and a box of crackers?" I suggested. "With a small altar hidden in the rear where he makes sacrifices to obscene gods."

It broke her up for a moment—all my friends tell me I'm a panic—but the mood passed and suddenly she was quiet, looking at her hands to avoid looking in my direction.

"I keep forgetting," she said.

"Forgetting?"

"That you really are what they call you. A preacher."

"You're also forgetting that it's past tense. I turned in my collar and knee pads a long time ago."

"Helen Spence doesn't believe that."

"Doesn't believe what?"

"That you really...resigned or unfrocked yourself or whatever it is you do. She said you still run some kind of a church out in California. Up in the mountains."

I paused for a moment to deal with a sudden surge of resentment that I hadn't known was there, covering the upset by checking the little car's rearview mirror. A pickup truck was on the road behind us. It looked vaguely familiar.

"Helen," I said when I was sure my voice was fully under control, "hasn't seen or talked to me for more than ten years."

"But it's true, isn't it?"

I took another time-out and checked the mirror again.

The pickup was closer.

And now I knew where I had seen it before.

As a general rule I try to avoid explanations. They can be painful. They do not satisfy. They get in the way of normal human relations. And besides, I'm not absolutely sure I know all the answers myself. Or that the answers I know are true.

This time, however, I was spared even the minor annoyance of inventing an evasion.

"Check your seat belt," I said, giving a tug at my own. "And pull that chest strap tighter."

She hesitated for an instant, but did it.

I checked the little red skate's instrument panel. There were no oil pressure, amp, or temperature gauges—just warning lights to let you know when everything had already gone wrong—but the manufacturer had given a passing nod to sports-car tastes by including a tachometer. I wondered what function it was supposed to serve in a car with automatic shift.

"We are going to have a little race now," I said, putting the pedal to the metal and trying not to show how I felt when nothing much seemed to happen.

"Race?"

"The truck behind us," I said.

The tachometer needle didn't seem to be going anywhere at all. I down-shifted from automatic to manual second, and things got a little better; the speedometer and tach began to move around the scale more or less in sync. The tachometer was only calibrated to 6000 and there was no red-line indication, so I took it to 5500—cursing myself for not having found out more about the car before I tried to drive it anywhere—and then dropped it back into automatic. The engine and transmission didn't like it and called me dirty names, but the speed kept climbing and there were no immediate signs of collapse. I took another peek in the rearview mirror.

No comfort.

The pickup was still gaining.

"Last time I saw that truck," I said, "it was a real mess. Barely chugging along on four cylinders. And the driver wasn't in such red-hot shape, either. But it sure looks as though they got both of them running again, doesn't it?"

A SERMON (CONTINUED)

Some courses run more smoothly than others.

Digressions occur.

Now and then a trial balance is struck; the unexpected threat of immediate extinction has changed more than one life...and not always for the better...

EIGHTEEN

The road was two lanes of fresh gravel over an old blacktop bed. Not exactly a wagon track, maybe, but far better adapted to the racing needs of a light truck than to those of a somewhat underpowered imitation sports car.

I checked the tach and speedometer.

Still no comfort.

Flat out and with all the time in the world to do it, the little car still wouldn't be pushed much beyond ninety miles an hour, which wasn't even close to being good enough to stay out of trouble. The pickup was now less than a hundred feet behind us, and its driver seemed to think we were already meat on the table. He made no attempt at deception as he swung left, gunned his engine, and prepared to crowd us off the world. I moved my left foot to be ready with the brake and dropped my hand to the gear selector.

Dana's eyes were showing quite a bit of white at the tops and bottoms as she glanced at the truck in her side mirror, then at me, and then back at the truck again. But she didn't ask any distracting questions, and I was grateful as the front of the mud-spattered vehicle pulled into range of my good eye.

Wait…Wait…Wait…

Now!

The gutless little toy bucked and wobbled as I swung the wheel, slamming my foot down on the brake and dropping the gear all the way back to manual first. But the suspension was—just barely—equal to the strain of the sudden skew-turn. The bed of the pickup trundled out of the way with inches to spare, and my right wheel played with the lip of the drainage ditch as we swung around to the reverse course.

"That truck," I told Dana conversationally as we climbed back through the gears, "has the weight and speed on us. We're a little more maneuverable, maybe, but we won't be able to surprise him that way again. So I guess we're going to have to try something else."

She tore her gaze away from the mirror where the pickup truck's image was beginning to grow again.

"Such as what," she said. "A rocket launcher?"

I nodded appreciatively. "That would be nice," I agreed. "But dang if I didn't forget to pack one in the lunch hamper."

"So?"

"So. You grew up in these parts; tell me, would you happen to know if the kids around here ever play a car game called chicken?"

Dana's eyes got even wider and they begged me to tell her I was joking. But I couldn't do that, and after a moment or two she turned back toward the mirror.

"Oh, shit!" she whispered.

I surely couldn't argue.

Looking down the road and measuring speed against distance, I decided the best chance was about a thousand yards ahead. A dry wadi had cut its way through the land there, and the roadway angled steeply upward over a culvert that had been designed for cloudburst conditions. I thought it might be just high enough for what I had in mind. Better than nothing, anyway...

I down-shifted but kept my foot off the brake as we hit the upgrade, then herded the little car through another skew-turn to reverse our course one more time as soon as I thought we were out of sight on the other side. The pickup was invisible to us now, as I hoped we were to it, and I forced myself to wait through a slow three-count.

"Close your eyes," I said.

"Crazy...*bastard!*" she replied in a choked whisper, and I couldn't help laughing as I steered the little red car into the exact center of the road and slammed the hammer down.

For a split second I thought I had made a mistake.

I had assumed that Greenteeth was driving the pickup, and that he would come charging over the incline at full throttle to find himself facing a head-on collision with no time to think. If it was anyone else—or if his reactions were a little slow—there would be precious little time for apologies.

But I wasn't wrong.

We were still nearly a hundred yards from the culvert when the pickup appeared. I had a single flash of Greenteeth's face as it registered a combination of shock, rage, and fear; could see his hands move as he twisted the steering wheel. And then he was gone.

The oncoming truck swerved violently to the right as we charged past. I was still in first gear, but the little car's speed lifted it off the roadway for a few feet after passing the top of the rise, and that kept me too busy to see what was happening behind us. But I could hear.

There is a special sound made by a motor vehicle coming to grief at high speed. It has been compared to everything from a bomb to the slamming of a great door, but none of these similes does justice to its peculiar resonance. Not a thing to be forgotten. It was this sound I heard as I regained control of the car—and kept on hearing in ever-decreasing installments as I headed for the main highway.

Checking the rearview mirror, I could see that things had worked out even better than I had expected.

Greenteeth must have been going at least seventy miles an hour when he lost our game of chicken and swerved to miss me. That would have thrown his pickup into a classic Hollywood-stunt roll. But it couldn't have lasted more than half a turn; the drainage ditch at the side of the road would have seen to that. Hitting it with all the unexpended energy of its unbraked speed, the truck's engine compartment must have been partially collapsed into the cab. Then the elasticity of the steel would be asserted, changing the simple roll into a twisting end-over-end cartwheel as the truck shed its doors, wheels, and anything else not too firmly attached to the chassis.

I saw the last dying bounce as we sped away.

And the sudden plume of flame as the fuel exploded.

I turned my attention back to the road.

"You're not going to stop, are you?" Dana said.

"No."

"He...might be alive."

"Good for him."

"And hurt."

"Lord, I do hope so!"

We rattled along the gravel in silence for a minute or two, and I could almost hear the thoughts forming and dissolving. Finally she turned one of them into words.

"Pull over," she said.

"I'm not going back," I told her. "And you're not, either. Maybe if I was alone. And armed. Maybe. But I'm not alone and I'm not armed, and we are going to treat that thing back there exactly as we would a wounded bear."

She wasn't listening.

"Just...pull over!" she insisted.

I applied the brakes with ill grace and brought the little red skate to a stop at the side of the road, ready to use argument or physical force if necessary to keep her from doing something I knew was both dangerous and stupid. But there was no need.

Dana's face was colorless and stricken as she opened the passenger door, but she made no move to get out. Unsnapping the chest strap that held her upright, she let the seat belt remain fastened as she leaned far to her right and made restrained but unmistakable sounds of distress.

Well, Jesus out of the boat...

Some kind soul had left a roll of paper towels in the glove compartment, and I grabbed it as I cut the engine, opened my own door, and hustled around to Dana's side. She had lost most of the lunch and was thinking about getting rid of the rest. It seemed a pity.

"Relax," I told her, bracing her shoulders and putting a hand under her forehead. "Let it happen."

There was a moment of resistance, but it didn't last. Then the tension went out of the shoulders, and I could feel a change in her breathing. The trouble wasn't over, but the crisis had passed.

We stayed that way for a minute or two, and I had my first undistracted opportunity to listen to the world around us. It was quiet, but filled with sound. Mountain silence is a little like that. But different, because wind and echo and tree grumblings are a constant, so much a part of the world that they no longer make any conscious impression except on those rare occasions when they stop.

The silence-sounds of this place were flatter, more personal, and I found myself responding to them in an unaccustomed way. Mountain background sounds can be a shield against loneliness. The components make positive contact with the world, connecting the gaps and affirming the eternal rightness. But sounds and voices in this place had no echoes; they came unseconded to the ear, offering only the cold comfort of singularity, and I wondered, irrelevantly, if this might be the real difference between Jake and me. New Mexico was no place for a man who sometimes needed refuge from his own thoughts.

Dana stirred and took a deep breath.

I waited a moment to see how it was going to come out, but the body slowly firmed and took on its own weight. She sat up. Wordlessly I offered the paper towels, and wordlessly she used one to touch up her forehead and her lips. Nothing to say. I closed the door as she struggled with the chest strap, and a moment later we were turning onto the interstate, headed for Farewell.

The drive back to the motel passed in silence, and I thought Dana was using the time to deal with a sense of mortal frangibility that can accompany a close look at skull-face, the Great Death.

But I had underestimated the lady. Whatever problems she might have had with that had evidently been left by the roadside along with the remains of the *garbanzos encurtidos*. This was something else, as I discovered when I stopped the car in front of her room before pulling into my own parking stall.

The safety belts gave her a minor argument, and she kept her mouth shut while dealing with them and unlocking the car door. But she turned to look directly at me before getting out.

Suddenly I could sense the cold anger of her *wa*.

"Goddamn you!" she said in a tone of rising fury. "You can fool Father Jake and you can even fool Helen. But I saw your face back there when you went at the truck. Anyone in his right mind would have been scared—I was ready to pee in my pants. But you were laughing it up and having a ball. You ought to be locked up! You enjoyed it, you crazy son of a bitch! *You enjoyed it!*"

An hour later I was still staring at the ceiling in the drape-darkened motel room and waiting for sleep that always seemed just a yawn away.

But some thoughts are circular.

Dana was right, of course. That was the hell of it. She had called the turn on me, and I hadn't replied, because there wasn't anything to say. Nolo contendere, Your Honor. No defense. Something wrong inside here, sir, some kind of short in the wiring. Be so good as to fix it, please. And make it snappy. I've been waiting all my life.

She was wrong about the Spences, though. I had never been able to fool them—especially Helen, with her cool appraisals and inescapable arithmetic. Or Sara.

Sara...

I tried to force my mind away from the picture of her face, appalled but fascinated, watching from the ground after I won $400 from four other divinity students who had bet me that I couldn't walk blindfolded around the crenellated battlements of Gailor Hall at Sewanee. Sara and I had used the money for a weekend in Nashville, and there was a soft spring rainstorm that kept us in the room...

Stop that!

Where had the craziness started? For the ten thousand and first time, I remembered the tree in my grandfather's backyard, the one with the tangle-foot band intended to protect it from bugs, small boys, and other pests. I had figured a way around the problem, and by the time the ladder was discovered, I was out of sight in the branches above, too far out on a top limb for my uncle Hammond to reach when he climbed up to get me.

My mother was having hysterics down below, and the look on my uncle's face said I was doomed the moment he got his hands on me, but I had climbed up there for a purpose.

"Look, Unca Ham," I said. "Tarzan!"

I let go of the branch above me and hung for a moment by my legs as I had practiced over and over on the jungle gym. And then I straightened my knees.

The screams that rose around me as I fell were counterpoint to a swelling sensation in my chest, a lunatic-happy laugh that would not be suppressed. It kept boiling out, hot and maniacal, even after the branch that was supposed to have saved me at the end of the fall turned traitor and tore itself from my grasp, leaving me scraped and arm-broken on the ground. My mother and my grandparents dismissed the incident—after the obligatory threats and the noises of protest—as the normal act of a five-year-old boy with an overactive imagination and time to watch too much television.

But not my uncle Ham.

He had been there, had seen the look on my face as I let go and started to fall, had heard the laughter that continued even after the "oof!" interruption of ground contact. And besides, as I discovered after he was reported killed while flying refugee children out of Biafra, there was a lot of that derangement inside him, too. All he said about it at the time, though, was to caution me against any further open demonstrations.

"Save it, boy," he advised. "Save it until you're ready to get full value."

I didn't understand, and said so.

"You're too young yet," he said. "Keep this stuff up now and they'll be dragging you around to headshrinkers, trying to find out what's the matter with you. A real pain in the ass..."

"Headshrinkers?"

"Brain mechanics, kid. People who work your head over until you're talking and acting—and thinking—just like everybody else. They call that optimum adjustment. Sanity. You wouldn't like it.

"So save the crazy stuff until you're grown. Or anyway, till you're bigger."

We never discussed the subject again, and later a lot of people told me I was too young to have remembered either the fall from the tree or the conversation with Uncle Ham. Which just proved how right he had been.

Random thoughts drifted insensibly into the landscape of dream: I was back in the tree at my grandfather's house, but the man climbing toward me wasn't Uncle Ham. It was night, and he was wearing black pajamas and there were traces of mud blacking on his cheeks and he hadn't come up there to help me. My hands were empty and I had somehow lost the M16 and the frag grenades. I climbed higher, but the branch bent under my weight and I had turned my leg around it, leaning forward to reach another when a sudden metallic-sounding snap sent me into space, ripping and scraping through the foliage below. I laughed, the same locked-ward sound as ever. It was so funny! Charlie had missed. I was home free, and all I had to do was keep from hitting the ground. Simple. No sweat…just a matter of timing: My clawing fingers found something solid, scrabbled, bent, almost tore free…and suddenly I was awake, all systems at full alert in a half-darkened room, my left hand closed and locked around a curved double bar of cold metal.

"Good," a voice beside the bed said. "Very good, *amigo mío*. But not nearly good enough! You are getting old and slow and you forget to bar the door, and one day the cats will be looking down at you."

I fumbled for the lamp switch beside the bed, releasing the metal hook to improve my reach.

"Hi, Robbie," I said, when light finally filled the room. "When did you get into town?"

In Farewell, no one ever seemed to knock…

A SERMON
(CONTINUED)

The perception of personal mortality can open the door of insight.

It can also close the window of introspection.

These reactions are individual; they depend upon us, personally...

NINETEEN

Roberto Vincente de Bonzo y Obregon—Robbie—was probably born to be a movie star. Or a gigolo.

He is almost too handsome.

Clear black eyes radiate warmth and luster from the ascetic face of an Andalusian holy man—an angelic impression only slightly marred by the dazzling and slightly feral intensity of a smile that would confound a whole convention of orthodontists. Not a face to sell oil stocks with, perhaps. Too many oil men with smiles just as sharklike. But their wives might have found it irresistible. If the army hadn't found him first.

Service instructors had made Robbie a first-rate helicopter pilot, and natural inclination had placed him at the controls of a gunship. During the twenty-two months he spent in 'Nam, he had won three combat citations, two Silver Stars...a single Purple Heart to cover the loss of his hands, both burned beyond reconstruction when he tried to save his door gunner after a stray bullet brought their chopper down during the evacuation of Saigon.

I hadn't known him there, however.

Robbie and I had met during the final days of his sixth stay at a charity alcoholic ward in Los Angeles, about the time they had decided they were running a medical-psychiatric facility, not a rooming house for strays like the silver-tongued crazy who had talked the attendants into forming a wine-smuggling syndicate for him.

Discussing his situation, we had agreed that a few months in the mountains, among people who didn't pity him and couldn't be bullshitted with the maimed-hero routine, might be an interesting vacation from skid row.

For the past three years now he had been flying water drops and fire-rescue missions on contract for the Forest Service. We both knew it was getting on toward time for him to leave, but the world down-the-hill was full of highly qualified helicopter jockeys, not many of whom were able to make a full-time career of their trade. And the stainless-steel prehensiles were still the first thing prospective employers seemed to notice.

"Old...and careless," he repeated now, enjoying his temporary ascendancy in the running game of stealth we had started playing about a year ago when he began studies with our *mahayana* master.

Robbie loomed over me, grinning with at least sixty-four teeth. One of the hook-hands was raised to tease me with my own key ring, held just out of reach.

"One day," he prodded, "I will be called to pick up whatever is left when the cats are through."

He was probably right.

"You didn't waste any time getting here," I said, deciding to change the subject. "What time is it?"

"Four o'clock."

"A.m. or p.m.?"

"Sixteen hundred hours. Give or take a few minutes." His eyes narrowed, and the blinding smile diminished by several thousand lumens. "Christ, Preacher, you look like hell!"

"Thanks," I said. "I needed that."

Heaving the body erect and tottering it into the bathroom, I gave myself the standard water-in-the-face treatment and a forgettable lecture on the virtues of clean living and regular habits. When both were done, I removed the eye and gave it a bath.

"That damn thing," Robbie said from the doorway, "leads a life of its own. You know? Lying there in the water, it still stares right through you. Weird bastard."

"Not if you don't stare back."

He grinned and thumbed his nose—no small accomplishment for a man with neither thumb nor fingers, but possible to one with the imagination of a mime and plenty of time to practice.

The shirt I had worn that morning was strictly for the laundry. No matter what Dana might think, it still held the adrenal fear-stench of a wearer who had measured the tide of the Styx, so I broke out another and elbowed my way into it while blinking the right eyelid to let it finish the nonemotional weeping that always goes with reinsertion of the prosthesis.

"Between the two of us," Robbie said cheerfully, "we are one hell of an assembly job, Preacher."

"But crafted," I said, "to a gnat's ass."

"Fuckin' A!"

The helicopter hangar was considerably more depressing than I had expected. Experts from the National Transportation and Safety Board had used half its space to lay out the forlorn remnants of the wrecked LongRanger, retrieved from the field where Prescott had crashed. Assembled under shelter and arranged to simulate their original interrelationship, the component parts took on the accusative air of a canine traffic victim: How could you do this to me?

Robbie circled the ordered mess with blank-faced concentration and then stepped warily through the litter, avoiding physical contact with the debris while making his way to the flattened remains of the cockpit and craning his neck to examine the inside.

"Avionics all screwed up," he said. "Too bad. Sometimes you can get an idea of what went wrong by seeing where the needles were pointing when the dial cracked."

What was left of the controls bore heavy brown stains. Robbie's nose wrinkled reflexively, but it was his only concession to normal squeamishness as he poked an exploratory hook into the tortured metal, scraping the dual tip of the prosthesis against various impediments until he seemed to find what he wanted. Kneeling carefully and supporting himself on one elbow, he bent his head to peer inside.

"We got a flashlight?"

I started to shake my head, then noticed a clublike five-cell model standing nose down on the mechanic's workbench.

"Maybe," I said, picking up the long-handled monster and checking the switch to see if it was working. It was.

Watching Robbie use his hooks could be fascinating, but it was a sometime thing, because everybody had a mother who said it wasn't polite to stare. Actually, he had told me that he didn't mind normal interest or even questions, so long as the interest was open and friendly. But I never could get used to it, and the opportunity to spy from behind while he was fully occupied was just too good to miss.

Clamping the flashlight in the left prosthesis, he leaned on an elbow and pushed the right hook back into the smashed cavity of the cockpit, squinting and maneuvering the light beam to examine something just outside the line of my sight. His movements were precise, controlled...altogether natural, and therefore a kind of miracle. Years of practice had done their work. An observer who didn't know better would have sworn Robbie was exploring the wreckage by sense of touch.

"Collective," he said finally, snapping off the big flashlight and standing up. "It's jammed wide open. Not set. Jammed."

I looked at him, waiting for more.

"Could mean nothing," he went on. "Crash impact could have done that, or it could even have happened while they were loading the scraps onto the truck to bring them here."

"But...?"

"But it could be something else. Yeah. With the controls set that way, the bird could kind of fly itself for a while. A very damn short while—but maybe long enough. These jets are a lot easier and safer to handle than the old piston types. You don't have to use both hands and both feet every damn minute. I mean, you can even scratch your nose or eat a sandwich without having to land while you're doing it."

"So someone else could have been flying the helicopter and then got out of it just before the crash. Or even set the controls for a short flight with Prescott unconscious in the pilot's seat?"

"Well..."

"Could you do it, Robbie?"

"Hell, yes! But that doesn't mean every damn fool on the face of the earth could bring it off. You couldn't do it, for instance."

"Because I can't fly a helicopter."

"Right."

"But someone with helicopter experience—maybe not a licensed pilot, but with enough training to be able to get a bird off the ground and down again without killing himself—someone like that could get it done?"

Robbie turned the idea over in his mind for a moment or two and then nodded. But slowly. "With luck," he said. "A lot of luck and good flying conditions, and if he didn't have to take the bird too far before he put it back on the earth. Maybe, with all that going for him."

We both took time out to look again at the wreckage, trying to imagine how it might have been.

"The crash site," I said, "was less than a mile from here."

Robbie nodded absently. "What time of day?"

"Early morning."

"How early?"

"About six, I think. Would that be important?"

"It could be." He looked at the twisted bits of machinery again and moved one of his hooks to scratch behind an ear. "I told you these jets are fairly easy to fly," he said. "I should have added that they can be a real bitch and a half to start sometimes. Especially at higher altitudes."

Farewell's part of New Mexico is a little less than a mile above sea level. He gave me a moment to recall that bit of information and let it sink in.

"Also," he said when he decided I was beginning to get the idea, "ambient temperature is a major consideration with jet engines. Remember the trouble we had a month ago getting the Forest Service bird to wake up and cook? All because we live at seven thousand feet and the temperature that day was a degree or two below zero, Celsius."

I remembered. It had been an emergency medical evacuation— some woman over at Twin Forks whose baby was coming a month early. The whole town had turned out with blowtorches to help Robbie get airborne.

"What I'm getting at," he continued, "is that high altitude and low temperature mean a real hassle when you're starting the day, and sometimes it's more than a one-man job, even if you know the bird pretty well and have all the experience in the world."

"So maybe Pres started the engine himself?"

"Maybe."

I gave it another moment's thought. "Or," I said, "maybe he had a little help...from a friend?"

Robbie smiled. "Someone he knew, anyway," he said. "Someone he would trust to give him a little casual assistance."

"You're saying he might have flown to the crash site himself. With the killer in the passenger seat beside him."

"It would work out easiest that way."

We stood staring at each other, occupied with our own thoughts. But after a while Robbie shook his head with a slow and heavy finality. "No," he said.

"No what?"

"No way."

The splendid whiteness of the de Bonzo incisors flashed once more, sardonic and challenging below the length of the Roman nose. "This," he said, "is all a crock. You never met the dude. I never met him. We never saw this old bird before it crashed. And here we are standing around making up a whole second-rate television script about it. Who you wanta be...Eliot Ness or Barnaby Jones?"

"Well, Ness is prettier."

The smile again.

"In that case, *amigo mío,* the role was clearly written with me in mind."

We spent the better part of the next hour inside the hangar, checking out the remaining physical assets of Prescott Helicopters, Inc., and trying to make sense of the books and business papers strewn around the office.

In the end, Robbie leaned back in the bookkeeper's chair and made sounds of sighing.

"Guy was losing his ass," he said.

"And all his fixtures," I agreed. "But the thing we've got to decide now is, would the family be better off trying to run the business or just selling it? Not necessarily as an entity; we might peddle the various components—the two remaining helicopters and the tools and the rest—and wind it up that way. You're the helicopter expert. What do you think?"

His answer was instantaneous: "Oh, Christ, start it up again, of course! You got to!"

I was surprised and I suppose my face showed it.

"I said this Prescott guy was losing money, not that he was out of business," Robbie explained. "We still have that JetRanger and the little Robinson. And the parts inventory. And that alone, *compadre*, is a gold mine."

He had unconsciously begun using the pronoun "we" in speaking of the business, and that was all to the good—in line with something I'd had in mind almost from the beginning—but I let him keep talking, and got a minor education in one facet of the fixed-base helicopter business.

"Running a parts inventory in a big town like Los Angeles or even Albuquerque is one thing," Robbie said. "Something goes bad on the bird, you can pick up the phone and the only question is do you want to pick up the part yourself or do they send someone over to deliver it. But out here in the boondocks, fifty miles from land or water, it's a different story.

"These birds are too expensive to let them sit on the ground, even for a day. So when a part goes sour, it's always panic time. You need to stock enough spares, and just the right ones, to keep flying. Make all the normal, predictable repairs. The hell of it is, those parts are damn expensive in themselves, and having too big an inventory can kill you just as quick as not having them on hand when you need them."

He got up and paced across the office to look out at the tool-and-parts shack, a small room closed off from the rest of the hangar by corrugated steel walls and heavy wire mesh window grids. The room was high security, two locks plus an electronic burglar alarm that was cut into a response grid at the sheriff's office. We had needed the keys and a phone call to the sheriff's dispatcher to get Robbie inside for a quick glance-and-guess inventory, and I had noticed the care with which he replaced the locks and rearmed the alarm when he was finished.

"Prescott must have sweated blood in the beginning, learning what he had to have ready on hand and what could safely be left to order as needed," he continued. "But he damn sure learned, and the inventory here shows careful attention. That was one big thing I noticed, by the way: Everything about this place is first-cabin. Clean and professional. Well maintained. You know there is a kind of a smell about half-ass fixed-base operations—dingy and rank, even when they're prettied up for company. But this place is just the opposite. It just doesn't make sense to me…" His voice trailed off.

"That the man who set it up and ran it this way would kill himself?"

Robbie growled, shaking himself out of the mood, and grinned at me again.

"Always, we come back to that."

"Seem to, don't we?"

"Well, then, since you've got a one-track—"

But he never got to the zinger, because that was when the first bullet hit the window beside him and we both hit the office floor.

A SERMON (CONTINUED)

We are the arbiters of our own fate. For we are the creators of our own dreams...

TWENTY

Some little towns are livelier than others. I had an opportunity to ponder on this during the moments Robbie and I spent belly-crawling toward what seemed like relative safety in the blind area just below the window.

Since arriving in Farewell three days ago, I had been threatened by a pistol-packing punk, set upon by three thugs, beaten by a deputy sheriff, nearly killed in a back-road drag race, and now I was under fire from a bushwhacker. A good, full social schedule. Exhilarating. But I couldn't help wondering what people had done for kicks before I came to town.

Another bullet angried through the window and buried itself in the opposite wall close to the plaster-dimple made by the first one.

"Shit!"

Robbie came to his feet like a spring-loaded knife blade, sprinted two steps into a rolling somersault, and came down on his feet, still running outside the office. I heard an occasional light footfall as he made for the access gate at the rear of the hangar.

That left the side door for me, and I decided to wait for the next bullet on the theory—not necessarily valid but better than nothing—that a man using the kind of rifle favored by snipers usually has to take time to work the bolt before each shot. Make the bastard hurry. Maybe spoil his aim.

I've always been an optimist.

The wait was a short one. My legs had already taken on a sprinter's set, and I didn't spare a glance to mark where the next slug landed as I let the sound push me along Robbie's track out the office door, jinking left and picking my way around the remains of the LongRanger en route to the parking-lot entrance, where I crouched and waited with my hand an inch or two from the knob.

Robbie was biding his time in a similar position at the back of the hangar, ready to go for broke. No need for talk. The two of us might be a bit out of our element trying to take a logical approach to the question of who was playing games with whom in the interbred business community of small-town New Mexico. But long-range rifle fire was something else again. A firefight is a firefight is a firefight, and this was a routine we knew by heart.

The fourth shot, when it finally came, had a slightly different sound, and I decided after a moment's consideration that it had probably not landed inside the building. But it was all pretty academic by that time. By then, Robbie was already out the back door and making quiet eel-like progress toward the covert rifleman via a weed-choked ditch we had both noticed at the edge of the helipad when we drove up, and I had popped out into the parking lot, run two quick steps, and taken a flying headfirst leap over the hood of my little rental car, landing in a roll and putting its none-too-substantial bulk between me and the sniper.

If all went according to the book, the next moves for Robbie and me would be a feinting pincers intended to whipsaw the rifleman, moving in on him step by step from two directions until one or the other of us was in position to do him some damage.

But we might have saved ourselves the trouble.

By the time I was ready to make my first diversion—no fun, but safer than it looks; the run would start at the sound of the next shot and was intended to put me at an angle that would make for awkward shooting if the sniper's nest was where it seemed to be—an automobile engine started up, just out of sight behind a hump of New Mexico landscape, and the sound of tires spraying gravel told us the war was over. For a while.

It could have been a little head game, of course. Many a hopeful lad had found his way into a body bag by forgetting that not all trappers wore fur hats. Our sniper might very well have had a friend primed to make going-away noises that would lure us into breaking cover prematurely. Surprise party is the name of the game for a bushwhacker. But somehow I didn't think anything like that was on the menu today.

In fact, I was beginning to have second thoughts about the whole scene.

Robbie was still out of sight, presumably working his way toward the sniper's shooting stand, when I noticed that our play-mate had given me a little extra chore for the late afternoon. The left front tire of the rental car was flat, and I could see that one whole section of the tread and sidewall had been sheered away as if by the stroke of an outsize battle-ax. The damage tallied with the caliber of ammunition that had knocked holes in the office wall, and explained why the final shot had sounded different from the others. The shooter didn't want any company on his way back to Farewell.

"Let it go, Robbie," I called. "He's split."

"I know it."

Robbie's head and shoulders emerged from the ditch about twenty feet from where he would have been within rock-throwing range of the sniper's presumed firing point. He was so damn good. I hadn't spotted a single false movement among the tall-grown grasses of the ditch.

If only the rifleman had stayed put for a minute or two longer...

"Son of a bitch." His voice and posture were eloquent of disgust as he ambled over a little knoll to where the shooter had been hidden. He poked around for a moment, picked something up, and came back to where I was standing.

"Careless mother," he said. One of his steel hooks was clamped delicately on the bright brass end of a cartridge case. "Must've picked up the other three but missed this one. Or just didn't give a damn."

He held the empty up to catch the dusk-slanted sunlight and examined it with close professional interest.

"Thirty ought-six," he said. "Nothing fancy, nothing expensive. But good enough. Hand loaded, which makes sense. Even sleeved and sporterized—if that's how it was, and it sure looks that way—those old service pipes like a slightly underweight charge."

He handed me the evidence.

I haven't Robbie's expertise, but even my unpracticed eye could make out the telltale reloading scratches and the slight imperfections near the base that are the mark of the reused center fire casing. It helped confirm the thought that had been forming in my mind ever since I'd seen the second shot group itself so neatly on the office wall.

"Piss-poor shooting for someone who went to such a hell of a lot of trouble," Robbie said, his voice still audibly irritated. "Four tries, easy distance, all the time in the world—but no meat. Awful!"

I handed the brass back to him. "Or very damn good," I said.

It brought him up short and cut off whatever else he'd had to say. He looked at me and then followed my line of sight to the flattened front tire on the little car.

"Remember when the shooting began?" I said.

He nodded, squatting to get a better look at the damage.

"We were talking," he said. "Something about…hell, I can't remember…oh, yeah: about Prescott and whether a guy like that would kill himself."

I nodded. "You were walking back and forth," I said. "Right in front of the window. Not thinking about it, just moving. Like a metronome. Three paces one way, three paces back. Robbie, you've been shooting rifles almost as long as you've been alive. Given the angle and the distance, could you have made a shot like that?"

He thought about it, but not for long. "Piece of cake," he said.

"And the next two rounds—you happen to notice what a pretty little group they made with the first one, there on the wall of the office?"

He could see where I was headed now. "Cover all three with a half-dollar," he agreed.

"And then the car tire…"

We both looked at it, double-checking the probable angle, lighting, and distance the rifleman would have been up against.

"Took that shoe off without so much as denting anything else," Robbie said meditatively.

"Not too shoddy, would you say?"

"It'll pass."

We took a few moments for private ruminations. Mine were unpleasant. And judging from the blank austerity that had spread over Robbie's features, his were no better.

"Whoever was doing the shooting," I said, spelling it out for both of us, "could have touched us off anytime he felt like it. His option. But he didn't feel like it. He wanted to send someone a message, not make work for the coroner."

Robbie was incensed. "That sucks," he said.

"We're alive."

"Still sucks!"

"Beats being dead."

He looked back at the empty cartridge, hating the inanimate brass in default of its late owner, and threw it as hard and as far as he could. He got a nice distance on the throw. Robbie's steel-arm accuracy with light missiles is myth and legend in our part of the mountains.

"Playing games," he said, watching the cartridge bounce on the concrete apron in front of the hangar. "Miss us close and watch us scramble. A fun-fragger!"

His face set in planes of grim rage, and the eyes, usually so warm, were like frozen coal.

"Never did get used to being shot at," he said. "You remember how some did? Even got to like it, thought it was the best game since Cowboys and Indians. Crazy! But I never did and I still don't, and whether you miss me or hit me is a detail; the main thing is how I feel when I hear the stuff whizzing around my head, and it makes me want to puke, and any son of a bitch thinks it's funny could get to be a total stranger…"

I saw no reason to interrupt.

He was playing my song.

"So…he wasn't really trying to hit either one of us. Just wanted to see us hit the dirt and fill our shorts? Terrific! Remind me to add his goddamn name to the Christmas list. I don't suppose you'd happen to have any idea how it might be spelled?"

"Not even a clue."

"Uh-huh." The eyes didn't believe me, but we'd known each other too long and too well to argue the point. "Well," he said, "if you ever do get one, maybe you could kind of let an old buddy in on the secret. Just for old times' sake. Think you could do that?"

"You'll be the first to know," I said. "But meanwhile…"

I let the word hang there, and after a long moment the icy face melted into another of those mega-candlepower smiles.

"Meanwhile," he picked up the sentence and finished it for me, "I don't suppose we are going to say a damn word about this to the local law, are we, amigo?"

That's another thing I've always liked about Robbie. Sometimes he can be a real mind reader.

We matched quarters for the job of changing the tire, and he swore I was using one with two heads, but did the job anyway while I hunted up some spare plywood to make temporary repairs on the broken window.

By the time both jobs were done it was dark, and we started back toward Farewell in silence, absorbed in our own thoughts.

Mine were pretty cloudy. Offhand, I could think of one or two people who might have good reason to want me—or maybe both of us—out of town. But neither of them had impressed me as being stupid enough to think that a few chunks of metal flying around would do the job. Robbie's reaction was only partially an echo of my own.

I wasn't especially fond of gunfire either, but the shooting had given me a prime case of the stubborns, which can be hell on wheels when it gets mixed up with curiosity, and now I could hardly wait to find out whether any of the feelers I had put out during the day had touched a nerve.

On the other hand, I was having trouble with myself.

Little by little, I could feel the beginnings of a mood I knew to be dangerous, especially in the present circumstances. I was beginning to take things personally. Bad news…

One of the most attractive things about playing poker for a living is that you keep score with money. Put it down on the table at the beginning of the game and change it for chips, turn them back into money when you're done, and count. That's how you find out whether you won or lost. No agonizing or philosophizing. No recriminations. Just simple addition or subtraction. Impersonal.

Other games can turn out something else without warning: Play the stock market and you're dealing with actual part-ownership of a business—with the lives and prospects of the people who work there. Too easy to find yourself identifying with the company, taking a personal interest in its fortunes. Letting the feelings get in the way of logical strategy and tactics.

But poker doesn't deal with anything real. Just money. Win it, lose it, spend it, save it, do anything you want with it; in the end it's still just money, a temporary marker that means absolutely nothing until and unless it can be exchanged for something else. Pretty hard to form any personal attachment.

Unfortunately, not everyone sees it that way.

Money impresses people. One of the downtown hotel-casinos in Las Vegas takes advantage of this. In the lobby, between the registration desk and the poker alcove, a million dollars—in cash—is permanently on display. It is in $10,000 bills; one hundred of them geometrically arranged for maximum visibility between two heavy sheets of shatterproof glass. Visitors are encouraged to pose for snapshots standing beside this visible symbol of the city's basic religious dedication.

Here it is, folks: money!

Examine it closely. Note the cunning artisanship of the engraver, the technical mastery of the paper mill. Admire the lifelike lineaments of the portraiture, the handsome symmetry of design. We'd like to let you touch it, smell it. Even taste it. But that's a no-no. So why don't you all just stand there and drool? Lots of people do.

Every now and then, of course, someone cracks under the strain.

True religious experience is like that.

Something snaps in the brain, and a voice as from above seems to say, *Go for it!* The usual—intended—result is an all-out assault on such hopeless propositions as roulette, the money wheel, or the slots. By the time sanity returns, considerable wealth will have departed.

But once in a while the impulse is more direct, and the new-hatched engraving-fancier decides on a little do-it-yourself social reform. Share the wealth. Guards at the casino are under strict orders not to interfere. The glass protecting the bills is high-test, shatterproof, and quite heavy. It was handled into place by a forklift. Watching the would-be thieves get it out of the building could be a show in itself, something you don't see every day.

And once they are off the premises, the problem of spending the proceeds would be considerable.

The $10,000 bills are real enough, purchased from and attested to by the Federal Reserve Bank. Legal tender of the United States. But they are rare. Few legitimate transactions of such size as to require such sums are carried out in cash; the Federal Reserve keeps a record of every $10,000 bill in current circulation—where it is and how it got there. Any attempt to spend the money would be an immediate prelude to arrest.

Such is the nature of reality.

And such is the reality of money. At best, it's a handy way of keeping score while keeping the mind clear for more consequential matters.

But the game in Farewell was getting serious. Personal. Emotional. Something other than money seemed to be involved, and someone seemed to think it was important enough to outweigh human life.

And as always, I found this difficult to believe.

Murder—casual murder, offhand and unthinking—is a daily occurrence in our world. Newspapers have long since stopped publishing accounts of any but the more interesting examples: the grisly serial slaughters by obviously demented life-collectors, the drive-by offings of fourteen-year-old rivals by fifteen-year-old street gang candidates, the quiet removal of wealthy spouses by ambitious gigolo-husbands. Anything more mundane simply isn't news.

Yet the fact remains that murder is a crime of almost incredible violence, the ultimate frustration of the individual and an act well beyond the real-world capabilities of most people. Psychopaths and sociopaths aside, when the moment of truth arrives, most men and women simply cannot pull that trigger even in defense of their own lives.

But it had happened here. That made the pot a big one. Call it two raises before the final card. No time for me to start having doubts about my objectivity. I was in for the whole ride.

"Think they're going to sell?"

Robbie's voice broke into the long silence just as we were reaching the edge of town. I dragged myself back from the distance. "Sell what, the helicopter operation?"

"Yeah."

"Already sold."

"Oh…"

The disappointment in his tone was so patent that I just couldn't let it alone. "Only temporarily," I said. "Part of an idea I have to see who was doing what to whom. Mrs. Prescott will own it again in the end."

He didn't reply at once, and I could almost hear the computations in his mind as he tried to select exactly the right words and phrases. The ones that would seem casual.

"In that case," he said, "I guess they'll be doing some hiring. A pilot, I mean…"

I started to give a straight answer, but couldn't resist the temptation to play the game out with him. Sometimes I'm a real bastard. "Beats me," I said. "That would be up to the new manager."

"Oh. Yeah, I guess he'd probably want to bring back the guy who was working there before…You said they had a second pilot."

"Not a chance."

"Say what?"

"He's already got a new job. And moved away to Amarillo."

"Oh."

Another long pause. It was getting too thick now. I decided to cut out the nonsense. And about time...

"Probably a couple or three more guys with helicopter experience living around here," I said. "And someone could always be hired from the outside. But that would be your problem, not mine."

"My problem?"

"Of course, yours. Look: You're a nice guy, Robbie, and good company and even moderately decorative in a Frito Bandito sort of way, but I sure as hell didn't get you out here just for that. The problems of who to hire and all the rest of it are yours because you're the new general manager of Prescott Helicopters. The boss!"

He looked at me, goggling, and I laughed.

"Who else could I trust?"

A SERMON
(CONTINUED)

Not all the dreams of mankind are worthwhile, of course. But some are worth dreaming—so strong and so real and so utterly satisfactory that even the vagaries of chance and the certainty of death cannot entirely destroy their power...

TWENTY-ONE

Introducing Robbie to the Prescott family was pure pleasure. I had already told Marilyn why he was in town, prudently withholding certain details concerning his personal history—and the prosthetic hands. If they were going to be a problem for anyone, I wanted to know about it up front.

But I had guessed right. If Marilyn noticed the steel clamps protruding from Robbie's sleeves, the only outward sign was an omission: She didn't extend her hand to shake and then withdraw it hastily, as too many people do. And the children did the rest. No shyness there. And no awkwardness, either. Just open and wide-eyed curiosity, totally devoid of pity or squeamishness and expressed in practical questions and demands for close personal inspection.

Marilyn started to intervene, but reconsidered in the face of one of the blinding de Bonzo smiles as Robbie rolled up a sleeve to let Bubba and Missy see how the prosthesis was fitted to his arm. The expressions of wonder and admiration were profuse and genuine, but faded into the background of accepted knowledge when Robbie demonstrated the grasping ability of his substitute hands by picking up one of the checkers from the Connect-Four game that was set up on the family room table. He was, he announced, the Connect-Four champion of California. Were there, by chance, any possible challengers on the premises?

There were.

Dana drifted in from the kitchen and stood for a minute or two in the doorway, nursing a Marlboro while taking in the scene. Robbie was holding his own at Connect-Four. Barely. She went on watching the game for a while and then grinned at me.

"You," she said in a voice audible only as far as my ear, "have nice friends."

Say this for me: I recognize a peace overture when I hear one.

"Speaking as an outsider, or...?"

"Bastard."

My turn to grin. "Takes one to know one."

Dana blew a lungful of cigarette smoke in my direction, then seemed to regret it and waved her hand to dissipate the cloud.

"Sorry," she said. "Reflex."

"The smoke or the hand signals?"

"Double bastard."

"My, but we're salty tonight."

"Speaking of which..." She made a come-with-me forefinger gesture and vanished into the hallway. I followed and caught up with her at the kitchen end of the passage, where she was pounding the unfinished half of the cigarette into a cutesy little ashtray formed to resemble an old-style peaked sombrero.

"Speaking of feisty, or salty, or whatever it was," she said when the last spark was out and she had made sure no one was around to overhear, "one of your other friends called. The motel referred him here, and I promised you'd get back to him as soon as possible. Was that all right?"

"Depends," I said.

"On what?"

"On who it was."

"Oh. Yeah. Sorry...I'm still a little bit shook—fuzzy—from that thing with the pickup truck today. Don't know what's wrong, really. But something."

I looked her over. The hand now unconsciously fumbling for another cigarette had a slight tremor that I didn't remember being there before, and there was a suspicious redness at the corners of the eyes.

"Try getting some sleep?" I asked.

That earned me an indignant snort. "Fat chance!" she said. "Ever since I got out of that damn little car, I've been shaky. Sleepy. Out on my feet. But go to sleep? No way, José. The eyes pop open as soon as the head hits the pillow, and I'm back there on that road with the truck coming at us."

I sighed inwardly but restrained an impulse to put my arms around her and make comforting noises. Gestures like that are rarely of much help, and they can lead to all manner of complication.

"Delayed stress," I diagnosed. "You know: kind of a short-run version of the thing they talk about 'Nam vets having. Comes of building up a big head of steam—lots of adrenaline pumping—and then giving it nowhere to go."

"Terrific! So what do you do about it?"

I shook my head. "If I knew a specific answer," I said, "I could probably get elected President right now, without opposition. But there isn't any that I know about. Everyone handles that, or doesn't handle it, in their own way."

"What's your way? Poker?"

Perceptive lady.

"Partly," I said. "Or, anyway, part of the reason I learned to play poker well enough to make a few dollars at it is because of what I do about the stress...which is a pretty evasive answer, I guess."

"Yes, it is."

"Okay, then. Try this: I deal with some of my feelings by going away from the place where they are. Not physically. Geographic solutions don't work. At least not for long. But you can go away in your mind."

Her eyes didn't believe a word of it, but she didn't interrupt, so I went on.

"Everyone has a different place. One to a customer, strictly personal service. Mine is a high meadow where the sun is warm and the breeze is cool. I sit there and try to understand an endless nonverbal lecture delivered by a holy man who died fifteen hundred years ago..."

Dana went on looking at me in silence through two complete lungfuls of smoke and then stubbed out the new cigarette beside the other one.

"I was right in the first place," she sighed. "You're crazy."

I drew back in mock astonishment. "Why, Miz Dana, ma'am," I said, "I surely do hope that I never went to give you any impression to the contrary!"

"Oh, to hell with you."

She turned away toward the stove, where the evening meal seemed to be in a relatively early stage of preparation, but caught herself and swung back immediately. She brought a scribbled bit of paper out of a skirt pocket and handed it to me.

"Almost forgot, in all this brilliant repartee," she said. "The call you got. It was from someone named Price. In Houston."

Mistah Dee Tee wasn't immediately available at the number he'd left with Dana. It was, a discreetly modulated Texican voice informed me, the twenty-four-hour number at his office, and he would be out of touch for an hour or so. But was there a number where he could reach me later? Mr. Price had left strict orders...

I thanked her kindly and was on the point of reading off the number of the telephone in my hand when I thought better of it and gave her the motel number instead.

She thanked me and rang off.

"If you go now," Dana said when I had put the phone down, "you'll be missing one of the great dinners of all time. *Carne estilo Nogales,* prepared by one of the truly great chefs of the great Southwest."

"Better than Helen Spence?"

She made an offhand gesture. "Helen got a late start," she said. "You have to grow up cooking this kind of food to really do it justice."

"May I assume, then, that the great chef you mentioned was a modest reference to yourself?"

"Who else?"

"Who, indeed."

I went over to the stove. The pot that smelled so good would be the simmering tomato sauce with beer. Odor intensified and resolution wavered as I lifted the lid. Chances were she had not exaggerated.

"Sherry?" I inquired.

"Just before serving," she said. "Otherwise it gets lost. Good?"

"Superb. But I still have to go."

"Triple bastard."

I considered this. "Sounds unscientific to me," I said. "But you may know more about such things than I do."

I ducked the half-empty pack of cigarettes she threw at me.

"On the other hand," I laughed, making a tactical retreat down the hallway, "perhaps not. In any case, you were asking how I keep from gaining weight after eating two breakfasts and a big lunch? Well, it's simple: I don't follow them by sitting down to a meal I like as much as *carne estilo Nogales.* That's my secret. Tell me, what's yours?"

I really don't know whether she would have thrown the little ceramic sombrero or not. But it was in her hand by the time I was in a position to duck through the family room to the front door, and I decided not to press my luck. The best way to handle a short-tempered woman is with your hat. Grab it and run.

A SERMON
(CONTINUED)

Most of us, however, dream small.

We live from day to day, from hour to hour. Our hours loom large; twenty-four hours is a lot, next week is the horizon. We live, as Thoreau said, lives of quiet desperation...

TWENTY-TWO

I hadn't been entirely candid about my reasons for leaving early. True enough, my usual food intake was one meal a day, and the amazing three I had already taken aboard were still keeping step with me. I knew they were there, and felt as though I needn't eat again for a month. But avoidance of temptation wasn't my only reason for leaving early.

The conversation with Robbie, before it was so pointedly interrupted, had given me the beginning of an idea, and I wanted a chance to check it out privately before talking to Dee Tee again.

Jake's office was dark when I pulled up at the church, but there was a glow from the sanctuary. The double doors in front were unlocked—I wondered, irrelevantly, how many big-town churches would dare leave them that way after sundown—and after only a momentary hesitation I let myself in and moved past the guest-book lectern and tract rack to the nave.

At first glance the place seemed deserted. Jake had built his church on the original southwestern plan of high windows and narrow roof, a style adapted to that elder world's need for defensibility against Indian attack and the relatively short lengths of wood available for ceiling beams. The only light was behind the rood screen, and the nearer reaches of the nave were in deep shadow. But after a moment I was able to make out a recessed side altar with two pews, probably used now and then as a chapel, and fixed on a single black-clad figure kneeling at the rail.

I stood still and kept quiet.

Years before, deep in the throes of those doubts that customarily assail young and overearnest postulants, the preceptor to whom I had confided my reservations and I had come upon Jake similarly occupied at solitary prayer in a chapel at Sewanee. The preceptor, my assigned guide to the world of religious enlightenment, had stood surveying the praying figure for a time and then turned away with a deprecatory shake of the head. "True believers," he said in a voice edged with icy contempt. "They always make more trouble than they're worth."

It was, I had thought at the time, a most peculiar attitude for a man in his position. But I was grateful to him for having said it when he did. The words had warned me against seeking any further advice from him about any serious subject. Another hopeful postulant, less fortunate, told me a few years later that he had confided his problems to the same man and was jocularly advised to put away such childish things and get on with "the real work."

Faith, he was informed, is for the consumers of faith—for the congregation. Not for the priest. He is the supplier. True belief can be a real career-killer for the minister, gets in the way of clear-thinking, practical administration.

My friend subsequently resigned from the ministry, as did I, while that preceptor, a clear-thinking and practical administrator if ever there was one, became a bishop—which I suppose might be considered a textbook demonstration of the sure wisdom of that hypocritical bastard's philosophy.

Of such is the new and malleable church-for-our-time raised high. There are no mistakes. And no coincidences.

Jake stirred, rising to his feet.

"Troublemaker," I said, making a noise to alert him to my presence.

He peered into the gloom. "That," he said, "could only be an ex-roommate."

"Or a bandit," I said. "Do you really feel safe enough to leave the doors unlocked at night?"

He didn't seem to think the question was serious enough to warrant an answer. But he offered a final small bow in the direction of the concealed host before turning to make his way toward me along the aisle, adroitly avoiding a double stack of hymnals someone had left in the way.

"Confirmation class tonight," he explained. "Normally, we'd hold it in the parish hall, but the furnace over there broke down again last week, and the fireplace really wouldn't heat a closet. No sense trying to explain the articles of faith to people whose hands are turning blue before your eyes. And what do you mean, 'troublemaker'? What have I done now?"

"Just a memory," I said. "Nothing important. But while we're on the subject of memory, how's yours? For local gossip, that is. Something from a few years back...?"

He shrugged. "A priest hears things, of course. But I don't know about repeating gossip."

"All in a good cause," I reassured him. "And all in aid of doing the job you got me out here to do."

He still wasn't convinced. But he waited for me to go on.

"Vollie Manion," I said, listening with my eyes as well as my ears, and twisting all the emotional antennae to full gain. "Dana Lansing tells me she went to school with him. A couple of grades ahead, but remembers him well. Do you know him, too?"

Jake didn't reply at once. But he didn't have to. The reaction was too strong and too immediate for it to have been based on anything Dana might have told Helen about our encounter with the deputy on the night Bobby Don Thieroux was killed.

"As I told you this morning," he said at last, picking the words carefully and trying to make them sound noncommittal, "I heard you had some kind of fight with him."

"He hit me, and I hit the wall," I said. "I guess you could stretch a point and call that a fight."

He waited for me to go on, but I didn't, and he used the silence to make up his mind about how much he wanted to tell me. I love Jake, but he has a glass head. Always did. And he had simply never done enough lying or evading during his lifetime to be worth a damn at it.

"Vollie was born in Farewell," he said. "His mother was Roman Catholic, and he was brought up that way. Went to a parochial school—Saint Joseph's, it's just down the road—until she died. After that, I understand, the county was his guardian and wouldn't leave him there. Trouble about it, but none of his mother's people would take him in, because they'd disowned her when she got pregnant without being married and wouldn't tell them who the father was."

"The county supported him? He was a public charge?"

"Oh, no!" Jake emphasized the denial with an emphatic shake of the head. "There was money. Had been, to support her, and it kept coming for him after she died."

"Money from where?"

"The bank."

The fog was getting pretty thick.

"You mean the bank—the bank itself—was supporting Vollie Manion and his mother?"

"Of course not." Jake was puzzled for a moment, but then his expression cleared and I could sense a similar easing in his emotional aura. We had arrived on safe ground so far as he was concerned. "I forgot you don't live in New Mexico," he said. "Some of the laws here are a little different. For instance, there's a legal blinder that can be invoked on personal trusts. The bank pays out the money, but doesn't have to tell anyone where it comes from."

I nodded, thinking about it. "Not the worst idea I ever heard," I said. "But there must be some way of getting at the information."

"Of course there is. A judge can issue a search warrant if someone convinces him that a felony is being committed."

"Uh-huh." I had reservations about that; there is always a back door. But I kept the doubts to myself. "All that must have been before you got here. Let's talk about the last few years."

Jake cleared his throat and we were back to foot-dragging. "Well," he said, and I could see him editing again, "Vollie had left the Roman faith by the time I arrived, and had joined this parish, such as it was; they were meeting in a storefront, trying to get enough financing to buy some land."

"And he helped?"

"As much as he could, yes." Jake stopped talking and I tried to wait him out again, but it was no-go.

"Dana didn't tell me too much about Vollie," I lied, "but I gather she didn't like him a whole lot. Was she the only one who felt that way, or were there others?"

Jake squirmed, but I was surprised to sense another partial relaxation. He didn't seem to mind the new direction the conversation had taken. I made a mental note to find out why.

"No," he said, "she wasn't alone. Vollie never did have many friends in Farewell, I'm afraid, and at first I just put it down to the fact of his illegitimacy. People stopped picking on him when he got big enough to defend himself, but the stigma was still there. This town can be small in more than one way. Only natural for him to throw up defenses."

"Such as covert sadism?"

Direct hit!

Jake's *wa* turned hot and cold and hot again all in the space of a second, and I knew I was zeroing in on the spot he had been trying to defend from the very beginning. But I couldn't simply crash on through. I needed his cooperation. And he was a friend.

"I can't discuss that," he said.

"Why not?"

"Seal of the confessional."

It was a real stopper.

Personal, private confession is most common, of course, among Roman Catholics. But it is not unknown in the Anglican communion. To the contrary, basic doctrine stipulates that "all may" confess privately if the need is felt, and "some should" do so, but "none must."

The majority of the faithful, not surprisingly, pay attention to the last two words and skip the rest, confining themselves to the much-less-demanding general confession that is a part of the communion service.

But Jake had said Vollie Manion was reared a Roman Catholic, so it might have been natural—perhaps necessary—for him to bring certain problems to the one-to-one intimacy of private confession. That would explain Jake's reactions when the man's name was mentioned, and might also tell me a lot more than he had intended about the nature of the sins acknowledged and redeemed.

"Okay," I said, "I understand, and we'll try to stay away from the sensitive area. But there are plenty of other things you can tell me—matters of general knowledge."

"Uh...maybe."

He still wasn't happy about any of this, and I couldn't blame him, but we had to move on before he could think of a good reason to shut up entirely.

"Vollie's too young to have been in Vietnam," I said, accepting his halfhearted nod in lieu of reply, "but talking to Frank Ybarra I got the impression that he hadn't been with the sheriff's department for any great length of time."

He hesitated before answering. "That's true enough."

He was on guard and nothing was going to be easy, but it was information I had to have. Now.

"Talking to Vollie himself," I continued, "I got the idea he'd been away from Farewell a few years ago, going to college in some other town. Is that right?"

Jake nodded. "He went to the state university. Did well there, too, I understand."

"Uh-huh. Did he graduate? Take a degree?"

"Well...no."

And there we were back on shaky ground again. I decided it was time to find out why, if possible.

"Was he ever in the service?" I prodded. "In the army or navy?"

Jake blinked, and I could see a whole phalanx of refusals forming up, ready to march.

"Old friend," I said gently, "all of this would be a matter of public record. I could get it the hard way if necessary. Have someone back in Washington go digging through the files. And I'll do that if I have to. But it would make things a lot easier—and shouldn't intrude—if you'd just tell me as much as you feel you can right now. We've known each other far too long to keep on sparring."

He nodded slowly. Reluctantly. "It's not that I don't trust you or that I don't want to help," he said. "But this is a lot more complicated than it seems, believe me."

"I do. And you know well enough that I'd never ask you, of all people, to do or say anything we know you shouldn't. But there really are questions here that I have got to ask, and answers I am going to get one way or another."

"All right." He took a deep breath, and I could feel the heat of his *wa* begin to cool slightly as he brought it under control. "Vollie Manion spent a summer working the harvest after he got out of high school, and then he went off to the state university."

"Scholarship?"

"No, the trust money still seemed to be coming in, though I suppose he did have jobs on the side to pay for extras. The usual thing."

I nodded, and he went on.

"At first he was going to study agriculture, I understand, but then he switched to public administration. Minor in law enforcement. Told people he was going to be a police officer, maybe in a bigger town like Albuquerque or Amarillo. He seemed to mean it, and I believe he was at the top of his class academically when he suddenly quit school and joined the army."

"Why'd he do that?"

Jake shrugged. "I don't know," he said. "At least, not exactly. He told people here that he felt he needed to spend some time away from school; he was going to go through the army's military police school, get three years of practical experience in the field, and then finish up the degree when he got back. But he didn't do it."

"Didn't what, go back to school?"

"Didn't do any of it. He joined the army, all right, but he never became an MP—something about an aptitude test—and he didn't stay in the army the full four years he'd signed up for, and he didn't go back to school afterward, either. Instead, he came back here to Farewell after a year and a half and joined the sheriff's department."

I started to ask another question. But Jake wasn't through talking; he had only paused for breath. "I think," he said with greater assurance than I'd heard in his voice before, "that this is as far as we'd better go in this particular direction. The next step would be one I couldn't answer. Sorry."

"Don't be," I said. "But I still need to get a couple more answers—on nonconfessional subjects—before we drop it for good. You say he came back to Farewell before his hitch would normally have been up. What kind of discharge did he get?"

Jake looked blank.

"Was it an honorable discharge," I said, "or some other kind? Administrative, maybe?"

"Why, neither," he said. "Vollie was released on a medical discharge."

That surprised me. The hulking gorilla who had enjoyed bouncing his nightstick on my skull had seemed in perfect health. Physically.

"Vollie got hurt in the army?"

"I guess so. Or got sick. Anyway, he was in the hospital for several months before his discharge."

"You're sure of that?"

"Oh, yes. I got a letter from him with the hospital's location and his identification number on the return address."

"But you don't know why he was in there?"

"No...would that be important?"

I started to say that it damn sure might be, but thought better of it. I could find out the rest if I needed to, but it was more important for the moment to get the answer to the next question.

"I guess it doesn't matter," I said.

"Then ask your last question and let's drop the subject. No offense, but this is really beginning to give me an itch in the ethics."

"Just one more, then," I promised, giving him a smile and trying to make the words seem casual. "You said Vollie didn't make it into military police work as he'd intended. So what did he do instead?"

"Well, as I said, he didn't stay in the service for the full four years. A lot of the eighteen months he did spend in uniform was used up going through basic training. And in the hospital."

"Right. But every grunt rifleman gets cross-trained to be something besides—a communicator or a medic or a clerk—these days."

Jake struggled with that. No reluctance this time, just honest effort, a snippet of information he'd never given thought to before. But he was willing.

"Oh," he said finally. "Oh, sure! You're right, Vollie did say something about the school they finally sent him to. And that may have been where he got hurt, now that I think of it, though he did tell me once that he enjoyed the work. But...I can't seem to remember exactly what he said..."

He broke off, sweating it, and I shut up to let him have his best shot.

His fingers drummed on the doorway, and he closed his eyes with the effort of recall.

I was about to tell him to let it go; it was something I could find out through regular channels, and probably not all that important anyway. But then he relaxed.

"Aerial gunner!" he said, smiling at the successful memory-gymnastics and also, I suppose, because I'd promised it would be the last question.

"The army made Vollie a door gunner," he said. "On helicopters."

A SERMON
(CONTINUED)

And the result?

We see the debris of such unexamined racecourse lives all around us…

TWENTY-THREE

The shortest route back to my motel led through the center of town, and I took it easy, letting the little red skate drift along at a pace well below the speed limit.

Nightfall had given a different face to Farewell's main drag.

The town was big enough to have a couple of medium-size shopping centers on its outlying edges, but they didn't seem to have done much harm to the original downtown commercial district. Stores that had branches in the semi-suburbs still maintained headquarters on Main Street, and I counted three drugstores, two supermarkets, five fast-food outlets, a pair of small-scale department stores, a clutch of dress shops, and five bars (cocktail lounges, their lighted plastic signs insisted) among the usual clutter of such miscellaneous enterprises as a shoe-repair shop, florist, record store, mom-and-pop café, hardware store, and hobby shop that filled the remaining space and elbowed for space on the side streets.

There was even a bona fide example of that most endangered of species, the single-auditorium downtown movie house.

And all seemed prosperous.

With one exception...

Unkempt and all too obviously abandoned, Farewell's single Main Street vacancy—For Lease: Will Renovate to Suit Tenant— stood at what appeared to be the main intersection; its architecture no less distinctive than the fading grime marks that spelled out Ranchers National in block letters across the faded Georgian revival front, proclaiming it a failed competitor to the Citizens National Bank, J. J. Barlow's stronghold, which faced it, bland-modern and marble-prosperous, from diagonally across the street.

Hard times for some, opportunities for others.

This, we are assured, is the essence of the American way: Where there are winners there have got to be losers. Survival of the fittest. Darwinian economics in action. Devil take the hind-most. Make up your own slogan. It's easy.

And surely a man whose living is derived entirely from a form of merchandising—you buy the cards from the dealer and sell them for the best price you can get—could have no possible objection?

Well, no. Not really.

I try to avoid playing poker with people who cannot afford to lose or with the emotionally disturbed, including the unhappy few who actually prefer to wind up on the short end. I do not take candy from babies, unless I'm really hungry, and the list of widows and orphans who have been the worse for knowing me is compara-tively short. But while I will always give a man burying money, and have even been known to put up bail, it simply does not do to find oneself overcome with compassion while seated at a poker table. I might very well lend a friend a few dollars to get back into a game when he gets broke, but I will most certainly do my very best to take every penny of it away from him again on the next hand. Any other attitude makes nonsense of the game and leads inevitably to abuses. The whole idea is to get rich at the other players' expense, and I have never seen anything wrong with this.

Poker is an amusement. A pastime. I play it professionally for the same reason Jackie Robinson played baseball and Bobby Fischer played chess.

No one is forced to sit down at the table, and those who choose to do so risk only money.

But the game played out at the main intersection of this town had involved far more important stakes, and neither the winnings nor the losses could be computed entirely on a spreadsheet.

Farewell had lost something of value. Something indefinable but deeply rooted in those notions of trust and neighborliness that are the whole basis of community in the parts of America that do not echo to the melody of steel canyons and concrete arroyos. A bank is a bank is a bank, and no one sheds a tear for the banker, no matter where he plies his trade. Considered as function, the role of the urban financier and his rural counterpart alike is to provide the pecuniary lubricant that enables the wheels of commerce and industry to roll. Without this contribution they grind to a halt. And mistrust, even in very small doses, has much the same effect on the operation of this financial machine as a handful of Carborundum in the bearings of a dynamo.

Trouble comes when this basic role is either forgotten or removed, even temporarily, from its paramount position among priorities. Bankers get rich enough in the normal course of affairs; impatience leads to error and error to disaster. Reality has no more sympathy for greedy optimism among bankers than it does for the same fault among poker players.

J. J. Barlow's bank had survived. Indeed, according to Dee Tee Price's information, it had even managed to make good its early reverses through adroit management of the opposition's ill fortune. Yet the coup could not have made him happy.

I had met the legless banker only once, but much of that encounter had been spent at a poker table—and there is no better way of forming an accurate assessment of a man's inner landscape. He was a willing and aggressive competitor. Barlow wanted it all, and he would try to get it all. But the tenor of his play, and of our conversation afterward, had shown me a man of clear perceptions and understandings, one who would value the game for itself even while bending every effort to win.

Such a man would be more likely than most to appreciate the nature of his responsibilities in a town like Farewell.

Which made it all the more difficult for me to understand how he had been able to rationalize some of the things that I knew, or suspected, about him. Especially the sudden rupture of relations with the late Orrin Prescott.

And that made no sense...

But I never got to tell myself why it didn't make sense, for suddenly I had something else to think about.

The traffic light that had given me the time for reverie changed to green, and the little car was already in motion when a momentary flare of light near the rear of the Citizens National Bank building brought my head swiveling around at full emergency speed. Having one eye can be a literal pain in the neck.

A door had opened and closed back there.

Waiting for the light, I had spotted J. J. Barlow's state-of-the-art Corniche parked under a streetlight at the curb just outside the ramp-equipped side door of the bank building, and when the door opened I had fully expected to catch a glimpse of the man himself. But no wheelchair emerged from the building, and there was no one visible on the street.

Obviously, then, someone had gone in, not out, and the sight of a sheriff's patrol car parked unobtrusively just down the block from the bank fostered a sudden urge to make three right turns and park on that same street.

It was ridiculous, of course. Also sneaky and stupid. Besides, I was in a hurry to get back to the phone in my motel room and find out what Mistah Dee Tee Price had discovered.

But I made the three turns and parked my car, switched off its lights, and settled back to get accustomed to the dim light.

That's always been a weakness of mine.

During the early stages of a game, I can seldom seem to resist the chance to pay for a look at another player's hole cards.

I waited in the darkness for nearly an hour.

Poker teaches patience.

And when Vollie Manion finally came back out of the bank and got into his car and drove away, I was about a block behind.

Following Vollie Manion was even stupider than waiting around to spy on him.

He had already shown an unhealthy fondness for beating the hell out of me. Taking the chance of giving him another—bigger and better—reason for indulging that taste was about as sensible as feeding caramels to a grizzly bear. But I couldn't seem to get my foot off the accelerator.

At first, he seemed to be cruising at random, turning corners when he felt like it and occasionally doubling back on his tracks, but it didn't take me long to see that he had a purpose. The deputy was trying to avoid the very thing that was happening to him. Trying to be sure of shaking off any possible pursuit.

The realization raised a regimen of questions.

The patrol car he was driving had the appearance of a standard black-and-white, with regulation decals on the doors and the usual light bar clamped to the top. But the sound of its engine and the quickness of its response from a standing start told me it was probably the sheriff's department's special pursuit vehicle. Most southwestern law enforcement agencies have them. They justify the expense as a necessary measure for control of illegal street racers. But the truth is that lots of people like to drive a really powerful car now and then, and back-road sheriffs are no exception. I wondered if Ybarra knew his deputy was driving the hot wheels tonight, and I wondered if Vollie was on duty or just doing a little street prowling on his own time. I would have paid good money to be able to tune in to the local law enforcement net for just a few minutes.

But I couldn't spare much time for wishing. As soon as I understood the purpose of his erratic course and speed, I began a series of countermeasures intended to make Vollie think he had succeeded, running through a series of such fun maneuvers as stopping at the curb and turning off my lights to let the patrol car gain a block or so before pulling out into the street again, or turning into a side road to make a quick U-turn that brought me back into his wake at a distance that would not mark me as a constant follower.

The little car that had performed so indifferently when matched against a pickup truck earlier in the day turned out to be well adapted to this kind of work, even to its paint job. Fiery red in daylight, it showed up as black under the amber glow of Farewell's sodium streetlights, offering me just the extra edge of anonymity I needed.

We kept at it, the patrol car leading and me following at the most erratic pace I could manage while still keeping the other car in sight, for nearly twenty minutes before Vollie finally seemed satisfied that he was alone and unremarked in the night world, and cut left to the highway leading out of town in the general direction of the Prescott Helicopters operation.

This presented another kind of problem: There were no side streets and no places to park. But there was darkness—street lighting stopped short at the city limits—and there was other traffic to mingle with and hide behind. Besides, it turned out that we weren't going far.

Less than a mile beyond the Now Leaving Farewell, Come Back Soon! sign, Vollie's high-powered car swerved left through oncoming traffic and bumped to a stop on the sand and gravel apron of what appeared to be a crossroads garage I'd noticed in passing earlier in the day. It was an all-night affair, apparently, and so were several places nearby.

I drove past them without changing speed or turning my head, but cut right a moment later to swing the little skate past a line of cars parked beside a peeling white stucco roadside establishment whose bulb-lighted tin sign proclaimed it Lupe's Famous / *Food * Beer * Music.*

The music was easily audible even before I killed my engine. And I could smell the beer.

Here was Farewell's answer to Broadway and the Sunset Strip—proof positive that sleaze is where you find it.

Lupe, I was told much later, was not a short form of Guadalupe, but the family surname (originally Lupidischikoff) of the man who had homesteaded a section of thin grassland here nearly a century earlier. Lupe had failed at farming, failed at ranching, failed at oil prospecting, and had been about to burn his sod shanty to the ground and strike out for California when the state decided to put a two-lane highway through the land. That gave him an idea.

He set up an old-fashioned gravity-feed gasoline pump he had found in Amarillo—some said he had stolen it from a man who died there under mysterious circumstances, but nothing was ever proved—and put out the word that he was a European-trained specialist in the repair and maintenance of all manner of motorcars.

Local people knew it was a ghastly lie, of course. Lupe had a hard time just getting his pump to work. But out-of-towners sometimes fell for it, and over the years he actually did acquire a rough working knowledge of the internal combustion engine and its various ailments.

Meanwhile, he married a Farewell girl—her pistol-toting father was determined to attend either a wedding or a funeral that day, and practical-minded Lupe opted for the wedding—and put her to work in a second business, a café that he set up across the road from the garage.

Call it symbiosis: Gas-and-repair customers could always expect their work to take long enough for them to consume a full meal. Plus extras. While hungry motorists who stopped there seemed frequently to need the services of a qualified mechanic to get their cars started again, and better-dressed wayfarers might even find their vehicles in such bad shape as to warrant spending the night in one of the tourist cabins / Clean * Reasonable that sprang up beside the café.

It was a good, full life, and Lupe enjoyed it hugely until his sons were old enough to join their mother in a lawsuit that put the old man in a rest home "for his own protection and conservation."

He died not long afterward, but the family continued to operate his crossroad enterprises for several decades before dry rot finally set in. Time changes all things, and one of the things it changed about Farewell was the route of the main road. The four-lane state highway that had brought prosperity to Lupe's garage, café, and cabins was now a minor county thoroughfare, and the various businesses located on it had been obliged to adapt to their altered circumstances.

By the time I saw it, a little gasoline was still being sold at the garage—the old gravity pump stood empty between two slightly newer Wayne electrics—but its main income was from renting space and tools to adolescent do-it-yourself mechanics who met there to tune and rebuild their Saturday-night wheels.

The café still sold a little food, but the kitchen was permanently closed by order of the county health department. Everything now came from a freezer via a microwave located behind the bar. The biggest seller was beer—spiked, for a fee, with white lightning—and a large share of the gross was from those few electronic games that could be kept working.

Doctors did well on the tetanus injections and suturing inevitably associated with such an establishment.

And cabins rented by the hour.

I parked the little red skate out of sight and walked slowly toward the front while looking for a place where I could see the garage without standing in full view.

It was easy to find. One of the few holdovers from the café's years of prosperity was an outdoor telephone booth bolted to the side of the building next to the pothole-and-gravel parking lot. It was a technological antique, relic of a day when phone companies cared enough about their customers to protect them from the elements. Two panes of glass were missing from the bottom of the old booth, and the door had suffered some mishap that made it hard to close. A chain that had once protected the telephone directory now ended an inch from its mooring, and the light socket at the top of the booth was empty.

But the telephone itself was in working order, and no one would be surprised to see someone making a call, no matter how long it seemed to take.

Wedged inside and resting my weight warily on the rickety seat, I had a near-perfect view of the garage—and immediately found myself looking at familiar objects. And people.

One of the recognizable objects was a motor vehicle. Vollie Manion's overpowered patrol car was in one of the work stalls. The hood was up and the sound of a power drill at work occasionally managed to muscle its way past the raucous country-and-western beat emanating from the café. A pair of overalled legs protruded from the engine compartment of the cruiser, but the angle was wrong for me to see whom they belonged to.

Also familiar was a pickup truck that sat forlorn and leaning heavily in what I decided was a meditative pose beside two other wrecks in the lot next to the garage. The driver's door and tailgate seemed to be missing, and the nose was bashed in; only two wheels remained, and one of those seemed to be rather loosely attached, but I had no doubt at all that it was the same unfortunate vehicle that had chased me down a lonely road on the other side of town a few hours earlier. Nobody else appeared to be much interested in it now, but I was at least mildly pleased to note that there seemed to be no major bloodstains around the cab. Always struck me as wasteful to kill someone by chance or error.

And here was Deputy Vollie Manion himself, emerging from the garage. Lounging in front of the office, hands in hip pockets and a beer-heavy sneer on his face, was Harold, the fledgling thug who had turned out to be so talkative after I offered to remove one of his eyes on my first early morning in Farewell.

He offered some brief remark as the tall deputy started across the road, and Vollie didn't seem to like it.

Or maybe Vollie was just in a bad mood.

Whatever the motive, reaction was swift and effective. Vollie turned with more speed than I would have expected in a man his size and brought his knee up hard into Harold's crotch, while seizing the front of his shirt in one of those peculiarly undersized hands. The youngster's feet left the ground and his eyes widened as the deputy brought his face close and said something that couldn't have been audible five feet away, but appeared to have the desired effect on the listener.

When Vollie let the youngster go, he dropped to the ground in a crouching attitude, nursing his groin.

The overall-clad mechanic who had been at work on the cruiser had emerged from the repair bay to watch the fun, and I was interested to see that this did, indeed, seem to be old home week. Lighting was poor and our last meeting, in the parking lot at the country club, had been a brief one, but the grubby splint of his right wrist identified him positively as the knife-wielding druggie who had initially seemed so insensitive to pain.

I sat still in the phone booth and wondered.

I wondered how well and how long those three had known one another.

I wondered if their conversation had anything to do with their erstwhile *compadre*, Greenteeth—a.k.a. Boo—and how his pickup truck had managed to get itself into such deplorable condition.

I wondered how competent good ol' Vollie Manion, the sometime helicopter door gunner, might be with a .30-06 sniper rifle, and if he went in for loading his own ammunition for greater accuracy. The notion didn't seem to fit, for some reason, but it was certainly worth a question. Or two.

But wondering is dull work when you don't get any answers.

I watched the three drift back inside the garage, their earlier difficulties apparently forgotten, and I wondered what possible good it could do me to go on sitting in the cold. Nothing more to see, and always the chance of being spotted if I kept hanging around there. I roused myself, keeping a close eye on the garage as I began to move out of my improvised hidey-hole...and got just the right amount of emotional advance warning to brace my right leg against the base of the booth and swing my right hand in a blunted lance to the midsection of the man who was moving in so quietly from the back of the parking lot.

The air went out of his lungs in a great huff of surprise, and his eyes lost focus, but the spring-handled blackjack he had swung at my head continued right on course, knocking a fair splinter of wood out of the door.

I hit him two more times—one left-handed hammer blow directly over the heart and a kite to the exposed nerve just below the nose—and he went down without another sound, mouth open and eyes lolling far back into the skull.

It was Greenteeth.

A six-pack of Coors on the ground beside him explained the errand that had kept him apart from his friends across the road, and how he'd been able to get so close without my feeling his *wa* behind me. A certain level of intoxication, even from a mild but long-standing beer drunk, tends to cloak the emotions.

But there was no time for philosophy.

A quick glance around the area assured me that our little set-to had not been observed. All the same, there was a good chance that someone would be driving by or coming out of the café at any time. And Boo's buddies would miss him—or the beer they'd sent him for—after a while. The newly vacated telephone booth seemed to be as good a hiding place as any, and I bent over the recumbent form to grasp it under the armpits.

His hat fell off while I was wrestling him into the booth, and I was pleased to see that our little meeting out on the road near Pemberton's home office hadn't been entirely without penalty. The coarse wavy hair at the side of his head was matted with long-dried blood, and his ear had been bandaged after some mishap or other. I wondered if there had been any internal damage, and surprised myself by hoping that there had not. Greenteeth's attempt to muscle me off the road hadn't been his own idea, any more than had our original encounter at the country club.

A doctor at the hospital where Dee Tee and I spent time after they sent us back to the world told me once that a man can rarely remember events immediately preceding sudden trauma resulting in unconsciousness. No time for the permanent memory to function, he said. I hoped he was right as I stuffed the unconscious form into the booth and made sure he was solidly perched on the seat. I wrapped his hand around the telephone receiver, snatched up the hat and clamped it on his head with the brim over the eyes, and shoved the six-pack out of sight beside his feet.

Then I wedged the door shut and got out of there.

Fun is fun, but the party was over.

I took the long way back to the motel, puzzling around the country roads until I found my way back to town in order to avoid driving the little skate back past the garage.

I'd had my look at the hole cards.

Pretty soon, now, it was going to be time to bet.

A SERMON (CONTINUED)

But there is more to the story than defeat.

There is hope as well.

There is love.

If in the midst of life we are in death, then equally in the midst of death we celebrate life…

TWENTY-FOUR

"**H**ey, there, you tinhorn peckerwood!"

I stared at the darkened ceiling of the motel room and let the tender cadences of Dee Tee Price's voice and persona do their soothing work. Sometimes talking to a friend can be better than an hour's meditation. And it beats little green pills all hollow.

"Spend half the day doin' chores for you," he roared, "and asking questions that could get me kilt if I wasn't talking to good close personal enemies—and then you don't stick around in one place long enough so I can let you know what I found out! Goddamn Bible-thumping highbinder!"

"Thanks, Dee Tee," I said. "I love you, too."

He chuckled. "They treatin' you okay?"

"Oh, sure. Only hurts when I laugh."

"Well, then, you got nothing to worry about for the next few minutes—especially if you happen to be an investor in the Citizens National Bank of Farewell, New Mexico. You're not, are you?"

I was beginning to wonder.

"I don't think so," I told him, squirming my head deeper into the pillow and rolling it sideways to clamp the receiver in place without having to keep my hand on it. "But it's been a long day, and I am not as sure of things now as I was when it started."

He didn't ask for an explanation and I didn't offer one. And that was just as well. I had managed a shower after returning to

the motel and even forced myself to pick up the phone and have
the operator get back to the Houston number that had been leaving call-back messages ever since sundown.

I pinched the nails of my thumb and forefinger into my thigh
to keep the eyes open and the mind in recording mode. "I gather
Barlow's bank is in trouble, then?" I said.

"Well, yes and no," Dee Tee replied. "Yes, it's in trouble.
But no, no one knows about it yet—except for you and me and
Barlow and whoever he's got in there helping him lie to the
federals."

"You're absolutely sure?"

Dee Tee's voice, usually rife with animal spirits, was curi-
ously lifeless as he replied. "No doubt in the world, good buddy.
And I got to tell you it hurts a hell of a lot more than I thought it
would. I think I told you Barlow and ol' Dee Tee go back quite a
ways…"

"Sorry, Dee Tee."

"Oh, hell." The tone changed again, and I could feel his gen-
erator beginning to pick up speed. "If there is one thing you and
me ought to know, it is that even the best can make damn-fool
mistakes and still be the best. It's not like it was the end of the
world, and right here and now I think I ought to warn you that
I intend to make some money on what I found out. Can't hardly
see any way not to. You got a problem with that?"

"No. Do you?"

"Hell, yes! Of course I got a problem with it—but I be damned
if I'm going to let it get in the way of what I do or who I am. It's
just that I got to admit I don't feel quite right about none of it."

"Then don't do it."

That got another laugh. "I'd feel even worse if I didn't. Gets
kindly complicated, doesn't it?"

I let that pass without comment and he didn't press. We'd
had a lot of time, back in the hospital, to confuse each other

discussing the various conundrums of ethics and society. No conclusions reached, but no need to repeat the exercises, either.

"Anyways," he said, taking up the slack, "I can give this to you in the short form or the long form. You're paying for the call, so which'll you have?"

I burrowed deeper into the bed. "Short form, please. I got a hunch I wouldn't understand the long version no matter how clear you made it."

"You do sound just a tad bushed, now that I think of it."

"You are a perceptive person. For a Texican."

He turned the insult almost absentmindedly and launched into exposition, leaving the good ol' boy accent behind as usual when discussing subjects he considered serious.

"The Citizens Bank of Farewell," he said, "looks real good on paper, and the federal examiners are satisfied, and in the general way of things I think it might have gone on that way for a long time. But it's not going to happen now, and not because you and I started nosing around, either. The sharks are already beginning to circle at a distance."

"How do you mean?"

"Well, I think someone's already smelled a rat. Not an official someone—this would be a trader, an outside hand like me, who makes his money turning information into leverage."

"What would the information be, and where would it come from?"

"As to what, I can tell you for sure, and it only cost the national debt of Ecuador in long-distance telephone bills to find out: The energy-loan paper Barlow's bank had to eat, early on. That was plenty bad medicine, but he handled them all right and seemed to come out smelling like a rose when the other bank in town, Ranchers National, I think they called it, got into trouble. You know about that, so we won't go over it again. But the hell of it is, it looks like Barlow was sitting on more trouble than he let on. There was also some kind of deal with the government of Haiti…"

That pushed the sleep clouds back a foot or two.

"When was that?"

"Just exactly when you're thinking. Two or three years before Baby Doc got kicked out."

"But—"

"No buts about it, buddy! That's exactly how it went down. The paper Barlow took was at twenty-five percent. Twenty-five! Lordy, a banker ought to be shot just for thinking of things like that! Why, that kind of interest is for people who break your legs if you miss a payment. No excuse for it. But that's what the loan was supposed to pay, and that's by God what it really did pay for about a year and a few months. Until they tossed Duvalier's pudgy little ass out and got in some new bosses, who naturally promised to pay everyone and then locked up the vault."

"Is any money coming out of Haiti at all?"

"Oh, sure. Some of the bigger boys had the muscle to get things rolling. Rescheduled the loans; fancy way of saying they cut the interest to something sensible and extended the time, and then threw in some money to pick up the slack. Barlow wasn't big enough to get in on that, and I kindly doubt he found anyone in the new government who would help out of the goodness of his heart, you know? But, glory be to goodness, you will never guess what I found out from a bank examiner who owes me a couple of favors."

"Barlow's books show the loans paying again?"

"Figure that out all by yourself, did you? Well, ain't that a caution! I tell you, boy, I always did think you had the makings of a banker. God knows you think crooked enough." He laughed again, but the sound was sad and hollow.

"How long has this been going on, Dee Tee?"

"Can't say for sure, but it would have to be two years at least, more, maybe, but that long for sure."

"In that case—"

"In that case, as you are about to say, he is going to have to do something right quick. Come up with enough money to square the books and cook the accounting to show that some other bank—in a foreign country or in the Caribbean where the examiners can't double-check him too close—took over the whole shebang."

I thought about that for a minute. "How much money are we talking, Dee Tee?"

"Oh, hell, just chicken feed, relatively speaking."

"How big are those chickens?"

"Well, Citizens' original share of the Haiti consortium—the part of a bigger loan that they contributed—was maybe fifty million. It could be a lot more or a lot less now."

"Sorry, you lost me there..."

"Well, see, all the other banks that had a piece of that particular package have already pulled out. Written the money off and taken their licking from their stockholders. Couple or three of the bank presidents got fired; one had to hold still for a takeover by another bank in California. Fact is, that's how I was able to find out so much. One of the losers took it kind of hard and told his sad tale to a few people."

"Uh-huh. But nothing like that happened to Barlow."

"Nope. According to the way his books tell it, he was able to do the same thing the bigger lenders did—reduce and reschedule. Might could take you a month of Sundays to unravel the mess, but I suspect that when you got done you'd find that he even took over some of their bum paper and showed it as a discount item."

"Lost me again, Dee Tee."

"Nemmine. You don't have to know all that. Only just that it's what happened here."

"Right." The receiver was biting into my ear, and I moved a little to ease it. "How much of the money do you think Barlow could have gotten back in payments before things went sour down there?"

Dee Tee took a moment to answer. Anyone else might have been fiddling with a pocket calculator, but I knew he was just sitting still with his eyes closed. Talent. He'd have made a world-class car salesman.

"Call it twenty-one million seven hundred twenty-six thousand nine hundred thirty-three dollars. And change. Give or take a million or so for grease along the way. Doing business with Baby Doc was always expensive."

"So the net shortage would be...?"

"Still damn near fifty, Preacher. On the books, anyway. It was a young loan, you know, and now he's had to come up with the servicing—payments, that is—out of his own pocket for a while."

"You're sure?"

"Couldn't hardly be any other way, unless some of the money was coming from his partner."

"Partner?"

"Hell, yes, partner. I told you he couldn't be handling this alone. He needed someone inside—on the board, and with an administrative title, too, just to be safe. You been there in Farewell for a day or two now, so you should have met some of the locals besides just Barlow himself. You ever run into a big fat dude named Edward Watrous? Nickname's Tiny..."

For some reason that bothered me more than it should have.

Suddenly the receiver under my ear was painful again, and I found myself squirming on the bed, unable to find a comfortable position. The temperature of the room was wrong, and the mattress was lumpy, and I wanted to be somewhere else.

"How sure are you that it's Watrous?"

"I guess some of what I was feeling showed in my voice, because Dee Tee waited a minute before he replied, and when he finally spoke I could detect a note of real concern.

"Preacher," he said, "you told me once that the most dangerous thing a poker player can do is to get emotionally involved in the game he's playing. Lets it get to having some kind of meaning outside itself. You remember that?"

I did, and there was nothing I could say, so I didn't say anything.

"About a year ago," Dee Tee said, "there was a little bit of shuffling among the officers of the Citizens Bank. Someone either died or retired—I don't know the straight of that and I don't really care—but Edward Watrous, Tiny, became the bank's treasurer and chief financial officer. Sort of drifted into the job, really. He'd been a director of the bank for years and he runs a lot of other things in Farewell, and everybody thought it was just a temporary appointment. But they never hired anybody to take the job full-time, and by now I guess nobody thinks much about it one way or the other."

"How about the guy who had the job before?"

"What about him?"

"Wouldn't he have to have been in on the scam, too?"

"Maybe. But maybe not, too, unless he was also the head bookkeeper or something like that, and I guess that wasn't the case. Ain't no trouble to cook a set of books. Anyone can do it. Hard part is to get away with it for any length of time."

"Well, you're making it sound pretty easy."

He shut up to let me stew for a while. So I did. Jake had brought me to Farewell to see if Pres Prescott had been cheated in the local high-stake contests, and I had come to the conclusion that he probably had not. But the more I found out about the town, the more apparent it became to me that cold decks and the other poker arts arcane just weren't in the same league with the kind of games these people liked to play. They didn't need the cards. They had a whole town for their game board: Take a walk on the Boardwalk. Take a ride on the Reading. Win the Irish Sweepstakes. Take a Chance. Go to Jail; go directly to jail, do not pass Go, do not collect fifty million dollars.

And how the hell long had it been going on?

And why did I find it easier to like Barlow and Watrous, who were looking more and more like the Black Hats every day, than I did Deke Pemberton—who just might be the only straight hand in the game? But I didn't have any answers, so I finally had to give up and ask the next question.

"Okay. So what's going to happen now?"

"Oh, it'll go on this way for a while maybe, if nobody rocks the boat. A few months. A year. More, if they got a lot of luck and a real dumb examiner and enough money to keep up the servicing payments. But finally, if nothing happens to change things for the better, somewhere along the line someone is sure to notice that the emperor is in his skivvies, and then it is going to be raining assholes all over east New Mexico."

"The bank will be bust?"

"That, or get itself swallowed up by something real big and hungry."

"What happens to the town? To Farewell?"

"Into the dumper..."

I kept waiting for him to add a qualifier, something to soften the edge. But he just let the words sit there, and I knew he was probably right. The loss of one bank had been bad for Farewell, but it was a survivable crash. Two would be complete disaster.

Poor Jake. If things went the way I thought they might, the church board was going to have some harsh things to say to him about his choice of friends, and about meddling in matters best left alone. Never mind the fact that such meddling comes with the territory in such a job, and never mind a murder—or two—along the way. They would be looking for scapegoats to blame for the sudden drop in local real-estate values, and he would be standing right there with a Kick Me sign pinned to his coattails. And I would be the one who put it there...

"You can still back out, Preacher," Dee Tee said quietly.

He could always read my mind, damn him.

"Yeah," I said. "I sure can do that, all right."

More silence.

"Okay, then, good buddy," Dee Tee said when we'd both done enough thinking and one-handed shadowboxing. "Other things: Messenger from the bank in Amarillo'll be over there with the cash money you wanted about noon or such a matter, tomorrow. Call you from the lobby of the motel if that's okay, but best do your business in private. Hellfire, I don't have to tell you."

"Noon's fine," I said. "And no. You don't. And thanks, Dee Tee."

"Well, then..."

There wasn't any more to say, and I could feel the numb fingers of sleep creeping up my neck again—this thing of staying awake in the daylight takes some getting used to—but Dee Tee wasn't ready to hang up yet.

"Listen, you silly bastard," he said, "I don't wanta hear about you doin' any dumb shit, now, you hear? Don't go winning no medals. You're used to dealing with fine, genteel, civilized folks like ol' Dee Tee, and everybody's not like that. You get careless, they'll have you for a midnight snack! I kid you not, buddy, they purely play for keeps around that part of the world."

"I heard."

"Don't suppose I could get you to let me send an old friend of mine in there with the bank messenger tomorrow—ex-cop, lives over that way? Got him a private detective license and a body-guard permit, all nice and legal, and he owes me. Big."

I had to smile. "I don't suppose," I said. "But thanks, Dee Tee."

"Yeah. Well...y'all take care, then. Goddamn Bible-thumper."

"You, too, bandit."

My eyes were closed and the lights were going out before I could get the receiver back into its cradle.

It was an old dream. Stale from the vault...

We were moving single file along the side of a hill, flankers out and a specialist sweeping the top of the ridge. Silence in the rain forest except for the sound of our boots and the inevitable wire-thin whine of insect life that becomes so much a part of existence that it ceases to be audible, except in dreams.

The first Charlie was a tree. It had been standing right there for a century, and it was as real as anything else in the world around us, except now it was a little brown guy in black pajamas, and he was going to kill someone for sure if I didn't stop him. The trouble was, I had never killed anybody before and I didn't know if I could do it and I really didn't want to find out and what the hell was I doing here anyway? My movements were too slow, like being underwater or trying to stir thick syrup—it was that kind of dream, the everyone-moves-fast-except-me thing; I knew it was a dream, except that I couldn't seem to get myself out of it. But before I had time to deal with that idea, things began to change around me and the M16 in my hands went off—silently, not much of a sound track in this one—and I could feel the heat and the bucking of the weapon as the little man in black fell down. Only now it wasn't a man anymore.

It was Sara. My Sara was there in the jungle, and she was wearing the yellow jumpsuit I had bought for her the day before I shipped out. She had seen it in a window and wanted it, but wouldn't say so because the money was getting pretty short. But I had saved a couple of dollars back for just such an occasion, and

I slipped out of the motel where we were staying and bought it and had it laid out on the bed with a bow and a card when she got out of her bath, and now she was wearing it and screaming and hugging herself where my bullets had ripped a bright red path across her stomach.

She dropped the sign she had been carrying.

Stop Murdering the Babies! it said.

I looked at the men in my squad, the ones standing on either side of me, but they had faces I didn't recognize, and we weren't on the hill in the rain forest anymore, either. These were National Guardsmen—I recognized the citizen-soldier patches on their obsolete combat fatigues—and we were on the park-neat campus of Sara's college, and the squad was getting ready to fire again. I shouted at them to stop, but my voice made no sound, and so I turned my own rifle on the frightened fuzz-face of the officer at the end of the file and switched the selector to full automatic.

He took a whole banana-clip, and it didn't seem to faze him.

"Fall down," I roared. "Goddamn you, you civilian shithead, fall down!"

And then I was awake with only the sounds of silence in my ears.

Darkness filled the motel room, but it was not the dream that had roused me. The door of the room had opened and closed— I was almost getting used to prowlers now—and someone was walking toward the bed. I closed my hand around a pillow and braced a leg to throw myself off the bed in the opposite direction but stopped a split second before giving my body the execute command. The visitor's aura touched mine, and it was neither threatening nor angry.

I relaxed and took a deep breath.

The air nearby now contained a faint scent of Marlboros, partially masked by musk and soap.

"If you've come in here with a plate of *carne estilo Nogales*," I said, "I still don't want any."

But my visitor hadn't come for a chat.

"Just shut the hell up," she said. "And move over."

A SERMON (CONTINUED)

Death may lie in wait.

Ruin may threaten.

Sometimes the shadow corners seem truly to contain all the terrors of childhood, formless and implacable...

TWENTY-FIVE

We slept late the next morning, but there was none of the strangeness that sometimes accompanies the first awakening with an unfamiliar bedmate.

Dana was startled, but not repelled, by the sight of my right eye.

I had removed and cleaned the prosthetic eye, storing it away in the case it shares with a twin, before lying down to talk to Mistah Dee Tee the night before. And had forgotten all about it—what with one thing and another—afterward. I don't own an eyepatch or use any other halfway measures, so she got the full treatment as soon as she rolled over to face me, and I lay perfectly still, awaiting developments. Reactions, over the years, have been various. You never can tell. But hers was the only one of its type that I could recall.

She laughed.

And after a startled moment, I laughed, too. And we kept it up for a minute or two and couldn't seem to get stopped, setting each other off again every time one or the other of us would begin to achieve some kind of control, while occasionally trying without notable success to form words. There was no occasion for hilarity, of course. None at all. But the laughter was real and not self-conscious, and while there may be better ways to start a morning than laughing with a pretty woman, I would have to say that I couldn't have named one at that moment. The world was beginning to look almost habitable.

"Oh, God," she said when things finally tapered off to an occasional honk of mirth. "I'm sorry! Well, no…sort of sorry anyway. I guess. But you looked so solemn, with that eye all drooped over in a kind of sunken wink. Did anyone ever tell you that you look like a drunken coyote when you do that?"

"Not lately," I replied with a fair affectation of stuffy austerity. "Coyote, you say? Gracious, goodness me—and here all this time I just took other people's word for it that I was the handsomest man they had ever seen who was intended by nature to be an ape. I'll have my secretary make a note."

"A memo would be better," she said, rolling out from under the covers and heading for the shower. "Get the damn thing in triplicate and roll all three of them into a tight little tube—"

I threw a pillow at her. She caught it in midair and swung it back at my head, and I grabbed it and she tripped and landed on the bed again.

And then we laughed some more. And after a while the laughter became smiles and there were no more words, and it was a lot later when we finally got into the shower—which was where we were when Vollie Manion came to take us both into custody on suspicion of armed assault with intent to do grievous bodily harm.

He was playing it a lot cooler than he had on his last visit; none of the aw-shucks country boyishness and no Gomer Pyle mannerisms. But there was an underlying threat implicit in everything he said and did, and I wasn't happy about the idea of Dana being involved.

I had been expecting something like this, of course.

Seeing Vollie with his companions the night before was really just the icing on the cake. Ever since the encounter with Greenteeth—I had real trouble thinking of him as someone called Boo—it had seemed obvious that someone was going to have to take some kind of countermeasure. So, considering Vollie's track record, a second arrest came as no big surprise. I had even taken a moment, on the off chance that it might be something like this, to put one of the prosthetic eyes into the empty socket before answering the door. But dragging Dana into it was something else again.

I decided to try a little reconnaissance-in-force.

"Just for the sake of argument," I said, stuffing the tail of a fresh shirt into my trousers and fiddling with my necktie while we waited for Dana to do her dressing in the bathroom, "can we assume that you've gone to the trouble to get a warrant or two this time?"

He shook his head.

"Don't need none," he said.

I sighed with what I thought was a fair approximation of friendly concern. "The last time we went through all this," I reminded him, "Frank Ybarra didn't seem too pleased with the way things came out. I even had a feeling that he might be going to holler at you a little when I was out of earshot. Was I wrong about that?"

"Frank's the boss. He can holler at anyone he wants, anytime he feels like doing it."

"So when this arrest doesn't stick either, don't you think you might be in a lot more trouble than you were the first time?"

"This one'll stick."

"Not if you forget to read us our rights again, it won't. And not if you forget to tell us who we are supposed to have 'grievously harmed,' and not if you try bouncing that damn nightstick off my head again, Mr. Deputy," I said. "This time there is a witness, and we'll either do it by the book, starting right here and right now, or we will forget the whole thing."

It was a fair bluff, but he didn't bat an eye. "This time," he repeated, "it'll stick."

"The hell it will, Vollie Manion!" Dana walked out of the bathroom with her damp hair neatly swept into a ballerina's bun at the top of her head and her eyes bright with anger. "You know damn well you're just doing this for meanness."

Vollie smiled and attempted what might have passed for a formal bow. "Why, Miz Dana, ma'am," he said, "I don't think I've had a chance till now to tell you how glad I am to see you back here in Farewell again. And to see you've made some nice close friends right off…" He favored her with an oily smile that did not reach his eyes.

"My!" he said, when she didn't seem to react. "Living off there in Las Vegas surely does seem to agree with you. I declare you even prettier than ever!"

This time he seemed to have hit a nerve.

Vollie had given peculiar emphasis to the name Las Vegas. It had been somehow aimed at Dana, and she had heard something in it that I didn't. Her eyes and the aura she had brought into the room with her went through a chain reaction of emotions from anger to shock to defiance and back to anger again in the space of a second.

"I still want to know who it is we are supposed to have assaulted," I said, breaking up the private exchange. "And with what deadly weapon."

He waited a moment before turning back to face me.

But he didn't lose the smile.

"The victim," he said, assuming a more formal tone, "was one Commencement P. Brown, a resident of this community. And the weapon was a motorcar. Driven by you."

He pointed a finger at me, and I hoped the relief I felt didn't show in my face.

"And occupied by you," he concluded, turning his attention back to Dana.

Knowing Greenteeth's name was a definite plus. It is embarrassing to meet anyone—even someone like Greenteeth—more than once when you didn't catch the name, except for a nickname such as Boo, at the first encounter. And when all the meetings seem to involve some form of physical violence, that kind of ignorance can be construed as outright social error.

Gauche.

Unforgivable, perhaps—though, when you think of it, a man saddled with a name like Commencement might very well prefer to be known as Boo. Or even Greenteeth.

The point, however, was that Vollie Manion seemed unaware that his friend Commencement and I had met at Lupe's café the night before.

It might mean anything, or nothing. But I was hoping it indicated that Greenteeth had been either too drunk or too surprised by the turn events had taken to remember just how he wound up sitting in the old telephone booth.

It would simplify things, I thought, if Vollie didn't know that I had seen him with his playmates.

I shook my head to register sad bewilderment.

"Commencement," I said with a puzzled note in my voice. "Commencement. Commencement? No, I'm sorry, Mr. Deputy, sir, but that name just doesn't seem to ring a bell. Truth is, I really don't think I have assaulted anyone named Commencement for—oh, two, three weeks now. Especially not in any way that would cause him 'grievous bodily harm.'"

"There was a Circumstantial, though," Dana said, picking up on the line. "You remember him? We assaulted a Circumstantial just day before yesterday."

"Why, now that you mention it, ma'am, I think that's so," I agreed solemnly. "But his last name was Smith, not Brown. And besides, we didn't really do him 'grievous bodily harm.'"

She sighed. "I suppose you're right. Let me see…has to be 'grievous,' you say? Not just 'moderate' or 'negligible'?"

"Nor 'inconsiderable,' either," I admonished. "Don't forget that."

Vollie's face was getting red.

"Commissariat!" Dana crowed, clapping her hands. "That's who he means, I bet. Commissariat. I don't know if the last name was Brown or not, but we sure as God did him some grievous bodily harm."

It had gone a little too far. I still couldn't feel any heat from Vollie's *wa*—he was truly unusual in that respect—but I didn't need to inspect his aura to know he was on the verge of popping his cork. One look at his face was enough. The red had drained away, and the sudden pallor was almost frightening. If we didn't quit soon, he was either going to kill one of us or have a heart attack.

Fortunately, there was a diversion.

The telephone rang and we all stood still for a moment, looking at it and waiting.

It rang again.

"Answer it or let it ring?" I inquired. "Or would it be for you?"

Vollie hesitated for another moment, but then nodded in my direction. "Hold it where I can hear," he said.

That was fine with me. I picked the handset off the cradle, held the receiver just under my ear, and made social noises to indicate that I was listening.

"Ayuh!" the caller said. "Be that you, Preacher?"

Mose Thieroux.

"Shouldn't wonder," I said.

"Shouldn't wonder what?"

"Shouldn't wonder it be me and shouldn't wonder I be listening—if'n you got something to say."

"H'mph!"

There was a pause, and I used the moment to evaluate Vollie Manion's reaction. He had recognized the voice, too, and I decided he was already regretting his decision to let me answer the call.

"If'n you was here or I was there," Thieroux said, "and if'n I was about thirty year younger. And if I didn't like you—and your pretty lady—I would jeezly sure muckle on to you one of these times. You know that?"

"Ayuh," I said, playing the accent for all it was worth.

Another pause. And then a faraway, unaccustomed sound that might have been a chuckle. Or might not.

"Anyways," he said, "how soon can the two of you get back out here?"

"Well," I said, looking at Vollie, who looked back at me dead-faced, "happens the lady and I are just a bit tied up this morning. What with one kind of trouble and another. I think I am going to be over to the courthouse for a while."

"Ayuh?"

I didn't know Mose Thieroux well enough to read him with any degree of confidence, but I thought I could detect the quiet sound of mental gears meshing. It occurred to me that I wished we were closer to the same age. It was interesting enough to be acquainted with him now; I wondered what he'd have been like in his twenties or thirties.

"Wellsir," he said, "you come on out here then, anytime you can. I got me some more of them Mexican bean. And water."

"Sounds good."

"And don't come alone, neither...Scenery hereabouts could stand improving."

"Shouldn't wonder."

One final pause.

"Ayuh, the hell with you. Come when y'ready."

He hung up.

Vollie took the handset from my shoulder, replaced it on its cradle, and then spent a moment or two looking at me with his head slightly cocked to one side.

"You know old man Thieroux?" he said.

I shook my head and blanked my face. "Never heard of him," I said.

He started to say something. But you could see him hitting the brakes and shifting gears, and instead of whatever he'd intended, he managed to keep his voice both level and casual as he said the second thing that had come into his head instead of the first. "Just seemed sort of odd, is all."

"Odd?"

"You knowing Mose Thieroux. I mean, seeing as how the victim, Commencement Brown—that is, the one you think has got such a funny name—used to work out there at the Thieroux spread."

His use of the past tense triggered an alarm. "Used to?"

"Well, sure." I could see Vollie beginning to enjoy himself, and I didn't like it. "Used to, until you done what you done to him thataway. Lord knows he won't be working there for a while. Nor anyplace else...if he ever get back to where he can work at all."

It didn't track.

Greenteeth had been in good enough health last night, give or take a few cuts and bruises. I certainly hadn't hit him hard enough to inflict permanent damage, and I almost said so before I managed to catch my fool tongue and shut my mouth around it.

"Sorry," I said when everything was under control. "I think you lost me back there somewhere."

"That a fact?"

"That's a fact."

"Well, that does beat all! I reckon, then, the things he told me—before he lost consciousness, you know—were just imagination. Said you and the lady, here, waited for him on a road outside town here yesterday, and then crowded him into the ditch playing chicken head-on. Smashed up his truck. Hurt him real bad."

I had an answer to that. And a question or two. But Dana spoke up ahead of me. "Lost consciousness?" she said.

"Oh, yeah, lost consciousness," Vollie nodded emphatically, looking at her but aiming the words at me. "Woke up long enough to give the statement. Front of witnesses, too, in case you were wondering. And then he went into a coma or something. People over there at the hospital say he might not ever wake up."

He paused momentarily, looking back and forth between us. "And if he don't wake up, of course," he went on, "what he said could count as what they call a deathbed statement."

He didn't say anything more after that, and neither did we.

Nothing to say.

We locked up the room—God knows why; people seemed to come and go through the doors in that place as though they weren't there—and got into the back of his patrol car for the ride to jail. It was getting to be a familiar routine. But this time was easier and less painful than the first trip. Vollie evidently didn't think either of us was going to run.

He didn't bother with handcuffs.

A SERMON (CONTINUED)

We do not yield to them.

We take up arms; they seem to flee before us. But ever and ever they return, altered in form but no less terrible for all that.

We are strangers in a strange land, unarmed and lonely upon a darkling plain…

TWENTY-SIX

The jail hadn't changed much.

There were a few more signs of life than on my last visit to the top floor of the courthouse: two trusties mopping up instead of one, a crickety old man in an ill-fitting deputy's uniform on hand in the booking room to fingerprint us and take the pictures, and a fat-bellied man wearing sergeant's stripes at the desk.

But we didn't have time to get acquainted.

The older man had just finished my profile view and was getting ready to take down the vital statistics when Deke Pemberton walked in and handed two papers to a sergeant.

"Judge Bronson's waiting downstairs," he said. "So let's get moving."

The sergeant seemed stunned to see Pemberton at the jail in person. "I be gawdam!" he said.

Pemberton looked at him without expression. "Something bothering you?" he inquired.

The sergeant took a moment to answer, goggling. "Well, I should hope to kiss a pig," he said finally. "Pardon me all to hell for staring, Counselor, but to what do we owe this unexpected pleasure, as the saying is?"

Pemberton glanced briefly in the direction of the booking room, letting everyone know he saw us.

"I have presented two writs of habeas corpus," he said. "They are for the individuals listed, who are my clients. If you have either or both of them in custody, you will present them forthwith before the Honorable Hilgard W. Bronson, magistrate of Farewell County."

He turned his gaze back to the sergeant, who was still sagjawed with disbelief.

"Well," he prodded. "Do you have them?"

The sergeant finally came to life. "I be gawdam," he said again, shaking his head. But he busied himself making notes from the faces of the two writs, and then motioned toward the booking deputy. "Bring 'em out," he said, "and take 'em downstairs."

Dana and I followed the old man out of the booking room and into the lobby. Pemberton's expression didn't change, but he led the way to the elevator and pushed a button that took us two floors down.

Setting bail appeared to be a cut-and-dried formality, and Pemberton was already signing the guarantor's statement when Frank Ybarra entered the little courtroom and told him to forget it.

"No bail," the sheriff said. "And no charge, and this is the second set of booking slips I have had to tear up for the same people and the same reason this week. Getting monotonous."

Pemberton didn't comment and Ybarra didn't seem to expect it.

"For a man who just got into town a few days ago," Ybarra said, "I swear you seem to have made one hell of a lot of friends in a hell of a hurry."

"Basic charm and a dishonest face," I said.

He nodded reflectively. "Desk clerk from the motel called me at home," he said. "Told me you and the girl were getting arrested. No sooner hung up than old Mose Thieroux was on the line, purely raising hell for me to find out what kind of trouble you were in. Now I get here, and the counselor's already on the scene, throwing writs around and posting bail."

He was looking at me, waiting for an explanation, but the lawyer's arrival had been as much a surprise to me as anyone, and I didn't have any answers for him.

Dana did, though. "Telephone in the bathroom," she explained. "I called my lawyer."

She turned a tentative grin in Pemberton's direction, and he surprised me by offering a kind of impressionist sketch of a smile in return.

"And Glenda Mae, on the switchboard, was listening in." Ybarra nodded. "So she called me. Okay, I suppose I under-stand...all except the call from Thieroux."

He was waiting for an answer again, but I decided there had been enough for the time being. No sense showing your hand if nobody's paid to see it.

"Angels," I said in my best prayer-meeting tones, "protect the just and the righteous."

He snorted and the black eyes called me a son of a bitch.

But "By God if they don't" was all he said.

"I take it my clients are free to go, then?" Pemberton said.

Ybarra nodded, then seemed to reconsider. "Miz Dana, yes," he said. "But I'd like to talk to the Preacher, here, in my office for a minute. If that's all right." There was a moment of silence when I could see Pemberton preparing to object. But I was curious about what the onetime San Francisco detective might want to say to me. And besides, if he'd really wanted to give anyone a bad time that morning, all he'd had to do was stay home and not answer the telephone.

"Just pleasant social conversation," the sheriff said with what he probably meant to be a reassuring smile. "No need to draw up another get-out-of-jail warrant, Counselor. You can wait right out in the bull pen if you like. Shouldn't take too long."

Pemberton shrugged. Reluctantly. "We'll wait," he said.

The rock that Ybarra had thrown into the wastebasket to check out my ersatz eye during our last session together was back on his desk—or he'd found a duplicate—and he busied himself hefting it from one hand to the other as he sat down, letting me settle myself uncomfortably in the visitor's chair across the desk from him.

"You," he said by way of opening the conversation, "are beginning to be a real pain in the ass."

I don't know what he expected me to say to that.

"Got you back up here," he continued when I didn't react, "with the doors closed and no fancy tape recorders running, to tell you that I am not real fond of private detectives."

I sat quietly and let him go on.

"The kind that have licenses are usually semicompetent sleazeballs when they're not outright blackmailers. And the kind that don't have licenses are a bunch of goddamn amateurs who get in everybody's way and mess up a professional investigation… when they're not off getting themselves hurt. Or maybe hurting somebody else."

The last five words, I decided, were the ones aimed directly at me, and they brought up a question or two that I had been wanting to ask ever since he told the judge that the assault charges had been dropped. But he didn't give me a chance to ask.

"I dropped the charges against you and the girl," he said, "because I am neither a fool nor an incompetent, no matter what you might think. I know that Commencement Brown—hell of a name to stick some kid with, isn't it; no wonder he likes people to call him Boo—that the stupid little shit was looking to ambush you out on that road, not the other way around, and I am pretty damn sure I know why, too. But I can't prove it yet, and you're not making things any easier."

I started to say something snotty like "Sorry about that," but managed not to, at the last moment.

"For your information," he went on, keeping the voice level but somehow edging it with ice, "and purely for the purpose of getting an idea through your thick head...you weren't the only son of a bitch following Vollie Manion last night. I borrowed a specialist from the Albuquerque police force on the day Bobby Don Thieroux died, and he's been keeping an eye on my deputy ever since. That's how I damn well knew that Boo Brown didn't get the worst part of his injuries in any accident. My man saw you coldcock him at Lupe's café and waited around to see him wake up again and then go across the street and go riding in the car with his good buddy, Vollie."

"Your man followed them from the garage?"

"Tried, but couldn't. Vollie put the hammer down, and he was driving a pursuit car that I have reason to think is the fastest thing— on the road, anyway—in this part of New Mexico. They were out of sight before the Albuquerque dick knew what was happening."

"And Brown turned up in the hospital, ready to go into a coma, after that?"

He nodded. "That's how it went down."

"But—"

"I told you: This is my investigation and I'll handle it my way. I don't need help from amateurs."

I turned it around, looking at the situation from his point of view and understanding why he felt as he did.

"You seem to have the professional investigation in hand," I said, keeping my tone noncommittal.

He sighed, flipping the little rock from hand to hand. "Well, then, since we understand each other so well," he said, "maybe you'd be good enough to tell me why you don't just haul your ass out of town and let me get on with it?"

It was a perfectly logical inquiry, but it wasn't anything I could promise to do. So instead, I decided to use the opening to try to find out what else he knew.

"Why...I play poker for a living," I said. "I thought you understood that; I came to your town to play in a couple of the games at the country club because I heard there were some fairly high rollers out there. Fact is, I believe there is going to be a game like that out there tonight. And if there is, I am going to play in it...unless there's some objection."

He leaned back, still hefting the rock in one hand, and whistled quietly through his teeth. "You're a liar," he said after a while.

I thought it over. "Likely so," I agreed. "But not about the poker."

"Uh-huh."

We sat that way for a bit, looking at each other and waiting for something to happen. But nothing did, and finally he leaned forward again, putting the rock down on the desk between his hands, and spoke his piece.

"You came to Farewell," he said, "because Jake Spence knew you from a long time back, and he was wondering if that game out there at the club might be crooked, and since you are a pro he thought you could find out the truth for him."

If he was fishing, he seemed to be at the right hole. But it wasn't my business to tell him so, and I deliberately blurred the focus of my one eye to make sure that my face didn't give him any answers.

"Well, you found out that the game is straight," he said. "Illegal as hell—gambling is, you know, in New Mexico—but I checked it out first thing when I got to town and found out it was okay, at least in terms of poker. Which, now that I think of it, isn't saying one hell of a lot."

I think that was bait, too.

"And now," he said, "we come to the Preacher. You say you make your money playing poker, and there are a lot of people who seem to agree with that. I know because I've talked to quite a few of them since the last time we sat in this room."

"Sounds sort of boring."

"Not at all. Like I said, I talked to some who thought they knew all about the Preacher—but then, damn if I didn't come across some others who gave me a whole different slant on him…"

He smiled a little, just at the corners of the mouth, and I knew what was coming next, and it seemed to me that he could have skipped this conversation and been the better for it.

"What they told me," he said, warming to the subject now that he had finally identified it for me, "was about a young guy, fresh-caught Episcopal minister he was, right out of that fancy big school they got back in Tennessee—Sewanee, the University of the South—and how he got into the army as a chaplain during the war over in Southeast Asia."

"Look, Ybarra…" I began. But he didn't seem to hear.

"Seems they shipped his ass over there, and he did a whole tour in the 'Nam and was sent back to the world without a single scratch on him. Happened that way for some. But about a month before he was due to come home, he got a telegram from the Red Cross telling him that there had been a sort of a war casualty in his family after all. His pretty young wife was dead. Shot to death by some damn-fool draft-dodging National Guardsmen during an anti-war demonstration…something like those shootings back at Kent State."

I had heard enough and I wanted out of there, and I started to get out of the chair to leave the room, but Ybarra's voice stopped me before I could move.

"You set still," he said, still not raising the volume, but hammering out the words. "If you can live through it, you can sure as hell listen to it, Preacher."

I took a deep breath and hated him and put my full weight back in the chair.

He was right. If I could live it, I could listen to it.

Any time.

"So the young chaplain wasn't there the day his wife died, and he wasn't there for her funeral, either," Ybarra went on in a calmer tone. "And they even say he never went to visit her grave when he did get back stateside. But he did some other things that were sort of odd. Not what you'd expect. He resigned from the ministry and he resigned from the Chaplains Corps, told them to shove the captain's commission he'd earned over there. And then he turned right around and joined up again. Enlisted. As a grunt."

I looked at him and through him and far away, not seeing his face. Or anything else.

"He was qualified for OCS or for a lot of the other schools the army has. But instead, he volunteered for advanced infantry training and went through that, head of the class, and then they shipped him back to the 'Nam as a corporal...just in time to be sent up to Khe Sanh when they decided to reoccupy the old marine base there. That was a hell of a fight, they tell me, and this fellow got a Silver Star for his part in it. Some said it should have been an even more important gong, but that's what he got... along with a Purple Heart he picked up as a flat-even swap: damn piece of ribbon with painted metal on it in return for his right eye."

Ybarra paused for a moment. "All straight so far?" he inquired.

"You could tell it that way," I said.

"Okay, then: At the hospital where they sent him, they began to wonder after a while if he was some kind of a nut case. Hell of a troublemaker. They were even thinking about getting him a transfer into one of the locked wards. But after a bit he seemed to pull himself together and quiet down enough that they could let him go. Some people, friends of his like Jake and Helen Spence and a few others, thought he would maybe have a change of heart and go back to being a priest.

"But he didn't. Instead, what he did was take to playing poker. Professional. Not for fun. Wasn't any too good at it in the beginning. Not enough experience, not enough patience. But he kept at it, holding jobs when he had to and paying his dues as he went, and finally it seemed like he sort of got the hang of the game and got to be one of the best in the trade, so they say."

"Hell of a story," I said.

"Ain't it?" he said.

"But I know a funnier one," I said. "See, there was this sheriff off in New Mexico and he got kind of bored with things around him, being used to a bigger town, and so he took to listening to every idiot story anybody wanted to tell him until he finally bored himself to death."

"Damn pity." Ybarra nodded and waited to see if I had anything more to say, but I didn't, so he went on. "None of this would mean very much," he said, "if the guy had just kept the money he won for himself, after he got to be good at the game, like anybody with good sense would do. But no. What the Preacher did with it was to buy up a whole little town over on the California side of the Sierra. Little place called Best Licks that used to be a mining camp and then was almost a ghost town for a while. Bought the whole shebang, mind you—houses, stores, equipment, even the old locked-up church—and opened it up as a kind of commune or refuge, or maybe just a hidey-hole, for people like himself that had a hard time fitting back into the world after spending time in some craziness like the 'Nam."

He paused for breath, and I think he really wanted me to smile at him and relax and talk and explain...which only showed how little he understood of what he had heard.

"Bullshit," I said.

"Is it?" Ybarra's eyes were bright. "Is it, now? I wouldn't know, myself. Only what people tell me. But the story gets even stranger the further we go. Because one of the ones I talked to said that nobody staying up there at the Preacher's place in the mountains even knows where the money comes from.

"Oh, they know he plays poker, all right. Sure! But they don't know what he does with the money. Truth is, they think he's some kind of high-grade hustler, ripping the government off for federal rehabilitation grants, and they think that is so funny that they will even come to the church he runs—holds Sunday services in the old church building he fixed up—because they think it's part of the scam. Go to church because they think it's all a game he's running on the government. Now ain't that the damnedest thing?"

I held my breath and waited out a long ten-count, but it didn't help a whole lot.

If Ybarra could find out that much with just a few telephone calls, then the story could get back to the mountains. To Best Licks. And that could destroy the whole thing. One way or another, he had found out the one place where I was vulnerable, and that was bad news. But a poker player wouldn't last long if he didn't have at least a little alligator blood in his veins, and it was getting on toward time for mine to do some work.

I gave him my blandest smile. "Hope you had a nice time telephoning here and there around the country and talking to people and all that," I said. "But I'm afraid I just don't see how any of this fits into what's been going on here in Farewell, New Mexico."

He smiled right back.

"Maybe it doesn't," he said. "Except it has come to mind that someone like the man these people told me about, like the Preacher, might remember that Orrin Prescott was a Vietnam veteran, too—just like the folks up there in his mountain town— and take the notion to sort of include him in the flock. One of his own, you might say."

I stopped smiling.

Ybarra didn't seem to notice. "So instead of just telling the Spences that the game was legit and letting it go at that, it seemed to me that someone like the Preacher might take to poking around sort of on his own, and get the idea that poker wasn't the only kind of game being played in this town. He could even decide that if Prescott's death wasn't suicide and wasn't an accident either, then it sure as hell had to be something like murder, because that helicopter jockey didn't die of pneumonia or a heart attack. And, you know, I wouldn't have a bit of a quarrel with that kind of thinking—except for one thing."

Well, Jesus out of the boat.

"And what might that be, Sheriff?" I asked.

"The verdict of the coroner's office in this case," he said, "was death by misadventure, and the word is already out that the National Transportation Safety Board, the agency that decides about things like that, is going to say the crash was due to pilot error. But I flew with Prescott a few times, including once when it was foolish because even the birds were walking, and he was as good with that damn eggbeater as any man who ever lived, so I do not believe for one minute that he made the kind of mistakes that could turn everything sour enough to kill him. Not in daylight and clear weather and with the machinery in good working order. And I sure as God can't see a man like him deliberately killing himself, neither, so that leaves nothing for it to be except murder, and I came to that conclusion all by myself, and I have been acting on it in my official and professional capacity... no outside help required."

"And so the Preacher can damn well butt out or get his butt kicked."

"The thought had crossed my mind."

I smiled again, with teeth, and put my hands on the edge of the desk in front of me and leaned some of my weight on them to bring my face closer to his, because I wanted him to hear every word I said and not think for a moment that they were anything short of sincere.

"You're a good man, Ybarra," I said, "and in other circumstances, or maybe in another place, we could get along just fine. Maybe that can happen here and now, too. But that depends on both of us being able to understand that I stopped taking orders and turning the other cheek and paying dutiful homage to my elders and betters about the time I got out of the army. If I am here in Farewell, it is because I want to be here, and if I stay, it will be because I want to stay. And if I go, it will be because I want to go, and it will be at a time of my own choosing."

This time it was his turn to wait. He did it well.

"You tell me that you know Prescott's death could be murder," I said, "and you want me to believe that you are and have been investigating it, and I do believe it. But that doesn't mean I am going to go away and lie down and go to sleep for the winter. The last time we talked, we agreed that a sheriff shouldn't have to run for office. I don't think you'd sweep a murder under the rug, because you're a better man than that, and it's my guess that you couldn't make yourself do it even if you wanted to. But you're still an elected official and you still have to live here and you have a stake in the town itself and you're still personally involved with the people who run things in Farewell. You wouldn't let one of them get away with murder, no. But you might very well handle the whole thing on tiptoe, very quietly, to keep from disturbing the status quo."

"Would that be such a bad thing?"

"Maybe not. I don't know. Not yet, anyway, and that's the whole point, Ybarra, because neither do you. We're both guessing, and we're both being influenced by factors that really have nothing to do with the facts in the case. From where I sit, there are at least three people on this earth who deserve to know exactly how Pres Prescott died, and who did it, and why. And they deserve redress."

He didn't like that.

"Redress, my ass!" he growled, breaking in. "Now you're talking like a high school poet. Redress. Don't be a bigger fool than God made you. If 'Nam and all the rest of it taught you anything, it should have been that there is no redress for a life. Can't be. Not in the nature of things. Unless you are talking about revenge, in which case—"

"In which case," I said, stealing the sentence back and finishing it for him, "I can go to hell. And I probably will, Ybarra, just to keep you company. But not today. And not for any reason like that. Of course nobody can redress the personal loss to Marilyn Prescott and her children. Her husband, and their father, is dead and he isn't coming back, ever, and no one can fix that. But someone stole—or tried to steal—something besides a husband and father here.

"Someone took a hell of a lot of money from Prescott, almost broke him and put him out of business, in the months just before he died. And someone is trying to finish the job now by stealing what's left from his survivors. And that, by God, is something for which redress is well and truly possible. Or am I wrong?"

He picked up the stone and put it down again and looked past me at nothing and snapped the middle finger of his right hand into the palm of his left and then slapped them both palm down on the desktop.

"All right, Preacher," he said. "We'll leave it there. You're right and you're wrong, but sitting here and talking about it isn't going to do anyone a lot of good, and I sure got other things to do besides worry about whether you get your butt kicked, and for all I know you got some things to do, too, and I am just too old and too tired to try and tell anyone, including myself, that I have got all of the answers."

Sounded fair enough to me.

I waited to see if he had anything else on his mind, and when he didn't seem to, I nodded in his direction and got up to leave. But he wasn't really done.

"One thing," he said when I got to the door, "and then to hell with you. I know there isn't a hope in this world that you have got enough sense to listen to anything I say, but there seem to be a few people here and there who set a good bit of store by you, and I just wouldn't feel right if I let you go without one final bit of warning, and it's this: You mind where you put your feet, Preacher."

I gave him one more smile—a real one this time. "Always do," I said.

"Uh-huh," he said. "But it takes a lifetime to get acquainted with a town like Farewell. To know who's doing what with which to who. You got nice friends. Particularly the girl; she's real good people. But you got a few aren't your friends, too, and I don't think you know all their names just yet. You're still a stranger...and that is enough to get a man hurt bad sometimes. Keep your eye open."

I noted his use of the singular.

Friendly.

And oddly comforting.

"Thanks, Ybarra," I said. "I love you, too."

A SERMON
(CONTINUED)

People change.

Motives become clouded.

The mysteries of the human heart and soul are deeper and more convoluted than all the books ever written and all the poems ever sung have tongue to declare...

TWENTY-SEVEN

Mose Thieroux's coffee was as good as ever, but his mood wasn't.

He had brewed up the second pot of the morning by the time Dana and I arrived—we had half expected a side-road confrontation with Vollie Manion, but he didn't show—and the first few minutes were occupied by questions (What the jeezly hell had been going on in there?) and explanations (Your sheriff's a nice enough guy, but he's got some weird playmates) and with pourings and sippings and expressions of pleasure. Dana surprised me by not lighting a Marlboro, and thinking back on it, I couldn't remember seeing her smoke all morning. But I let it pass without comment for the moment because more pressing matters seemed to be at hand. The room around us had turned silent again, and when I stilled my own center to touch the old lobsterman's *wa*, I found the spoor of something dark and ugly that he wasn't ready to talk about just yet.

"Great-grandkids okay?" I asked, more to create sound than anything else.

The warmth and pleasure were immediate. "Ayuh!"

A startling rictus that might have been an incognito grin—if nobody looked too closely and the day was cloudy—flickered for a brief second across the unfamiliar landscape of his face, and he ducked his head back into his coffee mug, perhaps to prevent it from reaching escape velocity.

"Little devils put a horny toad in my bed last night," he said. "Son of a howah! Scairt the livin' shit out'n me, and I lit a shuck after the two of them, but they got out the window and onto the top of the house and stayed up there till I was cooled down."

He sipped and snorted and sipped again. "Shouldn't wonder we'll get on right well," he said. "For sure they have got the makin's."

"Adoption papers coming along?"

More warm feelings, close to the surface. "Monday week." He nodded. "All drawn up. Just one more thing that you'n me got in common, Preacher: We use the same lawyer. That cold-pissing Pemberton bastid. Temperature goes down ten degrees anytime he's around, and I sure as God wouldn't want him on the other side of nothing I was interested in, I can tell you. But a feller don't get no Christless choice around these parts. Any other lawyer you could trust is too stupid to pour piss out'n a boot, and the ones smart enough to do the work would steal the pennies off a dead man's eyes. So it's Pemberton."

"Spooky bastard," Dana agreed.

Thieroux shook his head, weighed by the vagaries of human nature, but that unfamiliar smile-rictus flashed again as he looked at her.

"Son of a howah!" he repeated. "I am some glad to see this Bible-thumper had sense enough to do like I told him and bring you along. Ain't never been enough smart, pretty women in this world to suit me—and none like you in this house since m'wife died, b'Jesus."

He gave her a long up-and-down of frank admiration. "Was I even ten year younger..." he said.

And then, in an instant, the smiles and the warming mood were banished and we were back to square one. Thieroux downed the remainder of his coffee, got up for another cupful, and detoured on the way back to open the right-hand drawer of what

I had taken for an old-fashioned potato bin on the underside of the tall kitchen cabinet that stood by the pantry door.

"Kitchen's my office," he explained. "Do my business here, so the things I need for it are here, too."

The bin hadn't held potatoes for a long time. If ever. Instead, the space was occupied by files, neatly color-coded and arranged for easy access, beside what appeared to be an extremely sophisticated high-tech telephone equipped for data transmission. I glanced around the room, searching for the computer that I knew must go with it. Thieroux noticed, and nodded to the left of the cabinet's work surface, which I now realized was at desk height rather than at the drainboard level repeated elsewhere in the room.

"Bread box," he said.

Looking with unblinkered eyes, I could see now that it was somewhat too large to be a real bread container. The door at the front, I decided, would be the back of a fold-up LED crystal monitor, with the computer keyboard and drives concealed behind it. I looked a question at our host.

"Just cantankerousness," he said, pulling one of the files out of the drawer and bringing it to the table along with the coffeepot. "Showing my age. Never could decide whether I liked being alive in this part of the twentieth century. Got used to the furniture and the colors and the—hell, the whole world that I grew up with, and never felt at home with no others, so I go right on living in that kind of a world most of the time, because I got rich enough to afford it. But all the same, a man has got to make an exception here and there. Or die..."

He slapped the file down in the middle of the table and topped off all the cups of coffee before sitting down himself.

"Once't you woke me up and got me to moving and looking in the right direction," he said, opening the packet and handing me the topmost sheet, "it wa'n't too jeezly hard to find out what had been going on while I was asleep."

The paper in my hand was a rough summary, and some of it was couched in the arcane obscurities of New Mexico–style land descriptions. But the message of it all was clear enough: Doing part of the work by personal inquiry and part by long-range computer sorting, Mose Thieroux had followed a trail through two years of local real-estate transactions—and corporate shenanigans covering a period perhaps three times as long—to a single door. It wasn't anything you could take to a prosecutor or even to the civil courts as yet, and it involved a few offshore holding companies and corporate entities that might or might not be legally penetrable. But it was enough to nail down the main players.

"Llano Escondido Exploitation and Development," I said.

"In-gawdam-corporated." Thieroux nodded.

I looked at him expectantly, waiting for the other shoe to hit the floor, but the answer to my unspoken question wasn't on the paper he had given me, and he seemed oddly reluctant to spit it out with the rest of his words.

"Who?" I finally asked.

He swallowed half a cup of the good coffee and put the mug down, and his face declared that this was a bad day for the world and there was no fixing it.

"Man gets to be my age," he said heavily, "he had ought to know better than to go around looking for happy endings or pots of gold. Or friends he can trust. It would be nice to say that things was different once't; there are people this world who make a good living just from telling how it was better and nicer and you could depend on a man's word to be his bond, way back when. But the hell of it is, my memory is still too clear to lie to myself thataway, so finding out that people are still just people—like they always were—shouldn't make me feel so low in my mind, should it?"

"But it does," I said.

"But it does. I live out here and purt' near never go to town, but I hear things, 'most everything that I need to hear. Anything that's public property and quite a bit that's not. And a lot of the things I hear have got something to do with some business or other that I am in, because I am in a lot of different businesses. But mostly I am in the land business. Always have been. Found out real early that's where the money was and that I was some good at it, so you would think I would hear and know what was going on around me."

He was beating himself about the head and ears for failing to spot a gaffed game, and that didn't make sense to me.

"You weren't intended to hear or know," I said. "No one was. That was the whole idea."

"Ayuh," he said. "Makes no jeezly difference. Didn't take me the whole of one day to find out, when I got to looking in the right direction. But it needed a stranger, someone who didn't know the town of Farewell from a can of paint a week ago, to tell me what I should be looking for. The only reason I didn't see it right off was that I was sitting out here asleep. And because I done that, because of me being a damn fool, a man is dead who oughtn't to be—no, don't go lookin' at me like that, I mean Orrin Prescott, not my grandboy—and a lot of other people stand now to lose their ahss and all their fixtures."

It still sounded like a bum rap, but I could see arguing wasn't going to help much, and anyway I still wanted the answer to the question I hadn't exactly asked, so this time I kept my mouth shut.

"Forty year now," he said, "I been doing business with two men here in town who I trusted. Partnered them in many a thing and bought from them both and sold to them both and half the time no more than a handshake or a word on the telephone needed between us. Stood godfather to my boy, one of them did, and both friends to me. Or I thought they was, anyhow. Till yesterday."

He wanted me to break in now, take him off the hook. But all I could do was wait.

"For two years," he said, "Llano Escondido has been sitting doggo in the weeds, putting together a parcel of land a bit here and a bit there. Always through third parties and never enough to make a stir. Never enough land changing hands to rate more than a paragraph in the local paper. No two parcels to the same buyer, always just some corporation with a name like XYZ or Acme or How-Dee...and when you get to checking, it turns out that corporation is owned by another one and that one is off in the Caribbean or Liechtenstein or some damn place where it costs your eyeteeth to bribe someone to tell you who the hell it really is. One of the parcels they got even come from me. Not that I mind that too bad—kinda unfriendly, but business is business and I understand about it; ain't nothing I ain't done m'self one time or t'other."

He nodded reflectively, not seeing us or the room around him for a moment, but then came back to the world with a snap.

"But this about it, Preacher," he said, pointing a finger at me. "There is a big difference between sharp trading and thief trading, and the line of work you're in is one of the best ways of showing it: A man who wins his money by bluffing the other feller out of it or sucking him into a hand where he can't win is one thing—that's the game. But a man who marks the cards or mechanics the deck or is partnered with someone else at the table is something else again, and that is b'Jesus what we have got ourselves here. Putting the money in a bank account down in the Caribbean or in Switzerland and setting up five different dummy companies to make a smoke screen ain't the kind of thing a sharp trader needs. That's for a Christless pack of thieves, so there can't be no horse pukkey about how this was all just business."

He looked questioningly at me, but I couldn't see where he needed any answer. "No argument," I said.

He nodded and went on. "The parcels was all centered on one place, and a baby coulda seen it if he'd looked. Minute you told me what you suspicioned, I thought of the old Good Hope. And sure enough…"

He waited expectantly, but the name meant nothing to me and I said so.

"Ayuh. No reason you should know about it, I expect," he said. "Before your time. The Good Hope was an oil field—biggest strike ever in these parts and purt' near the only one, come to that—first deep hole got drilled here and the first one that spouted anything but dust. And people remember it because it was what people nowadays call tech-no-logical theft…pure unarmed robbery!"

His eyes went opaque with memory.

"The Good Hope came in just a little after folks learned how to slant-drill a well," he said. "Before, you just drilled straight down. That way, you could always tell right where a oil pool was by looking where the derricks or pump heads was setting. But with the jeezly slant-drilling, you put all the derricks in one place, and it can be miles and miles from the pool—all you do is slant the wells over to where it is, like someone using a straw to snitch soda water out'n his neighbor's glass. Nothing wrong with it if you got permission to get the soda…or the oil. But it's a scandal for sure if you do it on the sly."

I still didn't see what this had to do with a modern-day real-estate swindle, but he had my interest. "Scandal?" I said.

"Bet y'ahss, boy! People who brought in that old well—the Good Hope—had slant-drilled without telling nobody. They'd had one duster drilling straight down and knew they wasn't a drop of oil under their own lease. But they thought they knew where it was—and they was right! Only the man who owned the land it was under was a crazy furriner called Lupe—Lupidischi-something it was—who wouldn't sell to them, nor lease it neither. He was trying to farm the land at the time and wouldn't listen to nobody. So what they done was to drill on a slant, like I said, and tap into the pool down below Lupe's land without anyone being the wiser.

"Now, that don't seem possible, does it?"

I started to say I didn't know whether it did or not, but he didn't wait for an answer.

"Normal course of things," he went on, "someone would have caught on, of course. But this wasn't normal for the times. The hands worked on drilling the well knew just enough about oil to do their jobs. Nothing more. The tool pusher in charge of drilling told them what to do, and since he was one of the thievin' bastid partners in the well, he sure wasn't about to tell no one. So it got drilled and flowed for a while and then went to pump, and the partners got richer'n hell, suckin' oil out from under old Lupe's land without him knowing about it.

"Oh, sure—it all come out later. But by that time, the pool was damn near dry and Lupe'd finally sold off the subsoil rights to them, not knowing they'd been using them all along, because he needed money to build a café and some tourist cabins on his place."

I thought for a moment of the monuments to long-gone hope that I had seen the night before.

Some people don't seem to have much luck.

"Anyway, the bastids done it took their money and went away back east, and I heard they lost the whole kaboodle in the '29 crash. Good enough for 'em! But don't none of that tell us why someone would be wanting land around the Good Hope nowadays, does it? Nothing down in that hole no more. Just an empty dome more'n a mile down, under two horizons of rock. Hard to figure. Unless nothing was what they wanted."

He sat back to let me think about it, but it made no sense at all to me.

"Give up?" he said after a while.

"Well..."

"Dump!" Dana practically shouted the word, light breaking across her face and her fists hammering delightedly on the tabletop. "Someone wants that thing for a dump! Am I right?"

Thieroux nodded at her with real appreciation. "Ayuh! Thought from the beginning you'd do fine," he said, "but I was wrong. You will do some better'n fine, missy. Betcha. Ayuh! That's it, for sure as sure. What we have got here is a big chemical company that's been having one hell of a lotta trouble about dumping the dangerous damn muck that they throw away after they make the stuff they make. Don't matter what it is. The throwaway is toxic—hell, maybe even radioactive for all I know—and they want to build a whole new plant where they can get rid of the garbage without no trouble."

"You mean dump toxic wastes down one of the old wells?"

"Hell, no. I mean dump it down every livin' one of them! The wells is only just a bunch of thin holes leading down to the empty cave where that oil pool used to be. Sometimes water'll seep in and fill up the cave when the oil's gone, but it didn't do that here, so what you got is a jeezly big cavern way the hell and gone down yonder. Thing like that, you could go on dumping radium droppings and skunk piss for damn near ever, and if you done it careful and sly—like the way them bastids did when they drilled the holes in the first place—maybe they wouldn't anyone ever know what went on."

I thought about that.

"Or," I said, "maybe the Environmental Protection Agency would even give you a permit to do that. The whole idea, as I understand it, is to find someplace where the dangerous stuff can't do any harm. Maybe if you put it that far down...?"

Thieroux nodded. "Sure," he said, "it might be just the place. And then again, b'Jesus, it might not! Who the hell knows? Might be you just building a kind of a time bomb for my great-grandbabies to worry about when they get their growth. That's the whole thing, see: Nobody knows. Don't even know if the Christless dome's connected with the water table here. Or somewhere else you'd never suspect. Don't seem likely, but that's the whole trouble. They don't know! And they don't give a damn."

"They'd be caught," I said.

"They'd shit," he growled. "Plant the like of that, kind of jobs they could offer to people here, the kind of growth it would mean for Farewell—wouldn't nobody be looking too close at the deal. Hell, the chamber of commerce here'd welcome an atom bomb factory if they was money in it. I oughta know. Time was when I was just like 'em."

"All the same…"

"All the same what we have got here is someone looking to build something dangerous and someone else, right here in town, willing to buy up all the land they would need for it on the quiet. Real quiet. Because it is going to make him some richer'n God."

"How rich would that be?"

"Son of a howah, boy! Places like this is rarer'n balls on a heifer, and what ones there are is mostly took."

"So the price would be good?"

"You might say so. Feller moves quiet and don't spook the herd, he could get it for two, maybe three million. Sell it for five times that if he's in a hell of a hurry. Ten times the buyin' price—hell, more, maybe—if he's careful, or knows the right buyer. And they for sure knew who was going to buy. I made sure about that, one way or another. But the buyer wouldn't be interested unless he had the whole package. No use to him no other way. They got the deal made, but only if they can put all the land together."

"You're talking about Barlow and Watrous, then?"

He hesitated and took a breath before answering. "Ayuh," he said, his voice quiet again.

"Absolutely sure?"

The heaviness that had been on him when we arrived rushed back to perch on his skinny neck and shoulders now, darker and more oppressive than ever, and he answered from a place where the soul goes to mourn.

"They the ones," he said. "Spent all of yesterday trying to find where there could be an out. Trying to show myself where it could be some other way and it could be someone else working through them unbeknownst—a bank does that sometimes, y'know, fronts for other money—but the more I checked and double-checked, the more it got to be them. Hand-fed each other to get that land, double-dealing friends and strangers. Well, that's business and, like I said, I could live with it. Mighta done the same myself, backalong. But to kill the Prescott boy..."

"Maybe they didn't do that."

His head snapped around to face me suddenly, and there were lightning bolts playing back in the soul chamber behind the eyes, a cold electricity like northern lights, and the temperature of the surrounding countryside was sub-zero.

"Ruint him first," he said. "Took me three telephone calls to be certain sure. But I made 'em, and I am. They cut Prescott off at the pockets on three of the biggest whirlybird contracts he had, did it right easy because they owned the companies. That would've been just after he told them the first time that he wouldn't sell, I shouldn't wonder. Then when he still wouldn't budge—after him and Barlow stopped speaking—they bullied a few more of his steady customers into quitting him. And all to make him poor enough to sell the land and move. Goddamn them! All in the world J. J. Barlow had to do was tell Orrin Prescott what was going on. Orrin loved him. Was like a son to him. He'd've done anything. And kept his mouth shut about it, too."

TED THACKREY JR.

A winter of the spirit shook him for an instant, sweeping him along through the outskirts of lamentation. I could feel the quick tears of age rising from the bottomless well that is at the center of all exiles from Eden. But the moment froze, and passed, leaving an inner landscape mantled in cold, white fury.

"But, no. No! They wanted all the money and they wanted it all for themselves, and so they killed him instead. Murdered him!"

His voice had turned soft and almost gentle.

But the ice-edge of loathing remained.

"And now," he said, "they can put their souls upon the altar of the Lord...because their asses are mine!"

A SERMON
(CONTINUED)

Man's destiny, prepared for him by the hand of the Creator, is to become truly the son of God.

And a vital part of that process is the joyful injunction to love and defend and protest his fellow man; joyful for—admire him or despise him as you will—he is your only possible companion here in the living world...

TWENTY-EIGHT

Dana and I rode most of the way back to Farewell without talking, thinking our own thoughts.

Mose Thieroux had been in pain, hurting deep, and when a man is doing that, there is no point in trying to argue with him. Later, perhaps, he might consider the possibility that a land grabber and swindler might not automatically be a murderer as well...might not, in fact, even be an especially bad person, as such things go.

People are far more complicated than that.

And so are motives.

But for the moment the old lobsterman was sick deep in himself, not only with the thought that two men he had known and trusted might do murder, but that they could conspire so cleverly in business as to put together a major undertaking with neither his knowledge nor his participation.

Hubris is affliction, from any angle.

"I might not want any part of the jeezly deal," he had said. "Fact is, the more I hear about it, the less I like it. But that ain't the point, b'Jesus! I don't drink hot buttered rum on a summer morning, neither, but if I go where it's being drunk I like to have it offered..."

I wondered what his attitude might have been thirty years earlier. Or twenty. Or ten. Or even a few months. Some people grow up early and others grow up late, but it's painful either way.

Dana sat beside me quietly, face averted, staring out at the cold flatness of the landscape but not seeing it.

She seemed to be at war on two levels; it worried me that I could only find one of them.

Twice during the trip she fumbled a pack of cigarettes, and twice she put it back with effort and annoyance. It was obvious now that she was trying either to cut down on the smoking or stop altogether, and that gave me a minor-league case of the guilties.

Ever since the government started printing its warnings on the side of cigarette packages, the decision to smoke or not to smoke has become the very latest crusade of all the world's busies. I find this especially depressing because I haven't smoked since my second tour in 'Nam, and so am accounted to be on the Side of the Angels in what has suddenly emerged as the Crusade of the Self-Righteous.

In point of fact, I have no deep feelings on the subject one way or the other. And I am not much for crusades. I was never a heavy smoker, and quitting was almost inadvertent. Cigarettes were one of the few things that Dee Tee Price and I didn't bribe the orderlies to smuggle into the hospital for us, because it is dangerous to use an open flame anywhere in the vicinity of pure oxygen, and several of the people in our ward were apt to need oxygen at any moment.

When they finally turned me loose, it seemed a little silly to start again. So I didn't.

But that doesn't even qualify me for a gold star on the forehead, never mind sainthood, and what people now call the "smoking revolution" has pretty much had to get along without me.

I don't care who smokes what in my vicinity—well, I could make an exception for certain brands of cigar and a few of the sweeter, more heavily scented pipe tobaccos—and I find the presence of cigarette smoke far less offensive than the

simon-pure vaporings of nonsmokers who insist that everyone in their vicinity cease smoking simply because they have
deigned to favor a room with their delicate presence. They are
probably in the right; the Surgeon General says he has scientific evidence that ambient secondhand smoke is a danger to
one and all.

But the attitude is still arrogant.

And the steamroller methodology is enough to drive a reasonable man back to the tobacco counter.

When it became apparent, then, that Dana might be trying
to give up the Marlboros, it posed a somewhat delicate problem:
If the lady was trying to quit for her own sake, it was her business
and a damn good idea and I wanted to help in any way I could,
even if the best support I could give was to shut up and let her
fight her own battles. But if she was doing it for me, we were in
Indian country with hostiles behind every bush.

I am just not brave enough to let people make big, or even
medium-size, changes in their lives on my account. I don't
know enough of the answers, and I'm not sure enough of the
ones I do know.

Only heroes have to be heroes; the rest of us are exempt.

A gutless attitude, perhaps. But mine own, so if that's what
was going on, it was time to find a tactful way to call a halt...

But the subject changed before it ever came up.

The road connecting the Thieroux spread to the highway
had dipped into a dry wadi, the bed of a steam that holds water
only in the immediate aftermath of a rainstorm, and Dana
turned away from the window with a tiny smile at the edges of
her mouth.

"Pull over for a minute," she said.

I glanced at her and was pleased to see that she no longer
seemed interested in the contents of her handbag.

"If you are going to barf again..." I teased.

She pretended to take offense. "Just pull over, turkey," she growled. "And don't talk so much."

Oh.

Well, that was more like it, and I can't deny that the moments after the little car was safely parked by the side of the road were pleasanter without the faint taste-tracks of nicotine and tars. Score one for the angels. Concentration is the main thing on these occasions, and distractions should be avoided.

Not that they would have mattered much.

It had been several hours since the night before, and after the first minute or two I found myself wondering if added privacy was really worth the effort of driving all the way back to the motel. The morning was turning warm and we had just passed a secluded-looking pasture with a few trees clustered around a stock pond. Winter grass was tall there. And green.

"Uh...Dana," I began.

But she laughed, a bit shakily I noted, and moved an inch or two away. It was as far as she could move; the car was really as small as it looked. And I could have followed. But the climate had changed, and what had been sudden and heated was now warm and easy, and the time to follow up had passed.

"The district attorney in Farewell," she said when she was sure I wasn't going to press matters for the moment, "is Lionel Sparda. He lives on Yucca Street, or did the last time I was here."

"Fascinating," I said.

"So...do we go there, to him, or do we just go back and tell Frank Ybarra what we've found out?"

I looked at her and there was a sudden vertiginous moment of déjà vu: I had told Dana that it was her I saw, not Sara, and for the most part it was true. But in that moment it was a lie and the hair was red and the nails were bitten and the wide, trusting eyes were asking me why I was going away to join the army when I didn't have to and the answer was going to be one she couldn't accept.

I blinked, and Sara was gone.

But Dana's eyes were still the same, and suddenly I didn't want to explain anything at all, or stay in Farewell, or do any of the things that I knew I was going to do in the next few hours. So I wouldn't do them: I would turn the car right instead of left when we got to the highway and drive it to Amarillo and take a plane to Tahoe and we would drive back to Best Licks from there. Phone Ybarra from the airport, maybe, and give him the information I'd picked up from Thieroux and Dee Tee Price, and leave him to deal with all of it.

But I can lie to myself for only a few seconds at a time, and that's where I stopped.

"Neither one," I said. "We go back to the motel, and I get myself ready to play a game of poker tonight."

At first she didn't believe me, and then she didn't understand, and there was only so much that I could tell her.

But I did my best.

"Mose Thieroux is a good man, and he swings a pretty big hammer hereabouts," I said. "But what he knows and what I know—which is quite a bit more because I talked to someone that he didn't and I looked in some different places—is still not enough to do more than dim a few reputations around town."

"But Mose said Pres was murdered!"

"And that is just what happened, angel. Someone killed your sister's husband. Set up the crash to pass for an accident. Or for suicide, if anyone got to checking too close. And the killer's not going to walk away from it. That I promise."

"So let's tell Ybarra."

"Tell him what? That there is a new industry that might be planning to locate in Farewell if they can find a nice quiet place to dump their refuse? That we have some bad news about the town's only remaining bank? Ybarra is a good man, better than this town has any right to expect, but if we went to him with a tale like that and told him to arrest someone, he wouldn't know whether to laugh or cry."

"He already suspects old Vollie."

I grinned at her and shook my head. "Miss Big Ears," I said.

She actually blushed, but without real embarrassment. "The door to Frank's office is pretty thin," she said. "I got real tickled at that spooky lawyer, Pemberton. He came all over nervous, watching me put my ear to the door, and had to think up an excuse to leave."

"So you know Ybarra doesn't have enough to go on yet— maybe never will—and what we know about Barlow and Watrous wouldn't help him a bit."

"If Vollie was working for them..."

I leaned back to my own side of the car and reflected that necking by the side of the road like a couple of high school kids was a lot more fun than talking about malfeasance and murder. Or small-town social mores.

The moment had passed.

"Vollie may have been working for one of them," I said. "Anything is possible. But being essentially a gambling man, I would be willing to put a little money on the street at six to five or better that he wasn't."

That surprised her. "What makes you say that?" she asked.

"Character," I said.

There was a moment when she was going to say she didn't know what I meant. But she did know, and she didn't say it.

"You don't think those two would do it?" she said.

"That's right," I said. I reached out a hand to touch her cheek, and it was warm and soft and it didn't move away, but the gesture didn't touch anything deeper than skin, either, so I had to put the whole thing into words. For both of us, maybe.

"It just wasn't in them," I said. "They had tried to swindle Prescott out of his land, and when that didn't work they tried to break him in business. Put him in a more receptive mood. And when that didn't work either—and we know now that it sure wasn't going to—I don't doubt for a moment that they would have thought up something even meaner, because that's how things were with them, whether we can prove it or not. No doubt about it. But Dana, you have known those two men, or known about them, for most of your life. So ask yourself, could either of them do murder?"

"Well, during the war…"

"A lot of things happen during a war," I said, more sharply than I had intended. "But try this: Make a picture in your mind of J. J. Barlow or Edward Watrous actually, personally, killing Pres Prescott."

She gave it her best shot. I could see it going on inside her, and I knew when she came to the part where Barlow, in his wheelchair, and Watrous, with his immense belly, tried to physically subdue the Steelers' former wide receiver. Her mouth twisted with the effort of suppressing a laugh, and after a moment it broke through anyway.

"Oh, all right," she said. "Have it your way—they couldn't have done him. But Vollie…"

I shook my head emphatically.

"Deputy Vollie Manion is a certifiable crazy from dingoville," I said, "and there is murder in him, and if anyone in this town was capable of killing Pres Prescott—could handle the physical end as well as the emotional side of the job—it would well and truly be him. But the question that neither Frank Ybarra nor I can answer is why."

Her response was instant: "Money."

I just looked at her.

"Well, why not?"

"Can you," I said when I thought she was ready to listen, "imagine either Barlow or Watrous paying that hulking menace to kill someone?"

"Maybe…"

I shook my head. "No way," I said. "No way on this earth or the next. I have played cards with the two of them, and I even had a chance for a little conversation with Barlow later, and while he didn't strike me as competition for Albert Einstein, he's a long way from being Mortimer Snerd, and I'd guess Watrous at about the same mental capacity. So even if one or both of them really did make up their minds to have Prescott killed, can you see them putting themselves in the hands—in the power, forever and ever—of Mr. Deputy Vollie Manion? Can you really?"

The shine of certainty that had been on her face flickered briefly, and was gone. But she wasn't quite ready to concede anything.

"Well, who the hell knows?" she said. "A weirdo like Vollie, maybe he just did it because he thought it would please someone. I mean, he's still the little boy who liked to step on baby mice…"

I waited for her to think it through.

"Oh, all right, then," she said finally. "We don't know enough yet. But we can't just let it go."

"Of course not," I said. "But first things first: When I said someone was going to pay for what happened to Prescott, I meant financially as well as all the other ways. And the first installment on the financial end comes, I think, tonight."

She took a deep breath, putting her feelings about Vollie Manion aside for the moment and relaxing against the car door. You could see her mind at work around the edges of the proposition—pulling a thread here and worrying a knot there—while her hands lived a life of their own, dragging a single Marlboro from her purse and setting fire to the end of it without conscious volition.

"The poker game," she said.

I nodded. "The poker game."

More thought, and a deep lungful of smoke that finally brought full awareness of what she was doing. The gray pungency whooshed out of her in a pattern that was somewhat shaped by a really imaginative curse, and she killed the glowing tip of the cigarette in the car's ashtray.

But she had done her thinking and made up her mind, and side issues were not about to distract her.

"Okay," she said. "The money's the first step. But just don't let's forget there is going to be a second one…"

I certainly couldn't argue with that.

Back at the motel, I pulled the little skate into my own parking stall, unlocked the door to the room, and stood aside for her to go through it ahead of me. But she hung back.

Disappointment was more poignant than I would have expected.

This was really one hell of a woman.

"You mean it's all over so soon?" I said, trying to keep it light. "Usually they stay right up until I try to borrow money."

She stuck out her tongue.

"Borrow all you can find," she said, "and sing Irish ballads while you're doing it. But save it. I've got some unfinished business to take care of. In my own room."

"If it's another boyfriend waiting over there," I said, "I'll pull out his mustache, hair by hair."

"He has a beard."

"It'll go, too!"

"And three big brothers…"

"They die!"

"And three big sisters."

"We…negotiate."

That finally got a laugh. "You would, too, you bastard. No, it's just a letter I need to write. I'll see you later."

I groaned. "I'll be playing poker later."

"Then I'll be here when the game is over."

And with a quick peck on the lips she was gone, tocking away down the sidewalk on three-inch heels and giving me the benefit of a deliberately exaggerated hip motion with each step.

I went into the room and locked the door and took a shower, turning the tap gradually to full cold.

They say it helps. Sometimes.

The phone rang just as I was toweling, and I picked it up quickly, thinking it might be Dana. But it was someone named George Goodhue, from Amarillo, and I had to think for a moment before I realized that this would be Dee Tee's bank messenger.

I gave him the room number and was careful to wait beside the door to get him inside as quickly as possible.

But he was nonchalant.

An attaché case with double combination locks was in his right hand, and the left was in the pocket of his suit coat, and it stayed there even after the case was open on the bed and I signed a slip of paper acknowledging its receipt.

You don't win at poker by missing details, so I asked him about it.

"Just a precaution," he said easily. "You're not dressed quite as Mr. Price said you would be."

I glanced down and saw what he meant.

Dee Tee would have described a skinny gent in preacher black. I was skinny enough, but was wearing only the trousers I had pulled on in haste after the shower.

"Mr. Price said there was one sure way for you to identify yourself," the messenger went on. "He said I wouldn't have to tell you what it was."

I laughed. "In a changing world," I said, "it is nice to know that some things never change and that one of them is Dee Tee Price."

The messenger smiled politely, but didn't make any other moves—and kept his left hand where it was—until I had reached up and unscrewed the prosthetic eyeball from its socket and held it in my hand.

Then he relaxed.

"Just for the sake of conversation," I said, turning away to put the glass eye back where it belonged, "what would have happened if I hadn't been able to do that?"

"My orders were to open fire at once and keep it up until you stopped moving."

I looked at him in wonder, but he wasn't smiling anymore. He would have done it.

"When you are carrying a million dollars in cash," he said, "you absolutely do not take chances."

A SERMON (CONTINUED)

The ending of our verse from Isaiah, with its warning to those who would leave their fellow man no place, spells out the fate of those who will not heed: "…That they may be placed alone in the midst of the earth."

This is the living death prepared for those who, for whatever reason, would deny space upon the earth to others—that they stand, at last, alone…

TWENTY-NINE

Few people ever hear—and even fewer understand—the special language that is the inner fabric of high-stakes poker.

It is a colloquy in silence.

But J. J. Barlow and I held a five-hour, six-million-dollar conversation in that tongue at the Farewell Country Club that night. We were the only ones who heard the words. We were the only speakers. And when it was done, we alone knew it for a dialogue of rare and classical merit...

I had come to the club at the appointed time, with the double-locked attaché case in one hand and the legally executed deed to Prescott Helicopters, Inc., in my breast pocket. I was calm and rested, ready to play as well as I could for as long as it took.

But Barlow was late.

Pemberton had arrived on time. Of course. He entered the clubhouse on the stroke of eight, looked around for the others, nodded in my direction, and sat down to stare silently into space while he waited.

Dr. Woodbury came through the door a few minutes after Pemberton, accompanied by a younger man whom he introduced as a visiting colleague, a surgeon from Amarillo with a passion for high-stakes poker.

We recognized each other at once.

I had played against him and beaten him regularly in Las Vegas, Reno, and Tahoe. So had most professionals. He was known in poker circles as one of the most dedicated of the "Red Board" players—losers who enjoy public bleeding over their losses. I wondered if his Amarillo friends knew about this little quirk of character, and wasn't especially astonished when he pretended that we were meeting for the first time. It was sad and it was silly, and I wondered whether he might find some good reason to disappear before the game began. But he surprised me and stayed to play.

Tiny Watrous arrived a few minutes behind the doctor, sidling through the wide doorway with an effusion of good cheer and heading directly for the bar, followed by the car dealer who had been at the poker table with us earlier in the week.

That left only one seat empty.

The usual old-friends banter of a fading small-town day washed around me as I sat at a table in a corner of the lounge, nursing a glass of iced mineral water and keeping the toe of my shoe in close contact with the satchel of cash.

It was exactly $100,000 short of containing an even million now.

I had counted out that amount, in centuries, and folded it carefully into an envelope, which I slipped into the breast pocket opposite the one where I was carrying the Prescott deed. The two packets made a comfortable but just visible bulge in the coat. That was fine with me. I wanted both to be noted by the man I had come to challenge.

But after I'd waited more than half an hour, he still hadn't arrived, and the car dealer suggested we start without him.

I felt a little pang of disappointment. I had been primed for victory or defeat…but not for armistice. Still, Tiny Watrous would be in the game, and I consoled myself that I might very well strop my razor on his ample hide while waiting for the main action to begin.

We sat down and exchanged some of our dollars for chips.

A few glances were exchanged, and one or two eyebrows twitched, but there were no objections when I counted the full $100,000 onto the table and set up a neat row of $500 gray chips beside the reds, whites, and blues on the table before me. Rules of the table-stakes game prevent a player from buying the pot simply by having more money to risk than another player. He can raise only to the limit that an opponent is able to match, using the money or chips he has when the hand begins. If you need more, go get it after the hand ends and before the next begins.

Nonetheless, I could feel the covert measurings as we cut for deal.

Watrous won. He riffled, scattered, cut, riffled again, shuffled twice, handed the deck to me to cut, and announced that the game tonight would be seven-card stud—high only—if that was agreeable to all. It was, and we had already tossed in the ante for our first cards when J. J. Barlow arrived in a confusion of apologies and explanations.

A late customer and some late news.

And he had stopped to get some things out of his own safe-deposit box.

He turned a bland but cool-eyed stare on me. Would we give him time to buy a few chips—he glanced, not casually, at my line of grays—and get into this hand?

Silence and an offhand laugh from Tiny Watrous gave consent. The Red Board loser from Amarillo went looking for his third drink of the evening while Barlow counted out some of the things he'd found in his safe: The line of gray chips he bought just matched my own. And there was a bulge in the breast pocket of his coat that seemed familiar, too.

It's nice when everyone knows the same rules.

I nodded a greeting as he neatened up his stake, and our conversation began.

But at first we didn't really say much. Others at the table had come to play poker, too. We were all in the same game, and most of the preliminary hands were simply sociable, friendly moves intended to keep the party polite and interesting.

Barlow took about $700 from the Amarillo loser, backing an innocuous low pair against the Texan's possible straight and picking up another unexciting low card on the next round. He watched while the visiting fireman gradually hanged himself waiting for an inside jack that he needed to fill his hand.

It never came, of course, and they went into the final betting round with the loser trying to bluff and then throwing in his cards with a stagey groan when the banker finally showed three fives and two sixes against what everyone at the table already knew was a bobtail straight.

Barlow raked in the pot without comment. The lighting of the room kept some important parts of his face in shadow, but I thought I detected a hint of weariness around his mouth and in his motions.

Sounds from the loser were far easier to interpret. The anguish was horrendous; he called for still another bourbon and branch water, and we knew it would end shortly—the drinks and the financial drain would finally claim their due—but you could already see jaws clenching here and there around the table. A little stylized lamentation goes a long way. And the irritation was directed as much at Dr. Woodbury for having invited such a clown into the game as the offender himself.

I paid no attention and neither did Barlow. We had other things on our minds, and the very next hand gave us a chance to start saying a few of them in a way that was audible only between the two of us.

The deal had come to Barlow, and I stayed in the pot past the first round, pushing in $1,000 to back a concealed king-queen. He looked at the bet—sizable, perhaps, but not too unusual for this game—and met it, driving everyone else out of the pot and leaving us head to head.

My first open card was another queen; his was the ace of hearts.

I drummed my fingers for a moment, making sure I had his full attention, and then pushed $10,000 into the center of the table, a move that could have been roughly translated: *I had a long nap this afternoon and I'm feeling lucky tonight. How about you?*

Barlow looked at the money, looked at me, counted out twenty of the gray checks in a double stack of ten, played with them for a while, stroking and recounting, and then threw in his cards instead of meeting the bet: *Haven't been sleeping too well of late myself, and I feel like an amputated leg.*

I raked the pot over to my side of the table and kept my eyes on it, stacking and arranging the various denominations, while putting out feelers to test the emotional responses around me. With two exceptions, they returned only the echoes of astonished bemusement.

Something was going on…but what?

Even the compulsive loser from Amarillo found himself distracted, at least momentarily, from his own woes.

The exceptions were Barlow and Watrous, and I took an extra moment or two for a deeper probe into the fat man's unguarded consciousness.

But my first perception had been true.

His *wa* registered only the pure, timorous chill of helpless fear.

On another day, in another world, I might have pitied him, and in another life I might have felt compelled to try to heal the hurts and the heartsickness that had left him in such a condition. But this was not that day and not that world and not that life, and my only reaction in the here and now was to make a mental note to bet him into the wall the next time I caught him trying to bluff.

The deal passed to Pemberton, and my two down-cards were nothing, and I dropped out to watch Watrous and Woodbury haggle over a $400 pot that the doctor finally won on a sadly underplayed trio of tens.

Several more hands—two complete rounds of the table—passed before Barlow and I had another chance for serious discussion, and it came with me in the forced-bet trapping position just to the left of the dealer. This time I was holding jack-ten concealed with a nine of clubs showing and picked up another club, the six, on the next round, and Barlow decided it was time to take some of my money.

He had the king-seven of hearts showing and he offered $300 on the proposition that they were the visible evidence of a flush: *Guts, Preacher?*

I thought it over and tossed my garbage into the discard: *All the guts I need, friend. But very, very little stupidity.*

But it was catnip for the Amarillo loser. He met Barlow's $300, stayed to the final round, and finally pushed in his entire bankroll behind what absolutely had to be two pair—queens and jacks—with an ace kicker.

Barlow's inner sigh was almost audible as he uncovered the other two kowboys that had been his original hole cards, and cupped his hands possessively around the pot.

The visiting loser sat for a moment in silence and then began to swear, noisily but not expertly.

Woodbury put up with it, sharing our mutual disgust, for about sixty seconds and then rose abruptly to his feet. "Speak to you for a minute?" he said in an unmistakable tone of command. The loser followed him into an adjoining room trailing complaints that continued for a moment or two after he passed through the door and then stopped with the suddenness of a lightning bolt.

A minute or two—time enough for the thirsty to sip and the necessitous to visit the restroom—passed before the doctor returned to his chair. But he came back alone, and no one asked any questions.

The next hour or so was sleepy time again. Watrous rode a run of cards to the top of a $3,000 hill…and slid slowly to the bottom again as the laws of mathematics exerted their irresistible power.

Dr. Woodbury and the car dealer traded pots and insults, quibbling with great heat and good feeling over who should have stayed with what and for how many raises, while Pemberton played his usual grind game, winning an occasional medium-size pot and buying a succession of low ones on the first face card until I trapped him into a fair-size loss, just to keep him honest, and he had to begin the slow process all over again.

He did not tire.

He did not perspire.

I couldn't help wondering if there was anyone inside there at all.

And then came a hand that changed things. I had stayed for the third round of low betting, more for the sake of form than anything else, not too proud of the pair of sevens I was showing, but hoping for a third—or perhaps for a mate to the single ace that lay concealed on the bottom. But Barlow bumped the action with a bet of $1,000 to prove that the pair of jacks he was showing had friends and allies in the bushes: *Still in the game, Preacher?*

He was waiting for me to answer, and there was a moment when I was almost ready to let him have the pot. It wasn't much, aside from his bet, and I wasn't sure it was worth any real con-test…until he leaned back in the wheelchair and clasped his hands behind his head, eyes inspecting the ceiling in a gesture clearly intended to indicate that he just didn't care.

The hell he didn't!

I matched his $1,000 and bumped the price another twenty grays: *Still here, friend.*

The hands remained behind the head for a moment, but the eyes flicked toward me and he took a deep breath and leaned forward again. He matched my raise and we waited for the next cards. *Then let's boogie!*

Everyone else was out by then, of course, and no one seemed to have much to say on the verbal level as the dealer flipped an ace of clubs down in front of Barlow and sent the jack of hearts skimming across the table to me.

I almost laughed. Someone, somewhere, was playing a more interesting game than we were, and surely having more fun.

Barlow's face was a study in disgust, pondering the lost jack that should have been his. But he didn't know how much reason I had for similar feelings, and I certainly wasn't going to tell him. His pair was still best, and he put another $1,000 in play.

My nerve's still in good shape, Preacher. How's yours?

I matched him without hesitation: *Can't complain.*

The final two open cards landed on the table.

I caught seven of diamonds, giving me trips, and counted $5,000 into the pot: *Better let me have it, banker.*

Barlow's card was the king of hearts, no visible improvement, but he matched my $5,000 and raised another $5,000: *Not a chance.*

I waited a moment, to give the impression of hesitancy, and then put in $5,000 to see his raise and bump the action $5,000 more: *You're bluffing.*

He counted another twenty grays into the pot and sat back to wait for the final down-card: *The hell I am, my one-eyed friend.*

My down-card was an ace, and it turned a fighting hand into a dream situation. Barlow knew about my three sevens, but both of the aces were concealed. Unless there had been a miracle on his side of the table, the only question was how far I could milk it. I put another $5,000 into the pot just because it had been the last bet. And waited: *Up to you now, banker.*

Barlow studied the pot and studied his cards and studied mine and studied me and took a cool look at the chips he had left on the table. It came to about $70,000—a few thousand more than was sitting in front of me. He pushed the whole stake into the center: *Right back at you, son.*

It was a good move on his part, given the information he had available, and it was exactly the one I'd hoped he might make. But all the same I took a minute to run the whole set of possibilities through the mill again before making my own decision.

Two of the aces were in my hand and another had already gone into the discard, so there was no chance at all that he had paired the one he was holding. I had seen no other kings go down during the early rounds, so there was a bare possibility that he had one or more in the hole. Odds were against there being more than one, though, so that would make it two high pair for him at best unless there was a concealed jack. And that jack would have to be the last card he got, because the hands-behind-the-head gesture had told me that he didn't have one in the hole to begin with.

There was still a chance that he could beat me.

But not a good one.

Stack by stack, I lined up my entire table stake of grays, blues, reds, and whites beside his on the table. It left me about $11,000 short, and Barlow reached out to claim his extras, but I stopped him before he could touch the first stack.

"I'm going to raise," I said aloud.

There were immediate objections from everyone but Barlow. He knew what I meant and had, I think, been expecting it.

A few minutes after the last break in play, I had quietly removed the envelope containing the Prescott Helicopters property from my breast pocket and placed it on the table beside my chips. The envelope wasn't sealed, and I had printed the name Prescott on the face. I had seen Barlow glance at it several times. And since it was on the table, it could legitimately be considered a part of my betting resources in this game.

The banker's hand dipped inside his coat and came out with a filled-gold pen, which he handed across the table to me.

"Write a number on the envelope beside the name Prescott," he said.

"You know what's inside?"

"I think so."

"Then you say the number."

He looked at me narrowly, and I don't know what he saw, but it didn't seem to make him happy and he looked away.

"Two million," he said.

I wrote down the figure.

"Now write 'eleven thousand' below it."

I did that, too.

"Now your raise…"

I wrote "$100,000" under the other figures and put the pen down and pushed the marked envelope into the pot: *Back to you, sir.*

The room had gone entirely silent. Games at the Farewell Country Club had never been nickel-and-dime affairs, but they had never been like this, either. Breathing seemed to have been generally suspended.

Barlow had no chips left on the table, but like me he had made a few arrangements. He, too, had an envelope, and he opened it to disclose a sheaf of crisp currency. Quietly, he counted 200 thousand-dollar bills into the space beside his coffee cup, and put them in the pot: *I want that property, sir, and I mean to have it!*

I picked up the pen and wrote another "$100,000" below the first one. A call, not a raise: *That's enough for now. Let's see what made you so confident.*

I think almost everyone had expected me to raise again, but no one spoke and Barlow's hand was steady as he turned over his final down-card to expose the third jack.

He had caught trips the final round, and I had to admire the control it must have taken for him to avoid a show of elation after bluffing all the way behind a pair in the face of my exposed trio. The arrival of that final jack must have looked like a message from the Almighty.

It was good enough to beat my three sevens.

But not nearly enough against a full house.

I used the edge of a card to flip the two aces face up, and they leaned neatly beside the sevens.

There was a collective sigh.

"Jesus…" said Tiny Watrous.

"…Christ!" said Dr. Woodbury.

Barlow's face was rain-washed marble as I raked chips, cash, and marker deed into the open space before me. But he did not speak.

We were finally getting down to business.

A SERMON
(CONCLUDED)

God set the game in motion; God made the rules.

He showed us the choices and He left us to make the decisions for ourselves. Would you look upon the face of your judge and jury and prosecutor and executioner... and defender?

Try a mirror.

THIRTY

But Barlow needed kid-glove treatment for the next hour or so.

Pro is pro and amateur is amateur; he was one of the most talented nonprofessionals I'd come across in a long time, and the game he played, at his best, was so much better than anything else I'd seen in those parts that his main problem over the years must have been not to trim them too close to the hide or too regularly. This was a man who had the makin's.

There were flaws, however, and I'd spotted one on my first night in Farewell.

Barlow played poker like a banker.

He knew the game and he knew the mathematics and he knew the men he was playing against. He also understood the social restraints; he wanted to go on living in the town. But there was still a tendency to go for that last dollar. That last cent. Trimming Watrous that first night, he had not only decoyed his friend and sometime partner into an expensive miscalculation—as I had just done with the two concealed aces—but had taken it to an extreme that I wouldn't have considered, even though I didn't expect to see these people again once my business in Farewell was concluded.

Trimming a man is one thing; it's part of the game. Humiliating him for the sake of a few extra dollars is something else, and it told me things about Barlow, things about well-concealed pride and arrogance and basic voracity, that might otherwise have passed unnoticed in a lifetime.

And now there was more than greed and hubris on the line.

He had come so close to the Prescott property, to the final bit of paper that could save his reputation and his friends and his town and the whole life he had built for himself here, that he had been mentally rehearsing the telephone calls he would make to turn the Good Hope package into quiet cash.

But once again the parcel had slipped just out of reach. Now he was possessed—judgment impaired and fingers avid. His face was composed and his breathing was regular and there were no surface tremors to tell the story, but the heat of his *wa* filled the room around us and his challenges to further combat on the table were too many and too directly aimed at me to be anything but an incoherent howl of rage and frustration.

I waited patiently for him to regain the control that would allow our dialogue to continue.

We were down to just five players now. The car dealer, astonished by the sums that had suddenly started changing hands in this quiet game—and, I suspect, a trifle horrified by the apparent nonchalance with which Barlow and I seemed to make our bets—had decided it was past his bedtime.

Nobody tried to dissuade him. But nobody else moved to leave.

It took only a moment or two after the big hand to settle the mechanics; the supply of gray chips (the club seemed to have no higher denominations) was running low, and I sold Barlow about $100,000 worth, plus an assortment of flag colors to enable play to proceed, quietly concealing the tiny glow of relief that I would not, at least for the moment, have to dip again into the million-dollar bankroll that Dee Tee Price had so kindly provided.

Two people recently had told me that I have some nice friends, and both were right. The kind who will lend you a million dollars for a poker game, in particular, are not easy to find.

But the million had been a necessity. My only real concern about going into tonight's game had been the possibility that I might have to face J. J. Barlow without the resources to meet his basic money-power. To play for the kind of stakes I wanted, I had to come in with something really substantial in the way of a bankroll, and Dee Tee's satchel of cash was just the right edge for the evening.

Barlow's resources were still far greater, of course. No contest there. But poker players do not write each other checks; markers must be paid before you leave the table, and the cash he had brought with him was about what I'd expected when I was sure he knew what I was after and what I would offer in the game.

The $100,000 he had just laid out for chips was the last of his immediate cash. But, like me, he had other assets on the table—five envelopes bearing the return address of the Llano Escondido Exploitation and Development Company.

They were the game I had come to hunt.

I waited it out.

The doctor, Watrous, and Pemberton all played their usual games. Competent but not exciting. They knew Barlow and I had some unfinished business, but it didn't interfere with what they were doing and, in fact, gave it a certain added cachet.

Barlow's early heat gradually cooled. I could feel it happening when I reached out from the center of myself to touch his *wa*, and I could see it on the table as he slowly returned to the conservative betting pattern that was his base. He and Pemberton played a little chicken game with each other, buying the pot on the first round by a sudden high bet on the two closed cards and "accidentally" exposing them later to show that they had bluffed.

Pemberton finally bit. Sitting in the trapping position to the left of the dealer, he met Barlow's $500 raise with one of his own, followed it to a showdown...and lost about $5,000 backing a heart flush against what turned out to be a full house.

But it didn't stop him from buying the next pot, and another hour passed before Barlow and I were able to resume our conversation.

It finally happened on a hand where Barlow, Woodbury, and I were still in on the third round, with jack-queen showing in front of Barlow, a low pair for the doctor and two low clubs for me. I had a third club in the hole, and it was worth a few hundred to find out if I could catch two more. But Barlow's raise was $5,000.

The doctor was out at once, and Barlow sat waiting for me to make up my mind: *My luck's back, Preacher. I'm feeling better, and I'm winning.*

I looked at Barlow's open cards and knew he had at least a second jack in the hole—more likely a pair of jacks or queens. His *wa* had cooled to room temperature and he was thinking again. My clubs were just not good enough: *Maybe so. But luck's not enough to trap me into a hand like this.*

I folded, and reached down for the money satchel that had been waiting within touch of my toe since the game began. Time for it to make an entrance.

And it did. We live in a world of paper and plastic. Credit cards and checks move large sums of money around in a kind of never-never land that makes it all seem unreal. So the emergence of actual cash can come as a shock.

Conversation around the table lagged, lost direction, and then came to a full stop as I set out the nine paper-bound stacks that represented the rest of the one million dollars, arranging them in quiet concert with the rest of the cash that now over-flowed into the empty space at my side where the car dealer had been sitting.

"Uh, I really don't think…" Dr. Woodbury began, staring at the stake.

But Barlow was neither surprised nor impressed, and he stopped the doctor in midsentence with a small gesture of negation. "No problem," he said. "The Preacher and I understand each other."

I finished arranging the stacks of money and looked at the man in the wheelchair, and what he had said was true. All side issues and personal differences notwithstanding, J. J. Barlow and I understood each other right well. I wished I had known him in another time and another place. But this was here and now, and wishing has no place at a poker table.

The game resumed, and gradually, I think, the others forgot the sums now waiting on the table.

But I didn't.

And neither did Barlow.

And finally the time came to bring them into play. I had been waiting for just the right hand, and now it arrived. My hole cards were treys, paired. Barlow was in the forced-opening position, and he had started things moving with a pot-buying bet of $500. Watrous had stayed…and I pushed $5,000 into the center of the table and waited: *Luck still in, banker? Then how about your nerve?*

Barlow looked at my bet and thought it over for just a moment, and then pushed in $4,500 to match me: *My luck and nerve are just fine, Preacher. Never better!*

Watrous swore, folded, and turned his eyes away from the game. He knew what was going to happen now, and he wanted to watch so badly that he just couldn't do it.

Pemberton, dealing, threw Barlow the king of clubs. I caught the three of hearts. He bet another $5,000: *That is not much of a card, Preacher.*

I bumped him $100,000: *I liked it well enough.*

He met my raise and sat back to wait: *You know best, of course.*

I reached out to touch his *wa* again, but there was a cool shielding now, an ice-chilled wall of reserve that would not be penetrated. What a pro he would have made. I felt a pang of regret...and drove it to extinction.

Pemberton glanced between the two of us, and for the first time I thought I detected a trace of emotion. There was a tiny bead of perspiration on the very peak of his forehead. I wondered at it, then forced my attention back to the table.

Barlow's fourth card was the ten of spades.

Mine was king of diamonds.

He took a deep breath, brought out the gold-filled pen again, wrote "$2,000,000" on the topmost Llano Escondido envelope, and looked at me for confirmation.

But I shook my head.

According to Mose Thieroux, the banker had only options on most of the parcels. The only one he had bought outright was the Thieroux land. It alone was worth the figure Barlow had written. The rest were nothing much, so long as they weren't tied to the Prescott property.

"One million for all the options," I said. "And two million for the Thieroux piece."

For a moment, he was going to argue, but a look at my face must have told him it was no use.

I watched as he crossed out the million-dollar figure and replaced it with "$250,000" on the top envelope, repeated the figure on the next three, and then wrote "$2,000,000" on the bottom envelope.

Fair enough.

I nodded, and he pushed all four of the $250,000 parcels into the betting.

Your hand still look good to you, Preacher?

I glanced down at my cards and decided it did. I had a fair idea of what he was holding now, and his chance of improving was roughly as good as mine. But I had one advantage, and it came down to something Cherokee Bill Bear said to me years ago, a moment or two before he broke me on what had looked like a good even chance.

"I got 'em," he had said, "and you got 'em to git."

And that was the situation facing J. J. Barlow now, because I absolutely did not believe that he had two more tens at the bottom of his hand. Or another king, either.

I counted one million in cash onto the table beside his envelopes, and Pemberton dealt the next two cards.

Barlow got the eight of clubs.

I got the nine of diamonds.

He pushed in the envelope with the "$2,000,000" and waited to see what I would do: *This is the big one, friend. No more hands after this unless you pull out right now. Still game?*

That eight simply couldn't have been any more help to him than the nine was to me. There were still two cards to come. But nothing had changed. This was still poker.

I picked up the Prescott envelope and laid it carefully alongside Barlow's bet: *Game as I'll ever be. So let's find out.*

We were both all in now. Not a dollar and not a scrap of paper remaining beside either of us. So there was no point in keeping the hole cards concealed. Barlow flipped his to reveal the queen-jack combination I'd been expecting. I showed the table the threes that made a trio with their exposed brother.

And Pemberton, his forehead now—incredibly—agleam with perspiration, dealt the cards.

Barlow got a king.

I got an ace, and I could almost hear the snap of teeth as his jaw clamped shut.

"All right," he said aloud, with no audible trace of the pressure he must have been feeling, "let's see the final cards, then."

Pemberton, perhaps flustered or perhaps from habit, dealt them facedown as he would do in completing a normal hand. I turned mine to show the five of diamonds. No improvement, but I still had the trio of threes.

Barlow could beat me with an ace, a nine, or even a king.

He hesitated for a moment, his hand on the card, and then turned it faceup in the middle of the table beside the huge pot.

It was the queen of spades...

Barlow's reaction was minimal—a small, cold smile and a shake of the head. His eye caught mine for a moment, but there was no hint of despair or even of sadness. A game, he seemed to say, is only a game. Perhaps there will be others.

He was one hell of a man. It must have cost him a lot.

And he paid without a murmur.

But Tiny Watrous simply didn't have the price. The final, losing card was still on the table and no one seemed to have recovered sufficiently to pick it up or to start the task of raking away the money, chips, and envelope when the fat man told us what the final hand had meant to him.

His mouth opened and a small apologetic sound emerged. Not a word, exactly, but an unmistakable cry for help. His hand leaped spasmodically to the center of his chest, and his head turned beseechingly toward the old friend and physician beside him at the table. But before Woodbury could react, Watrous's eyes closed and the huge body rolled out of the chair to land with a crash beside the table where his world had just come to an end.

A BENEDICTION

The peace of God, which passeth all understanding…

THIRTY-ONE

r. Woodbury did his best.

Pemberton went to get a medical kit from the trunk of the doctor's car while I helped rip the coat and shirt away from the chest to reveal the deep scarring of major surgery. There was no pulse and no heartbeat, and I think Woodbury knew what had happened was beyond repairing, but he told me to call for an ambulance while he started cardiopulmonary resuscitation.

Looking for the phone, I got a surprise.

The Red Board loser from Amarillo was asleep in the lounge, a half-empty glass of something dark beside his chair.

I wondered, fleetingly, what he was doing there.

Remembering that Woodbury had introduced him as a brother physician, however, I detoured on my way back from the phone to tap his shoulder. I made it gentle. If he was drunk enough to need a major effort, he was too drunk to help. But his eyes popped open at once and came to sharp focus on my face.

"Wha...?"

"Are you really a doctor?" I asked.

He blinked and considered telling me it was none of my damn business. But I think something in my face told him that wouldn't be a good idea. So he didn't.

"Cardiology," he said, squirming to sit up. "I just play poker sometimes to...because..." He lost the thread and I couldn't help him find it.

"Dr. Woodbury could use some help," I said. "In the card room."

He blinked again, and I could feel him pulling parts of himself back from a great distance, but after a moment he heaved himself out of the chair and moved without a word in the right direction.

It was too late, though, and I think it had been so from the first. Tiny Watrous's body, naked to the waist, lay on the floor, and Dr. Woodbury was no longer astride it.

A long-nosed syringe—probably a heart-injectable stimulant—lay empty and expended on the table beside the fat man's abandoned playthings.

"Nothing at all?" said the poker-losing heart specialist from Texas.

Woodbury shook his head. "Nothing," he said. "Not even a single-beat reaction. I think something important must have ripped loose in there."

"Mind if I...?"

"God, no! You're the chest cutter, not me. But I was there five years ago when they did the bypass."

The younger man nodded absently, looking at the scarred chest, but reached out to accept the stethoscope Woodbury offered and then knelt beside Watrous's immense form.

"What happened?" he demanded.

Woodbury took a deep breath and looked at the rest of us, wanting someone else to explain. But no one spoke.

"I don't know, exactly," he said. "The game was almost over—which reminds me, what are you doing here, anyway, Tom? I thought you were going to take a cab back to town."

"I was." The voice was abstracted, its owner concentrating on the work at hand. "But I went to the bar first and had a drink. And another. And I think I fell asleep." He paused for a moment and looked up at his friend. "I owe you an apology, Bow," he said. "I let you bring me here in all good faith, and I should have warned you that sometimes I don't handle myself very well when I gamble. It's a problem of mine..."

He was talking to the other doctor, but his eyes were on me and he wanted to say something more. Woodbury was embarrassed, and cut him off in midsentence.

"We'll forget it," he said. "As I was telling you, the game was almost over. But a lot of money had changed hands in the final pot—millions! I don't know exactly what was going on, but when the hand was over, Tiny seemed to take it personally. As though it was his own money."

Pemberton cleared his throat to break in. "It was," he said. "Part of what was lost here was Tiny's. But it was my fault, Bow. My fault that it happened. That I let it..."

The doctor looked at the cadaverous attorney as though he had just lost his mind. "How...?"

"I am—was—Tiny's lawyer," Pemberton said. "And J. J. Barlow's. And Marilyn Prescott's, too, as of this morning. But not his..."

He nodded in my direction, and the doctor followed his glance for a moment, but then turned back to hear the rest.

"...and I tried to play God," Pemberton continued. "J. J. and Tiny were in a land deal, a big one, here in the county. I knew about it, and I realized before I took on Mrs. Prescott as a client today that there could be a conflict of interest. The pair of them wanted Pres Prescott's land. But I thought I could keep the two things separate. Work to the advantage of both sides."

Pemberton looked at me, but I had no comfort to offer.

I knew his intentions had been good. But I had also known, or suspected, that he would do exactly what he had done. And I had used the knowledge.

"I told J. J. about the Prescott Helicopters sale," he said. "I didn't know until we got here tonight that you were planning to use it in the game. But J. J. must have known..."

His voice trailed off as he looked around the room, discovering something I had noticed when I returned from the telephone.

J. J. Barlow was gone.

"Why the hell would he leave?" Dr. Bowering demanded. "Tiny Watrous was his best friend, and he was lying here on the floor..."

I thought I knew. But I kept my mouth shut and turned to look at the table. The money and chips were just where they had been when Watrous collapsed, but the envelopes containing real-estate documents were stacked neatly aside, bound by a single rubber band. Covering them was yet another envelope, smaller, with the return imprint of the Citizens National Bank of Farewell in its corner.

It appeared to be sealed, and a single name—Preacher—was written on its face in Barlow's hand.

"He couldn't stay," Pemberton said when the silence following the doctor's words became too heavy. "J. J. Barlow is a man with perfect manners. He wouldn't want to be around after a party's over."

The lawyer's glance was cool and sure. He had reached the same conclusion as I—and was going to do the same thing about it.

But the doctor didn't understand.

"I'd like to know," he said, "just exactly what in hell has been going on here tonight. And I would like to know about it right now, if you please."

Pemberton drew breath to explain, but was interrupted before he could say the first word.

"It's him!" the doctor from Amarillo said. "He's the one. I tried to tell you before, Bow, but you wouldn't listen to me. Well, maybe you'll listen now."

No one seemed to know how to reply.

It was as though there were two men crouching there beside Tiny Watrous's body—one of them the sure and scientific cardiologist who had wanted to save the big man's life, the other a self-flagellating hysteric who could emerge when the button "poker" was pushed.

It was the hysteric who continued: "This is the Preacher, and people think he's honest because he tells them he's a professional gambler before they start to play. But don't let the nickname or the black suit fool you. This man is death. This man is the devil! People come apart—people die—around him. By God, do you think this man here is the first...?"

I stood still and let him have his say, partly because I understood that he had to get the words out one way or the other, and also because he was too close to the truth as I know it to bother splitting hairs.

He wasn't saying anything I hadn't heard before.

Or said before, to the mirror.

"When we were introduced tonight, I pretended not to know him," the Texan went on, "and it was wrong of me. I know that. But the minute I saw him I knew something was going to go wrong. It always does. Only it never seems to go wrong for him. I've played against him in Vegas, Reno—lots of places. And in all those games do you know how many times I have beaten him? Never. Not even once. No one has ever seen him lose. Not one time. And don't try to tell me it's because he's so good at the game or I'm so bad. There's something wrong with a man who wins all the time!"

Myths grow like bindweed around anyone who learns to play the game of poker well enough to make his living at it, and myth is, by definition, a compound of lies and exaggeration. But this was a whopper of purest ray serene. Despite the circumstances, I found myself hard put to suppress a laugh.

Any poker player can get broke. And I do. Regularly.

Twice in the past year I had been cleaned out by rank amateurs who were having a good run of cards and playing them better than they ever had, or ever would again, in their lives. Such reverses are a predictable hazard of the business—one that is beginning to be recognized even by the Supreme Court and the Internal Revenue Service—and they happen to the very best.

And anyway, I'm not the very best. Except on certain nights...

"You invited him here"—the Texan was raving now, actually shaking a finger at Dr. Woodbury—"and when I finally spoke up to warn you, suddenly I was in the wrong and a sore loser and had had too much to drink and ought to go back to town. Well, how do you feel about it now? Now that...this...has finally happened?"

The doctor's face was reddening with rage, and I could feel the heat of it rising in him, but the answer came instead from the lawyer standing beside me.

"We think," Pemberton said in cadenced tones that contrasted sharply with the word-flood we'd heard from the Texan, "that you are a sore loser and you've had too much to drink and you ought to go back to town."

Woodbury's sudden flare of anger was back under control now, and he continued the reply. "This man came to Farewell at the invitation of someone all of us know and trust and respect," he said. "He told us the truth about his profession from the first, and he behaved decently and he was good company. He plays poker for a living, and he wins at the game. Of course he does. No one but a fool continues to play when he can't...or won't let himself...win."

The last sentence had been carefully aimed and fired for effect, and it hit dead center.

The Texan's *wa* winced away from the blow and cooled suddenly to room temperature and below, while his mouth opened to reply and then closed on the words that had been jostling for release.

We stood in silence, waiting for the ambulance, but it didn't come for a while.

I occupied the time by sorting the stacks of currency and arranging them tidily in the attaché case. There was a little room left after I was done, and I used it for the packet of deeds, liens, and sales agreements. I wondered if the bank messenger was anxious about the money. Probably not. Despite his obvious willingness to kill to protect it while it was in his care, it wasn't his and he was probably sleeping the sleep of the just, secure in the knowledge that it was someone else's responsibility for the moment.

I counted the cash end of my winnings and made out a deposit slip for my own bank in California.

The messenger would be going home a bit heavier than he had come and, the Texas loser's suspicions notwithstanding, I was considerably relieved to know things had turned out that way. This hadn't felt like a losing night for me, and it hadn't turned out to be one, either. But Dee Tee had loaned me the million—hadn't bought a part of my action—and if I'd wound up with the shorts I'd have had the job of finding some way to pay him back. Dee Tee is a friend, not a contributor.

Tiny Watrous's death was a sorry commentary on the value too many people place on money.

It is not worth dying for.

But reality is in there, too. Having money can free you to do things you enjoy most, put you in a position to be helpful to friends, and even cause some people to listen to your ideas who might otherwise prove impervious to all logic and reason.

Its lack has never made anyone happy yet.

And I was still solacing myself with such thoughts—using them to build a barrier against the nagging suspicion that the

Texas loser just might have been right about a few points—when the telephone rang in the lounge and the overnight waiter went to answer it.

He entered the card room a moment later and spoke quietly to Dr. Woodbury.

The doctor's face went very still.

"Thank you," he said. The waiter left the room and the doctor turned to face us.

"That was the hospital," he said. "They called to tell us that the ambulance has been delayed. There's an accident blocking the access road to the club. Someone missed the turn where the road joins the highway. Ran into a power pole and the wires touched off the...gas tank. It set everything afire."

He paused, and his face was a decade older in as many seconds. "They...said it was a Rolls Corniche..."

We got there as quickly as we could, of course, but there was nothing to be done.

The ambulance that had been dispatched for Tiny Watrous was still on the other side of the barrier, waiting for crews from the electric company to arrive and cut off the high-voltage current so that the raffle of power lines could be moved from the roadway.

But the Rolls's impact had skewed it free of the tangle, and it lay on its right side, turned 180 degrees from the roadway. County fire crews were on the scene and had managed to reach the car on foot.

It was dangerous for them to work in the vicinity of the writhing, sparking power lines. But they had somehow managed to put out the fire and were now at work on the left door of the car, using a specially built hydraulic jack to push the roof far enough away from the hood to allow them access to something that was wedged, blackened and hideous, in the driver's seat.

Something that had been a man.

A BENEDICTION
(CONTINUED)

Keep your hearts and minds in the knowledge and love of God, and of his Son, Jesus Christ our Lord...

THIRTY-TWO

Most of the night hours were gone by the time the various law enforcement agencies of eastern New Mexico were finally through with us, and even then there were still plenty of loose ends flying around.

Everyone wanted to get into the act.

You could hardly blame them. J. J. Barlow and Edward Watrous had been two of the best-known and most powerful figures in that town or that county or that vicinity of New Mexico. For them both to die on the same night—and after taking part in a poker game that was already taking on the patina of local legend—was better fare than the Farewell gossip mills had been offered for a long, long time.

Sheriff Frank Ybarra had "requested" that Pemberton, Dr. Woodbury, the Amarillo loser (whose real name, it seemed, was Thomas Alford Phipps, M.D.), and I join him at his headquarters for purposes of an "informal inquiry" into the evening's events. He provided a brace of patrol cars to make sure we got there with all deliberate speed, promising to bring all the personal cars and my rented one as soon as the roadblock was cleared. Pemberton and Woodbury bristled a bit; they were unused to taking orders from sheriffs or anyone else. But they complied—and it was just as well, as we discovered on arrival at the courthouse.

The word seemed to have gotten around pretty quickly.

Radio reporters from Tucumcari and Portales, a newspaper reporter and photographer from Farewell, and a television crew complete with live remote cameras and an on-air reporter from the station in Clovis were all waiting in the sheriff's parking compound to shout questions and demand a formal press conference as we filed into the building.

Ybarra stayed behind to block the way, promise information as available, and hold out the hope of an opportunity to interview the principals as "as soon as we are done with them."

I saw some of it on the air later, and it was a competent, nerve-soothing performance by someone who had done that sort of thing before. Ybarra's big-city experience came in handy in dozens of ways, and the smiling, low-key figure who appeared on those news reports was one who could have played the press like a cello anywhere in the country.

But the smiles disappeared once we were all inside, with no cameras turned in his direction.

"Will this take long, Frank?" Dr. Woodbury asked when we were all crowded into the elevator for the trip to the top floor.

Ybarra ignored the question.

I could feel his *wa*, and it was on fire.

"My questions will come last," he said. "There are a few other people who want a word with all of you before I begin."

This was true.

The elevator door opened to disclose a reception-booking area as crowded as the lot downstairs, and with far more pertinent questions waiting to be asked.

The coroner's office demanded precedence, citing the undeniable fact that both men had died suddenly of causes not yet determined. But Ybarra ruled in favor of a tall man from the district attorney's office, and Deke Pemberton followed him meekly into one of the two windowless interrogation rooms while Ybarra exercised a certain bleak tact in arranging the rest of us through the room so as to prevent a sub-rosa conference.

He wanted to compare the stories without pre-editing.

I waited it out with some show of patience. Poker is good training in that respect. It might even, I suppose, have been a good time for meditation and mantra, but some emotions must be experienced to the full if life is to be lived rather than merely observed, and the ones elbowing and jostling inside me were not to be put aside.

First, the guilt.

I had killed both of them as surely as if I had used a gun. No one had forced them to put themselves in a position where their lives might depend on a few real-estate fan-tans, and no one had forced them to buy cards in that poker game. It could even be argued, though less effectively, that the price they had put on their own lives was the same one they had put on Prescott's. But it made no difference. They had started the night alive and hopeful and seen life and hope evaporate before dawn, and it had happened because of me and because this was the only way that I could salvage something for the widow and children of a man who had died by their greed and arrogance.

I could live with that. But I didn't have to like it and I didn't have to like myself for having made the decision. The hell of it was, I guess, that Barlow and Watrous were basically decent men who had simply made a mistake and then compounded it in a way that fed upon itself, getting bigger and bigger until it had to consume them both. If they had acted in the beginning from greed, the things they had done in the end had been in an effort to make up for it, to save their town. The story was easy to understand because it is so familiar; each of us plays it out on his own scale sooner or later.

I had known Barlow and Watrous for less than a week, but I had liked them well enough to feel a personal loss.

If heightened awareness and a shortcut road to understanding of other people are the upside of poker, they are the downside, too.

And it hurts.

"Now you."

Ybarra's eyes were back to being the polished obsidian marbles I had seen at our first meeting, and his face said less than nothing as he motioned for me to follow him to one of the rooms located off the main bull pen, where two equally unreadable men waited. In that brief moment, I ventured a tentative probe in the direction of the sheriff's *wa,* but it touched only the cold solidity of a stone wall, and there was no time to search for an opening.

He ushered me into the room, stepped back, and closed the door.

"My name is Hince," the taller man said. "Jack Hince. I'm from the district attorney's office. This is Joe Cheli. He works for the coroner."

A thickset man whose eyes seemed permanently shadowed by heavy black brows nodded toward the only empty chair in the room, and I sat down in it.

Nobody offered to shake hands.

"Your full name?" Hince said.

I told him, directing the words toward Cheli, who appeared to be taking notes on a ruled yellow legal pad. Cheli spelled it back to me—incorrectly—and there was a moment of misunderstanding while we got it wrong a second time, and then got it right.

"But they call you Preacher," Hince said.

I said that was true, and they began a cross-tag game of interrogation about the events of the night and early morning, ranging backward and forward in time in a way that would have been impossibly confusing if I had been telling anything but the truth.

They were good at it; this was obviously an act they'd polished over a period of time, and under other circumstances I might actually have enjoyed the performance.

But it was late and I was tired and the words, "I want a lawyer," which would have brought the whole thing to a sudden halt, were almost out of my mouth before I realized that there had been a curious omission—a subject avoided—in the barrage of questioning.

At no time had either man mentioned the actual amounts of money that changed hands during the game.

I changed my mind and stifled my rising irritation and began paying closer attention to the world around me. Thinking back, I realized that the inquiries had actually covered the poker game. But lightly. The two interrogators had asked what time it was when the game started and when it ended, and they had wanted to know who had won and who had lost. But they simply hadn't seemed interested in the sums involved.

Hince and Cheli were no fools. Poker might be illegal in the state of New Mexico, and the deaths of two players—one of them during the forbidden event and the other immediately afterward—might form the technical basis for manslaughter charges against all participants. But they must certainly know better than to imagine that any such charges would ever be filed. The main effort, therefore, would be to establish the causes of death: Did the merchant die of shock because of the amount he had lost? Or won? Were the banker's losses sufficient to drive him to suicide?

And had the black-suited tinhorn cheated them?

But no such questions had been asked, which left only two possibilities: Either they had been told to avoid the subject, or it had never occurred to them because they knew the kind of stakes that were usual for the country-club game and simply assumed that this session had been the same.

I wondered which was true. But it didn't seem the time to ask.

The questioning continued, moving relentlessly back and forth across the same tired ground, with Cheli scribbling furiously on his tablet and Hince, I discovered through some not-too-careful observation, surreptitiously turning a hidden tape recorder off and on by tapping a floor button with his toe. The machine was either an expensive model or in poor repair: It had a low-frequency whirr that was clearly audible in the confined space. More than two hours passed in this minor mental exercise before Hince gave his recorder button a final tap and said, "Thank you very much. That will be all for now."

I stood up to leave.

"Oh, by the way," Hince said, "we'd like you to stay in town for a while."

"For how long a while?" I asked.

"We'll let you know."

Someone had been watching too many cut-rate television movies. Until now I had assumed I was dealing with competent adults doing their jobs. Perhaps I had been wrong. I turned back to face Hince and his beetle-browed teammate, being careful to keep my face in neutral and my diction clear.

"I assume, then," I said, "that I am under suspicion of having committed a crime here?"

"Uh...no..."

"Then I'll leave when it suits me."

"I wouldn't do that."

I took a deep breath and was about to suggest that Hince pick up the telephone from the table where we had been sitting and call his boss, when the door opened behind me and Ybarra's voice cut me off.

"That's enough, Preacher," he said. "Leave 'em be."

I swiveled and sent a grin at him.

"Why, hello there, sheriff," I said. "Welcome to *Sesame Street.*
I was wondering if you might be listening on the room tap."

Ybarra didn't seem to see the joke.

"All I said," Hince began, "was for him to—"

"You shut up," Ybarra amputated the rest of the complaint
with a single earth-scorching glare.

"And you," he said, turning the glare in my direction, "come
with me."

The money and real-estate documents from the poker game were
spread out neatly on Ybarra's desk beside the bank attaché case
when we entered his office.

I made a quick eyeball count of the various piles while he
closed the door and moved to his usual station by the window.

It all seemed to be there.

"Satisfied?" the sheriff asked.

"Looks right," I told him. "But I don't know any exact numbers for the money. Didn't have time to do much besides a snap-tally. And we left a lot of gray chips behind."

"If you left them at the club," Ybarra said, "they stay there.
And I wasn't asking if you were satisfied that you hadn't been
robbed. And you damn well know I wasn't."

True.

"In that case," I said, "I suppose the answer is yes and no."

The obsidian eyes hated me and wanted to do something
about it, but all he did was sit still and wait for me to go on.

"I'm satisfied that Marilyn Prescott and her children will be
financially secure now," I said. "What she chooses to do about the
land deal Barlow and Watrous were putting together is her own
decision to make. I wouldn't influence it if I could. Either way,
they'll be protected. So as far as that goes, I guess the answer is
yes."

"And the no part?"

"That's for Pres Prescott himself. He's still dead, and the man who killed him is alive."

Ybarra sat still for a while as though waiting for me to say something more. So we stared at each other for a minute or two, and then he got up and motioned for me to come around to his side of the desk.

"Pack it up," he said.

I opened the attaché case, flattened it on the desktop, and began piling the money inside while the sheriff spoke his mind.

"There's something missing from there," he said. "I took it. And I'm going to keep it. Before he died, J. J. Barlow signed over all those deeds and options to Mrs. Prescott, not to you, so I suppose he knew what you were doing and who you were doing it for. But he didn't stop with that. When he was done signing, he wrote a little note."

I remembered the small, flat envelope snapped inside the rubber band with the real-estate papers.

"It would make nice reading for that pack of yahoos downstairs," Ybarra went on. "The TV reporters and the newspaper gossips. But they are never going to see it unless I have to produce it in court sometime. So if you want to know what it said, I think I better tell you now. It was addressed to you."

I finished packing the little satchel and snapped the locks and looked up at him. "Do I have to know what it said?"

"No."

"Should I know?"

"No."

"Does it have anything to do with who killed Pres Prescott?"

"No. And I wouldn't tell you about if it it did."

That was the single bit of business remaining between us, of course, and this seemed like as good a time as any to bring it up. "You know who it was?"

"If I do, it's none of your goddamn business. I told you that before, and nothing's changed."

"Your man still tailing Vollie Manion?"

Ybarra's close-pent rage nearly spilled over then, and the *wa*, no longer concealed, was like a tiny sun burning in the center of him.

"You meddling son of a bitch," he said. "Two of the best men I ever knew are dead because of you, and a lot of people in this town are going to wind up pickin' shit with the chickens because of you, and a situation that was bad is now worse because of you, and you stand there with your little bag of money and you don't feel a thing."

It wasn't true—not exactly—and a part of me wanted to tell him so because he was a good enough man, and I do not need the disapproval of good enough men.

But there was nothing I could say.

"I got you out of that room because Hince and Cheli were talking like the assholes they are and always have been, and because they were telling you to do something that is just the exact opposite of what I want. And for right now, by God, what I want is what is going to happen!"

He paused for breath and to recover control.

I waited.

"What you are going to do," he said after a moment, "is to take your bag and go downstairs and get into that little red car that my boys parked out back and drive it to the motel and get your things together and get the hell out of Farewell before dawn. What you did for the Prescotts may be right and it may be wrong, but it's done now and so's your business here.

"I don't want to see you in Farewell County again, Preacher. Not tomorrow. Not next week. Not next year. Not ever."

I finally got back to the motel about an hour before dawn and considered getting the bank messenger up to take care of Dee Tee's end of the cash. But it had been a long night and not the most pleasant I'd ever spent, and I didn't want to make it any longer, so I decided on a compromise: Get a little sleep, leave a wake-up call, turn over the money to him then…and spend to-morrow afternoon in Amarillo.

It seemed like a good plan.

I was actually feeling quite proud of it as I unlocked the door to my room and stepped inside to find Dana sitting in the arm-chair, her eyes wide and something wrong with the corner of her mouth. It was bleeding. But I never got a chance to ask her what had happened.

Haragi, tardy with fatigue, warned of a presence—not neces-sarily human—just behind the door.

But not in time to avoid the sudden blow just behind the ear that sent me spinning, helpless and mortified, into a well of blackness laced with lightning.

It had no bottom.

A BENEDICTION
(CONTINUED)

And the Blessing of God Almighty...

THIRTY-THREE

Consciousness returned in fragments. I was in a darkness relieved by occasional flashes of light, but it took a while for me to realize that the flashes were made of real sunlight and not neural explosions.

I kept drifting.

Movie heroes and television policemen and other indestructibles get their skulls hammered with alarming regularity and seldom seem to suffer even the minor annoyance of a headache. Real life is different. The brain is not itself sensitive to pain because its section of the nervous system contains only receptors, not sensors. But it is a tender bit of Jell-O, sloshing around in the enveloping dura mater and protected only by the very thinnest of bone siding. It is all too susceptible to bruising and has absolutely no powers of regeneration.

A rap on the rock that seems little more than a love tap can put you in a wheelchair for life; a hard right cross can deprive you of the ability to speak. And a thug's blackjack can kill you as readily as a knife or gun.

My own skull was already in a state of reduced resiliency as a result of its introduction to the towel-clad power of Vollie Manion's nightstick, and it took a minute or two for me to gather the various parts of myself that had been scattered by its most recent encounter with something harder than itself.

At first I thought I had gone blind. Monocularity is not a normal human condition; the body is made to see with two eyes, you get used to it early, and the person who loses one of his eyes never really becomes accustomed to the altered state of the world. He merely learns to live with it. So on awakening I spent several minutes in a frustrating and unprofitable endeavor to examine my surroundings with an eye that was not only sightless but in fact no longer in my head.

Bits and shards of memory finally put a stop to that, but I drifted away again on a sea of blackness before I was able to put the information to any good use, and when I drifted back again I had those light flashes to worry about.

I finally nailed them down as real light, breaking up real darkness, in a real world that was in real motion.

But it was a smaller world than I wanted. The world I had left behind was largely vertical and I could move around in it at will. This one was horizontal and I found my movements severely restricted. My hands, for instance, seemed to be secured behind me by something that was hard and bit into the wrists when I tried to touch my face. Moving my head presented a problem, too. It was heavier than I remembered and had a tendency to loll against my right shoulder.

I was lying on my side, I concluded, in a small space with my face pressed against something bulky but relatively soft, and my back was being jostled from time to time against something hard and unyielding. The occasional flashes were sunlight coming in through small gaps in the trunk's sealing grommet, and the fact that they came from above reminded me of mortality, and I discovered that my mind, once distracted, was difficult to steer.

It strayed now to the final year at Sewanee, and for a moment or two I was kneeling in the organ loft of All Saints Chapel, staring blindly at the kaleidoscope-fracture of light streaming through the rose window and wondering if I was really cut out for the ministry.

Kyrie eleison. Christe eleison. Kyrie eleison...

I realized belatedly that I had spoken aloud, and the sound of my own voice, amplified but peculiarly deadened in that constricted area, brought me back to the present and told me that the world in which I found myself was the trunk of an automobile, and the sometimes painful jostling was because the automobile was in motion.

"Sapped," I said, speaking aloud again without having decided to do so and marveling—in some isolated part of the brain separate from external time and reality—that I seemed to have so little control over the matter. "Sapped down and cuffed and dumped into a car trunk like a bundle of tire tools. What an idiot!"

I heard myself laughing and it was frightening, because it took a while to be sure that it was me and because it was the kind of sound that usually comes from behind the doors of the locked wards and because it all seemed to be getting farther and farther away...

"Okay, sleeping beauty. It's wake-up time!"

Light streamed into the world and my eye hurt and I turned my head away from it, but the pain was fleeting and after a moment I was able to look up at an oblique angle, and the first thing I saw was Vollie Manion.

It brought a surprising sense of relief. That was how it had been possible to ambush me, wait behind the door and strike me down as I came into the motel room. Vollie. I had never been able to feel his *wa*, never had any warning about anything he was going to do.

He was standing over me now, dimensions somehow distorted—perhaps by the angle at which I was viewing him—and there was something else different about him, too, something that did not fit. But I was given no chance to analyze. He reached into the trunk, lifted me out with a kind of appalling ease, and set me on my feet.

I fell down.

"Get up, Preacher," he said in a voice empty of passion, "or I'll kick your ribs right through your lung."

I looked down at him and knew at once what had changed. It was the eyes. They were different, wider and rounder, and they seemed to be laughing, a cold and soulless mirth that had no joy in it and no remorse and no sense of life at all. I rolled obediently onto my face and gathered my legs under me and managed to stagger to my feet, feeling a trifle foolish and apologetic at having made such a production of it.

"See there! I knowed you could do it."

He looked me up and down. "How we doin', there, old-timer," he said, reverting to the Gomer Pyle impression he'd done for me at our first meeting. "Little shaky on the pins, are we? Kindly twitchy? Well, now, I know what'll do wonders for that. Sho! Y'all just turn around here a minute and let me get them cuffs off."

My sense of relief was humiliating.

My mind was still filled with oatmeal, and somehow it had just skipped over the fact that my hands were manacled behind my back. That was why I'd had so much trouble getting up. I turned slowly, moving like a man twice my age. It was the dream again, the one where you are the only one in slow motion, and I could see the little man who is the real me running up and down on the sidelines in some unimaginably remote place, watching all this and wringing his hands and screaming for me to come to life and get moving before they let the lions loose.

But as soon as my back was toward the deputy, I had something else to think about.

Dana was about twenty feet away, sitting on the ground with her arms handcuffed around a cottonwood tree.

The cut on her mouth seemed to have stopped bleeding, but there was a deep bruise on her right cheek and chin, and her nose was swollen. The eyes she turned toward me contained no hope at all.

Even after I was on my feet again, my movements were too slow to suit him, and Vollie let me know about it in a forthright and direct manner, planting a foot in the middle of my back to send me sprawling beside the tree next to Dana. I tried to roll with the direction of the fall, but the tenderness behind my ear turned out to be more than the minor blackjack-lump I'd hoped. Contact with the solid earth triggered new lightning bolts at the edges of creation and brought a sudden darkening and constriction of my already limited field of vision.

"Hug the tree, Preacher."

I extended my arms around the bole, and he replaced the cuffs with that same joyless twitch of a smile he had shown me before.

I took a deep breath.

First things first.

Something was wrong with the world: It kept having earthquakes that only I was aware of, twitching and bucking at unexpected moments. I settled myself against the bark and concentrated on getting it to stop.

Vollie didn't seem to care what I did. He walked back to the car—a nondescript Volvo I had never seen before—and reached into the trunk cavity I had lately occupied.

I kept an eye on him while working in the back of my mind to stop the earth tremors, and in that way discovered the identity of the resilient mass I had been wedged against during the ride to this place.

It was a man I had never seen before and, watching closely, was sure I would never see again.

Vollie had manhandled the torso and head upright and aside to get at something he wanted in the bottom of the trunk, and the body reacted in that sack-of-clothes way that always means the same thing.

I wondered who he might have been and how he had come to such a pass...and abruptly recalled Frank Ybarra's mention of having borrowed an accomplished urban tracker from the Albuquerque police to keep an eye on his suspect deputy. Evidently Vollie was better at spotting a tail than his boss had thought.

Vollie finally managed to wrestle the corpse aside and uttered a grunt of effort as he tugged a pick and shovel free and leaned them against the car's back bumper. Then he released the torso and swore as it jammed against the side of the trunk lid instead of falling back into its initial position.

I looked over my left shoulder at Dana. She was almost outside my field of vision.

"Can you hear me?" I said in a voice I hoped was too soft for Vollie to hear.

For a moment there was no response, but then her head nodded. Slowly.

I fought my way around to take a closer look. Her mouth opened and closed and opened again like a goldfish's, but no sound emerged. I noticed bruises on her neck and shook my head with enough violence to fire off the lightnings again.

"Don't try to talk," I said.

Her movements subsided and her gaze drifted back to the ground and her eyelids sagged. I looked at Vollie Manion. He was armed and he was in good condition and he was in control of this situation.

And I decided then and there that he was dead.

"Okay, there, Preacher. That's enough sleeping on the job. Time for work!"

Some time had passed, but I didn't know how much. The sun seemed a little brighter. I turned my head slowly to look up at the deputy. He smiled in that new cold and feral way and fumbled with a key ring affixed to the retracting clip on his belt.

His image was no longer distorted and the world was still around me. No visual temblors. I had been doing mental sorting games with my toes and fingers and legs and arms, and I was in control of them once more. But I took care not to display the slightest agility or coordination as I got to my feet, keeping my gaze on the ground and my shoulders weary. Not much of a hole card to go on with. But all I was going to get, and all a competent player ought to need. I heaved myself more or less erect and let everything sag a bit to one side. But Manion didn't try to help. He kept his distance.

"Trouble with you city boys," he said, rattling the pick and shovel he'd retrieved from the car trunk, "is you don't never get enough exercise. So I thought of a fun thing we could do...sort of a limbering-up thing? Get the blood flowing, like they used to have me do in the army."

He dropped the tools to the ground and stepped away, drawing the service revolver from its holster and holding it loosely in his right hand.

"Pick 'em up," he said.

I bent, and made a point of losing my balance, falling to one knee as I followed his orders.

The shovel, I decided, would be about right for what I had in mind. It was the long-handled kind, with a sharp leaf-shaped blade.

"What I want you to do now," Vollie was saying, "is to dig me a trench. You ever do that kind of work before? Sho not...I forget. You a man of the cloth, and they don't never get no palm calluses, now, do they? Well, what I want is, I want you to take that pick and break up the ground, and then I want you to dig a trench there, two feet wide and, oh, six, seven feet long. Big enough for two."

The last words seemed to amuse him mightily, touching off another fit of that chilling, joyless laughter.

I dropped the shovel beside me on the ground, swung the pick clumsily aloft, and sank it into the solid red clay at my feet.

"They'll be looking for us by now," I said, standing in the beginning of the trench and laying aside the shovel for a moment to get out of my coat. "Ybarra will be after you. The Spences and Marilyn Prescott will be wondering what became of Dana and me."

Vollie Manion just grinned at him.

"And they'll get curious about him, too," I said, nodding in the direction of the car trunk.

He went on grinning.

The deputy was leaning lazily against another of the trees in the little grove where he had brought us, the pistol swinging easily at his side. If I'd had the shovel in my hand right then, he'd have been in range. But I didn't and he wasn't and he knew it.

"Killing us isn't going to get you off the hook," I said. "Ybarra knows you murdered Prescott. He can't prove it yet, but he knows, and that's why the man in the trunk was following you."

That got his interest a bit; he hadn't expected me to know the identity of my recent bunkmate. But it didn't seem to dent his confidence.

"You're wrong about that, Preacher," he said, the death's-head grin now a permanent fixture. "Killing you and the girl—when I'm done with her—is going to take me off the hook real good, thanks to that neat little bag of money you was carrying."

I stepped back into the hole and picked up the shovel, and I don't think my movements were any shakier or less certain than I had been making them ever since he unlocked the handcuffs, but he had shaken me all the same. What with one thing and another, I had forgotten all about the attaché case and its contents. The legal papers would be no use to him, though their disappearance would cause no end of trouble back in Farewell. But there was more than a million in cash, and even at present-day prices a million can buy a lot of running space for a man who knows how to use it.

"Turned in your rent-a-car," he said, swinging the revolver carelessly by its trigger guard. "Took the keys back to the motel desk when no one was out front. They'll use the credit card receipt you signed and check the mileage and sign you off and never know a thing."

I put down the shovel and used the pick to break up another square of sod, staggering a little with the weight. He watched me without notable interest.

"What'll happen," he said, "is they'll figure you and the girl took the money and lit a shuck for Vegas. I mean, why not? You bein' a gambler-man and her being a hooker."

My good eye went toward Dana and I saw her shoulders stiffen when she heard the word. She did not look up, but I filed away the information that she was at least alert and reactive. It could be important.

"Reckon you knew that, didn't you?" Vollie said, enjoying himself. "About her being a hustlin' broad and all? Sho, you'd never know, lookin' at her, would you? But I seen the telex record ol' Frank Ybarra got back from the Vegas PD when he messaged them. Workin' at a legitimate job nowadays, there in Vegas, but had a license for more'n a year out to the Ranch, that fancy whorehouse town they got over there, before that. Musta been a doozy. You ever go there, Preacher? I did once't. Didn't see her, but whooo-ee!"

He nodded with pleasurable memory.

Dana's head was up now, the eyes alive again. But she was looking at me, not at Vollie, whose back was toward her. I gave her a covert smile—and a wink of the false eye—when that side of my head was turned away from him. I wasn't sure she saw it, but it was the best I could do.

"The way it'll go down," he said when he was sure he'd sucked the last drop of entertainment from the last word, "is that they'll get to wondering in a while where you two have gone, but they'll just check the police over yonder and they'll say they haven't seen you, and they'll go to checking at Reno and Tahoe and maybe at that little town—what do they call it? Best Licks! Sho…they'll phone someone in Best Licks to see if you there, but that's all there'll be. For a while."

I thought about it, and he was wrong. The bank messenger would know something was wrong when I didn't hand Dee Tee's money back to him on schedule, and he would call Dee Tee and Dee Tee would tell Ybarra…and the search would begin in earnest right then.

But it would still be too late.

"The Albuquerque police will want to know what happened to their man," I said, hefting another spadeful of dirt. "They'll come looking."

"And they'll find him," Vollie said. "Right where he is now. Dead, in the trunk of his own car. Parked at the Albuquerque airport."

It was a good, workable plan—given the information at his disposal and the million in cash—and even with the early start the others would have, I decided he would have a good chance of being out of reach before they got things sorted out.

Somehow or other, I had to distract him long enough to make just one all-out move.

"No good, Mr. Deputy," I said, leaning into the shovel and grunting with the apparent effort. "Too many killings. First Prescott. Then Bobby Don. Then the rented cop from Albuquerque. Then us. That's four. Five, if your friend Boo—Commencement, you said his name was—if he dies, too. They'll call it mass murder and it will get a lot of TV news time and newspaper ink, and there won't be any place on earth far enough or lonely enough to hide you."

The thought seemed to sober him for a moment, and he spat on the ground before him and his gaze locked into the middle distance.

"Had to kill Prescott," he said. "Tunk him on the head and put him in that whirlybird. Didn't know I could fly one of those things, did you, Preacher? Learned in the army; they cross-train the door gunners in case of trouble. Flew him to that field where I'd left my car and set the collective and away he went."

The memory seemed to restore his good humor, and he turned another one of those arctic grins in my direction.

"Had to kill him for the same reason I got to kill you. For my daddy...I knew from the first why my daddy couldn't tell anybody I was his'n," the deputy said. "It was my ma. Dirt, she was. Not a bad woman and not mean. But common as New Mexico mud. Never did know how she got close enough to a man like J. J. Barlow to have me...but I knowed it was him from the first time I could read. When I saw his name on the checks that come every month for my board and keep."

I stopped work to look at him.

"The checks," I said. "That's how you knew J. J. Barlow was your father?"

"Sure thing. Why for would he send the money if it wasn't for that? And they kept coming even after Ma died. I knew one day he'd come around, see that I was like him and not like her, and own me. He would've, too, if he hadn't got all busy with the gawdam football player the way he did. So when Prescott got in Daddy's way—I knew about that land deal he was into, used to follow him around without him knowing—I got him. And then there was you..."

The hole was getting deep, and I was standing in it. Too deep to make the kind of play I needed to make. But the other end of the trench was too far from Vollie and his gun. Somehow or other I had to get out of there and stand in range with the shovel still in my hand and the gun not pointed directly at me.

I risked a glance at Dana.

She was still looking at me, not at Vollie, and I reached out to try to touch her *wa*. It was open, but in pain. The return echo showed me terror and rage and despair that were almost an overload for the senses. I tried to tell her what I wanted, but knew it was no use. That kind of communication takes years. A lifetime. And we'd had only a day...

"What about me?" I said.

Vollie's eyes refocused, turning in my direction, but the grin persisted.

"You killed my daddy," he said. "Killed him just as much as if you took a gun to his head. I got no reason to stay behind in Farewell, now he's gone. But I couldn't leave without putting things square. A man owes that to his daddy..."

It was time.

I wiped my forehead with an arm and hefted the shovel as if to move to the other end of the trench, stepping casually up to ground level to do it, and spat dryly into the broken earth.

"Bullshit," I said.

The pistol firmed in the deputy's hand, pointing at my belly, and I guessed the caliber at .44 or .45, more than enough to knock me down if it hit me there. But it was the last chance I would ever get.

"J. J. Barlow your daddy?" I said, shaping the tone for maximum insult. "Not in this world!"

Dana was fully alert now.

There was probably no chance at all that she'd received the message I'd been trying to send. But she knew I couldn't let him kill us without some kind of return effort, and if she understood that, she might see that this was the time and that her position—behind Vollie, where he would have to move something more than his head to see what was going on—was perhaps our sole remaining asset.

"Barlow was a sucker," I taunted. "A born loser! Him your daddy? Hell, boy, that crippled pussy couldn't have sired a ten-pound turd."

Something was finally happening behind those ice eyes; a tiny hell-flame of fury had been lighted, and I could see the forefinger beginning to whiten on the trigger of the revolver.

"Your daddy," I said, "was a—"

But I never had to finish the sentence.

The frustrated hopes and unrequited insults of a lifetime were boiling, moving the muscles of Vollie's hand toward the point of explosion, and his lungs were filling for a shout of rage when he was momentarily derailed, forced off track by a noise from behind him.

Dana had screamed.

It was sudden, loud, startling, soul-piercing...and exactly what I needed.

Vollie's nerves, stretched to the breaking point with the effort of control and shocked by the unexpected sound, spun him toward her without conscious volition.

The pistol fired a single shot that went wild, and I swung the shovel at his head, hearing the chirr of air resistance as it responded to every ounce of strength I could bring to bear. There was an instant of wild elation as it connected with a solid metallic clang of bone contact that sent him sprawling—wide open for the killing-stroke that would have to follow.

It was good.

Almost good enough.

But almost doesn't count in poker or anywhere else.

I moved toward the fallen man, raising the heavy tool aloft for the second blow...and knew that I was dead. The blade end of the shovel was no longer attached to the shaft. The first blow had broken the handle, and I was left clutching the shattered stump while Vollie Manion, safely out of range, recovered himself and sat up with the pistol still in his hand.

He leveled it.

Fired.

And the world collapsed upon itself like the flame of a quenched candle.

A BENEDICTION
(CONTINUED)

...the Father, the Son, and the Holy Ghost, be among you...

THIRTY-FOUR

It should have been final, and there was a sense of shock—not entirely unmixed with disappointment—when I felt myself slipping back into the world.

The alpine meadow was so green...

And the Enlightened One had been speaking.

But survival is the chief instinct of all successful species; humankind has always given it top priority. So when I began once more to perceive light and sound—and pain—I was careful to do what both instinct and training had taught me. I lay still.

Bang, you're dead...

If I was swimming back to the surface of conscious life again, I knew it could only mean that Vollie Manion thought I was out of the play. Dead, or so nearly so as to merit no further attention. And the only way I could remain in the world was to keep him thinking that way. I closed my eye and began a cautious damage-control survey.

Item: *My left leg is numb, and I don't think it's working.*

Item: *My left shoulder hurts. I think it's broken.*

Item: *The right side of my head is on fire.*

I snatched the data from the printer and scurried off to my cave to analyze it.

My memory of the moments just before the lights went out was surprisingly clear: Vollie had shot me in the head. But he had been firing from an unstable stand, with a handgun, and apparently the bullet hadn't quite taken me in the ten-ring where he'd been aiming. That, I decided, would account for the raw and burning sensation just above my right ear.

But if he'd thought enough of the first shot to decide I was dead, what had happened to my left arm and leg? I turned the question around and over and upside down, and finally decided that neither of these conditions came as the result of a bullet wound. Son of a bitch must have spent some time putting the boots to me.

All right, then.

Time to risk a peek around the perimeter.

Opening the eye once more and bringing it to focus, the first thing I saw was Dana, and it took as much control as I had just then to restrain a scream of rage. Kicking me evidently hadn't satisfied Vollie at all. Dana was still handcuffed to the tree, but she seemed to be unconscious now, and her face had been further damaged. There was a terrifying show of bright blood on her dress and on the bole of the tree beneath her. I forced myself to look away.

Where was Vollie?

Scanning, not daring to move my head, I found the rest of the landscape vacant—a small grove of cottonwood trees near a dry streambed, one car parked nearby. Nothing in motion.

But sight is only one of the senses, and it was my ears that offered the next bit of information. I heard a grunt of effort and the grating of metal against earth and gravel behind me. Evidently I had been away for less time than I had thought; Vollie was still at work on the grave I had begun.

I set a separate watch to tell me of any change in the deputy's work pace, and turned my main effort back to personal inventory. Exploring, tentatively at first and later with more assurance, I concluded without actual experiment that I could count on useful response from my right arm and right leg and left hand, with limited cooperation of the left arm. The hand could hold, but the arm would have trouble moving it.

All right. What else?

I had fallen facedown, twisted away from the direction of the gunshot, and the broken handle of the shovel was still in my right hand, covered by my torso. The active left hand, attached to the semi-useful arm was under my right cheek...which accounted for the relatively wide arc of vision available to the good eye.

Something else...

Something sharp...

An insignificant pain in the upper part of my right thigh, almost unnoticed among the welter of other sensations, finally gave me the information I needed. The shovel handle had not simply snapped from strain when I hit Vollie. It had fractured along its grain, ripping at the end nearest my hand, but splitting cleanly—and sharply—at the other end of the break.

The stub in my hand could become a club or a sharpened épée, at my option.

I had a weapon.

Almost good enough. But unless I wanted a repeat of the last fiasco, it was going to have to be a lot better than that. I forced my mind through yet another survey of possibilities.

There would be the element of surprise, surely. The discovery that I was neither dead nor totally incapacitated might work well in my favor. But it was a blunted tool; Vollie would be on his guard. Still not good enough. Something more. Something strong. Something to keep him in one spot for just a moment. Just long enough.

And then I touched the answer.

My left hand, pinned beneath my cheek, moved a fraction of an inch as I covertly exercised its muscles for future effort, and the forefinger tapped my eyelid. Sensation and inspiration were almost simultaneous.

I worked the prosthetic eye out of its socket and grasped it in my palm.

I relaxed. I waited...

The body wanted sleep and the soul wanted to go back to the meadow in the Alps, but the essence of self could not allow it.

Time passed. The winter sun grew warm on my back, and a drone of insect life formed a background for the steady *crunch-ugh* of Vollie's labors behind my back. I forced myself to count out the seconds and record the minutes in order to remain at full power for the final effort to come.

But the work went on for more than an hour.

He must have wanted a deep grave...

Then, at last, he was ready. I heard a clang as the pick and the broken-handled shovel landed outside the trench, and the sounds of effort as he climbed out.

My *ki* was at full emergency pitch; I evoked *saika tanden,* the state of nothingness that leaves the self ready for all eventualities, and *shinki kiitsu,* the unity of soul, mind, and body.

His hand touched my left shoulder.

Vollie had intended to roll me over, but full use of the weapon of surprise demanded that nothing go as he had planned. As soon as I was past the point of balance, I brought my good right leg into play and completed the turn in a whirl and, disregarding the sudden protest of pain from my left shoulder, brought that arm straight toward his face, opening the hand to let him see the detached eye.

His reaction was all that could be hoped.

The sudden shriek of horror that came from his throat was almost feminine, and he stood for an instant paralyzed and helpless before me.

Almost lazily, I relaxed the left hand to let the eye fall and grasped the part of him that was closest and most secure. My fingers closed around his gun belt, clamping and binding, while my right hand brought the sharp point of the shovel handle upright.

I could feel him recovering, tensing, ready to break free, and I knew his physical strength would be far too great to resist if he could bring it into play. I needed one more instant of power, and used the full strength of my lungs to provide it.

My *kiai* was full-chested.

And effective. For one final, necessary split second Vollie Manion's huge bulk and menace stood transfixed, immobilized and defenseless as my left and right hands worked at death.

The wooden point of the handle flew upward as the entrapping belt drew him down upon it, and I heard myself shouting once again in triumph as it lanced through the center seam of his uniform trousers, penetrating the crotch and ranging unimpeded upward through scrotum, bladder, and bowels.

Pain broke Vollie's trance.

The howl that burst from his throat was accompanied by a great blow that flattened me, breaking my hold on his belt. He staggered backward, gouting blood as the sharpened splinter of wood was drawn free, and shrieked again as he discovered what had been done to him. I braced for a counterstroke, but it did not come.

The point of the wooden spear had done even more damage than I had hoped or expected. Vollie's second step was his last; his knees folded under him then, and he collapsed a few feet out of my farthest range, twitching and spasming in an effort to move legs that would no longer obey his command. The wooden blade had either cut or bruised the spinal cord; his lower body was paralyzed.

The sounds he made told the agony of fear that is always more terrible than any physical suffering. It is the imminence of death, unmodulated by hope. Dante described the sound well; it is the lamentation of the uttermost circle of damnation.

But finally it ceased.

And for a while there was silence.

"Preacher...?"

The sound of his voice came as a surprise. I had thought he was unconscious. Or already dead.

"Can you hear me, Preacher?"

I turned my eye in his direction and got a surprise. I could hear his voice, and I could feel his *wa* as well. Something had come loose inside him; something more than flesh and bone and nerves. I touched the *wa* again and felt the heat.

"Preacher?"

"That's what they call me."

"Preacher, Father Jake told me about you. He told me he knew you a long time back. In school. In the seminary."

"He talks a lot."

"No...please!"

The words and the voice were gentle, but the *wa* was hot to the touch. Vollie Manion did not mean to die alone.

"You were a priest. He said so. That was true?"

I considered lying, but couldn't see any reason. "Yes. I was."

"I was raised Catholic. With Catholics, it's once a priest always a priest. You can resign, but you're still a priest and you can still do the things a priest does, only you're not supposed to without permission. And it's the same for the Episcopal priests, isn't it?"

"Well..."

"It's the same."

"Yes. I suppose so. But..."

"Then hear my confession."

"*No!*"

What in hell was he getting at? I could feel the heat of his *wa* increasing, feel the weight and determination of his spirit, and it was swollen with the will to do murder.

"You got to!"

"I can't do that, Vollie. You need a license issued by the bishop, and I turned mine in a long time ago."

"But this is an emergency. You're the only one here. No one else is going to come. You got to! Listen: 'Bless me, Father, for I have sinned—'"

"Stop it!"

"Bless me, Father, for I have sinned…"

There was no escape, and I knew it. The emergency was real, and—no matter what he might be planning in his heart—I could not refuse to hear the confession of a dying man.

"The Lord be in your heart," I said, picking up the ritual, "and upon your lips that you may truly and humbly confess your sins, in the name of the Father and of the Son and of the Holy Spirit. Amen."

And then I could see it.

Vollie's legs weren't working. He had lost a lot of blood and he was weak, but he had brought a folding knife out from some hiding place and it was in his hand and he was using his elbows to move himself slowly in my direction. The confession was intended to keep me too busy to notice what else was going on until it was too late.

I took a deep breath, forcing my mind back to the thing we had begun and slowly turning the splintered shovel handle in my hand to make it a club instead of a spear.

"I confess to Almighty God," Vollie said, "and to His church, and to you, Father, that I have sinned by my own fault in thought, word, and deed…"

His voice droned on and his movement continued, inching closer and closer as he made his way through a litany of sins. Some of the things he confessed were childish; some sounded impossible. And some I could see were both real and disgusting. But none of it was anything I hadn't heard before, one time or another, and I had plenty of time to make sure of his continued intentions.

The *wa* turned fire-hot as he came to the end:

"For these and all other sins which I cannot now remember, I am truly sorry. I pray God to have mercy on me. I firmly intend am…uh…amendment of life…" The voice stumbled there, and I think there was a bare nanosecond of true repentance before he went on. I hugged the knowledge to myself and hoped it was real.

"…and ask you for counsel, direction, and absolution."

I took a deep breath.

His *wa* was hot again and he was far too close.

"Our Lord Jesus Christ," I said, "who offered Himself to be sacrificed for us to the Father, and who conferred power on His church to forgive sins…"

My right hand closed hard around the splintered end of the handle, and I tensed the arm as it lay across my chest. The angle seemed almost right.

"The Lord has put away all your sins," I said, taking careful aim.

"Thanks be to God," he said, tensing to spring.

"Go in peace…"

The time had come, and I brought the clubbed handle down with crushing force on the spot I had selected—the nexus between the brow and the bridge of the nose, turning the energy slightly upward to be sure of sending the end of the bone deep into the brain.

Vollie's body arched upward, eyes open, mouth wide for a scream that never came. And then it collapsed.

The knife fell from his hand.

The breathing continued spasmodically for another moment or two, and then ceased. The *wa* winked out.

"…and pray for me, a sinner."

The next few hours were never very clear to me.

I kept slipping back and forth between the cottonwood grove and other places, all of them equally valid, all of them equally real. Time has a way of moving things around, and one of the things it moves can be you. I think part of it was simply nightmare and may have happened later. But I'll never be certain, and it probably doesn't matter anyway.

It happened where I was sitting.

That's all I know. And it is enough.

As soon as I was sure Vollie wasn't going to move again, I took the spring-loaded key ring from his belt and crawled over to Dana's cottonwood tree to unlock her handcuffs.

But none of the keys seemed to work.

Patience is not a normal part of my character; I've had to learn it in order to play poker, and the game keeps me in practice—which was just as well when I discovered, belatedly, that I had been trying four keys over and over again for several minutes.

I struggled to concentrate, and finally located the right one.

She collapsed against me as soon as her wrists were free, and I could not find her essence, felt no presence of the *wa*. It frightened me, but there was a kind of cold comfort in the thought that my receiving apparatus might not be in the very best of shape either, and I cradled her head in my arms to try to assess damage.

The few bruises and cuts I had noted earlier seemed a little more pronounced now, probably because they'd had time to grow and mature. The new injury, the one that had produced all the blood, seemed more important, and I decided it was the reason I could not find her *wa* now.

The right side of Dana's head was distorted and raw, swollen as though from internal pressure. It had stopped bleeding now and didn't seem to need cleaning. All I could do was hold her and try to keep the sun from her eyes.

We had to get out of there. She would die if we didn't.

My left leg wouldn't work, and the arm wasn't much better—something else seemed to have gone wrong during the final engagement with Vollie—but I began dragging us, inch by inch, toward the car.

Hot sun raised the familiar rain-forest stench, and the whine of insect life filled the audio gaps between incoming mortar rounds.

I tried to crawl from my hooch to the APC, but it was no-go.

I couldn't see far enough.

Something was covering my eyes.

I reached up a hand to push it away, and the hand found something wet and sticky where my face should have been and I pressed my mouth against the earth to keep from screaming and finally a little hole opened up on the left side where the color had showed red instead of flat blackness and I could see some kind of overgrown beetle standing still on the ground, looking at me.

Neither of us moved for a moment.

But then he leaped away, and I looked around for my armored escape vehicle, but something was wrong with it and it was on its side with smoke coming from its side...

When I looked again, the APC was all right—standing up on its wheels; no smoke—but it had turned into a civilian-painted Volvo I'd seen somewhere. I decided I could accept that and started to crawl toward it again, but Sara was with me and she was wounded.

What was Sara doing at Khe Sanh?

I took her in my arms and covered her with my body against the incoming fire and tried to sort things out, but they kept slipping around and suddenly we weren't at Khe Sanh anymore.

The National Guard was at the top of the hill and they were firing on us and that was how Sara had been hurt and I reached for the M16 to return their fire and maybe get a couple of the bastards, but it wasn't there.

And neither was Sara.

"Dana!"

Her eyes had opened and her breathing was rapid and shallow.

"Dana!"

But she didn't hear me and the eyes closed again and her right leg began to spasm, kicking at the earth and the sky, and there was nothing I could do and after a while the breathing eased again and I was finally able to drag us to the car.

But Vollie had taken the keys.

They weren't on the key ring or in the pockets of his trousers or his uniform shirt. I checked him two more times, just to be sure my mind wasn't tricking me again, and then gave up.

Jump the ignition?

I crawled, crabwise without the help of the bad leg, back to the car.

No go.

It was one of those double-safe ignitions that lock everything when you take the key out. Jumping it would get you zip. Besides, I decided, taking another look at the controls, it wouldn't have made much difference if the key had been in the slot and the engine running.

The Albuquerque cop had rented a stick shift—easy on the gas and positive on the control. But not much use to a man with only one leg in working order.

I pushed myself back out of the seat and onto the ground. The sun had moved to shine in Dana's face, and I put myself in the way to give some shade, and she made a little sound in the back of her throat that might have been a moan.

I told myself that might be a good sign.

And then nothing happened for a long time.

The medics were late.

Sara's head was bleeding again and I kept calling for someone to help her, but no one seemed to hear and the sun was going down and I knew the National Guard would be there, in the bush, waiting for a sunset attack. That was the pattern they'd started two days ago, and say this for the Guard: Once the little bastards got an idea that seemed to work, they knew how to stick with it.

Their black pajamas blended with the late shadows.

Where had the car come from?

It was a make I didn't recognize and you weren't supposed to drive them onto the campus, and I had a feeling that I was connected with it in some way and I hoped that wasn't so, because I'd come up to visit Dana on a weekend pass and we didn't want to spend half our time explaining things to some campus policeman.

Time.

That reminded me.

The sun was lower in the sky now, and Charlie would be coming in soon. The car was gone and the APC was out of business. Mortar round, probably. We had to get out of here.

But Sara was hurt, and something seemed to be wrong with my leg…

My watch was broken, but the sun was at the top of the cottonwood across from me. It was midafternoon, or later.

The bank messenger must have put out some kind of alarm by now.

I hoped he was in good voice and Dee Tee had raised hell and stuck a prop under it. Absently, I glanced back at the car and noticed that the bank's double-locked attaché case was in there, standing on the floor in the backseat. Nice to know.

But I would have traded it willingly for just one sign of approaching human life.

Or one cupful of water.

I tried to pray. But it was no-go. The man I had just killed had his eyes open and he was staring at me, telling me I was a liar and a charlatan. The rebbe from Nazareth didn't seem interested and the Enlightened One had nothing to say on the subject and I was alone in space and time on a tenth-rate ball of mud flying around some third-rate star and surrounded by an unimaginable nothing.

"God," I said aloud.

"God...?"

I waited, but there was no answer and I knew there wasn't going to be one.

"God, you motherfucker! Where the hell are you?"

The medics finally arrived just before sunset.

I could hear the Hueys coming in, and hoped the security section had been able to give them a safe landing area. Sara had to get to a hospital.

I looked down at her, and something was wrong.

Her hair had turned white and there was a wound on her head and it was swollen half again its normal size and it wasn't Sara at all, it was someone else.

"Dana!"

What the hell was Dana doing in 'Nam?

And what the hell was going on with the evacuation chopper? The one easing down beside the cottonwoods wasn't a Huey, and it wasn't even military. It was a civilian JetRanger with the name Prescott painted on its side...

A BENEDICTION (CONTINUED)

...and remain with you always.

THIRTY-FIVE

Things finally began to take shape again about three days later. Robbie said I fought him and the deputy riding with him when they were loading Dana into a Stokes litter for the flight back to the hospital in Farewell, and kept it up even after I was in the helicopter myself and strapped down. Yelling something about Charlies and God and the National Guard.

And Sara.

"You seemed to think you were back in 'Nam and she was there with you," Robbie said. "Kept telling us something about how you hadn't been there when she needed you before, but no one was going to take her away from you now."

I thought about it, and remembered a little bit, and understood what it was about and why I'd said it, but didn't explain it to him or anyone else.

It was nobody's business.

My hospital room was on the third floor and I had a panoramic view of the town of Farewell, and it didn't look as though it had gone up in smoke because of the poker game or the killings or any of the rest of it, but I didn't really give much of a damn whether it had or not.

Jake visited me daily. He said the bank hadn't gone bust the way Dee Tee had thought it might. Marilyn Prescott had gotten acquainted with old Mose Thieroux while they were waiting around the hospital, he said, and they had passed some of the time talking about the land deeds and what J. J. Barlow had been trying to do, and they decided to go ahead with it.

Only it would be on the level—out in the light of day, where everyone, including the EPA, could have a say and decide how it ought to work.

"And the helicopter company's back on its feet," he said. "Got a brand-new LongRanger to replace the one that crashed, and your friend Robbie has had to hire an extra pilot already to handle the business that's coming in."

I nodded. It was about what I'd expected.

"How's Dana?" I said. "And where is she?"

"Dana's fine. She's here in the hospital, too, of course, and she's pretty banged up. I don't know how much you remember—you were in pretty bad shape yourself when they found you—but she's going to be all right. Her jaw is broken so she can't talk very well, and her face is badly swollen. She said she doesn't want you to see her until it's better."

I thought it over and decided that age and associating with people like me were beginning to make Jake a better liar. But not nearly good enough. There wasn't much I could do about it for the moment, though; my left arm was strapped to my chest and my left leg was beginning to move a little when I told it to, but I couldn't seem to feel much of anything down there and I hadn't tried to stand on it yet.

"The money?" I asked.

"All safe," he said. "It was still in the bag with the real-estate papers, and Frank Ybarra took personal responsibility for turning a million of it over to the bank messenger who'd reported you missing, so that much will be back where it ought to be by now. The rest is waiting for you."

I nodded again.

A big part of the bundle would go to the Prescotts, of course—for damages—and some of it to Dee Tee Price for being crazy enough to take the kind of chance on me that he had taken. The rest, I knew, could be mine if I wanted it. But the truth was that I never wanted to see a penny of that particular stake again. Ever.

"Thanks, Jake," I said. "Anything else I ought to know?"

"Not that I can think of. Oh...yes. Commencement Brown—Boo Brown—sends his apologies. He's here in the hospital and I talked to him and he wanted me to tell you none of what happened was his idea."

"He going to be all right?"

"By the grace of God," Jake said. "Vollie tried to get back in here the night after he arrested you and Dana, and I think it was to kill him and so does Boo. He says he and the others were always afraid of Vollie."

I sighed and wanted to shake my head, but didn't do it because it would have hurt. "Tell him to go in peace and sin no more; he is absolved."

"I did."

Frank Ybarra showed up later that day and stood for a long time at the foot of the bed looking at me out of those black-glass eyes.

"They say you'll be okay," he said finally.

"Glad to hear it," I said.

More silence.

"Do I owe you an apology or something?"

"No."

He stood there for a while longer, and then his face softened, almost imperceptibly, and he turned away.

"I'm sorry as hell, Preacher," he said, and was out the door before I could reply.

Deke Pemberton arrived on the morning of the fifth day.

My arm was loose from my chest again, but it hurt, and I was trying to find a position where it would be comfortable. There wasn't any, and I was looking around for an extra pillow when he appeared at the end of my bed and stood waiting for me to notice him.

"Counselor," I said.

He didn't reply at once.

I wished he had picked a different time to come calling and I wished he would say something. But everything else had gone wrong that day and, on balance, I couldn't see any reason he should be excluded.

"Barlow wasn't Vollie Manion's father," he finally blurted, by way of salutation.

I stopped looking for the pillow and looked at him instead.

"I was," he said.

Well, Jesus in a pear tree…

"Have a seat," I said. "But close the hall door first, all right? Thanks. Privacy gets harder and harder to find every day."

Pemberton sat down and put his hands in his lap, but didn't seem to want them there and tried putting them in his pockets, but that is awkward when you're sitting down, and finally gave up and let them perch on his thighs. It was an altogether astonishing performance for a man whose self-possession was usually so total and effortless.

"My family has some problems," he said, talking as if from a script he had been rehearsing for a long time. "Defects. They are genetic, nothing we can do anything about, and my father told me about them when I was fourteen. He apologized to me. Apologized for having begotten me, and wanted me to have a vasectomy right then so the…problems wouldn't be passed on to anyone else. But I was too young and it sounded so horrible that

I wouldn't do it, not even for him, and he warned me that I would be sorry, but I didn't believe him."

He paused for breath and I think he wanted me to interrupt, but I couldn't see any reason to do that, so I didn't.

"For a long time it didn't matter," he went on after a while. "I was too busy getting through college and law school and getting on back in Washington to bother about anything else. But then my father died and I came home for a visit to get things sorted out. And I met Ellie Manion."

The eyes were far away now, and I don't think he was talking to me anymore.

"She was just fifteen, but I didn't know that. She looked and acted older. And she seemed to like me. She was pretty and I wasn't used to having pretty girls smile at me, and we danced—it was a charity ball at the hotel ballroom downtown—and I had two or three beers and she had a flask of vodka with her and she spiked the beer with it and after a while we went outside and we drank some more in my car, and I raped her."

He licked his lips.

"I don't know why," he said. "It wasn't necessary. Thinking about it, I know she would have been willing enough. But I took her by force because it was what I suddenly wanted to do. I couldn't help it. And it wouldn't have mattered much, legally, anyway; she was so far underage it would have been statutory rape even if I hadn't used force. So it would have been a prison sentence and no law career, no nothing, for me if she wanted to go to the police. But she didn't. I took her to a doctor out of town—she had some cuts and some bruises on her face— and gave her some money and she cried but she finally calmed down and I thought it was over. And then she turned out to be pregnant..."

He stopped, breathing like a man who had run a long footrace.

"I got the vasectomy immediately afterward," he said. "At first she said she wanted to get married, but I found out that was only what her family made her say and they stopped pushing it after I set up a trust fund through Citizens Bank, with J. J. Barlow as trustee, to give her a comfortable income for life, and to provide for the child until he was grown."

He looked at me with a peculiar intensity.

"It was the only time I had sexual intercourse in my entire life," he said. "Do you know how far that sets a man apart from the rest of the human race? Can you imagine? I know the things people say about me here in Farewell. They think I'm odd. Different. If they only knew! But I swear to you, truly, I never thought that the child…that Vollie—"

He ran out of breath and his eyes bored into me for a second. And then it was over. His shoulders straightened and his voice, which had been teetering on the verge of hysteria, was controlled again when he spoke. "I am a man," he said, "and I do not ask sympathy or even understanding. But I have done you—and Barlow and the Prescotts—a great wrong. It cannot be compensated. But it can be confessed…"

I shook my head. "The Prescotts," I said. "Tell them."

"I did."

There was nothing more to say and we sat for a long time in silence and then he went away.

Mose Thieroux came in with his great-grandchildren.

"Court finally got around to doing the right thing," he said. "Want you to meet my daughter, Carmenita…"

The little girl smiled shyly at me and turned to hug her new father's skinny leg. "Ayuh," she said.

"…and my son, Moses the Third."

The boy grinned, too, but didn't hide. "Shouldn't wonder," he said.

Mose looked down at them, and I decided he might even turn out to be good at smiling. He seemed to be getting some practice.

By the seventh day I'd finally listened to enough lies about Dana, and went to see for myself.

The telephone at my bedside had a direct outside line, and I used it to impersonate an Amarillo newspaper reporter asking for information concerning Dana Lansing and that, after several switchings and referrals, gave me the information that she remained in "critical but stable condition." And told me where she was. The final nurse who talked to me had answered the phone with the words, "intensive care."

I put the phone down and got out of bed.

Verticality was still a bit unfamiliar, but I had been using the bathroom instead of a bedpan for a couple of days and I knew what to expect. The left leg was still about as responsive as a packing crate, but I could walk after a fashion and that was what I did, down the corridor to the elevator.

A couple of nurses and an orderly drifted by, but they were occupied with their own affairs and paid me no mind.

The nurse at the ICU was a different story, of course. But I waited her out, pretending to look for someone in the visitors' room, and finally she left her station to check something in one of the rooms.

I forced the leg to hurry down the hallway.

The first two ICU rooms were empty, and in the third a nurse was changing the I.V. on an elderly man who appeared to be unconscious.

I passed that door as quickly as possible, peeped into the fourth room, and was about to move on when I realized the half-covered face I was looking at was Dana's.

The eyes were closed and the ash-blonde hair had been shaved away and most of the skull seemed to be covered by a bandage that also concealed the side of her face that had suffered the most damage. She was on her back, connected to an array of monitors, and her eyelids were flickering…but not in a way that meant they were about to open.

I entered the room silently and stood by the bed.

The monitors didn't tell me much; I've had a little first-aid training, and my stay in an army hospital made me acquainted with a few bits of medical equipment and lore. But a modern ICU is a place of specialists and technology, and the only one of the glowing screens that meant a thing to me was the one with the sensors attached to the bandages covering Dana's skull. It was labeled EEG. Its signal was flat.

I took Dana's hand in mine and sat down to wait…

The nurse found me there later, and had a fit.

She said I would have to leave. At once. And when I didn't do it, or respond at all, she said she was going to call an orderly, and she did that and he came and started toward me.

"If you come any closer," I said, without turning my head, "I will break your arm and your leg."

It was ridiculous, of course; I was in no shape to handle him or his baby brother or an aggressive troupe of midgets. But something about my voice seemed to make him hesitate, and the nurse said she would call Dr. Woodbury.

The doctor wasn't in the hospital, but he arrived after about an hour and looked the situation over and told the nurse to go away.

"Dana doesn't know you're here," he said gently when we were alone. "She hasn't…there's been no brain activity since she arrived."

I didn't reply.

"You're still in bad shape yourself. The arm should be in a sling. And the leg…" His voice trailed off when he saw that I wasn't paying attention.

"I'll get a sling," he said finally. "And a blanket."

He went away and I sat still, holding Dana's hand.

Two days later, nothing much had changed and I took a few moments to go back upstairs to my own room. Jake had packed up my things from the motel and brought them to the hospital. I opened the suitcase and found the book I wanted, and the bit of ribbon, and spent a minute or two cleansing my hands and saying some words over a thimbleful of water, which I had put into a small medicine glass, and then went back down to the ICU.

The nurse paid no attention as I reentered Dana's room.

I put the glass down on the reading stand and kissed the bit of ribbon and put it around my neck and opened the book and began: "O God the Father, have mercy upon the soul of thy servant. O God the Son, have mercy upon the soul of thy servant..."

The nurse looked in and I heard her draw a sharp breath. But she didn't interfere.

"Depart, Christian soul, out of this world..."

Jake walked in behind me as I was invoking the trinity, and joined me in the final words. He didn't say anything else, and neither did I, and after a while he went away again.

After two more days they disconnected the life-support systems.

I sat with her for a minute or two after breathing had stopped, but it meant nothing. She had died in another place, in a grove of cottonwood trees where savages fought and inflicted pain for its own sake, and she had been there because of me and nothing could never change a single part of that.

I went back to my room and made a telephone call and began putting my clothes on.

AMEN

THIRTY-SIX

I signed myself out of the hospital and was on an airliner, west-bound from Amarillo, three hours later.

Nobody seemed to think it was a good idea.

Dr. Woodbury objected on medical grounds. "The scanners didn't show any major damage," he said, "but the nerves in your leg need rest and you could injure them permanently."

Jake Spence was worried about other things. "Helen wants you to stay with us," he said, "and Mose Thieroux said he invited you to spend some time with him and the kids. We don't think you should be alone right now."

Robbie picked me up at the front door for the ride to Prescott Helicopters' landing circle.

"You shouldn't be doing this, Preacher," he said.

"Tell me about it," I said sourly, and he shut up and just drove the car for a while.

The town was full of ghosts.

"J. J. Barlow was our sniper," Robbie said as we passed the Citizens National Bank. "He was a shooter from way back, alternate on the Olympic team twice running, helped set up the town rifle range."

"Loaded his own ammunition?"

"What else?"

Lupe's garage seemed to be closed, and there were no cars parked at the café.

"Marilyn and Mose exercised Barlow's option to buy the land," Robbie said. "I hear they'll be clearing it off to start building the new plant."

"The Lupe family?"

He favored me with a flash of the de Bonzo teeth.

"Cleared out the day they got the money. Didn't even bother to lock the doors."

We didn't talk much during the flight to Amarillo.

Helicopters—even fancy ones like the new LongRanger—are noisy beasts, and if the landscape of eastern New Mexico and the Texas panhandle is uninspiring from ground level, it is even more so from the air.

But we each had enough to think about to keep from being bored.

"When do you want me back at Best Licks?" Robbie finally asked when we were down and waiting for the courtesy bus to the airline terminal.

That earned him my very first smile of the week.

"I told them to sell your bed," I said.

He started to object, but I cut him off before he could begin.

"Farewell is your niche, Robbie. Your place in the world. You belong there. Best Licks is just for people who need healing. You're healed...and now it's time to go."

His eyes thanked me and said he knew I was right, but they contained a question, too. I thought he might ask it, but he didn't, and I was glad because I didn't want to hear my answer.

And when will it be your healing time, Preacher?

The arm still didn't work right and the leg was awkward, but I left the sling in an airport men's room at Amarillo and the cane under my seat on the airliner and walked to the motorized corridor ramp at McCarran International without a limp.

Some pains are more easily controlled than others.

I took a cab downtown and went into a casino where they know me, and I think it startled the bartender a bit when I ordered a bourbon and soda. He knows I don't drink when I play poker, and I don't come to Vegas for any other reason. But I knew I wasn't going to be playing poker this time, because a man needs to be on good terms with himself to do that. And for the moment I simply wasn't qualified.

Gambling is a world of difference.

It is clockless, peopled by liars, fools, cheats, madmen, cripples, and potential suicides—all largely governed by the larcenous—and the population was out in force today, turning their hands filthy on the handles of one-arm bandits and their pockets empty on games where the house edge sometimes climbs to twenty percent or more.

Ridiculous.

Insane.

But I was here by choice. I didn't dare go home to Best Licks in my condition, and I couldn't have stayed in Farewell, among friendly, sane, decent, honest human beings with loving families and good lives and bank accounts and insurance programs and a sure knowledge that the world is a good and sunny place.

For a while I needed to be here, in this place and among these people. Because sometimes you just naturally want to be among your own kind.

ABOUT THE AUTHOR

 Ted Thackrey Jr. was a Korean War vet, an author, and newspaper reporter who, after stints at several newspapers, ended up in 1968 at the *Los Angeles Times*, where he became known over the next two decades for his colorful news stories, columns, and obituaries. His novel *The Preacher* was an Edgar Award finalist that led to two sequels, *Aces & Eights* and *King of Diamonds*, and the movie *Wild Card* starring Powers Boothe. He also wrote the nonfiction books *The Gambling Secrets of Nick the Greek* and *The Thief: The Autobiography of Wayne Burke*, and ghostwrote more than forty books and several screenplays. Thackrey Jr. died in 2001.